SEEKING TWO LOVERS

MISSING LINK 1

LYNN BURKE

SEEKING TWO LOVERS

Finding my ex-fiancé beneath the man we invited into our relationship jaded my heart, and I refuse to share lovers ever again.

The dating app Missing Link offers me the chance to fulfill my desire of having two men love on me at the same time—without the crossing of swords.

Fate plays her games, and I end up separately dating two men at the same time, who as a whole, would be my dream come true.

The problem?

They're roommates. Best friends. And neither knows the girl they claim to have fallen for is one and the same.

When the truth is uncovered, I perceive the unrequited love in one's gaze and unrecognized feelings in the others.

But the fear of being set aside a second time comes too late.

I'm already in too deep.

1

LILY

No...no.

I scrolled through images of potential lovers the Missing Link app had paired me with, frowning over the number of couples smiling back at me from my cell's screen.

"No." I huffed the word. "What part of 'seeking two male lovers' don't you understand?"

"What?" Haley hollered from the kitchen behind me.

"Nothing!" I yelled a reply to my cousin and slouched into our couch we'd picked up at the thrift shop the week before. "Just bring in the wine already!"

Thumb back at it, I went on the prowl.

MM couple hungry for a boy toy.

FF couple seeking SWM.

"The hell?" I muttered, shaking my head.

"What's wrong?" Haley meandered into our living room and handed me a glass of our favorite chardonnay. Her purple and red dyed hair was pulled up in a messy bun, and she wore a long T-shirt, her favorite sleepwear.

I sipped and sighed inwardly at the cold wine trickling down my throat. She settled onto the cushion beside me and grabbed one of the brightly-colored pillows we'd gotten to offset the bland gray of the couch.

"Must be a glitch," I explained. "Missing Link is pairing me with MF couples who want a third to warm their bed, older males looking for littles...two dommes on the prowl for a big man to sub for them. Seriously—I did *not* check off BDSM or any kink boxes. There's got to be something wrong. I just want two other single guys looking to love on a willing female."

"Give it a rest. Look later." She hugged the pillow and took a long drink from her glass.

"I haven't gotten laid in like..." I tore my focus off my cell and tried to remember the haze of the last week. I hadn't done much other than lounge on the beach and drink wine while on vacation from the day job.

"Did you hook up with that guy from the bar last weekend?" Haley asked.

Bobby. Or was it Billy? Either way, he'd been a disappointing lay. "The cute redhead. Billy of the Pencil Dicks. Yeah."

Haley snorted a laugh and sipped her drink. "Seven days and you're desperate for it already?"

"School's out." I reminded her of my teaching job ending for the summer the Monday before. "I'm bored as fuck and reading too many menage romance novels. Of course I'm hungry for a thick, juicy cock or two. Billy's didn't do it for me. The guy didn't know how to use his fingers and tongue either."

"You need another job to keep you busy for the next couple of months."

"I'm starting at Carla's Cafe tomorrow morning." I went back to scrolling again.

"You are? How come this is the first I'm hearing about it?"

I frowned, recalling getting home from the short interview earlier in the week. Haley had already finished up work at Pieces, the clothing boutique she managed, an empty bottle of wine in her hand. "I told you on Wednesday that I started next Monday. *Tomorrow*."

"I was drunk." Haley gave her favorite excuse with a shrug.

"Bitch."

"Dickmonger," she shot back with a smirk.

I snorted a laugh rather than getting angry because she had a point. I liked dick, same as her. End of. My thumb went back to rolling to see what else I could find.

No...no...

"Oh! Now that's what I'm talking about." I sat a little straighter and set my wine on the coffee table in front of us. "This guy's easy on the eyes."

"Single?" She sounded interested, but not enough to scoot over to take a peek.

I frowned, scanning his info. "It says couple...but it's just a pic of this surfer-looking dude."

Zooming in, I made a sound of appreciation. He had half of his longer dirty blond hair tied back in a ponytail, and eyes as blue as the summer sky held the type of intense smolder that could melt any person's panties.

"Check this hottie out." Shit, I sounded like a needy whore.

That earned Haley's attention, and she slid closer to peer over my shoulder while I zoomed in further—on the thin gray sweats hanging low on his hips. That V and the obvious outline of the thick and juicy cock I'd been wanting...instantaneous lust hit between my thighs and made my drool factory wake up.

"Fuck. Me." Haley's breathy whisper sounded more like a groan.

I giggled, my core in complete agreement with her. "Yeah. I'd suck on that like a lollipop." I popped the P, and we both laughed.

"What's his profile say?" she asked, leaning in closer.

I swiped my fingers together over the screen and focused on his write-up for a quick skim. "Says him and his room-mate...best friends not partners...he's bi, his buddy is straight...not looking for anything serious. Shit." I grinned, shimmying on the couch. "They're local! Next town over!"

"Boom, baby."

I elbowed Haley even though a tiny zing of hope swept me up in excitement.

"With his buddy being straight, you won't have to worry about the two of them hooking up."

"Yeah," I murmured while Haley settled back into her corner to drink her wine and disappear into social media like she always did at night.

I didn't 'do' couples because I feared being set aside again when true love decided to shut down the fun of a threesome. Having experienced that once, I had zero desire for similar heartache.

My ex-fiancé had been gay as the day was long, and even though I'd speculated over that fact for years, we hadn't ever talked about it. From sixth grade when I first met Levi until I caught him on his back for our hot-as-hell premarital coun-selor we'd been meeting with at church, I had wondered about his sexuality.

We'd been taught that "choosing" to be gay was a sin. Levi had fought his natural tendencies his whole life thanks to our pastor and parents who'd been in agreement with everything preached from Simply Grace's pulpit.

But Zeke—Levi's husband now—had proven too much of a temptation, and they'd given into their yearnings.

It didn't matter that I had decided to end our engagement after a night of dancing with two hot guys grinding all over me, that I'd gone to Levi's apartment to break things off with him immediately afterward. Walking in to find Zeke fucking him on the living room floor had broken my heart.

I had tried my best to keep my hurt from Levi, not wanting to add to the guilt and shame I'm sure he had felt for cheating on me. But allowing those two strangers at the club to dry hump my front and back while sweating on the dance floor hadn't been much better.

I'd recognized in high school that Levi and I weren't meant to be together, but he'd been comfort for me, my safe place. Not easy to set aside, especially when we were expected to marry. But no matter how much our parents wanted us for each other, no matter how involved we'd been in the church as a couple, our relationship had been doomed.

I would always love Levi, but even though we kept in touch and chatted on the phone every couple of months, I knew we'd made the right decision.

We had both left the church. Left God. Left our parents.

At least mine still talked to and accepted me. Levi's father, the bastard, had shunned him for loving another man.

"Here." My favorite roommate tossed me an Andes candy, pulling me back from the past.

I dropped my cell to catch her gift. "Where'd you find that?"

"Shoved in between the couch cushions. Must have been from our movie marathon the other night."

"Mmm." I peeled the wrapper open with one hand and popped the yumminess into my mouth. Nothing tasted as delicious as chocolate and mint. "So good." I smacked my lips and sipped my wine, swirling the chardonnay over my tongue.

"Are you going to poke him?"

I picked back up my cell and swiped the screen to life. "Scott. Looks delicious in gray sweats. Yeah. Even if his best friend isn't up for a ride, I'm game."

"One is better than none," Haley agreed.

I clicked the poke button, hoping the photo I'd uploaded when creating my profile would be enough to get him to read my write-up. The red bikini I'd worn showed off the tan I'd gotten by spending hours every weekend on the beach with Haley. I'd gone with less makeup for a change. Unlike my usual messy bun like the one on top of my head, I'd had a fresh cut and blowout, blonde highlights accenting the darker wheat color beneath. The sun had hit me just right that morning, and I looked like a shampoo commercial. Or a bathing suit ad.

Hot—but not slutty.

"Think he'll poke me back?" I murmured.

"Hopefully, they'll both be poking you before next weekend." Haley chuckled. "There's nothing like having a dick in your ass and pussy at the same time."

"I've been spit-roasted." I reminded her of the last two male friends I'd hooked up with. Too bad they hadn't been into having their balls so close together for a guy-Lily-guy sandwich like I'd been fantasizing about.

"Stuffed full down below is the way to go."

I snorted a laugh and glanced over at my cousin. On the

petite side like me, she tucked her legs beneath her, barely taking up any room on the couch. It had been her whispered secret of a threesome over the phone that had started the fantasies in my head. The very dreams that had prompted Levi's and my attempts to sow our wild oats before settling down in holy matrimony.

How awry *that* plan had gone, but I didn't regret what we'd done.

We'd both ended up in better places.

Levi married to the love of his life and me moving across the country.

It had been Haley's idea for me to escape Philly after the breakup and move into her California two-bedroom apartment with her. She'd gotten me a job at Pieces, but I'd picked up a teaching position that same summer.

My parents weren't thrilled with my choice to leave them and the church, and they doubtless thought I lived a sin-filled life.

According to their beliefs I no longer held, I did.

Wine. Lots of cursing. Complete sexual freedom involving plenty of men—just not yet in the way I wanted. Haley had been the catalyst of my supposed downfall, and I loved her for it.

"What about you?" I asked her.

"What about me?" She continued to swipe across her cell's screen, her face deadpan.

"You haven't brought a guy home in weeks."

"Meh." She shrugged her shoulder and swallowed down the last of her wine. "I'm bored."

"Maybe you should be prowling alongside me for a couple of hot guys."

She shot me a single-raised eyebrow smirk. "It *has* been awhile."

"You don't mind the crossing of swords—make yourself a profile and find some love slaves you can boss around and watch do dirty things to each other." The idea of two men getting it on warmed me through, but I wasn't having it.

Nope.

"I wouldn't mind a harem of my own." Haley sounded all dreamy.

"Worshiping at your feet, obeying your every command."

"Damn right."

We both laughed. Haley had more confidence than I did in bed. She didn't hold back in stating what she wanted and how.

Not that I knew from personal experience.

We just had a completely open and TMI type relationship. Everything Haley did, I heard about. Everything I'd tried on since losing my religion, she'd enjoyed listening to as much as I did telling her.

We were a couple of heathens, hell-bent on sampling as much dick as possible—carefully, of course.

As long as the guys I hooked up with didn't attempt to boss me around or force their religious beliefs on me, we'd be golden. I got along with just about anyone except those whose dogmatism for their god came first in their life.

It was why I rarely went back east to visit my family. Being reminded of what I had once been twisted my stomach to nausea every time I thought about my prior existence.

Once I'd left to stretch my wings, that religious connection between us all had severed, and I found myself breathing more easily for a change. Funny, I hadn't realized how stifled I'd been until I'd escaped and found my freedom.

FaceTime and phone calls made it simple to stay in touch because I did love my parents, my two sisters, the brother-in-laws, and their kids.

I just no longer desired the life they all chose.

Perhaps I was immature and selfish, but I lusted for undivided attention—I did *not* want to share my lovers with anyone else.

Higher being included.

Scott's write-up didn't say jack shit about politics or religion since Missing Link didn't ask those questions when you went through their character profiling. But usually, people looking for poly relationships on an app weren't the religious type anyway.

I zoomed back in on those gray sweats, a shiver licking down my spine at the obvious ridge that promised a good stretch. My pussy dampened at the mere thought alone of taking his dick. Maybe his roommate wouldn't mind having his balls in close contact enough that I could finally fulfill my fantasy of being double-stuffed.

A shift on the couch lifted Haley's head. "Still checking him out?"

"Oh yeah." I sighed. "Even if Scott turns out to be a church-type guy, I'd still take his body on for a test ride."

He looked too damn delicious not to.

2

BLAINE

Grey and I sprawled out on the couch as our latest hookup gathered all the clothes I'd peeled off her a good hour earlier. She put extra sway into her hips while walking to the bathroom.

The second the door closed behind her, my best friend and I glanced at one another. He grinned.

I didn't.

"Dude." He chuckled quietly. "It took you for-fucking-ever to come. Was it her, or did you get all caught up in your head again?"

Closing my eyes, I rested back on the couch's arm. The woman Grey had found for us and brought home looked like someone from my past, and the sight of her had taken me to a place I'd rather not go.

To dark memories that continued to haunt me nine years later.

Nightmares enough to shrivel any man's dick. I was lucky to have gotten off at all.

"She reminded me of a woman...from there," I murmured as the toilet flushed in the distance.

"Shit." Grey stirred, but I didn't open my eyes. "Why the fuck didn't you tell me, B? I would have sent her packing without a second thought."

One thing about my best friend was that he always put me first. Every. Time. And I loved the hell out of him for it.

I shrugged. "I could tell you liked her."

"Shit. Doesn't matter if I think a woman is hot—she's a willing, wet hole to get me off, and there are hundreds more out there."

"You're a whore," I muttered what I often teased him about since the man *didn't* care what type of hole he found release in. Male, female, ass, pussy, mouth—he didn't discriminate.

"You okay?" Grey's serious tone made me crack an eyelid open.

"Yeah, man. No problem. But no more tall women with long black hair and blue eyes. Can't fucking handle that shit."

Just like I couldn't submit to thoughts of the same sex thanks to that bitch's husband.

My stomach pitched at the flashes in my head, images in vivid color captured by a traumatized child's mind.

Swallowing hard, I fought against the heat flaring inside me, the sweat rising to the surface of my skin that roused nausea in my stomach.

"So petite, blonde, and brown-eyed," Grey stated in his business tone that promised me he wouldn't forget. Ever. "Got it."

The bathroom door opened, and Grey hopped up to be the gentleman so I wouldn't have to.

I released a heavy exhale and closed my eyes again, trying to not give headspace to my past and how it had created the antisocial, insecure-as-fuck guy I had to look at in the mirror every day.

The hours of penance, the beatings. Sitting in a pitch-black cell of forced solitude and silence in order to better meditate on one's sins.

"Fucking hell." I scrubbed a hand down over my face, my teeth clenching up tight. But I refused to let in the light of our living room's overhead dimmers. I chose the darkness behind my eyelids because I *could*—it was *my* choice. I held the power over what I did or didn't do.

The couch dipped.

"You can open your eyes now, dipshit. She's gone."

"Fuck you." I kicked out with a leg, connecting with Grey's thigh. I still enjoyed my freedom to bask in the dark rather than look at him.

"I *suppose* I could offer up my ass if you really want it."

"Goddamnit, Grey." I shot him a glare, hating that he knew how to rile me up and control me at the same time.

"There's those hazel eyes I adore." He flashed a grin, and I kicked him again. With lightning-fast reflexes, he grabbed hold of my ankle and grasped tight. "Talk to me."

Strong fingers dug into my foot, rubbing until I sank back in total relaxation with a groan.

The fucker had hands to write poetry about.

"Have I ever told you how good of a buffer you are?" I asked.

"Yeah, but you can say it again. I'll take an ego stroke any day of the week."

"You get enough strokes of your own in as it is. Fucking keep it down from now on, would ya?"

"Sorry I get vocal when I jerk off." His voice held no contrite tone to speak of.

"No you're not."

"I'm just hoping you'll start to enjoy it someday." He waggled his eyebrows, and I shook my head, unable to help my grin.

"I don't do dick."

As if he needed to be reminded. The last guy he'd brought home had all but begged for a threesome, and I'd nearly lost my dinner on the kitchen floor.

"I've got a nice one." He grabbed his junk and flopped it back and forth beneath his mesh shorts.

"Mine's bigger."

"Yeah, I know." His tone lowered a bit, and he tossed my foot off his lap.

"So you *do* check out the goods when there's a woman between us." My turn to joke, thankful for something to help push the darkness away.

"'Course I do," he muttered, climbing off the couch and heading into the kitchen. "What horny, bisexual man wouldn't enjoy looking at a thick dick and heavy balls? Water?"

"Sure."

Grey brought guys back to our place just as much as he did women, but I didn't share in the fun on those nights.

And I also wasn't about to cross any further into teasing territory that might make things weird between us, even if I did think he was sexy for a guy. No fucking way would I mess up what I'd found with him. He was my best friend. My anchor. A soul mate if allowed that term for a platonic relationship.

Grey tossed me a bottle of water and crashed in the other corner of the couch again. "So."

"So," I echoed when he didn't continue.

"You okay?"

Goddamn him.

"I hate when shit gets riled up in my head," I muttered, turning to peer out the living room wall of windows overlooking the Pacific.

"Want to talk about it?"

"You know I don't," I snipped.

"You always feel better after you do." He pushed like always in his reasonable tone, the manipulative bastard.

"Did you like her?" I asked, ready to quit with the serious shit.

"Our hookup?"

I nodded, picking at the skin of my hands' callouses. Work kept my body in prime shape but was hell on my palms.

"Willing hole," Grey reminded me in his typical vulgar way.

"Someday, somebody is going to turn you inside out."

He didn't give me his usual spiel about never settling down.

I glanced over to find Grey studying my face. "What?"

He shook his head and guzzled water, breaking eye contact. Rarely was he the first to look away. The confident, cocky asshole took pleasure in making others squirm.

It was one of the characteristics that made him a good businessman. The fact he didn't love anyone but himself was the icing on the cake.

Well, he had feelings for me to some platonic extent.

Enough that he'd dragged me across the country after we graduated from high school, saving me from hell.

His rich-as-fuck father had paid his way through college while I'd been gifted the second bedroom in the apartment Mr. Scott provided for his use. I'd labored in exchange for money for the first time in my life, soaking in the California sunshine and slowly learning how to deal with and some-what move on from my childhood.

Shit still rose in my head like it did thanks to look-alikes and bits of religious rhetoric inadvertently caught on TV or radio, but at least I had my freedom.

Nine years and counting...no one from my life before had found me since I'd escaped.

I couldn't imagine what I would do if my past ever caught up with me beyond in my mind. As a child, I'd learned the hard way that runaways, even those heard speaking of leaving, would be found and properly punished.

And having grown into a man, those promises, the results of rebellion I'd seen and experienced, made me want to shrink in on myself.

Weariness settled into my bones from the hell my mind had dealt with all night while trying to get off to show Grey my appreciation. He always put in the hard work to bring the woman home for us. I should have wanted to sink into the couch and not move, but my feet grew as restless as my mind.

I got up without a word and gave my muscles reason to flex so I wouldn't feel the desire to escape even further than I'd done with my best friend. Fuck knew I wouldn't find a safer haven than living with Grey.

Only a few dozen steps upstairs to the second floor I all but had taken over and I shut myself in my bathroom. A hot shower would help to calm me, be the final push to allow sleep once I laid down.

But true rest wouldn't come.

It never did.

3

GREYSON

Turn you inside out.

Blaine's words echoed in my head long after he abruptly left me as he oftentimes did when the racket in his head grew too noisy.

If only he knew he'd done that to me years ago when I'd first met him in New Hampshire a few months after my mom had passed. I'd spent most of my time with him in the field separating my family's vacation house in the mountains from the compound he'd grown up on, desperate for an escape from my grief.

He'd been a quiet kid, like he too had seen heartache, so telling him about how Mom died had helped me deal. Blaine had told me he was sorry for my loss with a genuine look on his face, not the feigned condolences from my family's rich, fake friends.

He'd been a breath of fresh air from the stifling society where I'd been raised, honest with his feelings and thoughts in a way the upper class and powerful weren't. There were no polite but forced smiles and best behavior shit in order to better his station because of my family's money.

I'd needed something that summer to focus on rather than the emptiness in my heart, a reason to breathe without my mom.

Blaine had given me that. He was *real* and had become the friend I couldn't do without.

I'd never been allowed beyond the fencing to explore his home, but Blaine had somehow snuck out enough to keep me and my curiosity sated about the strange goings-on beyond.

His mess of dark hair and hazel eyes that made him seem like an old soul had drawn in my little bi ass once I learned about all things sex and hormones. Eventually recognizing his insecurities, his fears of never being good enough, had roused my protective nature to life and fused him to my heart.

After turning me inside out.

"Fuck." I stood and made my way to the wall of glass looking out over the dark night and gentle waves sweeping over the beach beneath the half-moon's light. No outdoor sounds reached through the windows, but I'd have been too fixated on listening to Blaine shower to settle in for the night anyway.

Hyperaware of his every move since first meeting him, I didn't miss much when it came to him. I'd known the appearance of the woman I'd brought home with me had bothered him, but he hadn't voiced a word.

"Shit." Lips pressing tight, I chided myself for being a selfish prick and not paying better attention to his body language.

It had been two months since our last hookup together, and my balls had been too damn ready to burst while having Blaine nearby.

My pipe dream.

My obsession.

My beautiful impeder.

All I had ever wanted, Blaine kept me from seeking more with anyone else. I'd become his rock, his safe place, and nothing would make me sneak over the friendship line and leave him floundering like I'd been after losing Mom.

His need for me far outweighed my desire for him.

Unrequited love fucking hurt, and yet I found a sense of fulfillment in being at his side. But I would never be able to stop the deep craving inside my heart for more.

His shower shut off, and I strained my ears for sounds of him moving around in his bedroom overhead.

Drawers opening and shutting.

Silence.

Did he stare into the pitch black like he'd done all those hours of being shut up alone as a kid? Did he fight the demons or bask in his liberation to choose an existence in darkness behind closed eyelids? Chances were, he had on a night-light as usual.

Turning toward my own bedroom on the first floor, I shut down my brain against my failure that might send him on a tailspin of upheaval and mental torture.

He'd dealt with enough of that before I'd offered him an escape from that hellhole.

Physically, he'd changed from the sickly-looking seventeen-year-old kid who'd snuck out of the compound and accompanied me when I left for the West Coast and college. Blaine had grown a few inches taller than my five-ten, and working a physical landscaping job had also covered his once-slight form with muscle, the California sun bronzing his skin.

But his eyes hadn't changed.

Gorgeous, more gold than green, his hazel orbs

continued to reveal the damage inflicted all those years ago. At least to me, the one person who knew what he'd survived.

Barely.

While I'd finished up college on my dad's dime and moved on with my life, Blaine had simply gone stagnant. He'd made a few friends at work, but his introverted ass never went out with them. I doubted he lowered his walls to let anyone delve too deeply into his inner workings.

I often wondered how much he didn't tell me too.

He might not love me in the same way I did him, but he'd entrusted me with his heart and mind.

And I'd been a blind fool with our hookup, the worst sort of friend.

A hot shower soothed the tension riding my shoulders, and I decided no more women, no more threesomes until *he* suggested it.

Because of his insecurities, Blaine didn't go looking for women on his own. Nor did he want to be alone with them behind closed doors. I sensed when he needed to empty his balls into something other than his fist and initiated for him, secretly getting off on the fact that I chose his physical interactions with the opposite sex.

I fucking loved the control since I wouldn't ever have it over his body in the way I dreamed of.

He'd gladly handed over management of his sex life to me years earlier at my insistence, and I'd watched him lose his virginity. I had drunk in the sight of his slack jaw and hazed eyes while ejaculating into a wet pussy as her mouth sucked on my cock.

I'd rather it had been *my* ass he'd pounded or vice versa, but beggars and all that shit.

"Thank you," he had whispered the second he'd caught

his breath after releasing, but I knew he'd meant the words for me rather than the woman between us.

For listening, for understanding, and for offering to all but hold his hand and see him through in becoming a man.

The Missing Link app made my job a shit ton easier since getting Blaine to head out to bars and pick up kinky women with me was like pulling teeth. It was tough to go on the prowl alone and ask a woman if she'd be interested in going back to your place for a three-way with your room-mate who had social anxiety.

The app dinged a few seconds after I finally settled into my bed for the night as though a sentient being offered a "You're welcome for that willing hole—how about another?"

Fucking cyberspace...a mind-reading alien intent on shifting through your brain and seeking out your every whim and secret longing.

I considered ignoring the notification since I'd put our shared sex life on hold, but it couldn't hurt to peek for the future when Blaine decided he was ready again.

I'd made our settings private, only allowing for exact matches to see our profile. Two men looking for a woman. No strings. No promises. Hookups only. Whoever the app allowed past our walls hadn't clicked the "Interested in rela-tionships" box.

They weren't searching for love.

Necessary since Blaine had none to give, and my heart already belonged to him.

I clicked on the poke from @S2L to check out who Missing Link thought might be a good fit for a bi boy and his best friend roommate.

The red bikini snagged my attention first, showcasing every gorgeous curve of her tight, little body. Her hip popped out in a sensual pose, highlighting her slim waist, the halter top swelling perfect apple-sized breasts.

Blonde hair highlighted by the sun, long enough for a man to fist when taking control, draped over one shoulder, halfway down her torso.

"Yes," I muttered, mentally checking off one of Blaine's requirements about hair color.

I focused in on the pic, needing to better see her face for the rest.

"Oh, fuck." I groaned and shifted my junk. Gorgeous dark eyes—no blue—black as coffee orbs with hints of Jameson hugging the pupils.

My two favorite drinks.

Full lips coated in gloss, perfect for sucking down a cock, smirked at the camera.

I considered rubbing one out but clicked back to read her write-up.

Twenty-four—young enough to just be on the prowl.

Enjoying life—always a plus when your thoughts aligned.

No BDSM—no problem since my dominant nature never leaned toward the pain with pleasure or tying some-one up.

Last check mark...

"Five-foot-three," I read, my lips turning upward. A tiny sprite compared to the two of us. "Perfection."

Blaine might not want pussy in the near future, but there was no fucking way on earth I would give up the opportunity to poke the hell out of her right back. Hope-fully, I could string her along until my heart's other half climbed aboard the ready-to-fuck train.

I hit the poke button in return which offered the option of communicating via direct messaging.

Having no clue what I'd brought onto myself by opening that door, I turned off my light and rolled to my stomach, ready for sleep since Monday mornings came too damn early.

The smile lingered on my lips, and hope welled in my heart even though over seventeen years of dreaming hadn't brought jack shit to fruition between me and the man I loved.

4

LILY

And I'd thought Monday mornings greeting a class full of second graders was rough.

Within three hours of learning the ropes and getting tossed behind the cafe's front counter, I was ready to prop my feet up and let some tears roll down my cheeks.

I wasn't a coffee drinker myself, but those who needed it and had to wait in line before finally having that first sip in the morning? Didn't they not know they could keep their grumpiness and bitchiness at bay by making a cup at home before dragging their asses out to start the day?

I hoped the fact it was a Monday morning accounted for most of the shortness and frowns I'd dealt with while smiling at every customer walking up to the counter.

Otherwise, I wasn't going to make it through barista training over the next couple of weeks.

Finally, my break time rolled around, and I went to the back room to get my cell.

"Is every morning like this?" I asked Cheryl, the shift manager rifling through the employee fridge.

"Busy as hell with everyone bitching about their lack of

foam or too much ice?" Cheryl closed the fridge door with her hip, her hands wrapped around a few boxes that looked like last night's leftovers. "Mostly just Mondays."

"Thank God." I pulled my cell from my purse. "I honestly don't know if I could handle dealing with coffee-fiend-needing-a-hit customers like this for six hours straight."

Cheryl snickered and popped a box into the microwave. "That's why you have a break halfway through."

I groaned. "Tell me it gets better."

"It gets better."

"Are you lying to me?"

She outright laughed. "When you have a bubbly outlook and a smile like you do, it gets better."

My face hurt from forcing grins all morning long, but my lips curved upward naturally at her praise.

"You must be a church person," she mused.

I snorted, knowing right where Cheryl headed. Others from Simply Grace Church had always said I'd been filled with the joy of the Lord, but they never considered the truth that someone could experience happiness without it coming from a higher being.

"I don't need to bow down to a god to be happy," I told her, my chin lifting a bit.

"I agree. That's just what my gram used to say." Cheryl glanced over at me. "*Filled with the joy of the Lord* and all that other God bullshit."

Yep. Nailed it. I shook my head. "I had enough of that back home—I live my own life now."

Her eyes softened, and in that moment, I understood we had more in common than dealing with pissy non-morning customers.

"The thought of religion makes you want to vomit too, huh?" she asked.

"Every bit of bile churns in my guts whenever I think too much about where I came from," I agreed.

"Same. Once I learned it was *wrong*—" she used air quotes "—to love another woman, I decided religion wasn't for me."

"Girlfriend?" I asked.

"Soon-to-be wife." She grinned.

"Congrats," I stated my honest-to-God opinion. Love, in my eyes, was love.

Period.

A minute later, I stepped outside into the sunshine, needing some fresh air. I didn't have enough time to trek across the road and down a block to hit the beach, so I snagged one of the empty chairs out front and rested my aching feet.

I saw first that my mom had texted, same as she always did on Mondays over her tea to wish me a blessed morning.

She must have forgotten that mine had started hours earlier and was almost over.

Dad's weekly texted Bible verse of the day dinged through as I typed out a greeting in reply to Mom's.

I didn't bother reading the verse he'd sent, just hit reply with a kissy emoji.

Levi had texted, and I half-squealed while bringing it up onscreen.

Boo: **We're adopting.**

My eyes popped wide before narrowing. "The. Fuck."

Levi didn't want kids...

I hit dial, my forehead dented with a deep frown that would leave a wrinkle behind.

"A dog!" he answered.

"You asshole!" I laughed, letting out a whoosh of air. "Seriously. What the *hell* kind of text is that?"

"One that would make you call me. I miss hearing your voice."

"Aw, I miss you too, boo."

"It's been awhile, so I figured I'd give you a buzz since school is out and you must be bored as hell."

"I was the past week, but I started working at a cafe just down the street from our apartment."

"Perfect job for you."

"Why? Because I smile all the time like I'm *filled with the joy of the Lord*?"

He burst out with laughter, and my grin stayed in place. Levi had never been as free with me as he'd become after finding love with Zeke. Shy and a numbers nerd, he'd been the silent eye candy on my arm for all our social activities surrounding the church.

"You sound happy," I said, a sweet ache blooming in my chest at the memory of his gorgeous green eyes that had always been shut off to me in a lot of ways. If only I'd truly taken note of that fact before the shit hit the fan between us.

"I am. I never knew...never expected to have this kind of love."

"Yeah." My smile faded, and I wrapped my free arm around myself.

"Any luck in finding your two lovers?"

I wanted to lie, brag about nonexistent men in my life over his happiness, but I had yet to find the same as he'd done in the year since our break-up. "Not yet," I spoke the truth along with a word to reveal my hope.

Which reminded me of the app I hadn't gotten a chance to check—

"When are you coming home for a visit? Zeke and I are

headed to Philly for the expansion of Humanity House's second location down there."

"The one where Pastor Ezra works?"

"Aaron's husband, yeah."

While mention of people from our past and catching up on all I'd left behind wasn't the way I'd choose to enjoy my break, hearing Levi's voice kept our few minutes from being uncomfortable.

"I have to get behind the counter again," I told Levi, headed back toward the cafe's front door.

"If you ever decide the West Coast isn't right for you, we've got a spare room in the condo."

"Boston means snow and cold." I shuddered while stepping into the cafe. "No thank you."

Levi laughed lightly, bringing my smile back. "Talk soon?"

"Promise."

He groaned. "You know I hate that word."

"Oops. I take it back."

Two minutes later, I resumed my position as smiling order lady without having gotten a chance to check if Scott had returned my poke.

Tall, dark, and handsome entered the cafe, ripping all thoughts of surfer blondie in the gray sweats from my mind.

Wide shoulders stretched out his green T-shirt with its Lionel's Landscaping logo on his prominent left pec. Dirty jeans...worn-as-hell boots covered in dust.

A working man who probably had calloused hands.

Shivers slid down my spine, and I lifted my focus back up his muscular form, my tongue flicking over my lower lip at the sight of how well he filled out his dirty, sweat-stained clothes.

For the love of all things holy...

Our gazes caught, and my knees went weak.

Shadows haunted his hazel eyes. Similar to what I'd seen in Levi's and never took note of until it was too late.

Unrest in his heart. Unhappiness in his soul.

My heart ached in that moment to soothe him as I'd always done with Levi.

But the man in front of me looked nothing like my geeky ex-fiancé.

A soft smile curved his lips, hesitant as though shy, and he quickly glanced at the chalk-written menu above and behind me while walking closer.

I swallowed hard, taking in the dark scruff along his jaw, the smear of dirt on his left cheekbone. "Hi." The usual huskiness of my voice intensified from the butterflies dancing in my belly. "What can I get for you?"

My cell number? A night in the sack? A blow job? Reverse cowgirl ride of your life?

I'd have pretty much agreed to anything in that moment while tingles raced between my thighs.

"Black coffee." Mr. Yummy gave me his eyes again, and another shiver licked down my spine. An olive green encased his pupils...going gold to deep nutmeg brown before the black center. Stunningly beautiful, a place a woman could easily get lost in.

Heat rose to my cheeks, but I forced out the upsell of fresh blueberry muffins even though others stood in line behind him.

His "Sure" rumbled with a low tone, ticking me in all the right places.

"Name?" I asked what I always did to identify a customer's order.

"Blaine."

I echoed his reply in my head, imagining whispering it while he sank balls deep into my body.

Wet. Panties.

Shit. I bit my lower lip and handed him his receipt, cursing that I didn't have time to flirt or jot down my number on the back of it.

He ambled off to the side while I forced myself to give the next customer my attention.

I'd rather have been Cheryl working alongside me who took over his order and got to hand him his coffee and bagged muffin.

I could feel his stare, and goosebumps stayed firmly in place along my arms.

"Blaine?" Cheryl called, and he moved in close.

Our gazes clashed again, his shy smile making me swoon.

Cheryl elbowed me the second he turned away, breaking out into song about the joy of the Lord and earning her an elbow right back.

"No God bullshit, remember?" I whispered harshly. "Unless you want puke all over your shoes."

She laughed at me, but my gaze followed Blaine out the front door. "Tell me he's a regular."

"I've never seen him before," Cheryl said, taking the next order from my hand.

"Damn." I let out a heavy exhale and forced a grin—definitely not from the Holy Spirit—and faced the next customer.

"I'll take a cinnamon dolce latte with three shots of espresso, one pump of hazelnut, and extra whipped cream." Her snooty voice had me thinking I wanted to reply that I would rather leave her hanging and go back to bed, but I kept my smile in place.

"And can I interest you in one of our warm-from-the-oven blueberry muffins?"

"Too many calories," she sniffed.

As if the drink she'd ordered wouldn't already put her over the daily limit if she truly counted.

The second she stepped off to the side, I glanced out the cafe's front windows.

Mr. Yummy had disappeared.

My smile dissolved, but I decided all wasn't lost. I still might be able to snag Scott with the gray sweatpants who had a V and bulge to die for.

5

BLAINE

At the quiet singing of the barista, nausea had set in my stomach. I'd been familiar with that song about the joy of the Lord—*too* much. The gorgeous girl who had waited on me stated the same way I'd felt at hearing the damn tune.

The mention of God made her want to puke.

I wondered over her story while sipping my coffee and striding back to the jobsite. Studied the image of her I'd taken in my mind while devouring the muffin she'd suggested I buy.

Delicious—and I expected she was too.

Big brown eyes with dark lashes, glossed lips, petite... everything Grey's and my hookup from the night before hadn't been.

Any other normal guy would have flirted, hell, even outright asked for her number when they felt the interest brew in their balls like mine had at the sight of her.

Not for the first time, I hated my insecurities, wished shit had been different for me so I could open my damn mouth and be *normal.*

Once I ambled back the three blocks I'd walked earlier, I'd finished my break snack, and the slight kick of excitement I'd had collapsed in on itself. I picked up where I'd left off on the job, spreading sand to ready a new patio for pavers, but my head refused to focus on work.

I wondered if the coffee girl's skin would be as smooth beneath my fingertips as it appeared. Would she be turned on by my calluses and rough hands? Or did she not prefer the hardworking type of man who didn't have any softness left to offer at all?

Fuck.

I swiped my forearm over my sweating brow, lips pressed tightly together. As if I had *anything* to give such a woman other than my dick and an orgasm or two.

Since when did I even think about a woman?

Still frowning, I grabbed a few papers off the pallet. If Grey knew I'd considered asking a girl out, he'd have been all over my ass until I relented, fought off my nervousness, and took life by the balls.

Had he been with me, he'd have done the deed himself, saving me from discomfort.

Jealousy should have itched beneath my skin at the idea of Grey touching the coffee girl—I'd seen her first—but the thought of him shoving his dick down her throat while I sank into her slick pussy gave me a chub enough that I had to adjust myself before kneeling down to set in the next line of blocks.

I loved sharing women with Grey, even enjoyed watching him with them if I wasn't in the mood to fuck. The man had magic hands, and according to the people he brought home, his dick was just as gifted. Hell knew he could move his hips like a male stripper. Kind of hard to not notice when he made a woman all but cry beneath him.

Not that I would ever tell him. Like I'd said, he didn't need any help in stroking his ego.

"Blaine!"

"Yeah?" I hollered back at Wyatt, my boss, having recognized his deep raspy voice without seeing him.

He rounded the house I labored behind, and I sank back on my haunches.

"What's up?"

"How's it going?" His head swiveled while taking in the patio I sweated over, his bright blue eyes hidden behind shades and his dark hair and scruff just as sweaty as mine.

"Good. The base didn't need much fixing after I ripped out that old shit." I motioned toward the pile of old pavers I'd cleared first thing that morning. "Just a bit of stone dust and the sand."

Wyatt nodded, and I bent forward to put another new block in place. I didn't mind my boss watching me work. He'd been the one to train me and trusted me enough to leave me on a job alone.

"I was checking in to see if you needed help, but it doesn't look like Davidson calling in sick set you back."

"Nope," I said, tapping the block with a rubber mallet to settle it evenly with the one beside it. "He okay?"

"Asshole is hungover."

I nodded, having heard that excuse before. My drunken right-hand man missed more Mondays than he showed up for. Wyatt had a soft spot for the guy. I'd never asked why since I wasn't one to sit and shoot the shit.

"Looks like you have a couple days here at most," Wyatt said.

"Could be the entire week if Davidson doesn't show up tomorrow though."

"He promised he'd be here."

"I'll believe that when I see it," I grumbled.

Wyatt made a noise of agreement under his breath. "I landed that contract for the Sunrise Condos buildings."

"No shit!" I sat back again, grinning up at him while squinting. "Fucking cool."

"Right?" He grinned, flashing perfectly straight teeth I couldn't help but envy.

There'd been no yearly dentist checkups when I'd been a kid, no option of an orthodontist to fix my crooked lower teeth.

Just another insecurity to add to the shit in my life.

Grey had offered to pay, but I'd taken enough handouts from him in our nine years together.

"When do we start?" I asked, refusing to fall back into the trap like I'd done the night before and on my walk home from the cafe.

"They want two guys full time—and I was hoping you'd take on the management of the property."

I blinked in the bright sunlight, sure I'd misheard. "Seriously?"

"Yeah, man. You've proven your worth time and again. No one shows up like you, works their ass off without complaint. Fuck, if I had deeper pockets, I'd offer you another raise."

Wyatt had given me one six months earlier, and I'd been beyond thankful for his generosity.

"You're the hardest worker I have, Blaine. Wish I could clone the fuck out of you."

Warmth swelled inside my chest at the words of praise. If the guy kept talking like that, I'd fall into platonic love with him like I was with Grey.

"I appreciate it," I told him.

He dipped his head. "Same. I'll let you know what's up

with Davidson in the am, but if he calls off again, I'll make sure you've got a grunt to help you finish this by Friday."

"Sounds good."

"I put the business sign in the yard out front—sorry I didn't replace yours from the last job."

Part of our contracts allowed for us to put up advertisement signs in customer's front yards, and the one I'd had in my company truck had gone missing.

"I need to order a couple more, so I'll be sure to grab you a few."

"Thanks."

Wyatt ambled back the way he'd come, and I focused back on doing a good job to keep the positive reviews coming in for Lionel's Landscaping. The busier Wyatt was, the more security I had.

Even if the new management position didn't come with another pay raise, the knowledge that my boss trusted me to represent his family business made me smile all damn day.

When Grey got home later that night, he pulled up short, blinking at me where I stood in the kitchen, grinning like an idiot while making spaghetti.

"Did you go out and get laid all on your own?" he asked, his voice raised in disbelief at my rare display of jolliness.

"Wyatt's offering me a management position—he landed that Sunrise Condo contract."

"Get the fuck out." Grey set down his briefcase and shrugged off his suit coat. "That's fucking awesome."

The previous twenty-four hours had been a roller coaster, diving into shit from the looks of the woman we'd shared, to chugging upward from the sight of coffee girl then cresting at the news from Wyatt.

An hour later, my brain rushed back downhill over the

news Grey watched on TV behind me while I finished up our dinner dishes.

A young girl, barely legal, had filed charges of childhood rape—against a well-known TV evangelist.

My stomach emptied right there on the floor, spaghetti, beer, and bile splattering over the marble tile.

"Fuck!" Grey hopped off the couch, the TV shut down and the clicker tossed, clattering on the living room floor. "Sorry, Blaine—I didn't change channels fast enough— fucking hell."

Another eruption gagged me, and I coughed, bent over with my hands on my knees.

Memories slammed into my brain, and I shook, eyes wide and staring at the reddened mess I'd made so I wouldn't focus on the images in my head.

Grey laid his hand on my lower back, rubbing while offering me a wet paper towel. "Okay?"

I nodded, swallowing hard against another heave. Grabbing the towel, I blinked and straightened. After a quick swipe of the damp cloth over my face, Grey spun me, pulling me against him.

A shudder ripped through my body, and I sank into his embrace, my cheek on his shoulder, my arms limp at my sides.

It wasn't the first time Grey had held me upright and offered his strength when mine left me.

"I'm so fucking sorry," he murmured, his breath hot on my hair.

"Not your fault." My voice rasped from acid rawness.

"Go hop in the shower. I'll clean this up."

I pulled away, shaking my head, coolness sliding down over my front where his body had provided much-needed warmth. A deep yearning to take advantage of his heat swept through me, but I stayed steady. "No. I'll do it."

The stench of vomit clung to my nose long after I scrubbed the floor, and it took a hot shower and a thorough scouring of my teeth to erase the effects of past memories.

Fucking bottoming out in my head did me in every goddamn time.

Weakness continued to plague my knees, and no matter how much I tried to focus on the present, my thoughts wandered to my sister.

With dark hair and bright hazel-green eyes, she'd been a spitting image of our led-like-a-lamb mom—and in our leader's sights when I'd left.

At thirteen, she'd been a budding beauty, and our dad had pushed her into our leader's focus whenever he'd been able to.

I feared what had become of her, if she'd been soiled like I'd been. Used up and left a mere husk. Incapable of feeling good emotions for longer than fleeting moments.

Guilt rose to choke me as I lay in bed, my eyes clenched tight. Leaving her behind hadn't been easy, but if I had stayed at the compound, I would have rested six feet beneath the soil long before my time. I'd been near the point of suicide when Grey offered to take me away from the only home I'd known.

Selfishly, I'd agreed.

And not a day didn't go by that I didn't mourn the only family member I'd loved—and left.

6

GREYSON

By morning, the feel of Blaine in my arms had faded, and a scowl etched on my face. A near sleepless night made me bleary-eyed and grumpy as fuck. Longing to fix the shit of Blaine's past had haunted me every minute, and the only conclusion I found was to do away with the cult once and for all.

If the compound emptied, its leaders suffering for the hurt they'd caused dozens of people, then perhaps Blaine would gain emotional healing and be able to move on with his life.

He'd told me enough of the nightmares he'd lived that if proven true would disband the sheep-like flock of followers from the man they looked upon as a god. And possibly put the asshole and his wife behind bars where they belonged.

But how could I expose what went down behind the chain-link fence, especially knowing Blaine wouldn't ever be able to take part in any court case brought against them? Merely hearing about a similar situation to what he'd endured had brought up his dinner the night before and left him weak.

And I wouldn't be able to hold him, be his strength, as he took the stand to help do away with the fuckers.

Lips in a grim line, I settled back in my office's chair the first minute I could spare from work and rang my father back home.

"Grey*son*, my *son*." His usual greeting revealed his grin, but my lips didn't twitch.

"Dad." I sounded shorter than I'd intended.

"Everything okay?" he asked, his tone flatlined by mine, all business.

"What do you know about that compound back behind our vacation home?" I asked rather than answering.

"The people keep to themselves and are well respected. Pious. They're rarely seen in town. Why? Is something going on with Blaine?" Concern filled his voice as it always did whenever we spoke of the man he saw as a second son.

I hadn't ever told my dad about the full extent of abuse Blaine had endured at the compound, and I wasn't about to uncover the truth of his hurtful past without permission. Ever since Mom's accident, Dad and I had become wicked close, but I refused to reveal secrets that weren't mine to share.

I'd been a little kid lost without his mom, and Dad had the love of his life torn from his side. We'd clung to each other, but no matter how close or good our relationship, nothing could replace what we'd lost.

Being ten years old and having to hear your dad sob while alone in his bed every night does shit to a kid's brain. Makes you recognize insecurity and fear abandonment— even if it takes years to put a name to both.

At least Dad fully understood my feelings for Blaine when I'd come out to him, and he'd agreed to keep my unrequited love to himself. It had been at Dad's prompting for us to leave the East Coast where my love might feel safer and heal from the bit of trauma he'd known about.

"He'll be fine," I stated, hoping like hell I spoke the truth. "Any chance you could get me the name and number of that detective you used a few years back? I've got shit that needs dug up and exposed for what it is."

"Anything for you and that boy of yours," Dad stated quietly, his gruff voice an attempt to hide his generous spirit I'd inherited.

As his only offspring and still seen as the golden child he'd always believed me to be, I knew Dad would give me whatever I asked for, same as always—same as I would do for those I cared about and loved. He might not have the nurturing heart of a mother, but he offered all he could.

Same as me.

I jotted down the information and promised to call him later with my findings.

"Before you go..." He paused, a rare display of insecurity in his tone.

My brow furrowed. "Yeah?" I asked when he didn't continue.

"Would you be averse to me dating again?"

His words took a few seconds to compute in my head. Dad hadn't shown interest in other women. Ever.

Dad. Dating.

A sweet exhale deflated my lungs, and I found myself grinning just as the clouds outside my office windows broke, allowing beams of sunshine to create rectangles of light on my office floor. "It's about damn time. Seriously, Dad. I hate that you've been alone for the last nine years without me."

"It's been good." His tone sounded like a smile. "I've done a lot of healing, worked through my grief. Dahlia says I've made amazing steps toward living again."

Dahlia. His therapist—his person from what I'd figured out with how much he talked about her.

"It took you long enough to realize she's the one, Dad."

"She really is." He sounded all dreamy like he gazed off into the sunset, imagining her in a white dress walking hand in hand with him on the beach.

I scrubbed a hand down over my face. Fucking romantic sap. I tended to keep that part of me under lock and key since Blaine wouldn't ever accept my loving words and dreams lavished on him.

"You have my blessing," I told Dad even though he hadn't asked for it.

"Thank you, Greyson."

"Love you."

"Love you more," he kidded back as always, and I hung up a few second later, my throat tight.

I'd often wondered if he hadn't dated since Mom's passing because I would see it in a negative light. Sure, we'd lost the woman we'd both loved, but life continued, and I longed for him to be happy.

Mom would, I didn't doubt. Even at ten, I'd known she'd wanted the best for him—same as she had for me.

Fuck, did I miss her soft smiles and kisses goodnight. The tender arms of unconditional love and affection I used to soak in.

A deep yearning for nurturing slumbered inside my heart like I was still ten years old, but I couldn't ask Blaine for it. It had been enough that I could give him just a taste what I yearned for.

But the memories of Mom that my conversation with Dad had brought to the surface had me wishing for more. I realized how much I missed out on in life. Dad was moving on...did I have it in me to look as well?

I blinked at the information I'd written down, pulling myself from grief that still made me wish things could be different between Blaine and me.

Dan Higgins, PI, would give me something else to focus on. Lucky for me, he was in his office and had a few minutes to spare.

Without naming Blaine, I went into some of what he'd experienced in the compound, explaining the punishment boxes and the whipping post in the village green he'd been tied to a few times.

My free hand clenched my chair arm, and I had to force myself to relax. The cold coffee I'd been sipping didn't do much to ease the tension in my guts that always cranked up when thinking or speaking about Blaine's past.

I also went into what Dad had said about the cult members but told Higgins it was a front for the sick shit the leader and his wife did all in the name of God.

"Infiltrating the compound won't be easy or cheap," Higgins stated once I finished.

"Money isn't a concern," I assured him, my stomach still in knots. Just the tales of what Blaine endured made me nauseated. I couldn't imagine what he'd dealt with—enough he puked at the mere mention of religious sickos. "I just want—*need*—to expose the truth."

Higgins didn't speak for a few seconds. "How far do you plan on taking this if the stories you've heard aren't hearsay?"

"As far as possible. I won't rest until the lying assholes abusing innocents are behind bars. But there's more."

"I'm listening."

I inhaled until it hurt, ready to reveal a secret Blaine didn't speak of but I'd wondered over with the haunted look in his eye the night before after puking all over the kitchen floor. "There's a young woman named Sarah Mitchell who lived at the compound as of nine years ago. Dark hair, hazel-green eyes. She would be around twenty-three now."

"Someone you know personally?"

"Close enough." I offered what I could about Blaine's younger sister. "I'd like whatever news you can find on her first."

"My schedule doesn't allow for much right now, but seeing as you're a Scott, I'll make the time."

After a brief overview of his charges, I promised to wire him the retainer fee, thankful as fuck for my surname and assets. Coming from money had its benefits even if it left me with a handful of true, honest friends. Dad and Blaine being the ones I sought out when I needed anything. I could count on the two of them to not bullshit or manipulate me.

Once we hung up, I filled my lungs to bursting and slowly let it leak out in attempts to ease the tension in my shoulders.

"You're a broody bitch this morning."

I glared at my secretary who'd waltzed into my office without knocking. Another of the few I considered friends, Meryl knew she could get away with murder when others in my employ wouldn't dream of speaking to me in such a way. Or entering without being invited.

"Lucky for you," she said, striding across my office, "I took an early break and stopped by Darlene's."

My frown dissolved as Meryl set a box of donuts on my desk. "I fucking love you." I all but groaned the words.

"I know."

I popped open the box and shoved half a chocolate iced donut into my mouth. A groan *did* escape me.

"Personal or business?" Meryl asked, perching her pert

ass on the corner of my desk, arms folding beneath the swell of her double-Ds.

"Personal."

"Need to vent?"

I shook my head and shoved the rest of the treat between my lips.

Fucking icing...sickeningly sweet perfection created at Darlene's Donuts a block away. My weakness. The donuts were kick-ass all on their own, but the chocolate frosting... goddamn chef's kiss.

And fuck, did the treat do its job of settling my emotions even more.

I'd handed over the case to Higgins...I could trust him to find the truth.

Meryl sat and waited as though expecting me to spill the thoughts lingering in my head, but Blaine's issues and what I planned to do about them weren't something she needed to know.

"Rough night," I finally said. "Didn't get much sleep."

"Woman or man problem?" she prodded, and I shook my head.

"Neither. Just...other shit. Nothing serious."

"You're sure?" She peered down at me, studying my face with a mixture of empathy and curiosity.

"I'm sure." I snagged another donut and nodded toward the door. "Thanks for the mood-booster, but I've got a ton of shit to do."

She snorted and straightened, smoothing her linen skirt with manicured hands. "Are you done being a broody bitch?"

"Thanks to you." I grinned up at her and winked even though it felt a little forced. "You're the best, M."

"Don't you forget it." She turned and walked off but

paused after opening my office door. "It's my birthday Saturday. Just saying."

I huffed a laugh over what me and her partner had secretly planned to celebrate her thirtieth, and she let herself out. My smile lingered for a few more seconds, and wanting to stay in a good place mentally, I left the investigation to Higgins in my mind. Work could also rest on the back burner a little longer.

My cell sat atop my desk beside the donut box, and I grabbed it, leaned back in my chair, and swiped it to life. Face ID activated, my home screen popped up. Two swipes to the right took me to another screen full of personal shit.

Missing Link's three-heart rainbow logo had a little red heart in the top right corner.

Grin widening, I opened the app.

Bikini girl, @S2L, had sent me a simple **Hi** message, and the green circle of availability beside her name meant she was still online.

Hi back, I messaged quickly before she disappeared.

I waited, refusing to chew a fingernail or tap my fingers on my chair's arm in my impatience. A message popped up, and I released a rushed exhale, surprised I hadn't noticed I'd been holding my breath.

@S2L: **I don't usually play the aggressor, but your profile tickled me in all the right places.**

I chuckled, typing out a response. **Which parts?**

@S2L: **Of your body or the write-up?**

Both, I went with while settling into my chair, ready to soak up whatever ego stroke she offered because after that chat with my dad and the aftereffects of grief, I was in desperate need of affirmation in any way, shape, or form.

@S2L: **As if you don't know you look hot as fuck in gray sweats.**

My dick thickened a bit in my briefs, and I palmed myself, getting a little more comfortable in case bikini girl wanted to get frisky online.

@S2L: **Like my handle suggests, I'm seeking two lovers. Nothing serious, just a good time to fulfill some fantasies. And you state you have a roommate...**

I had some *fantasies* of my own about said roommate.

"Fuck." I stretched out my neck side to side before replying, **Care to share what you've been dreaming about?**

@S2L: **I could be persuaded to over dinner and drinks.**

Bikini girl was careful even if she was only twenty-four and sowing wild oats, but until Blaine was on board with sharing another woman with me, getting together as a threesome might not be on the ticket.

He's got major social anxiety, and I always vet the women I meet on the app before bringing him into the equation. I typed out the mostly truth Blaine didn't mind me sharing with potential hookups.

@S2L: **You're a good friend.**

I wanted to be a fuck ton more. **I try. I'd love to go out with you, and if things go well, I'll get him to help fulfill some of those fantasies you have.**

@S2L: **That sounds like a delicious plan.**

Damn right, it did.

Do you have any hard limits? I asked what wasn't shared on our initial profiles.

@S2L: **No scat play, no golden showers. No bondage, I don't like pain with my pleasure, and I'm not a big fan of the crossing of swords if you know what I mean.**

I imagined my cock coming into contact with Blaine's and swelled fully, my length pressed hard against my pants. A ridge not easily hid throbbed along my thigh.

Thank fuck for private offices where no one but Meryl entered without an invite.

I squeezed my dick, rubbing my thumb over the swollen head, contemplating my weekend and how long I would have to wait to meet up with her.

Friday, I was hosting an office gathering at my house—surprise birthday party for Meryl—so that shot down that night. I didn't want to wait for Saturday.

Tonight? Yachtsman's Club? I suggested a bar I often went hunting in. Oceanfront and a few blocks from my home, the hotel's restaurant offered a sexy, dim interior and rooms easily rented for the night if a woman preferred to stay on neutral turf.

@S2L: **Gotta work. Wednesday night too. Are you up for Thursday?**

"Am I." I chuckled. **I'm up** *now*, **but I can wait for Thursday.**

@S2L: **Tell me more.** She sent along one of those smirking, side-eyed emojis along with a purple devil.

Demanding little minx—playful too. **Tell you or show you?**

@S2L: **Those sweats revealed all I need to know...if that pic is really you.**

It is, I assured her. **But what I'm packing right now is even more impressive.**

@S2L: **If that's the truth, you've definitely got yourself a date, Scott.**

A hot-faced emoji accompanied her message.

I hoped she didn't mind being bossed around because I couldn't function any other way. **Wear red. It's a good color on you.**

@S2L: **Does the fulfillment of my fantasies hinge on my ability to obey demands like that?**

If the woman looked as good in person as she did in her picture, I'd be on board with giving her whatever the fuck she wanted regardless of her lack of interest in being told what to do. Hell, I could easily be persuaded to be on the submissive end if it meant getting her on my cock.

Would you *please* **wear red?** I found myself grinning again while hitting send. Since when did I beg?

@S2L: **Thanks for the compliment, and I will—if you'll wear those sweats.**

Another laugh rumbled through me. **Yachtsman's isn't a sweats and hoodie kind of bar. Maybe afterward?**

@S2L: **Sigh. Does your roommate look as good as you do in those delicious things?**

Better. I typed out my response and bit down on my lower lip at the memory of Blaine wearing sweats the night before when I'd gotten home from work. Slung low on his hips, the sharply defined V disappearing beneath the waistband—and no fucking shirt.

My dick jerked beneath my hold.

No man wore gray sweats like Blaine Mitchell.

@S2L: **Damn, I'm in trouble if that's really true.**

I blew out a breath, wishing I could type the "You and me both" that would out my obsession with my best friend and let bikini girl know I wasn't as averse to the crossing of swords as she was. Bikini girl...

What's your real name, beautiful? I couldn't help but ask. Rarely did hookups on Missing Link offer that sort of truth, my name included, but I found myself more interested in the young woman than usual. Perhaps it was her blunt honesty and the lack of drama I tended to find too much of. Sure, the girl sounded needy—but in the best way possible.

@S2L: **Lily.**

I rolled her answer around in my head before saying it out loud in my suddenly stifling office. Imagining Blaine whimpering her name while sinking deep inside her pussy caused pre-cum to ooze from my slit.

Fucking hell. Even if he wasn't up for another hookup that soon, I needed to get between Lily's thighs.

Can't wait for Thursday. I tossed in a winking emoji.

She replied with a kissy face, then: **I'm not against seeing evidence of** *that.*

"Shit." I scrubbed a hand over my face, sure I misunderstood.

You don't want a dick pic, but you want to see my cum? I typed out, too damn curious to let her last message go without explanation.

@S2L: **Yes, please.**

God*damn…*

"Fuck it." I didn't jerk off in my office, but something about our light banter had me going to the point that I didn't give a flying fuck if Meryl walked in again without knocking. It would serve the woman right, maybe teach her a lesson she refused to learn otherwise.

I pulled out my dick, wrenched my dress shirt up beneath my chin, and rubbed one out within a matter of a few strokes, my focus on the image of Lily in her red bikini. Those pert tits, the tiny waist, the swell of her hips…

Sticky white painted my abs, and I heaved for breath, my clean hand shaking while taking a picture of that evidence she'd asked for. I made sure to capture my grip on my still-hard dick. If Lily wanted my cum, she was going to see where it came from too.

I hit send, tingles of euphoria settling into my fingers and toes while my breathing slowed.

Lily replied with a lip-licking emoji, then: **It looks like you could use some help cleaning up.**

I groaned another curse, wondering what the fuck had gotten into me. I never sexted while in the office. Ever.

I don't normally do this at work, I let her know.

@S2L: **Mmm. The thought of me must really do it for you then, huh?**

I'll admit to enjoying our conversation, but that red bikini... I trailed off my words, once more going back for another good look.

@S2L: **Those sweats...**

An image came through, stealing my breath.

Pink panties...a slender hand shoved beneath.

Another image flashed before I could fill my lungs, creamed fingers splayed on a taut belly, the pinkie resting beneath the edge of the satin like she still tickled her clit.

"Fucking. Hell." I gulped, my dick considering another go.

@S2L: **See you Thursday, Scott.**

I swallowed hard, my head falling back against my chair.

Two days, and I would hopefully get a taste of what smeared over her fingers.

But even better would be a call from Higgins. Hopefully, he'd find some leads into finally helping me set Blaine free so we could enjoy Lily together.

7

———

LILY

"Your tall, dark, and handsome was in this morning."

I moaned while tossing my purse into one of the employee room's cubbies. Turning, I found Cheryl smirking at me. I propped my hands on my hips. "Are you shitting me?"

"Nope." Her smile widened. "He asked about you."

"Get. Out!" And after I'd spent the morning getting myself off a half-dozen times once that sexting session with Scott of the Gray Sweats had ended.

"His face was beet red when I asked him if he was looking for someone—he'd been craning his neck for a peek behind the counter."

"Seriously?"

"The poor guy fumbled his words but spit out he wondered where the coffee girl from Monday was."

"He called me coffee girl?" A grin spread over my face, my insides going all gooey over the fact the shy man had given me a nickname.

"Yep." Cheryl perched her sunglasses atop her head, readying to head out for the day. "Any chance you want to trade shifts tomorrow? Janine is looking for someone to cover her—"

"Yes!" I cut Cheryl off, and we both burst into laughter.

"Good, cuz I told him you'd be in when we opened at six." She bumped me with her shoulder while passing, making for the back door. "You're welcome."

"Holy hell," I whispered, my stomach alight with butter-flies. Switching out shifts meant I had Wednesday night off...

I considered messaging Scott to see if he was up for moving our little date by a night but quickly shut that idea down. If tall, dark, and handsome of Lionel's Landscaping came in the next morning, I wanted my evening free.

Just in case.

I'd shown my entire messaging thread with Scott to Haley—except for the naughty pics I'd sent him—and she'd groaned her jealousy.

Me: **You'll never guess who came in looking for me this morning.**

Haley: **Get the fuck out!**

Me: **Right!?! What should I do?**

Haley: **Why choose? Ride that wave as far as you can.**

I snorted a laugh even while knowing my family would consider me a whore for wanting two guys at the same time. "Nothing wrong with sexual freedom," I reminded myself, refusing to live beneath guilt from teachings that were no longer pertinent to my life.

Me: **I'm going to.**

Haley: **Good.**

Me: **Loves you!**

Haley: **Loves you more, you lucky bitch.**

My smile stayed put long into the evening shift.

Scott had left me a message on the Missing Link app when I finished work at seven.

Scott: **Send me a selfie. I want to see those big brown eyes.**

I just got off work and look like shit, I messaged while hoofing it to my car in the back lot.

Scott: **Don't care.**

Snorting, I climbed into the Ford I'd snagged for a whopping three grand. While it appeared to have lived a full life, its paint faded and fender banged up a bit from its previous owner, the thing ran like a dream. The engine purred, and I cranked down my window—yes it was *that* old.

I checked myself out in the rearview, deciding to keep my hair back in the ponytail. A quick reapplication of gloss and I lifted my cell, tilting my head just right to catch the sunset's rays coming through my windshield.

Brown eyes appearing more golden in the fading light. I straightened my shoulders, let out a full exhale, and snapped the pic.

While not as sexy as I'd have liked, at least I didn't have bags under my eyes.

I sent the image and backed out of my spot, determined to not look at his reply, if I got one, until I parked at home.

A notification came through. Then another...and a third.

The second I stopped at a red light, I swiped my screen to life.

Scott: **It really is you. You're beautiful.**

Scott: **Those eyes. Those lips. I hope I get the chance to devour them.**

His last line surprised me. Most guys went straight for the whole, "Your lips would look good wrapped around my cock" line when complimenting my mouth, letting me know without question what kind of lover they'd be.

Selfish as fuck.

Scott: **I want to nose along the smooth skin of your neck, breathing you deep into my lungs. I'll bet you smell sweet. Bet you taste even better.**

I smiled as heat rose to my cheeks. Another message came through before I could reply.

Scott: **If you need to see more evidence about how excited I am to meet you in person, just say the word.**

His wink emoji made me giggle.

A horn blared behind me, but I typed out a **Yes, please** anyway, making the asshole behind me wait.

I stomped on the gas and peeled out, desperate to get home to see what else Scott had messaged. Butterflies jittered through my stomach, enough to make my hands shake when I put the car in park five minutes later. I picked my cell back up.

Scott had sent a five-second video of his hand wrapped around his hard cock. Pre-cum beaded and smeared—and my pussy pulsed when he shot ejaculate toward his camera.

"Oh God." I bit my lip and lifted my phone closer to my eyes, tapping the volume button and then replay.

Heavy breaths filled my ears.

One low groan at the first spurt of white.

My core clenched at the sound. There was nothing on the face of the earth sexier than a man's guttural noises while coming.

Fingers shaking and pulse thrumming, I typed out, **Hot. As. Fuck.**

Scott: **Thought I'd gone too far when you didn't reply right away.**

I was driving home, I told him and grabbed my bag, intent on the indoors so I could get myself off.

Scott: **Give me a peek at whatever color panties you're wearing right now.**

I snorted, shaking my head. Unshaved, not showered... yeah, no. I paused in my rush up the stairs. **Maybe later.**

He sent three sad faces and one puppy dog eyes emoji.

The horny bastard.

I enjoyed our banter, the sexy chatting and teasing. He seemed a bit bossy but laid-back too, like he appreciated life and didn't take things too seriously.

Was it possible to totally have the hots for someone without having met them in person? What if he was a lousy kisser? Would that gorgeous dick make up for where he lacked?

I expected it might—I hadn't enjoyed a good stretch in far too long. Billy of the Pencil Dicks hadn't done more than jab a few times before filling the condom. No clit play, no fingers, just straight on fucking. The second I'd kicked his ass out of my bed, I'd gotten myself off.

Fifteen minutes later, I did the same, but to thoughts of Scott and his big dick rather than a fantasy.

Haley had wine waiting for me.

I slumped on the couch, my skin rosy and hot from the shower—and the message I'd sent of the white lacy panties covering my freshly-shaved pussy. "Want to see the latest?"

She held out her hand, and I gave her my cell without a word, smirking while sipping my wine.

"Oh my god, he sounds like a sweetie..." Her voice trailed off while reading the first couple of messages about my lips and neck. "A video?" She waggled her eyebrows and pressed play.

Her eyes bugged out at the short teaser, and like me, she lifted the cell closer, pressing that volume-up button.

Scott's low groan hit my ears, and I bit the inside of my lip.

"Holy shit, that's hot," she murmured, tucking her hair behind her ear. "Like, seriously hot."

"Right?" I sounded like a breathless whore.

One more replay and she tossed the cell at me. "You lucky *bitch*," she repeated what she'd called me earlier in the day.

"What if he's an asshole in person?"

"With a dick like that, who gives a shit?" Haley settled back in the corner of the couch and lost herself in her cell.

"Did you get on the app?" I asked, waiting for Scott to reply about my panties pic.

"Too busy. Too tired to fill out a bunch of questions."

"It's worth it," I told her and took another sip of chardonnay.

A notification popped up, and my pulse jumped.

Scott: ***groan***

I could imagine that sound in my head and played it on repeat until I fell asleep later that night.

———

Tall, dark, and handsome showed up at the cafe at ten-thirty, sweaty and dirty like he'd been on Monday. So damn delicious-looking that my knees went weak.

All thoughts of Scott pushed to the back of my mind the second my gaze collided with the hazel eyes I remembered all too well.

"Hey," I said, smiling as he approached the counter.

Pink stained his cheeks beneath the dust and dirt, and

his gaze flitted up overhead at the menu board. "Black coffee?"

He muttered no hi, nothing but an order that sounded like a question.

"Sure thing, Blaine."

His focus jerked back to my face. "You remembered my name."

"You're not a man easily forgotten." I looked up at him through my lashes, my flirty tone so damn obvious any guy could take the hint.

He smiled, revealing a crooked eyetooth that didn't distract from his gorgeousness one damn bit.

"Blueberry muffin?" I asked, ringing up his coffee.

"Sure."

"Dinner tonight?" I tossed out as he handed over a five.

Blaine blinked, swallowing hard like I'd lashed his feet from beneath him. "Um..."

"Sorry," I rushed to say, snagging the bill he'd held toward me as heat flooded my cheeks. Cheryl had said he'd asked after me, but maybe he didn't like forward girls. Maybe—

"H-How about a late lunch instead?" Blaine's suggestion barely escaped his mouth, and he swallowed again.

I could work with shy. Hell knew, no man could be worse than Levi.

My smile widened as I handed over his change. "I'd love that."

"T-Tomorrow? I have to finish up the patio job and should be done by one. Maybe one-thirty." His words left in a rush, and he struggled to hold my gaze.

"Meet you here?" I suggested, realizing I would need to take it easy on the poor guy.

"Here. Tomorrow." He nodded, his focus flitting toward

me a few times as he stepped off to the side to wait for his order.

"Hi," I said to the next person in line, for once not having to force a smile.

I caught Blaine's gaze again before he headed toward the door, and I fluttered my fingers, jittery as hell.

Two dates in one day—but I doubted I'd get laid twice in those hours. Blaine was hot as hell and filled out his dirty work clothes enough to spin my head, so I didn't mind waiting for him to make a move. Even if it took a few lunch or dinner dates.

He seemed the type that would be worth the wait.

8

BLAINE

I asked a girl out for lunch—and I hadn't even gotten her name.

She was so damn pretty, and her smile made my knees weak. I almost drowned in her sparkly dark eyes, could barely keep my thoughts straight. How the hell was I going to sit across from her at a table without my usual buffer to ease my nervousness?

"You got this." I shook my hands out at my sides, striding down the sidewalk toward the cafe on Thursday for my date. "You *need* this." My self pep talk fell flat.

I'd never had a woman on my own, and the thought of it, while exciting, felt...off. Strangely unnatural.

I'm too dependent on Grey.

Everything good in my life was wrapped up in a neat package with him. What would happen when he was ready to move on from sharing a place with his best friend? Start something serious with whoever turned him inside out?

My stomach twisted.

I would be left to scramble on my own, *live* on my own, without his emotional support and strength.

The idea of a life without him made me just as sick, but I realized it was time to pull up my big boy boxers and do something alone for a change. Hitting bottom the night before had opened my eyes to that truth, and while I loved Grey, I needed to prove to myself that I could stand on my own two feet for when he eventually left me on the side of the road after finding his soul mate.

If things went well, if coffee girl and I ended up connecting and we met up enough times I was comfortable with her alone, then I would tell Grey about her.

Fuck knew he didn't fill me in on every hookup he'd had since moving to California—

She stood outside the cafe, her long blonde hair pulled back in a ponytail, large sunglasses covering her eyes. Still dressed in her work uniform, same as me, but mine was dirty from finishing up the job two blocks away.

I swatted at my thighs, dust from cutting pavers billowing around me while I walked toward her.

While I couldn't see her eyes, her head swiveled my way, and her smile stole my breath. Could she be any more beautiful?

My legs shook while I moved closer, my own grin making an appearance even though my insides quivered like Jell-O.

"Hi." She spoke first, her husky tone shooting lust straight to my balls.

"Hi." I stopped a few feet away, hands shoved in my pockets, mind blank to everything but her. Petite to my six-plus feet. Narrow across the shoulders unlike mine. Fairer hair to my dark.

But those lips slathered in gloss...I hungered for a taste, my damn mouth watering at the thought of flicking my tongue along the lower.

"So." Her smile widened. "Where did you want to grab some lunch?"

"Oh. Yeah." I cleared my throat while tearing my focus off her mouth, suddenly wishing to sink into the ground. I hadn't done any checking into what lay close by. "Um..."

"There's a sandwich bar a few blocks that way." She thumbed over her shoulder opposite of where I'd come from.

"Sandwiches are good." Fuck, I sounded like a moron.

She let out a soft giggle and spun, allowing me an eyeful of her pert little ass.

I bit back a groan and moved to her side, needing to give my libido a break before I stiffened fully and really made a fool of myself.

"I-I never got your name." I spewed yet another thing that would surely clue her into the fact that I was a total loser.

"Lily." She offered her hand without losing stride, and I clasped her smooth palm.

Instant electrical currents rushed up my arm, sliding over my torso to tingle my balls.

"Blaine—fuck, you already knew that."

She laughed again, and I forced myself to release my hold on her. "You have working-man hands."

"Sorry?"

"Don't be." She clenched her fingers I'd held into a tight fist, and like a hopeless romantic, I imagined it was because she wanted to hang onto the feel of me same as I'd done.

I loosened my own clasped hand at my side, letting out a heavy exhale. "I've never asked a girl out before," I blurted, my face heating.

Lily glanced up at me, and I wanted to rip those damn sunglasses off her face so I could see her eyes. "Seriously?"

"Yeah." I wiped my palms on my filthy jeans. "I'm...not good at this sort of thing. Communicating. Social stuff."

"I think you're doing just fine." She patted my arm, then squeezed, the lingering touch and soft smile still curving her lips settling my insides the slightest bit.

"I heard you talk about puking when your co-worker sang that song on Monday." More sewage from my mouth, but I figured she ought to hear the reason I'd found the balls to speak to her.

"The joy of the Lord bullshit?" she asked with a snort.

A grin flashed over my face as yet another piece of my insecurities melted away. "I've felt that way for years." I wasn't about to tell her it had happened the night I'd vomited over our kitchen floor. "You grew up in a church, I'm guessing."

"Yep." Lily didn't sound too thrilled about her past. "You?"

"A cult." I'd never admitted that to anyone but Grey, but something...*tangible* drew me to Lily. Like she got me, could understand me without having known me for more than a fast minute.

"How long has it been since you escaped?"

The wording she chose intensified my feeling of connecting with her, hitting me hard in the chest. "Nine years—not fucking long enough."

"Only one for me, and I hear that loud and clear." Lily smiled up at me, sending those jitters back through my insides even while I wanted to wrap her up in my arms and kiss away whatever darkness she might hide away inside her like I did.

I held open the sandwich shop's door, and she passed through, a cloud of vanilla swarming over my nose.

Of course she would smell as delicious as she looked.

My mouth watered and continued to long after we ordered at the counter and found a corner table to tuck ourselves away into.

She'd taken off her sunglasses and finally gave me her eyes as we settled across from one another.

I stared, wondering how the fuck I could feel so much for someone I knew so little about.

She stared—and smiled, easing some of my anxiety. "So."

"Yeah." My own grin felt lopsided, and I kept my lips closed to hide my crooked teeth. Heat flooded me, and I glanced around the shop.

"Were you always shy, or did the cult do it to you?"

Well, fuck.

My grin faded, and I rubbed a hand over the stubble along my jaw.

"Shit," Lily muttered. "Sorry. I tend to open my mouth a lot without thinking first."

Strangely enough, I wouldn't mind her mouth opening for me in other ways even though I'd never had a woman go down on me. But for some reason, I didn't mind her probing at the personal shit either. Maybe she felt the same thing between us, whatever it was, and wanted to figure it out. Maybe even expand on it a bit.

"I, uh, was always shy, I think." I cleared my throat. "But growing up on the compound definitely didn't help matters any."

"Does it make you uncomfortable to talk about your childhood?"

I'd only ever spoken to Grey about that shit, and even he didn't know all the details. "I'm not fond of it," I told her, sitting back in my chair and laying my sweating palms on my thighs, determined to keep them still. "Honestly, it was horrid. The shit of nightmares—and I still have them sometimes. It wasn't pretty."

"I'm sorry." Warmth filled her eyes, as though she understood. "I had a good childhood, well, it had seemed that way until I grew up and decided to make my own decisions about what I believed in. It took a lot of shit to get me where I am today, but I'm not sure I would change my past. It created who I am."

"I would change it all," I stated without hesitation, but the image of Grey floated through my mind, heating my chest like it always did when I thought of him. If I hadn't grown up on that compound in New Hampshire, I wouldn't have met my best friend, my semi-other half.

Our order number was called out from behind the counter, keeping me from overthinking. I hopped up to retrieve our lunch.

We ate a few minutes in silence, taking care of the hunger we had due to working all morning.

"Tell me about this job that makes you look like you could use a swim in the ocean," Lily said.

Heat rushed to my face again. "Sorry I'm filthy."

"I don't give a shit—just making an observation. Personally, I find your appearance ten times hotter than a man dressed in a suit and tie."

She hadn't seen Grey in *his* work clothes.

I blinked the image from my mind, wondering why I'd even gone there.

"Landscaping," I muttered.

Lily smirked, glancing at the logo on my shirt. "I kinda figured that one out on my own." Her dark eyes sparkled like she flirted.

We fell into easy conversation about what we both did for a living, neither of us touching on the topic of our past again. That connection had settled inside me like a carefully-laid boulder, situated in such a way I wouldn't ever forget its presence. Finding out she enjoyed chardonnay over beer, loved to lay on the beach and just *be* as the sun baked into her skin, and taught grade-school kids caused flowers to spring to life around the garden she'd created inside my mind.

"You're beautiful." I'd blurted an interruption, cutting her off mid-sentence about her piece-of-shit car she'd gotten for a few grand to haul her ass around town.

Pink highlighted her cheekbones. "Thanks."

I swallowed, glancing down at the napkin I'd crumpled atop my plate.

"You're pretty damn hot yourself."

Barely lifting my head, I met her gaze. I'd seen lust aplenty, but more than mere want for release radiated from her eyes.

"Can we do this again?" she asked, her tone more husky than bell-like. "Because I'll be honest, Blaine. I'd really like to get to know you better."

"There isn't much to know."

Nothing worth a damn, anyway.

Lily leaned onto the table, her gaze steady. Searching. "How about you let me decide that for myself?"

Because I could easily fall for you, and where would that leave me when you find out I'm nothing special?

"Blaine."

"Hmm?" I blinked her back into focus.

"How about we exchange numbers? Text a little bit. Chat some more. I'd love to get together again, but I'm also open to just being friends if that's all you're able to give right now."

I could always use another friend.

Not that anyone would ever take Grey's place.

"Sure. I'd like that."

We ambled back toward the cafe a few minutes later, walking closer than before, our sides brushing on occasion. Each and every time, tingles raced through me, and I kept my hands shoved in my jeans pockets so she wouldn't see them shake.

I followed her to her beat-up blue car, an eyebrow raising at its age.

"She's old and a piece of shit, just like I'd said," Lily said with a laugh, "but she's dependable and gets me to and from work. *And* she's all mine." The possessiveness in her tone layered yet another bit of beauty to the land of Lily inside my head.

She'd escaped too. Experienced freedom from a stifling past.

And goddamn, how I wanted to haul her up into my arms, squeeze her tight, and devour her mouth.

Stepping back, I cleared my throat. "Talk soon?"

Her smile sprinkled a few raindrops over the flowers she'd sown in that garden. "Definitely."

My legs shook while walking back to the job site to pick up my work truck, but I'd never been happier.

I carried around the secret of Lily in my heart, just as possessive over what she'd created inside me as she was over that POS car.

9

GREYSON

I ended up working late and didn't have time to run home to shower before my date with Lily.

Heading out for the night, I texted Blaine what I often did when on the prowl for a hookup. He shot back a thumbs up before I even walked out of my office.

He'd been quieter than normal since the evening I hadn't changed the news station quickly enough. My usual pushing for him to open up and talk about shit went ignored, worrying me even more.

Blaine didn't do well when he got inside his head, but I loved him enough to respect his boundaries.

Some of the shit he'd gone through he'd shared briefly and never touched upon again. The last thing I wanted to do was bring it to the surface of his mind and start back up the nightmares he suffered from for years after moving to the West Coast with me.

At least he hadn't shouted out in his sleep since then—not that I'd have minded crawling into bed with him and holding him until he quieted and rested again.

I missed having him in my arms like that but certainly

didn't wish those dreams to return. To have a man bigger than me shivering and shaking, clinging to me with grasping hands, outside sex…

In those moments, I felt needed and loved, able to give the nurturing I missed out on.

And secretly craved.

Perhaps once Higgins dug up some dirt—and hopefully exposed the truth about the cult—Blaine would be able to move on.

Pushing aside thoughts of home, my best friend, and longings that would never be fulfilled, I climbed into my car, ready for a drink.

Maybe a good fuck if Lily and I hit it off. With how we teased and messaged each other, I had high hopes.

I pulled into the valet out front of Yachtman's and handed over my keys as an old blue clunker puffed smoke and stopped behind me. The car appeared ready to shit the bed, and I went to turn away—until my gaze slid over the windshield and the driver behind the wheel.

Her.

Bikini girl.

I grinned, and she climbed out of the car, hitting all my goddamn feels with a simple clash of gazes that knocked my world off its axis, same as the first time I'd seen Blaine.

My breath left my lungs like I'd been punched in the gut.

Hair in soft waves over her shoulders, a shift of her body sent tresses over the hint of cleavage that played peekaboo with a blouse meant to tease. It was white with a deep slash across the chest, offering a tantalizing view to make men's mouths water. She wore a flirty skirt—also not red—and strappy heels that made her legs appear longer than possible for her petite height.

She handed over her keys and moved toward me with purpose, assurance and sensuality with every step swaying that damn skirt I wanted to sneak beneath. Not once did she glance over at my vintage Ferrari, and her slow perusal over my designer suit didn't light up a calculating gaze like it did with some dates. Nothing but lust rested in her eyes when she finally lifted her focus to my face.

Fuck yes.

"Scott?" Her low, husky tone hit my dick with a shot of lust-filled adrenaline, and I held out my hand.

Her small palm slid over mine, and I lifted the backs of her fingers toward my mouth. I always went by my surname when meeting with hookups, so I didn't bother correcting her.

"Lily, I'm assuming?" I brushed my lips over her knuckles, bummed as fuck she'd chosen to ignore my...*request* she wear red.

Pink stained her cheeks even though she didn't text like an innocent, her pupils dilating enough that I knew we headed down the track I'd hoped for.

"You're taller than I expected," she stated bluntly, tilting her head back to hold my gaze.

"And you're even more gorgeous in person."

"Flattery will get you everywhere," she said with a laugh that didn't sound like contrived flirting to weasel her way into my wallet like most of the women I'd gone out with in the past.

I joined in with a chuckle, my dick ready to roll whenever the fuck she wanted. While I normally would have gone straight for the sex talk, I tucked her hand in my elbow and led her into the restaurant because her honesty was refreshing as fuck.

Alluring as hell. Same as Blaine had been at ten years old.

And I decided I wanted more than just a quick romp between the sheets.

"Good to know," I said, "but maybe later?"

"Maybe later," she agreed, glancing up at me again with those big eyes a man could lose himself in.

"I hope you like seafood."

"As long as its cooked and not wrapped in seaweed, I love it. Otherwise?" She shuddered.

Another chuckle left me at her honesty.

The hostess led us to one of the private nooks I'd reserved for the night, pouring the chardonnay I ordered before leaving us alone.

I lifted my wine glass in the dimness lit by a lone candle flickering between us. Soft instrumental music filtered through our little corner, helping to set the mood of an intimate dinner. "What should we toast to?"

Lily licked her lower lip, and I wondered over the flavor of her gloss, how well it would taste on my tongue. "To new adventures."

"And to fantasies fulfilled?"

"Yes, please."

We both sipped, and I stared as she swallowed. "I enjoy hearing you say those two words."

"As bossy as you seem, I'm not surprised."

I barked out a laugh at her candid reply. "I think I like you, bikini girl."

"Feed me, put on those gray sweats for me, and I'll make my decision about *you*." Her dark eyes flirted, chubbing my dick back up.

"You're a tease."

"And you aren't?" she shot back before sipping her wine again.

"Touché."

"So, what do you do for fun, Scott?" Lily set her wine aside, and in that moment, I realized she wasn't some shallow young woman out to strictly sow wild oats. She also wasn't just hungry for dick but personable in a way I hadn't expected from someone on the hookup section of Missing Link.

She intrigued me enough that no sixth sense of wariness tingled in my brain. Add in that she hadn't given my car or my tailored suit worth more than her car the time of day, and I was on board with doing the same.

"Surf. Work."

"You work for fun?" One of her eyebrows arched upward.

"I love numbers—"

She snickered, shaking her head.

"What?"

"Please don't tell me you're an accountant."

"Financial advisor."

"Thank God."

I tipped my head to the side, watching as she took a long drink from her glass. "Are we going to bookmark that for later or...?"

"Ex-fiancé."

"Ah. The man must have been a numbers geek."

She nodded. "We're still good friends, but he has a husband now."

It took me a few seconds to process what she'd stated without a hint of anger lacing her words or tone. "Would that have anything to do with the whole crossing of swords limit?"

"Yep." She popped the P, and I had to fight off the grin wanting to escape my lips at her refreshing truthfulness.

Fuck, Lily could easily sneak her way into my life, same as Blaine and Meryl.

"How badly did he hurt you?" I asked, wondering over how jaded she might be.

"No more than I hurt him."

We stared at one another, a heaviness settling over a conversation I'd expected to be lighthearted and flirty.

Our waiter arrived, breaking the tension.

"Lily?" I offered for her to go first.

"You can order for me."

She hadn't even looked at the menu, so I did as suggested, choosing the grilled halibut with smashed fingerlings and tomato butter for her. Lily made a low sound of appreciation in her throat.

"And for you, sir?" our waiter asked.

"I'll have the Dungeness crab cioppino."

"Can I have a glass of water too, please?" Lily asked as our waiter gathered the menus.

"Of course." He left us after a brief nod, and I turned my focus back on Lily, some unnamed part of me pleased as hell that she'd asked me to order for her.

"Do you enjoy spending time at the beach?" I asked, praying like hell she'd say yes since my back yard consisted of one and I spent a lot of my free time riding the waves.

"I've been known to hang out one too many hours baking in the sun and cooling off in the salt water, yeah. Haley and I both. She's my cousin. We share an apartment over on Danson Street."

"How long have you been on the West Coast?"

"Am I that obvious?" she asked with a light laugh.

"You have a slight accent that sounds a hell of a lot like Philly."

"I do not."

"You do too." I grinned and repeated a word she'd said twice in the last few minutes. "Wooder."

"Water."

"Exactly," I said with a chuckle.

She laughed along with me. "I did grow up in Philly. You?"

"Boston. New Hampshire in the summers."

"Do you miss the East Coast?"

"Not one bit," I admitted without hesitation. "I hate the snow, the cold."

Lily fake shuddered. "Me. Too. I'll never move back there. You couldn't pay me to."

I wondered if that ex of hers had any bearing on her dislike of the eastern part of the US but wasn't about to bring back in that seriousness from earlier. "Your write-up said you're a teacher."

"Mmm." Lily swallowed her sip of wine and nodded.

"I'm guessing you like kids."

"I enjoy teaching them, but I have zero interest in having any of my own, if that's the info you're probing for."

Score another point for the near-perfect woman with the gorgeous eyes.

"Your mom isn't on your ass to give her some grandkids?"

Lily waved her hand. "My two older sisters already took care of that problem."

"So, you're free to live your future however the hell you want."

"Yep." Again with that popped P, her eyes lighting with... life.

I found myself leaning forward, wanting to know more —learn everything I could about Lily who didn't hold back with her thoughts. She didn't play games, which I could appreciate, and until we finished our dinner, I decided I *had* to hang onto her until Blaine was ready again.

I hadn't mentioned him.

She hadn't asked.

And I chose to keep it that way, wanting to enjoy her all to myself for the time being.

"So." I eyed her over the table, and she leaned forward as though gravitating toward me.

My groin took note, stirring in my suit pants.

"I'd love to invite you back to my place for another glass of wine."

She ran a fingertip along the rim of her empty glass. "I don't go home with men on the first date."

"Your place?" I pushed, my interest too damn stirred to give up easily.

"Haley is at our apartment, and one eyeful of you, and she'll try to steal you away from me."

"*Am* I yours for the night?" I couldn't but help ask, not hating the idea of the possessiveness hinted at in her voice.

"I was hoping so."

"We are in a hotel," I tossed out, fingers mentally crossed because I wanted—needed—a taste of Lily.

Her slow smile had me thickening fully, and I knew in that moment, I would get to see what color panties she hid beneath that skirt before the night ended.

10

———

LILY

I hadn't lied to Scott. I didn't go home with hookups.

Haley and I had a pact: our place or neutral ground, neither of us needing anything super fancy as long as we got off.

Scott paid for our dinner, and I took his offered hand to help me from my seat. Rather than releasing me, he twined his fingers through mine. Warmth ran up my arm, straight to my nipples.

Already hardened from the heated gazes he'd been giving me over dinner, they ached, chafed from the bra plumping my breasts up a bit. Dampness already coated my panties and had from the second I'd laid eyes on Scott in his dark gray suit. He hadn't pulled his hair back like in the picture on Missing Link, and his blue eyes were lighter blue than I'd thought. Absolutely fucking gorgeous with a hint of gold around the pupil.

No calloused palms on him but alluring all the same.

Besides, I had a generous memory that kept the vision of him in sweats fresh in my mind.

The second the elevator closed us in to speed us up five stories, he turned on me.

With how his messages had hinted at dominance, I'd expected a good slam against the wall, fingers clasping my neck even. Scott cradled my face in his hands instead, peering into my eyes. "You didn't mention kissing as a hard limit."

The image of Blaine shot through my mind, but I rose up onto my tiptoes because I could.

Freedom to be.

To live.

Scott brushed his lips over mine, a breathless whisper of a touch, and I knew trouble awaited around the corner. My legs went weak, between my thighs pulsing with a fresh surge of arousal.

I grabbed hold of his hair and opened my mouth, whimpering as his tongue stroked along mine in a lazy dance of seduction.

His hand splayed over my lower back, and he pulled me closer.

The fucking bell dinged, and the elevator's doors slid open the second his hard length pressed against my belly.

"Fuck," he groaned, grabbing my hand once more.

Yes, please.

I blinked up at him while he led me down the hallway, unable to keep track of the turns or even what room we headed toward in my lust-filled body and mind-blowing numbness from a simple brush of lips and tongue.

Kissing Levi had always been comfortable, a sense of home I'd never had with anyone else. The lip-lock I'd shared with Zeke had been hot, panty-melting, but no butterflies had rushed through my belly, swirling straight through to my head like with Scott.

He brought us to a halt before a door and glanced down at me. "Okay, beautiful?"

I realized I still stared up at him. Enthralled, my lips tingling and desperate for more.

So much trouble.

"You're one hell of a kisser." I barely breathed the words.

"You haven't seen anything yet." He swiped the key card, turning the light green. A push on the handle and he entered, tugging me in behind him.

For a man to be as arrogant and assured of himself as Scott, I expected he would deliver.

Hell, how I hoped he did.

He slid his suit coat off and tugged his tie loose.

I kicked my heels from my feet and set my purse aside, my insides a riotous mess of the best sort.

Not once did we look away from each other.

Light spilled in from the window on the far wall, shadowing his face enough that I couldn't make out his eyes other than the fact they were pale.

He took three steps toward me and hefted me with his arms, pressing my back against the door—gently but with serious intent.

I giggled with a bit of nervousness, but my legs wound around his waist, my hands finding his hair.

He kissed me senseless, taking his time to lick and nip over my lips. "So goddamn delicious," he groaned into my mouth, spearing in his tongue for another taste and stealing my breath. "Fuck, I want to devour every inch of you."

"Yes, please," I gasped out as his teeth scraped over my chin with a tender bite.

Scott nosed at the place his teeth marked me, and I lifted my head, tilting it back to rest on the door. He pressed soft kisses to my neck, flicks of his tongue and his rumbled sounds of appreciation causing need to pulse through my core.

Wetness slid from between my thighs, soaking my panties, and I wiggled, seeking out something to rub against.

He lifted me higher like I weighed no more than a feather pillow, his mouth finding the peekaboo cut out in my blouse.

"Vanilla," he whispered as his nose slid over my skin between my breasts. "So sweet. Take it off for me."

Scott stepped away from the wall, his hands firm on my ass, giving me room to pull my blouse from my body. I didn't make him ask for the bra, just ripped that damn thing away too. Before it fluttered to the floor, my back hit the wall again, and Scott wrapped his lips around my right nipple, nipping at the hardened nub.

"Oh God." I grabbed hold of his hair, swallowing hard as he suckled, sending shots of lust straight to my clit. "So good...holy shit, that feels... Damn." Biting on the inside of my lip, I tried to keep my whimpers contained as he gave my tits more attention than any man ever had.

Every stroke of his tongue, every scrape of his teeth, shocked charges through me, amping up my need to explode in a spasm of orgasmic pulses.

Who knew a woman could hover on the edge of a climax from mere nipple play?

The mouth on that man...

"Scott." I gulped, torn between wanting to yank his head away from my chest and press him closer.

"So sensitive." Hot breath wafted over my stinging nipple. "You are so fucking fine."

He moved fast, spinning my head.

The bed cradled my back before I could blink.

Scott stood over me, looming in the dim city lights filtering through the hushed room. His tie fell to the floor, and with every flick of a button down his dress shirt, my pulse picked up pace. He moved unhurriedly, slowly uncovering smooth skin, a lithe swimmer's torso with bitable pecs and ripped abs.

"Oh God," I moaned at the sight, sure I'd died and gone to heaven.

He slid his slacks and briefs down in one shove, and I gulped.

"Yes." Like a breathless whore, I stared at his hard dick. Perfect length. Perfect girth. I couldn't wait to feel the stretch, the fullness of him inside me. My fingers twitched to touch as drool flooded my mouth for a taste of his salty precum.

Scott chuckled while pulling a condom from his wallet before tossing the first beside me, the second to the floor where his pants lay. He grabbed my ankles and yanked me to the bed's edge, hands rising beneath my skirt until he bunched it at my waist.

"Red." He huffed a chuckle at what covered my soaked pussy. "Goddamn, Lily."

"You like?" I fingered the edge of the dark red panties I'd decided to wear for him—because I'd chosen too, not because he'd demanded it.

"Fuck yeah." He dropped to his knees and leaned in close, filling his lungs with a noisy inhale. "The scent of you is making my mouth water."

A shudder ripped through my core as he pressed a kiss atop my clit. "Mmm." His chest rumbled.

My legs splayed open, and I grabbed hold of that luscious hair again, biting my tongue to keep from begging him to kiss my aching core.

"Needy little girl," he murmured as though reading my mind, running his nose over my panties from clit to ass and back up again. "Soaked through for my cock."

"Scott…"

He licked over the lace, his tongue nothing more than a tease.

"Scott," I whined again, thrusting my hips up toward his mouth. "Please."

Sliding a fingertip along the edge of my panties, he lifted his head, peering at me from between my thighs with pale eyes full of fire.

I expected dirty words, filthy talk from how he'd teased online, but the second he bared my pussy to the air, he leaned in, his lips closing over my clit in a suckling kiss.

My hips bucked, gaze ensnared by his as his tongue flicked over my sensitive nub. "Oh…holy fuck, Scott. Shit."

He lapped and kissed again. "So fucking sweet." His growly tone hardened my nipples to tight points. "I could eat this pussy for hours."

Dead.

Fucking *dead*.

That rumbled voice, the words…

I humped up against his face, moaning like the dick-needy whore I was. "Give me your fingers," I demanded in my lust after torturous minutes of him making out with my clit like it was my tongue.

Two slid in before I could inhale, and my breath caught.

Right there—what man knew how to crook his fingers on the first stroke and land a woman in the lap of euphoria?

"Be a good little girl and soak my hand," he murmured against my clit and nibbled.

My body contracted, curled inward as his demand rushed over me. Climax waves rolled through me—erasing all thoughts from my mind other than *holyfuckingshityes*. My pussy clenched around his fingers, his hot tongue flicking at my clit to keep me falling. His hums and groans fed my body's frenzy until my release left me lax, empty of energy.

I lay like a rag doll, whimpering and gasping for oxygen as he lapped at my cum with lewd slurping noises.

Wrecked...by mere fingers and a tongue worthy of a gold medal.

"Fuck, Lily." He sat back and wiped his hand across his wet mouth before he grabbed the condom and sheathed up. "Flip," he commanded, and I lazed over like a limp noodle, too buzzed to give his bossy ass any shit.

His hands grasped my thighs, yanking me up onto my knees, and I pressed my face into the mattress, my core aching to be filled even though the rest of me felt spent. My skirt spilled forward toward my ears, and Scott didn't even bother taking my panties off. He pulled them aside and sank into me with one slow push.

Stretched the fuck out in delicious bliss...

"God," I moaned the word like a curse, my back bowing even more to suck Scott deeper into my body.

"Ah, fuck." He squeezed my cheeks apart, baring my asshole to him, but I didn't care—he stuffed me full of his hard dick, and I couldn't think beyond how delicious he felt buried deep inside me. "So hot. Tight."

I made some sort of garbled, strangled noise, fisting my hands in the comforter when he didn't retreat and thrust right away like I craved.

His length jerked inside me, but he didn't move, his groin hot against my ass cheeks.

Panting, I wiggled, needing something...more.

"Be still," he stated, his thumbs gliding up through my cleft to feather over my asshole.

Another whimper left me as I bucked toward him, ignoring the strands of hair across my mouth, sticking to my lips. "Please. Fuck me," I groaned, dragging out the "e" like a petulant child.

He chuckled and pulled back, his thickness dragging along my inner walls and sending another rush of arousal through my blood. I'd come harder than I had in months from his fingers and tongue playing me like a violin, but at the friction of his length inside me, my pussy hopped back aboard the "get off again" train.

"This ass..." Scott squeezed my cheeks and took his time filling me with one slow glide.

"Yes," I moaned, shivering even though sweat readied to break out over my heated skin.

Lust rippled over me as he bottomed out with a groan, and I arched my back deeper, pressing toward him.

"Again," I breathed the word, and bless his gracious heart, he gave me what I asked for. Smooth thrusts, slow undulating rocking of his hips like those damn male strippers who drove women worldwide to salivating with their dance moves.

"So wet." He ran his thumbs around where he stretched me while dragging out, slick pads sliding over my asshole as he sank back in.

I opened my eyes and craned my neck, needing to see him move.

And move he did, his abs rippling with every slow thrust, his hips gyrating rather than straight on thrusting like they were made for fucking a woman senseless.

Trouble.

"Fuck." I moaned and slammed my eyelids shut again as he continued to rim my puckered hole with his thumb. Watching him fuck me would ruin me for any other man.

He was that good.

That…delicious.

I could visualize those hips, those abs, behind my closed eyelids, ramping up my lust, the wetness he glided through.

He applied pressure to my ass, teasing rather than breaching.

"Touch yourself for me, Lily. I want you to come all over my cock."

I groaned and obeyed, sliding my fingertips over my clit like he did to my asshole, because there was no way in hell I wasn't getting off a second time with his perfect dick wrecking me.

He started moving faster but no less sensuous, rocking into me hard enough that he hit my cervix. A tap to my pucker, and he whispered, "Let me in."

I bore down like I did when playing with myself, and his thumb slid inside my body without much resistance. "Christ are you hot inside here," he groaned as though through gritted teeth, finger fucking my ass in opposition to his length in my pussy.

"Fuck," I drew the word out, smooshing my face against the mattress, and strummed the hell out of my swollen bundle of nerves, the closest I'd ever been to fulfilling my fantasy.

"Yeah…fuck yeah. You're a soaked mess. So. God. Damn. Perfect." Words rocked from his lips in time with his hips. "Fuck, I wish I could fill you with my cum."

Aaand, at that image he created in my head, I erupted, shrieking my release. Scott slammed into me harshly until I collapsed onto the mattress, every inch of me tingling, my breath escaping in hard pants.

He followed me down, grunting and rutting into my pulsing pussy until he shuddered, his dick swelling and twitching inside me. "Hell, woman." Hot exhales ghosted over my neck, and Scott pushed his hips tighter against me, the tip of him jabbing my cervix.

I hissed at the slight hint of pain, and he shivered again, resting some of his weight against my back. Sweat lay like a sheet between us, hot and slick.

"Okay?" he murmured against my ear, that tongue of his lapping up the side of my neck and sending shivers clear to my toes.

"Mmhmm." Completely spent, I soaked in the warmth of his hard body pressing me deeper into the mattress.

"Stay with me tonight," he whispered and flicked his tongue out to trace the shell, causing goosebumps to ripple over my skin.

He sounded...needy, something first impressions hadn't suggested Scott would be.

At all.

The desire for *more* I'd never experienced before, to nurture and soothe him, swam through my blood.

I should have lit out like a scared little rabbit with all the feels he woke inside me.

But I didn't move.

11

BLAINE

I lay on my bed, staring at the ceiling, my dick hard and my thoughts on Lily. Even though I'd sounded like a moron when we'd had lunch together, she'd still asked for my number. She wanted to get to know me.

Was she blind?

Deaf?

Or did she see beyond my obvious insecurities and social shortcomings?

Grey had, and I'd learned to relax around him, to be comfortable in my own skin when with him. Could I reach that place with her? Given enough time, I supposed I could. I grabbed my cell off the table beside my bed and pulled up her name.

Coffee girl.

Even knowing her true identity, I couldn't help but grin. Lily would always be associated with coffee and sweet blueberry muffins in my head. Add in the memory of the subtle scent of vanilla that hovered around her, and saliva started to pool in my mouth.

Ignoring my aching dick, I typed slowly...deleted a few letters, started from scratch...backspace two words...

"Fuck, I suck at this." I scrubbed a hand over my face and backspaced everything I'd typed out. "Do it, chicken-shit." Lips in a firm line, I went with one short and to the point question. **Would you like to have dinner with me tomorrow night?**

Grey had a friend gathering at our place, a surprise party for his secretary, and I didn't want to have to hide in my room the entire time like usual whenever he had a get-together. I couldn't handle the noise, the laughter, all the... bodies in our space.

It was always too much.

I hit send before I could overthink asking Lily out for a second time. Staring at the line I'd written, I waited. Chewed on two fingernails. Released an exasperated breath when she didn't reply within five minutes.

"Get over yourself," I muttered.

I hauled my ass out of bed and hopped in the shower, needing to take care of the buildup of cum I'd been ignoring since our lunch together. Running with the first fantasy to pop into mind, I envisioned trailing my hands up the back of Lily's thighs while sinking into her sweet body.

She would be tight. Hot. So tiny compared to me...fuck, she would feel divine wrapped around my dick.

I fucked into my fist, imagining her heels pulling against my ass as she moaned and begged me for more.

The shower beat down on me as I jerked myself, my lips parted in a pant, water droplets slipping over my mouth. My balls pulled upward, and I tugged them down with a groan.

Open up, I imagined Grey telling Lily, watching as he held her head, shifting her mouth toward his hard cock. He would smear his pre-cum over her lips before shoving over her tongue.

I shuddered—and came with a hissed curse, spurts of white shooting through the air to land on the tiled floor.

"Goddamn." I gasped for air, my skin twitching as a final ooze of cum dribbled from my slit. I wiped it free with my thumb and rinsed it off in the shower.

Grey would have sucked his finger clean.

My dick twitched again, and I chuckled.

Since when did I jerk off to thoughts of a woman and have a memory of Grey make an appearance? Sure, we shared—a lot, the only action I'd ever gotten—but he'd never been a part of my spank bank. Hell, if he knew, he'd call me a kinky fucker and laugh.

A few minutes later, I collapsed back on my bed, deciding to ignore whatever had caused Grey's words and body to appear in my fantasy of fucking Lily.

No text from her waited for me.

With a curse, I turned off my light, hit my pillow a few times to fluff it up a bit, and buried my face in the feather-stuffed cotton.

It'd been a hell of a long day, and the hot shower had been the perfect muscle relaxant. I passed the fuck out and didn't have one damn dream for a change.

———

My cell rang, jolting me from sleep.

Six in the morning—I'd fucking overslept.

"Goddamnit!" I hopped up and grabbed my cell.

Coffee girl.

I grinned and swiped to answer, my morning wood making a full appearance. "Hey."

"Good morning to you too." Her normally husky voice sounded breathless like she'd been scurrying around. "Just got your text—didn't want you to think I was ignoring you."

"It's okay."

"I'm running late for work, but I wanted to say yes to your dinner invitation."

"Great. Awesome." I slammed my eyelids shut, cursing inside my head.

Her laughter curved my lips. "I'm *starving* for some pizza if that works for you?"

"I can always eat pizza."

"I gotta run, but text me where you want to meet and I'll be there," she promised, her still-breathless tone sending lust twitching through my groin.

"Will do."

Grinning like an idiot, I yanked on my work clothes and sprinted out the door without my coffee.

Grey had already left for work—if he'd been back at all. Wouldn't have been the first time he'd fucked his way through an orgy of guys at some hotel rather than bringing them home where I would have to listen.

I barely made it to the new jobsite on time, and Wyatt showed up a half-hour later with coffees in hand.

"You're stuck with me today," he said, handing over a cup.

"Davidson?"

"Gone."

I straightened, blinking, wondering what the fuck had happened. "What?"

Wyatt barked out a laugh. "No...not like that. I had to let him go. Calling in hungover earlier in the week and not showing up the rest..." He shrugged.

"Shit. I'm sorry to hear that."

"His loss."

And my gain, I thought as we set to work. Davidson had been a decent enough guy, but Wyatt was one hell of a hard worker, his easygoing nature allowing me comfort enough that my self-awareness didn't get swamped with insecurity.

We labored alongside one another without difficulty, getting shit done long before I had expected to. Having finished two hours early, I headed to the cafe on the other side of town.

Lily had already left for the day, a co-worker of hers told me.

Probably for the best since my stopping by might be seen as a bit much since we had dinner plans.

I got home with a blueberry muffin and coffee in my stomach, butterflies rippling around enough that nausea grew.

After a long shower and impatient as fuck, I texted, asking if she wanted to meet for an earlier dinner.

Prince Pizza at five? I shot off, my face aching from smiling so damn much.

Coffee girl: **Can't wait!**

A text came through from Grey before I set my cell down. **The caterer for tonight's party is showing up at the house in a half hour. Any chance you can get home early to let them in? I'm fucking stuck in the meeting with Joseph I. Devonshire III and can't escape.**

Already home, I texted back. **Early day.**

Grey: **I owe you one.**

He didn't owe me a goddamn thing, but I'd never tell him that. **Just leave me to my peace and quiet tonight,** I texted.

Grey: **Sure you don't want to join us?**

Me: **No fucking way.**

Seeing as how I had the entire second floor of his house to myself, the party would go on unaware of the recluse upstairs.

But I wouldn't be there like I normally would have, and Grey would honor my boundaries by not even coming upstairs to look for me after I snuck out.

Me: **I'll help clean up in the morning.**

Grey: **You're the best. Enjoy whatever it is you're going to be doing while I'm getting drunk and having a blast.**

If only he knew my plans. My insides tightened a bit over the fact I kept something from my best friend, but I wasn't yet ready to share Lily. For once, I'd taken a step out on my own without him, and I loved the feeling of independence.

Until I walked toward Prince Pizza, my stomach in knots.

I missed my damn buffer, the one who set me at ease, the hand I could hold in my head while taking steps forward in life.

Lily had seemed excited for our date. We'd had a good lunch together...what if I made a fool of myself and who I was turned her off? There was no way in fuck I could pretend to be something I wasn't.

"Blaine!" she called from behind me, and I stopped, turning.

Lily rushed up the boardwalk, hair fluttering from the ocean's breeze. Pink flushed her face, her easy smile relaxing my insides. "Hey!" She beamed up at me, lips parted, chest rising quickly with each inhale. "I thought I was late."

"I wouldn't have minded waiting." In that second, caught by her beauty, I would have twiddled my thumbs forever. "You look really nice."

She popped out a hip, pulling my gaze over her summer

dress the color of sunshine. "Thanks. You clean up pretty good yourself."

"Oh." Heat rushed to my face. "Yeah...I didn't come straight from work."

"I see that." Her focus slid down over my black T-shirt and jeans. "Tall, dark, and handsom*er*." She winked, and I swallowed a laugh, my insides twitching.

"Hungry?" I asked, nodding toward the pizzeria rather than point, which would betray my shaking fingers.

"Starved."

I thought about offering my arm but shoved my hands in my pockets instead. "How was work?" I asked, as we fell into step beside each other.

"Long. Boring. I watched the door all morning long, bummed when no gorgeous landscaper came in to see me."

My cheeks went ten shades of red. "I, uh, started at a new jobsite today on the other side of town."

"So, no more butterflies and breathlessness for me?" she asked with an exaggerated teasing sigh.

Goddamn, this woman.

"I, um..."

She bumped me with her shoulder. "You aren't used to compliments, are you?"

"No." I pulled open the oceanfront restaurant's door, the heavy scent of garlic and baking pizza hitting my nose harshly enough that my mouth flooded with drool.

A hostess sat us in a booth beside the front window, and I buried my still-hot face in the menu.

"Blaine."

"Hmm?" I lifted my focus—barely.

Lily smiled at me from across the table, her eyes kind. "Do I make you uncomfortable when I state my mind?"

"Not uncomfortable, no." I cleared my throat, glancing

out the window. "I'm just...not used to this. I've never dated before."

She didn't respond, and I turned my attention back toward her.

I'd expected her to look at me like I had two heads or some such shit, but she simply smiled without a trace of teasing or discomfort over my weirdness. "So you said the other day."

I'm repeating myself like a moron who has nothing else to talk about.

"That's the best compliment *I've* ever received," Lily stated, her glossed lips in a sweet curve that eased my embarrassment.

My grin felt crooked, and I shrugged. "You seem pretty special."

"Is it too soon for me to swoon over you?" she asked with light laughter, fanning her face with her hand.

Seeing as how she'd pretty much done the same to me the second I'd first laid eyes on her, I didn't think so.

I shook my head and relaxed in my seat, knowing I was going to have the time of my life on our second date.

12

GREYSON

I had ten minutes to shower at the office that morning, thankful yet again for how Meryl insisted I keep clothes on hand.

It wasn't the first time I'd arrived late for work in the same clothes I'd worn the day before. Meryl had simply rolled her eyes and promised to get me coffee. While quickly washing the scent of sex off my body, I replayed the night in my head.

Lily's candor, her lack of fake-assed bullshit like I experienced with most female hookups, had been refreshing as fuck. Others on their best behavior, trying for perfect in their looks and manners, hadn't impressed me one bit.

But a woman with a level of confidence and inner happiness that sparkled through her eyes without feigned emotions? Toss in her sweet spirit that gave me warm fuzzies inside like only Blaine could do, and yeah.

Lily was all that and then some.

The memory of the way she'd given me her body, the complete submission she offered with just the hint of demanding when chasing her orgasm, made me come harder than any release a pussy had squeezed from my balls before.

She'd also woken up a sense of longing inside me for something more than a mere hookup or quick fuck whenever the mood struck.

Perhaps it was time to find something like Dad had done with Daphne...to fulfill needs I was ready to admit still lay deep inside me regardless of my relationship with Blaine.

Add in the fact the sex had been fantastic, mind-bending, and I realized I was open to the possibility of more with the little minx.

Lily had crashed into a deep sleep after we'd finished. I'd stripped her skirt off her, moved her beneath the blankets without her waking, and stared like a creeper at her while she lightly snored. I'd heard and seen men pass out after having my dick, but not a woman.

Dick drunk, I'd mused, smirking, but she'd woken me up with those lips wrapped around my cock long after my alarm should have gone off and hadn't. It was like fate fucked with me.

Late for the office or enjoy a good morning blow job that I feared would entwine us a bit more than either of us intended?

The way her tongue laved at my frenulum, shoved into my slit like she was cum-hungry...I couldn't say no.

Didn't really want to, regardless of the hairs rising on the back of my neck.

I'd given her the mouthful she'd begged for, wishing I'd had time to fuck her into the mattress. She'd denied me, stating if we fucked, she'd never make it in to work. Passing out after sex was her thing, she'd claimed, and Christ how I wanted to lay waste to her body and crash beside her to creep as she dreamed.

The scent of vanilla and sex filled my nose hours after leaving the hotel room, or perhaps it was just my memory as I tried to focus on work, but goddamn, the woman had gotten under my skin.

I'd texted her once when I'd have preferred to blow up her phone, but I refused to come off as desperate. We used Missing Link for a purpose, and neither of us were looking for anything serious. But fuck, did I want to see her again. Sink into her sweet pussy—her ass if she'd give it to me—and rock her world, sending her tumbling into oblivion while her soft hands soothed over my skin, tugging me closer.

The noises she'd made...her beautiful response to my kisses over her body—

"Mr. Scott?"

I blinked from my dick-stirring thoughts, giving Mr. Joseph I. Devonshire III my full attention across my desk from me. My biggest client was demanding as hell, arrogant as fuck, and full of himself enough that he gave my ego a run for its money.

"My apologies. Meryl?" I glanced behind him toward the woman seated on my couch, pen and paper in hand. She'd saved me time and again when I couldn't bear to listen to the man drone on. "Coffee, please?"

"Of course." She smirked as though knowing I suffered from the evening before. "Mr. Devonshire?"

He barked out his drink order, and she left us.

If only it'd been to silence. The man didn't know when to shut the fuck up. If not for how I profited off his investments, I would have told him to take a hike. While I didn't need his money in the least, I sure as fuck enjoyed it. Having lived with Blaine's shared memories of poverty, I knew a man couldn't have too much put away in his accounts.

Blaine made good wages at his landscaping job, but I would never have him lack for anything again. I didn't get to call him mine, but I provided for him in every small way he allowed.

If only he held interest in the physical as well. Lily would look good on him. Between us. Our marks and cum smeared all over her petite body.

Even better would be her loving on Blaine while he allowed me to do the same.

Heart heavier than usual after a perfect lay, I rushed home two hours later, lucky to not be caught speeding.

The caterers had set up for Meryl's surprise party in the open concept kitchen and living area, same as they'd done a few times before at my home.

Blaine had already escaped to the second floor, so I left him alone. He never joined in the parties I threw, choosing solitude to the noise and mingling people that made his skin itchy.

I didn't push, no matter how much I wanted to help him gain more of a social life, no matter how much I desired to have him by my side—where I wish he realized he belonged. My entire office knew of my best friend, were curious as fuck to meet him, but he refused to make an appearance. He hadn't come from money like I had, didn't have social graces or the ability to pretend instilled in him since childhood.

But I loved him regardless and had zero wish to change him.

I gave him his space, but thoughts of him lingered in the back of my mind, same as ones of Lily while Meryl blew out the thirty candles I'd insisted light up her cake. All twenty-three in attendance sang her happy birthday at the top of our lungs, but my cell buzzing in my jeans' back pocket had me checking. Just in case Blaine changed his mind.

Higgins, the PI.

I made a quick escape to my home office and shut the door against the ruckus, barely answering in time.

"It's amazing what a little money will get inquiring minds these days," Higgins said the second I greeted him.

"What'd you find out?" I stood in the middle of the dark room, my entire body tight.

"That place is completely off the grid. Sequestered like that damn Shyamalan movie but without the monsters."

"Oh, there's definitely monsters," I disagreed. "They're just in human skin."

"On that, I have to agree from what I've seen so far. Public punishments. People shut away in small metal boxes, just like you'd claimed, but when they're freed, the leader… he kisses their feet and leads them into what appears to be the temple or main gathering room."

"You managed to get inside the compound?"

"Let's just say I have eyes in the sky through black market means."

Drones of some sort, I figured.

"And Sarah?"

The sound of papers shuffling reached through the cell I clutched tight to my ear, my heart racing over what he might have uncovered about Blaine's sister. Would it set Blaine's mind at ease? Stir up enough darkness that he'd crash into a deep depression I wouldn't be able to help him escape?

My fingers curled into my palm, itchy for a soft hand—

"According to records, the cult leader, Abraham Quell, was married to a woman named Clara, but the younger woman I've seen countless times walking at his side and holding his hand is no stately raven-haired beauty."

My lips pressed tight at the memory of what I'd exposed Blaine to with our last hookup—but even more worrisome was where Higgins headed.

"There's no record of Clara's death, but no woman I'd seen since keeping watch over the compound matches her description. There's also no record of Abraham Quell remarrying, but it sure as hell looks like that's the case. I'm going to send you an image...hold on..."

I put my phone on speaker, and a texted image came through.

My breath caught before I let out a curse at the slightly grainy headshot. She had the same hazel-green eyes as her brother. The same cowlick just left of center in her hairline. An identical deeply furrowed line between her eyes that pulled her dark brows low, portraying deep sadness.

Sarah could have been Blaine's twin.

"That's her," I croaked.

Higgins let out an audible exhale. "She's pregnant."

"Fuck." I rubbed a hand down over my face, pulling at my jaw, my stomach turning inside out. "Quell's?"

"That would be my guess from what I've seen."

Eyelids slamming shut, I cursed again, knowing how that news would wreck Blaine. "Find everything you can," I stated through clenched teeth. "I don't care what it costs or how long it takes. We're toppling this fucker's supposed kingdom to the ground."

Higgins assured me he'd only just begun, and with the intel he'd gathered within a matter of days, I trusted him to get the job done sooner than later.

But my mind wasn't so easily put to rest. I hated withholding truth from my best friend, but what choice did I have? Until I accomplished what I'd set out to do with the investigator's help, I needed to keep the shit I'd stirred up to myself to save him anxiety, nightmares, and emptying his guts all over the floor.

Forcing the scowl off my face, I went back to the party, putting on my mask of an ease and lightheartedness I definitely didn't feel. Thank fuck for all those lessons when I'd been a kid.

A sudden longing for Blaine swelled over me like a crashing wave, but another hit me just as hard for my bikini girl.

I liked Lily. A lot. Loved her bubbly, flirty nature, the way she didn't filter her thoughts before spewing them out as most of those mingling in my living room did. Kind smiles and soft touches, no qualms, no pretenses. Just...simply her.

Same as Blaine, even though his personality was the complete opposite. Quiet. Introverted. But with honesty and true friendship I could trust.

He was my other longed-for half, and Lily...she soothed a part of me I'd recognized sat empty since Mom had passed. She'd barreled into my life with one app's pinged notification, and I craved more.

Fuck, did I want.

I didn't just lust to get her into my bed with Blaine on the other side of her. My heart yearned for that image in my head to become reality. The three of us fully sated as I expected a romp in the sheets would leave us, me and my best friend spooning the hell out of her tight little body. She would fit perfectly, and not one thing I'd seen in her would turn Blaine away.

She would be perfect for him—for *us*.

Me.

Unease stirred inside me, that goddamn poking intuition I hadn't pinpointed until that moment. I named it inside my head for what it was—fear of abandonment.

Having your mother ripped from your life at the age you needed her love and edification the most had bonded me and Dad together and had us both sitting with therapists, but the wounds remained.

I loathed the feelings of insecurity that lingered, keeping me from pursuing any type of relationship with a woman.

But I'd always had Blaine, and he'd been enough.

He might not be ready to meet Lily, like his quietness the previous couple of days suggested, but something inside me grew restless as the night wore on. Perhaps it was the news I'd gotten from Higgins or the need for quiet, the rest and sense of belonging I felt with Blaine.

I texted him after everyone nibbled their chocolate cake and finished off a couple more bottles of champagne. **We have cake. Sure you don't want to come down and have some?**

It took him a good fifteen minutes to reply, just long enough that I considered heading up the stairs to check on him.

B: **I'm good.**

My fingers tapped out a text before I could second-guess myself, the image of the three of us together too vivid in my head to let go. I hated being needy, but I couldn't stop the urge to be proactive. **So, I met this girl...**

B: **Yeah?**

Me: **I think you'd like her.**

B: **Not really interested right now.**

Exactly as I'd figured, but for the first time, my selfishness wanted to push him past his limits. An idea lit in my head, and my stubbornness proved too strong.

Me: **You and I are going out for drinks tomorrow night. No excuses. I miss my best friend.**

B: **What if I have plans?**

I snorted a laugh. **Nice try.**

Next, I texted Lily with a location and time for the following evening.

Bikini girl got right back to me with a **Bossy.**

Grinning, I repeated the texted order.

She sent me an eye roll emoji.

Me: **I have someone I want you to meet.**

It took her an hour to get back to me, but her simple **OK** set my mind more at ease than it had been all day.

I just hoped the feeling carried over to the following night.

13

LILY

Blaine was shy as hell and just as adorable.

I wondered if he was a virgin, but with how he watched my lips move, I expected he thought about having a taste. All he had to do was initiate and I'd gladly be on board.

Usually, I enjoyed going after what I wanted, but I refused to scare the guy off by coming on too strong. Bad enough my compliments shifted his gaze away from me, sending his palms down along his jeans as though sweaty.

He was the opposite of Scott in every way, but no less alluring. I'd had Scott, but I yearned for Blaine too. Imagining having the both of them?

Holyfuckingshityesplease.

My brain got the better of me, weaving all sorts of naughty fantasies. Being spread out like a feast for both men, loved on in the way I'd always craved. Enjoyed. Cherished.

Okay, so that last one had long-term connotations in my opinion.

Sure, I'd headed to the West Coast to find myself and a

couple of lovers, but even when joking with Levi about doing that very thing, I hadn't considered a serious relationship. It was why I kept to the hookup part of my favorite app.

No drama, no ties.

Just dick and fun times like a hopefully double-stuffed Lily.

A prickle of shame rose inside me, shit from the past attempting to make me feel like I committed a sin by exploring my sexuality. Ignoring those thoughts didn't come as easily as usual, and I pushed aside my second piece of pizza, no longer hungry.

Blaine continued to scarf his down, and I found myself smiling at how he went all-in with his food, no finesse like Scott, even making a few smacking noises with his lips.

He paused in his chewing when he realized I stared at him. "What?" he asked me around the food in his mouth.

"You're...refreshing." I chose the word carefully, even though Scott's superb manners hadn't been a turn off either.

Blaine finished chewing and swallowed while I planted my elbow on the table and rested my chin in my upturned palm.

"Are you going to stare at me while I finish?"

I couldn't help my smile. "I like watching you eat. It's kinda sexy."

"My manners are shit," he muttered and swiped pepperoni grease off his lips.

I'd rather have licked it away. "You certainly wouldn't fit in at some swanky restaurant that has a dozen different forks laid out on either side of gold plates."

"Do you eat at places like that?" he asked quietly, stilling as though I was about to break his tender heart.

"Fuck no." I huffed my answer. "I might have decent

table manners thanks to my strict mom, but I'm not good at keeping my thoughts to myself. Imagine a fancy dinner where everyone is quietly discussing the latest fashions or politics, and I tell the person beside me a little too loudly that the salmon smells like a dirty you-know-what."

Blaine burst out into laughter, and my grin took over my face.

"See?" I said, knowing we'd drawn a few glances from others in the restaurant.

Shaking his head, he went back to his dinner.

He finished off the pizza while we chatted—me mostly —about the usual get-to-know-you stuff people did on dates. He wasn't one to expand on my inquiries, so I demanded we play fifty questions.

An hour after he finished off our dinner, I knew his favorite everything. Color, food, drink, teams in every major sport, books, TV shows, movies...

He loved Andes candies *and* chardonnay.

Score major points for the shy guy smiling at me, sitting a bit more comfortably in his skin.

"Want to get out of here?" I suggested.

"Um..." He stilled again.

"There's a bench out there." I thumbed toward the empty one outside the pizzeria's window spilling light over our table. "We can sit and wait for the sun to set."

"There's an ice cream shop next door," he suggested.

"Then let's go."

It took us fifteen minutes to decide on the flavors we wanted, but I ended up bypassing all the unusual ones that sounded decent in favor of my favorite.

Mint chocolate chip.

He did the same.

We sat licking our cones while overlooking the

Pacific, shoulders and knees touching. Golden rays glanced off the water, and I kept my sunglasses firmly in place. People strode along the walk behind us, and dozens littered the sand in front of us, lounging or playing.

A volleyball game ran at high intensity a bit off to our right, but not loud enough to be interrupting more than the rest of the din surrounding us.

"Do you like the beach?" I asked and flicked out my tongue to catch a drip of melting ice cream about to hit my thumb.

"I'm not a fan of salt water or thoughts about what lingers beneath the darkness out there, but I like the sounds of waves crashing on shore." I'd finally gotten him comfortable enough that he spoke in full sentences, no stumbling or stuttering.

That fact gave me hope for getting him into bed at some point.

"Me and Haley are down here all the time—or we used to be before I started working at the cafe. I'll nap in the sun on my days off. You should come with me sometime."

Blaine didn't respond, and I glanced up to find him watching me, his own melting dessert smearing over his fingers.

Snickering, I slapped the napkin in my free hand around the one he clutched his cone with.

"Shit." He muttered a few more curses while cleaning his fingers.

"Were you staring at me?"

"I like watching you eat," he repeated what I'd said to him about the pizza chowing-down.

Laughter rippled through me, and holding his gaze, I slowly licked around my ice cream cone.

Blaine gulped audibly, and I nodded toward his hands. "It's gonna drip again."

"Shit." His turn to lick.

My turn to stare.

We were a couple of horny twenty-somethings, one too shy to do jack shit, the other afraid of sending a good thing running before she got a chance to sample the goods.

"I like you, Blaine." I bumped his shoulder and kicked my sandaled feet back and forth since my legs were too short to rest my heels on the boardwalk.

"I like you too, coffee girl." His voice teased just enough to send heat flushing through me.

We sat quietly while finishing our dessert, the sun slowly sinking on the horizon. I thought about watching sunsets back home, never once seeing the ball of gold disappear behind anything but houses.

My parents had been so involved in the church that we'd never gone anywhere on weekends, never took any type of vacation out in the country.

While the West Coast wasn't the sticks with the solitude and serenity nature offered, it held a beauty of its own. Smiling people, laughter as they enjoyed the ocean. Others jogging along the water's edge, driven to better themselves and their health.

So much...life when all I could remember from back home was coldness—more from the lack of emotional warmth I'd felt outside Levi's friendship.

"How did you end up out here?" I asked without really thinking about the consequences of a heavy conversation.

Blaine stared out over the water, his hands resting on his thighs. I wondered if he would answer, expand on what we'd touched upon when we'd gone to lunch. "It's a long story," he finally said, his tone quiet but not guarded like I'd expected.

"It's still early," I suggested.

I wasn't looking for something serious, but the stirrings of desire for more with him didn't agree. I wanted to know if the connection I felt with Blaine was more than just the physical attraction that simmered between us.

"But if you'd rather not get into the shit of your past..." I let my voice trail off and forced myself to be something I usually wasn't.

Patient.

14

——————

BLAINE

S he stated the words as though the cult I'd mentioned briefly before our lunch together had stuck in her brain.

"You used the word escaped," I reminded her of what she'd said rather than giving her a straight answer.

"Yeah." Lily blew out a breath. Her head turned in my periphery, allowing me freedom to glance down at her profile again. "I feel like I've done most of the talking."

"I enjoy listening to you."

She smirked and shoulder bumped me. "You're cute."

"You're beautiful."

Our gazes caught, and that sense of her being a kindred spirit I'd felt the first time I'd spoken to her settled firmly in my head. Her dark eyes piercing through to the deepest parts of me as though *seeing* me like no one else ever had. Although noise surrounded us, silence seemed to swell in a bubble, encasing the two of us in our own little world.

Want became the tangible thing between us, and I itched to lean into her personal space and taste how much chocolate mint flavor lingered on her tongue.

"Are you going to kiss me or what, Blaine," she whispered, "because I gotta be honest—I'm dying over here."

My breath left in a rush.

"Too forward?" she asked with the first hint of insecurity I'd seen in her.

I didn't kiss too many of my and Grey's hookups, choosing to enjoy watching him make love to a woman's mouth.

But I wanted that with Lily.

My hand shook, but I cradled her cheek in my calloused palm, my heart jackhammering in my chest.

I can do this...

She licked her lower lip she hadn't reapplied gloss to after the ice cream, sending blood to thicken my dick.

"Yeah, I can," I whispered more as encouragement to myself and pressed my mouth to hers.

Sighing, she parted her lips, and our tongues met in the middle. Beyond delicious, so much more addictive than I'd imagined, she wrapped my brain up in plastic wrap, closing me off to everything but her.

Soft strokes of her tongue that *did* taste like chocolate mint.

Delicate skin beneath my hand.

Quiet whimpers and moans—hers and mine.

I teetered on the edge of something vast, something frightening...something I never thought I would find or could have outside Grey. Longing to swan dive into oblivion rushed through me with every stroke of her tongue, every soft sigh she emitted over my lips.

"Come home with me," Lily whispered against my mouth.

I pulled away as the world popped the bubble around us with vivid color and detail. Her black pupils swelled, thick lashes blinking. Flushed cheeks, the delicate skin around her lips reddened from my scruff. Rubbing my thumb across them, I nodded even though my heart attempted to explode from my chest and my dick throbbed in its prison.

I stood and helped her to her feet, our fingers lacing together without thought on my part. She led me down the boardwalk.

"Where are you parked?" she asked as we scurried across the road toward the metered car lot.

"That end." I motioned over my shoulder.

She released her hold on my hand, pulled her cell from her small purse, and texted me, her fingers shaking like mine would have been were they not clenched at my sides. "That's my address."

Swallowing hard, I nodded at the vibration of my cell in my back pocket.

"No expectations, Blaine," she stated quietly, grasping my forearm and peering up at me, her eyes luminous in the fading sunlight. "I just thought we could hang out. Get to know each other better. Maybe kiss some more if you want."

"I want," I blurted the words, heat rushing to my damn face for at least the tenth time since our date had started.

Her smile lit me up inside, casting bright sunlight over the garden she had planted in my soul. "See you soon."

I nodded like I'd been clubbed upside the head, watching her walk away.

"Fuck." I scrubbed a trembling hand down over my face and turned, grimacing at the discomfort in my groin.

I'd never gone home with a woman before. What the fuck would I do? She would keep the conversation going when I felt like a dumb idiot, and I liked her. I longed to try for more but had no fucking clue how to make the first move.

Grey always did that.

I just followed along where he led, doing what he suggested since he knew as a man what I would enjoy, what would get me off.

Big boy briefs, I reminded myself, turning my truck's key with shaking fingers.

My stomach rolled again, but more from excitement than anxiety.

"You got this."

I snorted a laugh at myself. What twenty-seven-year-old man needed to give himself a pep talk when a woman claimed no expectations?

The seven minutes it took to get to Lily's apartment she shared with her cousin Haley felt like twenty hours. Even with the air conditioning on full blast, my back grew as sweaty as my palms. Until I climbed out of my truck, I had to swipe my forearm across my forehead.

Lily waited for me on the sidewalk in front of her apartment building, her sundress billowing around her knees with the evening's hot breeze.

"Hey," she said, grabbing my hand again as soon as I drew close enough. "I thought you weren't going to follow through."

Goddamn red face.

Again.

"You're a tease," I muttered, not at all upset she'd pretty much figured me out within a matter of hours. I was so damn obvious.

She snickered and tugged me toward the building's front door. "I love that color on your face is all. And now that I'm getting to know you a little bit better, I expect you won't go running off."

"Only because you're a hypnotizing serpent I can't say no to."

A very unladylike snort ripped from her. "In your own little Garden of Eden, are you?"

"Could be..." I bit back a smirk and decided to flirt a bit. "Are you the devil in disguise?"

"Maybe." She winked up at me and unlocked the door to their fifth-floor apartment the elevator had spit us out right in front of. "Come on in...if you dare."

My shoulders relaxed, and I moved past her into the small kitchen.

"Ignore the dishes in the sink. It's Haley's day to clean up, and they won't get done until eleven-fifty-nine tonight." Lily set her purse on the small square table. "Want some wine? I've got chardonnay and chardonnay."

While I enjoyed white wine better than beer or shots, I needed to keep a level head. "Water's good."

She poured one for each of us from a Brita filter in the fridge, and I followed her into the adjoining living room. Plants took up space on the windowsills, bringing the outdoors into the small space. A well-worn couch sat in front of a flatscreen atop an end table turned sideways, colorful throw pillows angled in the corners.

Lily sat smack dab in the center, and I settled in beside her.

"My parents—hell, my entire family—were super involved in the church."

I shifted to face her, my nervousness dissolving a bit at her choice of conversation. She'd said no expectations, but I doubted she'd want to dive back into what I thought I'd been obvious about not wanting to share.

But she could, and I would listen.

"I understand that all too well," I murmured, my heart

hurting for her even if she'd experienced only a fraction of what I had as a kid.

"I grew up beneath a shit ton of rules, obligations, expectations...and even though my parents believed they were doing their best in raising me, I've come to recognize how emotionally empty our household was."

She peered at me as though waiting, and I nodded my agreement, giving her that much at least.

"Were you told to trust God when things got tough and you didn't know how to handle your feelings?" Her question wasn't probing, sounding more like she wanted to create yet another bridge between us.

Perhaps she needed me to open up too, to meet her halfway before we could move forward, which I definitely hoped to.

I decided on sharing what I could without pulling too much darkness up from where it festered in the deepest part of me. "That and our leader who we'd been told heard directly from God."

Lily nodded. "Same. God's man and all that bullshit. I did everything asked of me, volunteered to help out around the church whenever I could. Worship and servitude were our life, the reason for our existence."

"And questioning that supposed truth?" I prompted, wondering how much we truly had in common.

"It was considered rebellion against God's word."

"Were you punished?" I asked quietly, my breaths slowing even as my heart rate rose along with a thread of darkness.

Lips pursed, Lily furrowed her brow. "My parents weren't abusive, but they didn't spare the rod, that's for sure. Once I hit my teenaged years, I had electronics and the freedom of hanging out with friends outside church taken away."

Better than being locked in small, dark spaces where no food or water was allowed. Or being forced to kneel and accept lashes—and the aftercare that hurt more than the leather biting across my back.

A shiver slid over me, raising the hairs on my arms. I rubbed at them while swallowing a hint of bile, determined to stay in the light while with Lily.

"Do you keep in touch with your family?"

I studied the callouses on my palms, fighting the urge to pick at them as memories continued to press upward and turn my stomach. "No."

"It was that bad, huh?"

"Yeah." I tried for a smile through my nausea, shifting on the couch and lifting my focus back to her face.

No pity shone in her eyes, just a kindness that promised understanding. "Have you figured out who you are outside your past yet, Blaine?"

Fucking loaded question, but it gave me something else to think on.

"Some," I finally answered after a lightning flash of memories from the previous nine years. My stomach settled a little at the reminder of how far I'd come, the escape Grey had made possible for me. Warmth spread over my chest. I owed the man more than I could ever repay. "You?"

"I like to think so." Lily's tone lightened. "It's nice to stretch my limbs and just swim in the ocean of life, know what I mean?"

I did to some extent, but I had yet to take off my life jacket.

Greyson.

"What haven't you done yet?" she asked. "What's on your

bucket list you've been dying to scratch off but haven't allowed yourself to do?"

Her questions struck hard. I'd never considered a future beyond working every day and resting in quiet at home. Sure, I enjoyed the hookups with my best friend, but I didn't strive for more. Didn't push myself to breathe fully and *live* even though he prompted me almost daily to stretch my wings and fly.

Perhaps it was time for me to do more. *Be* more. Open my eyes wide to all the world had to offer. Kick my legs against the current and learn how to slice through the ocean of life like Lily spoke of without a buoy holding me up.

"What's on your mind?" Lily prompted when I couldn't find an answer.

"That we hardly know each other but we share the same past. You understand what's in here." I tapped at my head. "You scare the fuck out of me, but I kind of like it."

She smirked. "I scare you, huh?"

"In the best way possible."

Her smile faded, and blinking, she glanced away.

"Hey." I grasped her chin without thought, same as Grey often did to me, turning her to face me. "I'm not comfortable around too many people, and even though I'm nervous as hell around you, you also make it easy for me to be myself. I only have that with Grey, and he's like...a staple in my life."

"Grey?"

"My best friend." My focus dropped to her mouth and back up with jarring force for my mind. "I really want to kiss you again."

The light and laughter returned to brighten her eyes. "You're giving my brain whiplash."

"Can I?"

She closed the distance between our mouths, her small

hands grasping at my shirt. That sense of rightness rushed through me once more at the softest touch, the sweetness of her on my tongue.

I wanted to lay her back on the couch, cover her with my weight. Touch and taste every inch of her skin. Slide my aching length inside her body like my tongue did with her mouth.

You belong to me.

Shivers rushed over me at the echoed words from my past, tensing my muscles. Instinct pulled me away from Lily before my brain caught up to what I did.

"What's wrong?" she asked, her fingers falling from my face as I leaned back.

Grey isn't here. Fuck, I can't do this...

"N-nothing." I let out a nervous laugh, rubbing my palms down my jeans as I scrambled to get a hold of myself. My pulse thundered in my neck as darkness pressed upward like a bubbling cauldron. "Um...bathroom?"

"Second door on the right," she said, motioning toward the hallway, and I hopped up the best my throbbing balls allowed. Of course, they wouldn't shrivel at the hated words. "Are you okay?"

"Yeah," I choked out. "Be right back."

Why couldn't I make a move on my own when those voices rose? Why did I need to grab onto that damn life jacket within seconds of finally letting go?

The answer to that last question sat heavy in my chest, memories fighting to escape the box I'd buried inside my mind.

Grey was the only one who gave me the freedom to choose when it came to sex.

I couldn't fucking handle it without him, couldn't get

over the...speed bump Quell and his wife had erected between me and taking pleasure because I wanted it.

Would I ever be able to hold that key on my own, or was I destined to need Grey for the rest of my days?

That thought didn't bother me—in fact, it only made me wish for him all the more. He was comfort and home to me.

Always would be.

For the first time, I admitted to the truth that I didn't want a life without him, woman in the picture or not.

He'd texted, I noticed after shutting myself away in Lily's bathroom to get a grip on my focus. He'd invited me down for Meryl's birthday cake, and I felt guilty as fuck for keeping the truth from him. He assumed I sat in my room, sheltered away from his group of friends.

So, I met this girl, he replied after I declined.

I stared at that message, wishing I was ready to tell him I'd done the same and how I wanted to invite her home to meet him.

Grey: **I think you'd like her.**

Keeping it short since Lily waited for me out on the couch, I told him I wasn't really interested. He shot back quickly, laying down the law. We were going for drinks the next night, and I wasn't allowed to complain.

Me: **What if I have plans?**

The asshole knew me too well—even if he wasn't aware of where I was or the fact I had a willing, gorgeous woman in the other room who would probably gladly spread her legs for me if I asked.

Grey: **Nice try.**

"Fucker."

Erection completely gone, I emptied my bladder and washed up before heading back to my date.

Of course, it had only taken one simple conversation with my anchor to once more set me free.

15

———

LILY

Haley dragged her ass into our apartment at five in the morning.

I'd gotten up for work a few minutes earlier and had the coffee pot brewing since she'd be home sooner rather than later.

"Need." Her one word made me chuckle, and she slumped down at the table, resting her forehead on the wooden surface.

"Wild night?"

"Something like that," she muttered, unmoving.

"Two dicks or one?"

"One massive one." She sighed. "And before you get all excited, he didn't know how to use it."

"Three-pump chump?"

"Hour-long fuck fest that has me sore as hell—and not in the good way. Damn jackrabbit had no finesse whatsoever," she grumbled, her shoulders slumped.

I bit back a giggle while putting the teakettle on for me. "Why didn't you just fake it to move him along?"

"I came—three times thanks to my own hand," she said,

"then begged and pleaded like a moaning whore for him to finish. Damn dirty talk didn't do jack shit to make him bust a nut."

"You could have told him to stop."

Haley let out a sigh and turned her face toward me, her cheek still on the table. "He liked to kiss while he fucked," she all but whispered the words.

"Ah," I murmured while grabbing two mugs from the cabinet.

Haley had a thing for mouths, men who could rile a woman up with their lips and tongue on hers. She'd been raised by a narcissist for a mother who held back on affection and edification unless it benefited her in some way. Haley still suffered from that shit, even though she didn't speak much about it.

Her mom had lost her marbles and ended up in the psych ward after stalking the marriage counselor she and her husband used before divorcing.

The same man Levi and I had gone to for premarital counseling and ended up inviting into our bed. I had seen the way Zeke and Levi looked at each other whenever we met in his office or at church. Neither of them had given me the same heated gazes, making the intense yearning that radiated between them clear.

There'd been no room in that bed for a third after we'd crossed the line into supposed sin. But things had turned out just fine, and I'd been given my freedom to explore more of what the world had to offer.

"Next time you should take charge and show the man how to move," I told Haley.

"Meh. Too much work."

I set a steaming mug in front of her, black, my mind flitting to Blaine and how he took his the same. A smile curved my lips.

Haley pushed upright and sipped, moaning and smacking her lips, tresses of her mangled hair falling from the messy bun atop her head. "Delish."

"So, why'd you stay the night?" I sat beside her and wrapped my hands around my hot tea.

"Couldn't fucking walk."

I snorted as she sipped again.

"How was your date with Blaine?"

My smile came back full force.

"Shit. Give me the details so I can be jelly and call you a bitch."

I outright laughed. "No sex."

"What?" She blinked, her sleepy eyes widening. "And you're all but glowing like that?"

Shrugging, I twisted my mug around. "We definitely connected, just not physically. I really like him."

"Did you at least kiss the guy?"

"Yep." I bit back a bigger grin.

"Shit. That good, huh?"

"Yep." My smile slowly faded as I remembered how he'd pulled back abruptly as though my touch, my mouth, had burned him. "He got uncomfortable though."

"Explain."

I did, and she frowned when I told her I didn't ask Blaine about his actions, that I didn't want to pry and make him even more uncomfortable. I'd already shared how shy he was, the type that needed patience and kid gloves.

"Scott texted me while he was in the bathroom too," I said. "Just dropped a time and location for a date tonight."

"He's a bossy asshole," Haley muttered, finally sitting back into her chair.

"It's kind of sexy," I said with a shrug. "And it gives me a chance to act like a brat rather than restraining myself and being *patient*." I feigned a shudder to get a snicker out of her.

"So, what are you going to do if he wants to hand out swats for disobedience?"

"I'm not getting Dom vibes from him."

Haley snorted. "As if you even know what to look for."

"I devour BDSM books even though I'm not interested in the lifestyle myself, thank you very much."

"It's *fiction*," she scoffed.

"I like to think some get it right," I argued, "but whatever. It's just an escape, something to do while lying on the beach being lazy."

"So, you're going to meet Mr. Bossy tonight, or are you hung up on tall, dark, and handsome?"

"I know I should feel guilty for hooking up with Scott on the same day I went on a date with Blaine—"

"Shut up with that bullshit," Haley snipped at me, frowning, her dark eyes flashing. "You're not tied down, and you're free to do as you damn well please."

"Sometimes the voices from the past..." Lips pressed tight, I shook my head.

"I get it, Lil, really, I do, but you've got to squash the fuck out of those thoughts when they rise. They're wrong. A manipulation to keep you feeding off a pulpit and lining the pockets of its leaders."

I blew out a slow exhale, knowing she spoke truth.

"*Live* while you can," Haley continued. "Enjoy the fuck out of every day and find who you *are*, not what you were told to be by people who are still sleeping in the dark ages. Now, back to Blaine. What happened next?"

He was a much easier subject than my religious past, one that made my heart rate tick a bit higher. "We sat and ended up talking for another hour. He got offered a management position with the company he works for, but it's still landscaping-type stuff. He's definitely not the office and desk kind of guy."

"You must be dying to get those calloused palms you keep talking about all over your body."

"God, yes," I groaned the words while hopping up for a second cup of tea. "My hand got lost in his, but the gentle strength in his grip, the clasp of his fingers…" A shiver licked over my skin, and I released a heavy exhale.

"Then what?"

I shrugged, my back to Haley. "He left."

"You just let him go?" Her voice rose at the end in surprise. "Even without a goodnight kiss?"

"Yep. He…seems like the type who's worth waiting for."

"Relationship material?" She eyed me as I turned and once more sat my ass down. She knew full well my stance on getting serious before I had a chance to knock off all my single bucket list items.

"More the timid kind of guy, and I'm dying to see if he's the same in the sack. He's so sweet, and there's more than lust between us, that's for damn sure." I hadn't told Haley about his growing up in a cult since it wasn't my place, but I'd shared he came from a religious background like me.

"I'm not looking to settle down," I reminded her— *myself*, "but I like him enough to want to spend more time with him. See how much we have in common. Connect." I shrugged, my head more wishy-washy than I liked.

"And if he has a pencil dick and can't even use *that*?" Haley sipped.

A memory flashed through my head, and I bit back a smirk. "He's definitely thicker and longer than a damn pencil."

My cousin's head whipped up from her coffee. "And how exactly do you know that if all you did was kiss?"

"It's kind of hard—pun intended—" I snorted a laugh "—to hide what you're packing when you're turned on as fuck."

"Mmm." Haley smirked and propped her elbow onto the table, her chin in her hand. "Tell me more."

"We'd sat on a bench by the ocean for awhile, shared our first kiss there, and when we got up to leave, he stood before I did. Jean-covered bulge all but in my face." Warmth rushed through me at the memory, my mouth's drool glands waking up.

"Well, hopefully Blaine of the Thick and Juicy Cocks has talent below the belt," she muttered.

I laughed again. "I already gave him a nickname—Mr. Yummy—but I like yours better."

"It's because I'm the fucking queen of nicknames."

Still smirking, I glanced at the clock. "I need to get moving."

"And I gotta go back to bed, but first, when are you seeing him again?"

"Blaine?"

"Yeah."

"Sunday we're going to spend the day at the beach."

"I'm jelly." Haley pouted.

I scratched the back of her head as I passed, and she leaned into the touch—starved for affection. I ambled toward the hallway, ready for a shower to help wake me up.

"Oh, hey!" Haley called.

"What?" I hollered back, not stopping.

"So, what's up with Scott? Are you going to meet him tonight like he demanded, or are you hung up on getting Blaine's big dick inside you?"

Laughter erupted from me, my body tingling at the image her words created in my head. If only Scott's roommate wasn't in the picture...

I imagined myself between him and Blaine.

"That would be spectacular," I moaned quietly, my core clenching.

"What?" Haley hollered.

While I'd gotten myself off after Blaine had left the night before, I ached for more. "I'm going to obey this time," I shouted back and shut myself in the bathroom, proud for stretching my wings with the whole "why choose?" thing even though bullshit from the past lingered enough that a twinge of shame ate at my insides.

I eyed myself in the mirror, the leftover makeup I hadn't removed smeared from sleep. My hair looked like a rat's nest. Too bad it hadn't gotten that way from a nice romp between my sheets with Mr. Yummy.

"You're free," I reminded myself quietly. "Guilt has no place in your heart or mind. Take life by the balls and live while you're still young."

Determined to do just that, I hopped in the shower to ready for a day of fake smiles and taking people's hard-earned cash for too-expensive coffees.

I had a hot date with Scott in the very near future that promised a lot of laughs, sexual tension, and eventually, the type of release I knew he could give me.

Ride the wave...

Hot water pelted me as I considered Scott and Blaine. I wasn't invested enough with either of them to feel a tug toward one over the other, and I didn't want to be. Choosing shouldn't be necessary, and I wasn't sure that I could if faced with that possibility.

Once more, the idea of a threesome sent lust through my

body, but Blaine was definitely too shy to toss me onto a bed, let alone one where another guy waited for us. Curiosity kept me interested though. I would hang with him until I figured out what was what between us.

And Scott?

Maybe his roommate was hot as fuck like him. Hell, maybe Scott had talked him into helping me fulfill some of those double-stuffed fantasies and they'd both be waiting for me at the restaurant later that night.

A girl could hope.

16

GREYSON

Blaine and I sat at the high table we always tucked ourselves away into at Shadow's Lounge, the darker corner making it easier for my best friend to relax. I didn't get him out too often, but the quieter bar had been one in the past that didn't make his feet itch to head home after a single drink.

I sat with a cold beer in hand, him a glass of chardonnay as usual, chatting about daily life shit, which I'd done intentionally to make him relax, his defenses down. For some reason, he seemed antsier than normal, but I was running out of time.

Only ten minutes remained before Lily was set to arrive, so I took a deep breath to spill why I'd really dragged his ass out with me.

"So, that girl I was telling you about..."

Blaine shot his gaze to my face from his wine glass, his brow furrowed slightly. "You didn't."

"Yeah. She's gonna be here soon."

"Grey—"

"I know you said you aren't ready, but she's...she's

fucking perfect." The memory of Lily's appearance, her laughter, the noises she'd made while coming all over my dick sent blood to my groin, stirring me to life. "You're going to like her, I just know it. She's everything our last hookup wasn't, and she has the most gorgeous smile..." My voice trailed away as I studied my best friend.

He picked at his callouses like they'd done him wrong, tension rather than annoyance radiating off him and his furrowed brow.

"What's up, B?" I asked, needing to get whatever bothered him from his mind before Lily showed up.

"I lied," he blurted, his shoulders immediately sagging a bit like confessions always did to him. The fuckers in his past *still* affected his ability to ignore guilt over every goddamn little thing.

"About?" I pushed when he didn't explain on his own.

"I-I wasn't hiding upstairs last night during your party."

I blinked, processing what he'd said. "Where the fuck were you?" The higher tone of my voice stated surprised-as-fuck, loud and clear.

"With a girl."

An instinctive grin split my face before his words fully processed in my brain. "Get the fuck out!"

He glanced around the bar with typical Blaine embarrassment tinging his cheeks pink. "I really like her. Like, *really* like her."

My smile faded, alarm bells clanging in my head and heart.

Danger ahead. Tragic...life-altering...

I swallowed hard. "Tell me about her." My demand escaped a bit ragged when I should have been thrilled to hear he'd finally stepped outside his comfort zone.

Religious background, just like him.

Left her previous life behind, just like him.

Finding out who she is, just like him.

He didn't need to use the word "connection" to explain what he'd found with her—I could see it clear as anything on his face and in his eyes.

Blaine was enamored with the girl, and with every word passing his lips, my heart ached a little bit more.

Had he found his other half? A woman who would *see* him, be able to empathize with every nightmarish memory he couldn't banish from his head? Someone who would hold and soothe him with understanding in their heart rather than selfish desires for physical touch like I tended toward whenever he needed me?

"Did you fuck her?" I spewed the question, cutting him off mid-sentence about how her yellow sundress had been like sunshine.

He swallowed audibly, glancing once more at his drink. "No."

I shouldn't have been pleased by his answer but the heaviness inside me lightened at his confession. "Why not?"

Blaine wouldn't ever give me the words I longed to hear more than anything, but I held my breath. Wishing. Hoping. Fuck, wanting to pray.

"We kissed." He shrugged, still not meeting my eyes.

"That's it?" I asked my throat tightening over the thought of him leaving me behind. Abandoning me.

My guts clenched.

Fucking hell.

Blaine rubbed his palms down his thighs like he always did when nervous. "Yeah. I couldn't...not ready for that on my own just yet."

Not exactly the answer I hoped for, but that meant he was still partly mine.

But for how long? When would he finally realize he didn't really need me to find release with a woman?

"She's got this infectious laugh," Blaine went on while I fought to find words or still my rioting insides. "Sparkling—happy—brown eyes. She's brought a garden to life inside me, bursting with color."

I blinked and stilled except for the rushing beat of my heart. He'd become a goddamn romantic.

My eyes stung, and I forced my lungs to fill as Blaine went on about his coffee girl as he referred to her. He sat up a bit straighter, his smile returning full force, a sight I hadn't seen in a long-as-fuck time. I stared as he all but told me he'd fallen in love with a girl after knowing her less than a week.

A shattered heart lay inside my chest, bleeding and weeping by the time he ran out of steam.

Blaine stared at me, his grin dissolving at the agonized look no amount of carefully feigned expressions instilled in me as a child could keep off my face. "Grey?"

I shook my head, unable to talk.

"Say something."

What the fuck could I say? Definitely not that I was happy for him because that would be a goddamn lie. Telling him I hated whoever the fuck she was because she would take the one I'd loved forever from my side would ruin the friendship I'd made myself content with.

I tore my focus off my best friend's steady gaze, my insides twisted and morphing...dying.

Lily walked in the front door.

She wore a strapless, tight-as-fuck red dress with lip gloss that matched.

My chest squeezed for a different reason, and I drank in the sight of her, breathing a bit easier. Where death from

Blaine's words had begun to create a zombie of my barely beating heart, she returned life.

Hope.

Her hair tumbled down in gentle waves over her bare shoulders. Heels with straps that wound up over her calves made her appear taller. Half of her thighs showed before the dress's hem hit, skin golden and begging for love bites and hickeys.

She hadn't noticed me or felt my stare, her gaze roaming over the people at the gigantic bar in the room's center first.

"Grey?" Blaine's voice pulled my focus off her feminine perfection. He still studied me, leaning onto the table, and I realized my face had changed from the crushed appearance mere moments before. "What?" he asked.

I cleared my throat, having no choice but to spew the truth. "She just walked in. The girl I wanted you to meet."

Blaine turned his head, and breath held, I readied to drink in his expression as his eyes landed on Lily for the first time.

His face lit up—but with recognition. "Lily's here," he said.

Because I'd invited her...wait. Blaine hadn't told me his girl's name.

No. Fucking. Way.

I jerked my focus off my best friend for Lily.

She turned our way, catching my gaze.

Blaine's.

Mine again.

Surprise widened her eyes, and my heart slammed inside my chest.

"She's the girl you were telling me about?" I asked Blaine while holding Lily's gaze and sounding like I'd swallowed jagged shards of glass.

"Yeah." The happiness in his tone hadn't faded one bit, the clueless fuck.

I tore my focus off Lily to find his eyes gleaming while staring at her. Pink flushed his face. "Blaine."

He glanced at me quickly, and I swallowed hard. "She's the girl I was with Thursday night. The one I asked to meet us here."

His grin flatlined. He blinked, confusion furrowing his brow. "What?"

"Lily."

"My Lily?"

Blaine saw her as his.

Fuck my life.

17

LILY

My slow amble into Shadow's Lounge halted like I'd hit a brick wall.

Scott.

Sitting with Blaine.

Sure my mind played tricks on me, I took in Scott's steady gaze—almost horrified widened eyes.

Blaine grinned at me like I was a burst of sunlight through gray clouds.

Scott swallowed so damn hard I could see his throat working from across the lounge.

Shame slammed into me like an eighteen-wheeler.

They're going to think I'm a whore...

My stomach turned inside out, but another thought rushed into my brain, giving me whiplash.

Had the two guys played me?

Gaze flitting back toward Blaine, I noted his flushed cheeks, the same shyness and excitement I'd seen every time we'd been together.

No way in hell he'd been faking those emotions.

So, what the fuck?

Lips pressed tightly together, I forced my feet forward as the two men turned toward one another, sharing a few words.

My knees wobbled in my four-inch heels, but I made it to their table, my height putting me on their eye level as they sat atop the stools. Neither stood to greet me as their gazes remained locked over the table.

"What the actual fuck?" I managed to spew out, my voice low and haggard, my stomach twisted tight enough it forced the oxygen from my lungs.

The men still stared at one another, but Blaine no longer smiled.

Scott cleared his throat but still studied his...friend?

"Scott?" I pushed when he didn't speak.

He finally turned to face me and slid off the seat to stand. "It's Greyson."

Damn liar.

"Greyson Scott," he continued as my anger swelled inside me. "And I just found out that you already met my roommate."

Ohholyshitandthensome.

I sped through conversations with both men, recognizing that perhaps a smarter person might have put together the truth.

But I'd never been the brightest star in the sky.

By the looks on the men's faces, I knew neither had been aware I'd been seeing them both.

Guilt crept up like rancid bile, churning and making my mouth water with the need to vomit. My anger dissolved, leaving me on the verge of trembling. "I'm not a whore," I gasped out, shoulders rounding in, hands clutching my purse against my stomach.

Blaine hopped up and grabbed hold of my arm, his

callouses scraping over my skin with a gentle caress. "Sit. Please."

The chair hit the back of my ass without my being aware I moved, and strong hands grasped my waist, lifting me onto the high seat without effort. Had I been in a better frame of mind, I'd have swooned for sure.

Gorgeous hazel eyes peered into mine, Blaine's face close enough to kiss, near enough I could read the turmoil in his mind. "This is a clusterfuck," he muttered, his hands still holding my waist.

"It could be fate." Scott—Greyson's low murmur turned both of us toward him, and Blaine moved away, taking his warmth with him.

Coolness slid over me, pebbling my skin, but Blaine tugged a free chair closer to me and sat down.

"It's a what-are-the-chances situation," Blaine stated, once more rubbing my forearm, "but I don't think you're a whore."

"Neither do I," Greyson stated, holding my stare. "You're twenty-four, unattached, and enjoying the smorgasbord of life."

God, he sounded like Haley.

Blaine pried my fingers from my purse and clasped my hand. "I want you to stay," he murmured as though reading the instincts in my mind, shame telling me to get the hell out of there regardless of what they said.

"Me too." Greyson scooted his chair closer until our knees touched. That sense of neediness I'd gotten from him on our date rose again—and I liked it.

I couldn't find words, my brain buzzing, still fighting to put my situation into unfiltered light I could make sense of, but I pressed my knee tighter against his.

Greyson had said he and his roommate shared women,

that "B" was too shy to find hookups on his own, but Blaine had stepped outside of his comfort zone for me. Add in the easy conclusion of Greyson still wanting me and some of the tension eased from my body.

What were the chances, Blaine had said.

Seriously. Haley was going to have a fucking field day.

"This is awkward as fuck," I blurted suddenly, laughter escaping harshly enough that I clasped a hand over my mouth.

Both men grinned—first at each other, then at me.

"How the hell did this happen?" I asked, voice muffled from my palm.

"I only use my surname on Missing Link," Greyson started, and I remembered he'd never used his roommate's full name either, "but if I'd told you the truth when we met... I'm sorry for lying."

"It wasn't a lie," I said, dropping my free hand to my lap where my purse rested. Blaine's hand stayed wrapped around my other atop my thigh. "Not really." My lips curved upward as familiar heat swelled up inside me at Greyson's— Grey, Blaine had called him—stare.

He didn't hide the desire, the draw I could feel between us, same as on our date Thursday night. Memories of his fingers, his tongue, those gyrating hips that fucked his dick deep inside me flitted through my brain, pebbling my nipples and causing pulses to wake between my thighs.

This girl had wished on a magical star like a damn Disney princess, and perhaps it *was* fate like he had suggested that made my dream of the two of them being a packaged deal come true.

A smirk lifted the corners of Greyson's lips as though he knew where my thoughts had gone.

"So, now what?" Blaine asked.

I tore my attention off Greyson to find him studying his roommate. Did he see the physical attraction between us? Could he feel it as potently as I did? But most importantly, did it bother him? Rubbing absently at the goosebumps along my arm, I studied the two men looking at one another, lost in what seemed some sort of silent communication.

Greyson had told me he was bi and that Blaine was straight, easing my mind over the whole crossing of swords between the two men, but watching them eye the other raised the hair on my nape. Love rested in both their gazes, but a definite hint of more than mere platonic emotions lay behind Greyson's eyes. Did Blaine know, or did Greyson keep those feelings closeted up in his heart?

Blaine peered at his best friend like those blue eyes of his were his safe haven. His home.

His anchor in an overwhelming world.

A look I'd seen before in Levi's eyes when I'd caught him staring at Zeke.

An unpleasant shiver slid over my skin, and I scooted to the edge of the chair before my mind even made a conscious decision to escape the inevitable heartache in my future.

Blaine tightened his hold on my fingers, both men turning toward me at the same time.

"It's your call, Lily," Greyson stated quietly. "B has the hots for you, and you *know* how I feel and what I want when it comes to you."

Blaine shot a glance between us. "Did you two..."

Greyson kept his focus on me but remained quiet—leaving it up to me to answer. He hadn't told his best friend we'd fucked. Would the truth make Blaine release his hold on me? I tightened my grasp on his hand.

Unable to voice what could hurt my heart after less than a week of knowing him, I nodded at Blaine.

No trace of jealousy, no grimace lined his face.

His eyes went dark, pupils swelling like the idea of his best friend and I together made him hard. "Fuck," he muttered, rubbing at the stubble on his jawline.

"You missed out, B," Greyson said, a hint of teasing and definite relief in his voice.

A rushed exhale of breath I hadn't realized I'd held flagged me in my seat, but tension coiled low in my belly as the truth of what I'd found flickered to life inside my mind and swelled into bursting light.

Greyson and Blaine *shared women.*

A shiver rippled through me, settling lust, pure and hot, between my thighs.

"What's going on in that pretty little head of yours, Lily?" Greyson asked.

I couldn't say it outright. "You, um…know my handle on Missing Link."

"S2L." It wasn't a question, but his eyes lit with even more hunger, potent enough I needed to shift on the chair.

"Yep," I squeaked rather than popping the P with assurance and confidence.

"You two are killing me," Blaine said. "What the fuck is going on here?"

"Our Lily here is seeking two lovers," Greyson supplied, his blue eyes full of fire and still focused on mine. "It's how we hooked up on the app."

Blaine let out a low groan that pulsed longing through me.

Wet. Panties.

The red silk thong I'd worn had officially been ruined. I prayed like hell there wouldn't be a spot on the chair when I finally got up onto my wobbly legs.

"I...I met both of you—had no clue Blaine was your roommate."

"Easily done seeing as how none of us dropped names."

I gave Blaine my full attention, needing clarity before my brain could move on. "You aren't angry? About my sleeping with Greyson?"

"No." He didn't hesitate to answer, but his brow furrowed slightly. "I've never..."

His voice trailed off, but he didn't need to expand. I'd been his first and second date, meaning he'd never been alone in a bed with a woman before.

My entire body throbbed, skin tight and itching, nipples hard at the thought it had been me who'd made Blaine wade into the waters of life, wanting to swim on his own.

Would Greyson's presence hinder forward progress—

Blaine pressed his mouth to mine, stealing my breath and answering my unspoken, cut-off question. His tongue stroked between my lips, his hand finding the back of my neck. I melted into a puddle of arousal, whimpering.

"Fuck." Greyson groaned the word out, sending another shot of lust through me.

Blaine pulled back, our gazes locked, both of us panting. Red gloss smeared over his lips, and I handed him a napkin with a trembling hand, motioning toward his mouth.

"Leave it," Greyson said, his tone low and rumbling. "It's hot as fuck."

Nervous giggles lightened my chest.

Blaine set aside the napkin without using it, pink flushing his face, but his eyes remained dark with want while staring at me.

I realized he'd become completely uninhibited, and nothing would hold him back.

Because of Greyson.

A red flag should have waved frantically in my head, but the promise in his eyes...

I tore my focus off Mr. Yummy for his friend and found the same desire in heated blue irises.

Neither Zeke nor Levi had given *me* such hungry looks.

I gulped and squeezed my thighs together.

I shot off a second wish and mentally crossed my fingers because those two boys were too damn sexy to deny.

18

BLAINE

"Can I get you something to drink?" The waitress pulled me back to reality, and I watched as Lily fumbled, fighting to right her brain in order to form words too.

"She'll have a glass of chardonnay," Greyson replied coolly as though unaffected by our what-the-fuck situation, and Lily offered him a grateful smile as the waitress hurried away.

The shock of my Lily being Grey's girl had taken me a few to work through in my brain. Jealousy should have raged—would have for any normal guy—but strange relief flooded me.

I'd finally found a woman who interested me enough I'd left my comfort zone, and she also wanted the man I needed to survive.

I had kissed her in public without thought, without hesitation. All because my life jacket sat beside us.

He gave me the ability to take pleasure in Lily.

The night before, I'd been half-sick with nervousness, unable to initiate what she and I had both desired. But being with them both felt right in ways I'd never experienced with other hookups.

Lily is no hookup.

I breathed the scent of vanilla into my lungs, wanting nothing more than to pull her into my arms again. She was a forever-type girl.

And I longed to know her inside and out. Mentally, emotionally, and physically—with Grey.

"So, how did you two meet?" he asked, sitting back and relaxing when all I wanted to do was head back to our place and let loose in what I yearned for.

His calmness radiated across the table to me, and my shoulders relaxed as though he steered me by autopilot. Such relief came in allowing him to drive the wreck of my life.

"He showed up at the cafe for coffee on Monday morning," Lily answered, and I let her tell the story, the words flowing from her easy as rain. She'd been smitten by the tall, dark, and handsome she'd referred to as Mr. Yummy in her brain.

Heat flooded my face at her compliments, the arrival of the waitress with Lily's wine intensifying my embarrassment.

Lily took a sip and made a husky noise of approval that thickened my dick again.

"All I got was his name, and we didn't even have a chance to chat because of all the other coffee fiends lined up behind him."

She muttered a few other annoyances about people rushing for work and in a hurry for coffee when they could very well make their own at home rather than drop five bucks on the too-expensive shit they served.

"When I found out he'd come in the next morning and

asked for me, I about died." She pretended to swoon, hand on her chest with a roll of her eyes.

Grey smirked at her drama, his gaze often flitting to me as Lily's story spilled from her lips in rushed, excitable words.

"My shift manager offered me to switch on Thursday, and of course, I said yes. Then he walked in—"

"Lily."

She cut off abruptly at Grey's gentle interruption.

"Let B speak."

"Sorry." She nipped at her lower lip. "I tend to talk too much when I'm nervous."

"It's okay, but I'd like to hear how he felt the first time he saw you."

Big brown eyes turned toward me without an ounce of annoyance over Grey's ending her word vomit I'd been enjoying.

I opened my mouth, and my answer spewed out. "Hot. Insecure. Overwhelmed. Dry mouth. Jittery insides."

Lily's smile shone over the garden in my heart, bursting new life from darkness.

"She asked me to dinner, so I wasn't the one who made the first move," I said, holding her gaze.

"But you suggested the late lunch instead," she murmured.

I nodded. "The words just spilled. I didn't think first, or I never would have asked you out."

Lily's eyes softened with understanding.

My heart stuttered in my chest as that bubble seemed to wrap around us again.

"And?" Grey prompted after a few long seconds of her and I staring at one another.

Clearing my throat, I gave him my attention. His focus

flitted between me and Lily, his expression unguarded and open.

Not the façade he usually put on with hookups, the one ingrained from childhood. Fake and pleasant, suave and smooth to attain whatever he wanted. For the first time with a woman between us, he was Grey. The boy I knew like the back of my hand, the man who didn't hide shit from me.

He feels the same as I do.

My breaths shortened at the thought, a strange ache spreading over my chest at his desire for honesty—and more than a one-night stand with Lily.

"We talked," I finally answered after swallowing hard. "Connected."

Lily threaded her fingers through mine, clasping my hand on her thigh again.

"Somewhat similar upbringings made conversation easy," I told Grey what I'd already shared before Lily had shown up.

Grey studied my face as though wondering just how *much* I'd told her. Still, no jealousy showed in his eyes over the fact that another person had made me comfortable enough to talk about some of the shit of my past.

He was the only one outside the compound who knew what I'd experienced.

"We went back to her place and kissed," I said, shrugging and trailing off.

"And that's it?" Grey pushed.

I nodded.

"You didn't want more?" Grey asked Lily.

"I did," she answered quietly, "but Blaine seemed... unsure." She squeezed my hand. "Not ready."

I could feel Grey's stare.

"Why?" He eyed me, needing an answer in a way I'd

never seen before. Greyson Scott didn't have an insecure bone in his body...

At least, I hadn't thought.

"You know why." I stated the truth quietly to set him at ease, and our gazes stayed locked.

Grey's eyes asked how much I'd shared with Lily—about my inability to enjoy the thought of sex without him, the buffer I'd told him countless times I needed.

A slow shake of my head answered his question, lessening the intensity of his gaze.

"Do you two always do this silent shit?"

Her question broke the seriousness of the moment, and Grey and I grinned at each other.

"It comes in handy when we have a woman between us," Grey answered.

Lily gulped her wine, choking as it went down the wrong tube.

I rubbed her spine, soothing until she breathed easy. My hand stayed on her lower back, the desire to tug her close, wrap her up in my arms, and hold her for Grey's loving rushing through me.

My jeans became a prison again, my pulse picking up.

Lily dabbed at her lips with a napkin, and I imagined Grey's mouth on hers, those whimpers she'd emitted the night before while kissing me filling my ears.

I shifted on the barstool, my groin tight and aching.

Grey caught my gaze again, his eyes stating he suffered along with me. One nod of encouragement from him, and I inhaled until it hurt.

"Will you come home with us?" I asked Lily, surprised my voice had any tone to it at all.

"Yes." Lily hadn't taken more than a breath to consider.

A sense of power swelled inside me, and Grey clasped

my shoulder as we stood. His hand lingered, warmth radiating down through my arm.

"Proud of you, B." His whisper close to my ear sent a shiver of goosebumps over my nape.

Lily's and my hand found each other's as though they wanted to be clasped, and for a split second, the three of us were connected physically, me being the center focus.

So right...

A punch of something satisfyingly sweet throbbed in my chest.

Grey's hold dropped from my shoulder, leaving a sense of loss behind.

My free hand flexed at my side as I imagined entwining my fingers with his, walking hand-in-hand with both of them. Strange flutters rippled through my stomach, but I pushed aside what felt like want to focus on the present.

We stepped out into the sunset, stopping on the sidewalk.

"You're riding with us," Greyson told Lily, pulling his keys from his pocket. "We can pick up your car tomorrow."

"Bossy," Lily muttered, but no trace of annoyance lit her husky voice. Her lack of argument stated she agreed to spend the night in Grey's massive bed with the two of us.

My dick pressed against my jeans' zipper, uncomfortable as hell all jammed up in its prison even while that garden inside me bloomed, bursting with life.

"I'll be your chauffeur," Grey said, hitting the unlock on his car. He opened the back door, ushering Lily in and motioning me to follow.

The second I slid onto the back seat beside Lily, I pulled her in tight against my side.

I still grinned like an idiot, hard as hell and completely comfortable in my own skin in the first time in...forever.

I kissed the top of Lily's head, breathing in the sweet scent of her. "Are you okay?" I asked her quietly as Grey climbed in and started the car.

"Never better." Cheeks flushed, she glanced up at me, her brown eyes sparkling with energy I could feel zapping across every inch of my skin. "I...I was thinking about the two of you last night."

"Really?"

She let out a shaky exhale and laughter that sounded more like a giggle.

So damn cute and lighthearted my chest swelled with giddiness too.

"Care to expand on that statement a bit?" Grey suggested from the front seat.

Lily's smile faded, her focus flitting toward the window.

"Lily," Grey pushed when it became obvious her mind had gone a different route than she'd planned or expected.

She inhaled deeply but kept her attention on the passing cars. "You both know I came from a religious background."

"You're not a whore, and you have nothing to be ashamed of," Grey bit the words out, a trace of anger in his voice I heard whenever shit from my past rose up to sicken the thoughts I would spew to him.

"But having two dates in the same day, craving one and sleeping with the other..."

"Hot as fuck," Grey stated firmly, his eyes on the road.

"And if it had been someone other than your best friend and roommate I'd been out with?" Lily prompted.

"I knew B would want you, so swaying your mind away from whoever that fictional asshole is would have been easy."

"Is he always this arrogant?" Lily asked me, a hint of smile on her lips.

"Get used to it." I kissed the top of her head, squeezing her tight. "You're here now—with both of us. Who cares what it took to get to this place?"

"Preach."

Lily laughed at Grey's command. "Is he always this *bossy*?"

I caught Grey's gaze in the rearview mirror, those blue eyes of his hinting at teasing. Promising a good time.

"Yeah. He is." And I liked it, I realized, needing to shift on the seat to adjust my junk.

A lot.

19

GREYSON

I loved B, but him uninhibited, no hesitation or unease with snuggling and loving on Lily in my car's back seat? Yeah.

Never had I ever seen such a beautiful sight. I wanted to watch him strip her down, worship her tight body and lose himself in the soft, hot heaven of her pussy. I imagined his groan at feeling how tight she would be around his length, and my own thickened in my jeans at the memory.

He hadn't been comfortable alone with her the night before, and that truth stroked a solid one over my ego, giving me the hope of hanging onto him a bit longer.

His eyes, his body expressions, revealed he'd fallen for Lily and was all in for whatever their future held. I wondered if she saw his truth and what she felt about it.

I glanced in the rearview, my gaze snagging onto Lily's dark eyes. My breath caught at the delight and joy that shone in their depths and the sweet smile on her lips. She gave me a saucy wink, the heat in her gaze keeping me from feeling like a third wheel.

B wasn't the only one tumbling head over heels for her.

Would sharing Lily cause problems if the two of them decide to make a go of it on their own?

The thought of losing him hurt like hell, but to never touch or taste Lily again didn't sit right in my mind either. She was so refreshing, and the soft femininity of her clicked pieces together inside me as though working toward a healing I'd never expected to attain.

If my heart didn't already belong to B, if I didn't shy away from relationships with women, I could have been in his shoes.

I remained quiet while Lily told B how we'd met, pulling out her cell to let him read over our texts.

"Oh, shit," he murmured over what I couldn't see.

"Right?" Lily agreed. "Here. Let me turn up the volume… watch it again."

I heard myself groan through the cell's tinny speaker.

She'd shown him the short video of me coming.

B released a hiss as though his jeans strangled him like mine did to me.

"And check out my reply," Lily murmured with a giggle.

"Fuck." He rasped the word a second later.

"Panties pic?" I asked, my tone ragged at the memory of those creamed fingers and the pinkie tucked beneath the satin.

"Yeah."

"She's sweeter than any woman I've ever tasted," I told him, and Lily let out a whimper.

"I want…" Blaine's rasp shivered my skin, and I once more met his gaze in the rearview.

I nodded at the question in his eyes, my chest swelling over the fact he required my encouragement.

"Can I touch you?" he whispered to Lily.

"Yes, please."

Christ, that needy, breathless voice made pre-cum ooze over the insides of my briefs.

Clothing rustled, and I wondered if she shimmied her skirt to her waist or if Blaine had been brave enough to slide his hand up her thigh.

Lily moaned.

The not being able to see about killed me. "Is she wet for us, B?"

"Yeah," he barely managed.

They kissed, and I watched as long and as often as I could without putting my car and its precious cargo in danger.

Blood rushed through me as I fought to keep from speeding to get the fuck home already.

Blaine pulled back and shoved his fingers into his mouth. His deep groan leaked more wetness from my slit.

He'd never done such a thing with any of our hookups. Ever.

The second his fingers left his mouth, Lily grabbed his head and pulled him in for another kiss like she was desperate to lick her arousal from his tongue.

"Christ, you two are so fucking hot. I can't even..." I grabbed my balls, squeezing and cursing over the few miles between me and heaven.

"I want to taste you too." Lily's whisper to Blaine rolled my eyes back into my head, and I gritted my teeth.

"Let her, B. Please...fucking let her," I pleaded for what I'd yet to see.

No woman had put her mouth on his dick, only their hands. While he'd never mentioned blow jobs as a trigger, I'd often wondered because what sane man didn't want a hot mouth and tongue wrapped around their dick?

Blaine watched Lily rather than my eyes in the mirror as

she scooted to the floor and rearranged herself to access his zipper and the thick ridge I knew waited for her.

He shifted, laughed a curse.

She giggled.

"Oh, fuck," he groaned the word, his tone rumbling ball-tinglingly low as his head fell back against the seat.

Welcome to the world of blow jobs, my love.

I bit my tongue, ears straining for the little utterances leaving Blaine's lips. Moans and gasps tightened every muscle in my body to spring over the seat to join them. Curses and her whimpers while she sucked him flooded my mouth with drool.

A fucking orchestra of lust-inducing music to my ears, a moving near-crescendo to my body that seized my balls up tight against my groin.

Don't blow, don't blow.

I cursed, needing to strangle my dick.

"Give it to her, B," I demanded, my voice as shaky as my hand attempting to tug down my balls.

Before I bust a nut like a goddamn teenager in my jeans.

"Lily—" Blaine's voice cut off with a guttural moan that shivered my skin. A delicious sound I'd memorized with his every climax I'd been lucky enough to hear over the years.

Beautiful.

I hissed through my clenched teeth, my one-handed grip on the steering wheel ready to snap the metal beneath it.

"Shit. I'm sorry," he muttered a few seconds later.

"Don't be." Lily's husky voice hinted at pleasure, a crooning happiness over a mouthful of cum.

Fuck, did I need to give her another load to swallow down.

"Come here." Blaine's murmur whispered over my skin like a caress, and goosebumps rose over my arms.

I glanced back to find Blaine clasping her neck, their mouths once more fused. A peek of tongue rushed adrenaline and lust through my blood.

Goddamnit.

Teeth gritted, I pulled into my driveway, every cell, every atom in my body on the verge of explosion. I imagined Lily felt the same considering she faced having her fantasies fulfilled.

I parked. Turned off the car. Contemplated grabbing her up and fucking her against the nearest wall.

But I wanted more—for all of us.

And that started with the man I loved beyond life. I needed him to be free for the first time with a woman. I lusted to soak that shit up, edge myself while watching him finally let go, because finding release after that would be fucking fantastic.

Legs shaking, I led the two of them to my bedroom, thankful as fuck the cleaning crew had come through earlier in the day, putting new sheets on my bed.

Lily and Blaine still held hands, trailing along behind me, but stopped in the middle of my room as I settled into the lone chair facing the king-sized mattress and down comforter.

Blaine's eyes flared with heat when he realized what I planned even though my body tensed to devour like a ravenous animal.

I grabbed hold of the chair's arms and gripped tight to keep from being a selfish asshole. I wanted him to have this...needed it more than I did release.

Lily glanced from me to him in my periphery as I held his gaze.

"What's he doing?" she whispered.

"He's going to watch."

You—I'm going to watch you, baby.

Blaine swallowed hard as though he'd heard my thought before turning his focus on Lily. "Are you okay with that?"

She gave me those dark orbs, heat and need slicing through my skin and causing blood to pool in my groin. "Take it out," she whispered at me, reaching to tug Blaine closer.

Fuck. Me.

The little minx had a bossy side too.

A groan escaped me, and I unzipped and eased my aching groin from its prison.

Watching how they tasted one another, Blaine's hands sliding down her back to cup her gorgeous backside oozed pre-cum, eased my firm grip's slide over my length.

Lily pressed against him, grinding with every squeeze of his strong hands.

I stroked my cock, no trace of jealousy coursing through me—just an insistent need to step behind my best friend and wrap my front to his back, feeling him up like he did her. All that hard muscle, firm backside against my groin. His scent filling my nose as I ran it along his nape while he made her whimper—

"More," Blaine groaned against her mouth, sending another pulse of lust through my core. "Please."

The poor, horny bastard had reverted to single words, his mind and body needing beyond what I had ever seen.

Not that I'd have been much better if I'd attempted to speak.

Pieces of clothing shed beneath their trembling hands, gasped breaths and stolen kisses between stripping one another fueled the flames inside me to the point I panted for oxygen.

Lily stood bare before him, eyes wide and luminous, staring as she tipped her head back to hold his gaze.

Blaine cradled her face in his hands, his dick long and thick, straining toward his belly button. "I..." He swallowed hard but didn't glance my way like he usually did when unsure.

A tingling of a fucking awful sixth sense skittered up my spine, but my love for him demanded I give him what he needed regardless of my heart. I would take pleasure in seeing his wings unfurl.

I *would*.

Shifting on the chair, I pulled my wallet from my back pocket and retrieved a condom. A quick flick of my wrist landed it on the bed behind Lily.

He eyed it. Eyed her.

Biting my tongue, I gave him the chance to make that move without verbal encouragement from me—but Lily led him, pulling back from his gorgeous body and climbing onto my bed.

Blaine followed willingly, without hesitation, blanketing her with his weight and, settling between her spread thighs.

My throat went tight even as my dick jerked as though seeking out my hand.

His ass flexed as he ground against her, both their moans ringing in my ears, and my fingers wrapped around my length again.

Fucking hot as hell...

Soft skin, his golden tan, rippling muscles, and gentle curves. Grasping hands and whispered curses.

I hadn't realized I'd clutched the chair's arm with my

free hand until Lily turned her face, her molten eyes catching mine.

Holding my gaze. Full of longing. Desire to ease the ache spreading through my entire body.

"Christ." I gritted my teeth and hissed while gliding my palm over my slick head.

She licked her lower lip, those damn dark eyes of hers begging for more.

I groaned and rocked up into my fist.

Blaine pulled away from where he'd nuzzled her neck and glanced at me, his pupils blown wide, eyes hazed with lust.

I longed for him to ask me to join them—prayed he didn't.

Please her...fucking hell, take *for once in your life, B.*

His focus flitted back toward her face, and he slid down over her tight, little body.

"Oh, God." She gulped, her hands finding his hair as he buried his face between her thighs. Her legs rose, knees tight against his head, holding him in place. "Shit...so good."

Fucking hell...

A choked, garbled moan barely escaped Lily's parted lips, and she bowed. "Blaine!" Her shriek cut through my room, seizing my balls up tight.

The wet sounds of Blaine eating at her pussy, his moans of appreciation over her sweet cum sent tingles down my spine.

I gripped the base of my dick and squeezed, willing him to hurry the fuck up already before I lost my shit.

He shifted back onto his heels, grabbed the condom, and sheathed up regardless of the way his hands shook.

Lily reached for him, and eyes locked, they came

together in one long, agonized groan of pleasure that rocked me to my core.

My Blaine, my love, had finally taken another step toward freedom, and although my heart ached in my chest, happiness rushed over me like a massive swell.

I imagined the tight clasp of her heat around him, the slick wetness of her cum easing his thrusts into her tight pussy. Heaven...and it was hell having to observe rather than enjoy what I remembered all too well.

Lily tore her gaze off Blaine's flushed face, watching as I stroked down over my cock regardless of my tumbling emotions.

"He's so fucking hot," she groaned the words, her gaze on my hand.

Blaine glanced my way, panting, his eyes still hazed—and needy. "Yeah," he whispered and flicked his tongue over his lower lip.

What. The. Fuck.

My breath caught, but I told myself I'd heard meaning he hadn't intended, that the licking of his lip had nothing to do with his wishing for a taste of the slickness coating my cock.

"Oh..." Lily's back arched beneath Blaine, pulling his focus off my dick.

Our gazes clashed, fire rushing through me.

"Yes, Blaine...right...there." Lily gasped.

"Grey—" Blaine's voice choked off and not because he needed me to finish what he'd started.

He *wanted* me with them in that moment.

Fuck being unselfish.

Heart racing, I strode toward the bed, shoving at my jeans as I went. A fumbled kick rid me of shoes and clothes from the waist down, and I climbed onto the mattress beside

Lily's head, my focus intent on her parted lips as my fingers found her hair, wrapping up tight.

Crowding close, I held my dick out in offering, ready to demand what I needed if she didn't open wider.

"Yes," she whispered, grabbing my ass and yanking me in.

Wet heat surrounded my head, and I groaned, blinking in the sight of Blaine dipping in and out of her sopping core. Wetness smeared around his groin, coating his drawn-up balls.

I lusted to suck on them, to lick her cream from the soft flesh. Ease a finger into his hole, stroke his prostate, and feel those jewels against my tongue as he fucked his load inside her.

"Fuck," I cursed through clenched teeth, sliding my hand down over Lily's breast, thumbing her nipple on my path toward her core.

Blaine sat onto his knees between her splayed thighs, rhythmic thrusts rocking her mouth over my cock.

Sweet, sweet pussy...bare and pink.

My mouth watered, and I slid my fingertips over her swelled clit.

She jolted beneath us, and I lifted my focus to Blaine's face as she writhed, whimpering and choking on my dick.

Sweat lined Blaine's forehead, his lips in a thin, grim line.

Holding back. Waiting for her.

He glanced up, catching my stare. My balls pulled up tight, all but disappearing into my body at the haze of passion and unadulterated lust in his black pupils. Had I not known any better, I would have sworn he wanted my hands on him in that moment.

I pushed against hope that sprung up inside my heart. I'd reached the end of my tether.

"Come," I rasped out the command he always obeyed.

Blaine gasped and buried deep, a shudder ripping through him.

A pinch of my fingertips sent Lily along with him, both of their cries of release rushing my climax through me.

I pulled from Lily's slack mouth and unloaded my spunk all over her tits and neck, streaks of milky white glistening on her flushed skin.

"*God*," she moaned the word, her fingers trailing over her chest, smearing my cum toward her slit still pierced by my best friend's cock. So goddamn beautiful in how she'd given herself to my love, I could barely breathe. "You killed me."

A sweet smile, a gentle giggle left her mouth, and I shuddered on an inhale, my dick going limp in my hand even as my heart seemed to swell inside my chest.

Blaine gazed down at her, his gaze soft, his dick still buried inside her as she fingered her clit.

He bit his lip.

Watched her smear my cum around where he penetrated her. No disgust shone on his face, and he made no move to escape my spunk she painted over his groin.

Fucking hell, Lily would be the death of me. She gave me so much hope.

"Fuck that sweet pussy, B," I told him, knowing how far up inside her he'd lodged and how he tended to stay erect even after blowing his load.

Blaine's face went a deeper shade of red, and he rocked against her.

"Make her come again," I rasped out, settling onto my ass beside Lily.

A flicker of need crossed his features, and he thrust shallower but hard enough that she gasped, her back arching.

Her fingers closed over her clit, and she shifted beneath him, chasing another orgasm.

I sank back and enjoyed the show, strangely satisfied in a way I'd never been before. My dick stirred at Lily's moan of pleasure and the sight of her curves jiggling, the droplets of sweat falling from Blaine's forehead onto her taut belly as he continued to fuck in and out of her.

"So goddamn beautiful." Unable to help myself, I leaned forward, licking over her tits, coating my tongue with my bitter, salty cum and Blaine's sweat.

"Scott," she whimpered and grasped at my hair, yanking my mouth toward hers. The tang of chardonnay and sweetness of her faded the flavor of my cum from my mouth.

"Come all over his cock, little girl. Take what your gorgeous body needs."

"Want...you...too." She gasped between Blaine's thrust, the words whispered into my mouth filling me so goddamn full of longing my heart once more ached.

"Later," I promised and sealed my lips over hers, swallowing the cries the man I loved pushed from her lungs.

20

LILY

Thank all things holy for the hard bodies bracketing me in the large shower because my legs had zero life left in them. My pussy ached in the most delicious way possible from Blaine's thick and juicy cock, my skin singing as two sets of hands soaped my body.

Greyson cradled my front as Blaine worked his calloused palms over me from shoulders to heels. Blaine's wall of hard, hot muscle caressed my back while *Grey* reacquainted himself with every inch of my skin, cleaning off the cum he'd gifted me with.

I'd called him Scott while coming, but I would get it right when not flying high as a kite.

The memory of him lapping up his cum, tasting his own spend, sent a shiver over me. I'd never seen a man do such a thing. Then to let me suck it off his tongue?

HolyfuckinghellIwantedtodoitagain.

And again.

And again.

I wanted Blaine's spunk on my lips, Grey licking them clean—

Blinking the image from my mind, I focused on the dripping hair and vivid blue eyes in front of me.

"Where's your mind, little minx?"

He would taste Blaine given the chance, I had zero doubt.

If he hadn't already done so with one of their past hookups.

And Blaine certainly wouldn't be averse to it even though Grey said he identified as straight. I didn't question that truth either. I wondered if I pushed the two of them to cross a line they hadn't before...

My core pulsed at the flashing image of the two men lip-locked.

Interesting.

And troubling because what the actual fuck? I shouldn't have desired any type of sword crossing, tongues included, but the thought of Grey and Blaine together...

Disgust over my want should have twisted my stomach, not sent my girl bits into a burst of *yes, please.*

I reached behind me, clasping Blaine's neck, and he bent willingly, nuzzling into my neck, his lips soft and roaming.

Grey watched Blaine's path of open-mouthed kisses over my skin, his eyes darkening.

Without jealousy.

Also interesting...and not so upsetting, I acknowledged as the soreness between my thighs warmed and slickened.

"So now what?" I murmured, catching Grey's gaze again after answering his question with one of my own.

"We crawl back into my bed and snuggle the hell out of you so you can sleep since we denied you that post-fucking blissed state you enjoy so much."

"A Lily sandwich?" I asked, one eyebrow raised in question, butterflies erupting in my belly.

Blaine groaned against my skin, his large hands palming my breasts, lifting them.

Grey thumbed over my aching tips his friend held toward to him, and I shuddered, my breath catching as Grey's gaze lifted to the man behind me.

Or would he prefer a Blaine sandwich?

Go*ddamn*it, I thought I'd been dead set against any male-on-male action. Feared to see it unfold, agonized over being set aside again.

But...why didn't my throat tighten? Why wasn't my chest squeezing the oxygen from my lungs?

"Do you two ever...touch each other when you're with other women?" I asked in a rush—my usual word vomit before I thought the question through.

Their gazes clashed, and Grey's eyes shuttered. "No," he answered quietly for both of them, once more giving me his attention.

I expected a question in return—like *did I want them to*, but Grey kept quiet.

He turned off the water, and I shuffled over the thoughts and feelings flitting through me as they gave me their undivided attention, using a couple towels to dry me.

Perhaps I wouldn't be averse to the idea of them interacting if an *equal* sharing remained between the threesome. Two guys together were always hot as hell in books and in the porn videos I was definitely drawn to.

Would Blaine allow Grey's touch?

Would Grey lose himself in the man he obviously loved?

Would I be set aside if that barrier lay in wreckage beneath masculine racing hearts and hungry hands?

I imagined sitting back and enjoying the show, watching Blaine enjoy Grey's gorgeous body. Or perhaps my tall, dark, and handsome would offer himself to his best friend who'd been by his side for over nine years.

The idea of both men giving and receiving created a deep ache inside me, and not from fear.

I wanted to watch Grey unleash all that passion he held back when looking at his best friend.

I lusted—bit back a moan—over the thought of Blaine offering himself up like a Sunday dinner to be worshiped. Devoured.

Iamsogoingtohell.

But I found its opposite seconds later as Grey lay me down on his bed, once more cradling my front, Blaine snaking his way beneath the comforter to spoon my backside.

Warmth bracketed me.

A radiating energy that should have kept me wide-eyed and hungry for more dick.

Satiated bliss sank my muscles into the softest mattress I'd ever felt instead.

I passed the fuck out with a smile on my lips and a gentle, addictive ache in my chest.

———

A hard dick pressed against my ass crack, fingertips dancing over my hip bones.

I blinked my eyes in dim light from a way-too-early morning to find gorgeous hazel orbs inches from mine. Sleepy green and gold, Blaine's irises lay bare and unshielded.

"Morning." His exhale hinted at minty toothpaste.

I made an agreement noise without opening my mouth and killing him with my morning breath that had to smell like sewage.

Lips and teeth nuzzled my shoulder, and I focused on the hard length between my cheeks and the fingers drawing circles ever closer to my core.

"So soft...warm. Fuck, I could touch you for hours." Grey draped my leg back over his hard thigh and ran his hand once more to my waist.

Blaine wound his fingers in my rat's nest and pulled my face closer, his forehead resting on mine. "Do you like his hands on you?"

Grey feathered his thumb over the top of my pubis, and I shifted, trying to help him along.

"Yes." I all but moaned the word as my body woke with full force.

"Like a sweet rose," Grey whispered against my ear, his teasing caress not dipping low enough to ease my ache. "Petals satiny soft." He lazed a fingertip along the crease of my thigh, knuckle barely brushing over my labia.

I wondered how many other women got to wake up to Blaine's sweet breath and Grey's gentle touches.

Jealousy swirled like a toxic witch's brew in my stomach at the thought of anyone but me between them.

Blaine pulled back. "What?"

Guess that stiffening of my body hadn't gone unnoticed.

Grey's hand slid down over my core, cupping my pussy, and my body went pliant as his hot exhale caressed over my ear. "What?" he repeated Blaine's question.

"Do you..." Shit. I did not want to sound like a jealous bitch. "Do you guys always do this?" I spewed out anyway, needing the answer one way or another.

"Do what?" Grey pushed, his index finger tracing over my damp slit.

I fought the need to shift, to encourage him to slide inside my body.

"Wake up your hookups with mind-blowing sex?" I blurted when he continued to tease, not giving me what I needed.

"We never allow a woman to stay the night," Grey said, his words ghosting over my ear and rippling goosebumps over my skin, "and you're no hookup, Lily." He sucked on my lobe, and Blaine watched him while trailing his thumb over my lower lip.

Good God almighty, what had I gotten myself into? I tumbled headlong down a steep slope, my heart ready to crash into their open arms.

At least, it seemed Grey and Blaine held them wide, ready to catch me.

I-I hadn't wanted anything serious. I wanted to live, taste all life had to offer...

"Is that true?" I asked, my heart fluttering.

"Yeah." He smiled at me with a hint of shyness, and goddamn him, my insides melted.

I pressed forward and kissed him, morning breath be damned because he needed assurance—even if I wasn't sure I was ready to give it.

"You two are so sexy together...make me so fucking hard." Grey's groaned words, the twitch of his cock along my ass crack had my core clenching.

I tore away from Blaine and angled my head, taking Grey's mouth. "Fuck me," I murmured against his lips.

"You want my dick deep inside this sweet hole?" he asked, sliding two fingers into my pussy.

"Yes, please."

Grey rolled, grabbed a condom from the bed side table,

and closed back in on me, sheathed and ready to rock my world with those damn hips of his.

He lifted my thigh and sank into my body with one slow glide, both of us releasing noises of absolute pleasure from the delicious friction.

Grey's hands tightened on my hips, and he moved inside me like he would if putting on a stripper show for a crowd of women. Body undulating, hips flowing in and out like water in a sensual wave of *fuck yes.*

"The way you move..." I moaned, my eyelids fluttering closed.

Blaine closed his mouth over one of my breasts, and I gasped, my eyes popping back open.

"Yes." I grabbed at his hair, holding him close, my gaze catching on his flexing forearm hidden between us.

He jerked off in time with Grey's pumping hips—in sync —both men's breaths and moans heightening in unison.

"I want you to come all over my cock, Lily." Grey slid his fingers down over my pussy, rubbing around where he rocked into me, up and over my clit.

Blaine pressed in closer, his teeth scraping over my breast as the slick head of his dick smeared over my thigh with every tug on his length.

Dead. I'm literally dead and flying with angels.

Tingles raced from my nipples to my clit, and I ground back against Grey.

I wanted to beg him to touch me, to strum the fuck out of my clit, but my bladder lay near bursting.

My body awash with heat, I burned from the inside out.

Should have fucking peed, damnit!

"Need you both to come," I whimpered. "Please."

"You first," Grey growled into my ear, his hard chest

pressing against my back while those hips of his wrecked me in the best way possible.

"Can't," I gasped out as his dick poked at my cervix. "Gotta...pee."

"Don't care." Grey slammed back into me, ripping a moan from my lips. "Need to feel you squeeze the life out of my cock, drain my balls. Soak my bed if that's what it'll take."

Blaine tore his lips off my breast and claimed my mouth with a deep groan at Grey's haggard voice. Wet heat erupted against my thigh, and Blaine shuddered, whimpering while ejaculating on my skin.

"Fuck...Lily..." Grey cursed...at the noises Blaine emitted while releasing. "Please."

I gave into his desire and let my climax pull me under.

No urine squirted from my body, thank *fuck*, but in those seconds of euphoric bliss of having Grey drag and shove through my pulsing core, I wouldn't have cared if I'd wet his mattress. Would have served him right for being a fucking god of delicious dick.

I giggled while coming down, assigning another nickname to the man releasing into the condom deep inside my body.

Grey, God of Fucking.

"What's so funny?" he muttered the second he came to a gasping rest, his body and breath hot along my entire back, his hands in a possessive hold on my waist.

"I...um..." My face warmed, and Blaine peered at me with the most beautifully sated eyes I'd ever seen in my damn life.

"What?" he prompted, his slow smile sending a tingling warmth through my chest.

"I might make nicknames for people?" I stated more like

a question. "A...surname sort of thing. It's an unfortunate habit of Haley's I picked up."

"What's mine?" Blaine asked.

"Um..." I called him Mr. Yummy, but the name Haley had assigned to him had been in my brain long before she'd voiced it. The idea of stating that one out loud heated my face. God knew, it would embarrass the hell out of him.

Grey slid his hand up my torso and pinched my nipple. "You've gotta tell us now. Not letting you out of this bed until you do."

"That's not exactly a punishment," I stated with a giggle, wiggling my ass against his groin even though I *really* had to pee.

"Mmm, I beg to differ. You have no idea the agony I could inflict." He licked over my nape, clear up to my ear while easing his dick from my pussy. "I'm the god of climax withholding."

"God of Fucking, more like it," I murmured the name I'd given him absently, lost in the sensations of his lips beneath my lobe.

Blaine barked a laugh, and Grey chuckled. "He does *not* need that ego stroke. Tell me that's not really what you call him in your head."

"Um...it is? But surfer dude was first."

Another laugh rumbled through Blaine's chest. "Appropriate."

"What's your name for B?" Grey asked, still laughing, and Blaine blinked, lifting his eyes off me for his best friend.

"Mr. Yummy?" I squeaked, and sure enough, Blaine's face flushed same as it had the first time I'd let that nickname slip around him.

"Surely you can do better than that for our boy," Grey stated with a huff.

"Blaine of the Thick and Juicy Cocks," I blurted and bit my lip while realizing what he'd said about his best friend.

Our boy.

Hope embedded in my heart, the kind of excitement I didn't know what to do with.

The cheeks in front of me flushed a deeper red, and Grey snickered against my ear. "Right on both accounts," he said, his tone hinting at teasing—and honesty.

Which meant he'd checked out Blaine's dick a time or ten.

"Our boy called me coffee girl before he knew my real name," I said, tugging Blaine back against my front in case his embarrassment sent him rolling from the bed even though I really needed to get up too. "What about you?" I asked Grey as he finally gave my neck and ear a rest, laying his head against the pillow beneath mine.

"Beautiful perfection," he murmured, stroking a hand through my hair.

Flutters of wings erupted through my heart as Blaine pressed his lips against mine in a chaste kiss.

"I like his name for you better than the one I gave you," he whispered and snuggled in close. "It's accurate as fuck."

21

BLAINE

I woke again when the sun shone bright through Grey's gauze-like curtains. A peek at the clock beside me showed it was after nine. Curling onto my side put Lily's face inches from mine, and I stayed there, watching her sleep.

Grey's hand lay lax on her hip where it'd been last I remembered after she'd scampered to the bathroom and back again, keeping her close against his chest.

Her golden hair spilled over the pillow, beneath her shoulder, tickling my cheek. Face relaxed, she seemed like a dream, an angel, sent down from God above—

Fuck.

I closed my eyes against the romantic thoughts that bordered on religious and threatened to bring bile up the back of my throat.

There was no God, were no angels, and certainly was no damn heaven beyond what we created for ourselves.

I was convinced of that, and evidence settled heavy in my guts over how supposed prophets of said God behaved in His name.

Forcing my eyelids open, I once more studied Lily's

beauty, knowing she would silence the shit in my mind. In sleep, she rested, her mind and mouth quiet, skin unlined by frowns or smiles. Even though we didn't touch, I could feel the connection between us as though I pressed my entire length along her soft curves.

Would she still want to lay between us if she knew the truth about the cult I'd been enshrouded in my entire childhood? Would she understand how I'd been tainted, parts of me ruined beyond repair? Would she even care?

The way she had responded to my initiations of sex, welcomed me into her slick heat, that tight sheath of a pussy I'd never felt the likes of...

Fuck.

Morning wood returned even though I'd emptied against her thigh a couple of hours earlier.

Unable to keep my fingers off her, I tucked a wayward strand of hair behind her ear. She shifted, her lips parting a sweet exhaled sigh.

Grey propped up on his elbow, half-mast eyes blue as the morning sky peering over her shoulder at me.

Our gazes met, and strange flutters rippled through my chest, heightening my breaths.

Lily had asked us in the shower if we'd ever touched each other when a woman lay between us. Sure, there'd been a few unheated brushes between our skin but nothing intentionally sexual. Grey hadn't ever instigated anything between him even though I felt sure he'd wanted to on more than one occasion.

He liked dick, after all.

I'd never considered doing so until that moment, his eyes solely focused on me where no embarrassment or insecurities clambered in my brain.

Her words, the idea she'd put into my head didn't disgust me as it should have.

After I'd fled the compound, I vowed that no man would ever touch me again, but how often had I sunk into Grey's open arms when waking from a terrifying nightmare? How often did I soak in his warmth, find myself clinging to his naked torso when fear chased on my heels, creating an emptiness inside me that no one but him could fill?

And how often had my emotions been calm—and still I yearned to feel his arms around me?

Something kindled in his gaze, a warmth beyond friendship, a longing that tugged on my heart.

And my dick.

Both he and Lily had referred to me as their boy.

Did Grey *want* me? He teased the fuck out of me, but did his love he claimed for me go beyond platonic?

More importantly...did mine?

The shuddering pulse in my throat suggested mine might, and the welling of pre-cum at the slit of my stiff dick agreed I wasn't as straight as I'd claimed.

Hot shame should have curdled my insides, sent bile rushing up the back of my throat, but a sense of relief swept through me, as though I'd come home.

The entire foundation of my world cracked, and I blinked, trying to make sense of what shouldn't be.

What I'd never considered.

Grey's lips lifted slightly as though he read the recognition on my face.

Unnerved, I glanced down to find Lily awake and watching me study my best friend. A similar want as Grey's rested on her face, and the truth slammed into me with enough force to catch my breath, completely ripping away that feeling of comfort from mere seconds before.

I would have to choose between them at some point.

The perfect coffee girl who stirred life inside my heart or my best friend, the man I saw as my soul mate.

Sure, Lily had fantasies about having two lovers, but three wouldn't survive long term. Eventually, she would want the diamond ring and picket fence—and Grey could provide both from his deep pockets with an ease I would never attain.

The thought she might choose him caused pain to lance through my entire body.

"Gonna go make some coffee and tea," I whispered and rolled, giving them both my back. My shoulders slumped as I grabbed my boxers off the floor and yanked them up over my ass. "No rush to join me."

Morning wood deflated, I escaped the eyes I could feel burning my back for the kitchen where I could breathe easier.

Grey and I had always stuck to our pact about one and done when it came to hooking up with women, and we'd never had an issue.

But Lily?

A definite bend of the rule he and I had agreed upon years earlier. I wanted more with her, and if how Grey couldn't keep his lips off her was any indicator, sniffing her hair and neck, I knew he felt the same. Sure, he loved touching women, but I'd never seen him so...possessive over a body laying between us.

The memory of his words from the night before crashed into my head.

He'd outright *told* her she was no hookup.

Where the fuck did that leave me? I'd just recognized and admitted my desire for him in my thick-headed skull, and he wanted her. A woman who would offer him the love and attention he craved—yet feared—from losing his mom at a young age.

Friendship aside, Lily could give him everything I couldn't.

I wasn't enough.

The two of them joined me as I was about to lose my shit and sink into darkness. They drank their coffee and tea, chatting about everything and nothing while I whipped up some pancakes, keeping my back toward them as much as possible to hide the emotions roiling inside me.

Heaviness settled over me, and no amount of Lily's giggles or flirting shone light on the garden inside me that sat in dim quietness.

I plastered a smile on my face, but I could feel Grey's scrutiny from across the table, letting me know I hadn't fooled him with my pretending all was right in our world.

"Work sucks ass." Lily pouted.

"So call in sick and spend the day in bed with us."

Her cheeks flushed at Grey's words, but she shook her head. "Between the fuck god and his best friend's thick, juicy dick, I'm out of order for a few days."

Grey made a noise of appreciation deep in his throat while I snickered at the nicknames regardless of the heaviness in my chest. "When can we see you again?" he asked her.

I jerked my head toward Grey even though the one and done rule had definitely fled the house. He stared at Lily with hearts in his eyes.

She looked at him with the same.

Darkness slithered its way through my mind, and

rubbing a hand down over my face, I held my breath, waiting for her answer. Hoping for just one more taste before they realized they didn't need me in bed with them.

"Next weekend?" Lily suggested.

"The *whole* weekend?" Grey asked, lifting her hand to trail his lips over her knuckles.

"Um...sure?" That husky voice of hers, once more breathless with need, chubbed my dick up as I released an unsteady exhale.

Grey finally gave me his attention for my agreement, and as usual, I followed his lead. Happily in the moment, even though I knew a shredded heart lay in my future.

I would never be good enough for Lily on my own, didn't have riches tucked away in the bank like Grey, wasn't the type of guy who could take her out for a night on the town if she wanted to party until the morning hours.

Their outgoing personalities fit together like two jigsaw puzzle pieces.

A gorgeous couple. Dazzling, I realized, glancing between the two of them. Sexy as hell.

Fuck, my heart hurt.

Grey got up from the table when Lily claimed she had to jet out of there for her shorter late morning shift, but she insisted she'd just take an Uber back to the lounge where we'd left her car.

Lily leaned down to press a lingering kiss to my lips, keeping me in my chair. "Thank you for a wonderful night, Blaine. Next weekend can't come soon enough." Her dark eyes sparkled like fireflies in the darkness inside me, bringing a bit of hope that I wouldn't bend beneath depression's press.

A minute later, Grey and I sat across from one another again.

Alone.

The sweetness of vanilla had dissolved from the air we breathed, the quietness of the house almost stifling.

"What's wrong?" Grey asked, breaking the stillness between us. He settled back in his chair, legs spread, one hand cradling the coffee mug on the table in front of him.

Recognizing the determined glint in his eye, I knew I wouldn't be able to just walk away or toss some bullshit excuses his way.

"I didn't want her to leave," I offered one of the truths bouncing around in my head.

"Same." He blew out a breath.

"I hoped to spend the whole day in bed with the two of you." I offered him another thought from the recesses of my brain.

One of Grey's eyebrows popped upward, and those blue eyes of his delved deep inside me like they'd done earlier that morning in bed. "Not just her?" His voice hinted at teasing, but his intense gaze didn't.

I glanced around the table covered with our dirty dishes and empty orange juice glasses. "No," I finally answered, unable to give him my eyes.

"Why not?" Of course the fucker would push. He'd seen my unease, had probably sensed it before I named it in my own damn mind.

Grey was aware of a lot of the shit in my head—but I had kept some from him.

I felt confident in our friendship in that he wouldn't be disgusted and kick me to the curb, but laying myself completely bare would bring pity I had no wish to see on his face.

For the first time, a deep-seated yearning pushed against

my reluctance to open up fully and reveal every last horrid piece of me.

I wanted Grey to know me inside and out. Craved it desperately.

Regardless of Lily and the situation among the three of us, there could be no barriers between us, and that started with the truth I'd kept from him.

"Those boxes he locked us in." I swallowed hard, forcing myself to lift my head.

Grey nodded, already aware of how Abraham Quell dished out punishment on those who failed to follow his teachings.

"After our discipline..." I rubbed sweaty palms over my boxers that had ridden up to cup my shriveled cock, my brow furrowing.

Grey leaned forward, elbows onto the table, palm outstretched. "Hand. Now."

I laced my fingers through his and was able to fill my lungs again.

"They took us into the temple and showered us with love to show their forgiveness." My throat tightened against the breakfast gurgling in my stomach.

"Love."

I nodded at Grey's quiet statement.

"Was it sexual?"

Unable to find my voice, I jerked my head in a nod. Tremors rippled over me, and I shuddered hard enough he got up, yanked me to my feet, and wrapped his solid arms around me. One along my lower back, the other hand grasping my nape, keeping my cheek tucked against his shoulder.

Grey clutched me to his hard, bare chest, and I burrowed into him like I'd done dozens of times before.

Eyes wide, I refused the darkness to suck me down, my focus on the coffee pot atop the counter beside us.

"Both of them?" he asked quietly, no trace of pity in his voice.

Only anger.

"Yes," I whispered, wetness hazing my vision.

"Fuck." Grey squeezed me tighter. "Tell me everything," he demanded. "I want it all, B. Let me help you carry this fucking burden. Please."

The pleading in his tone was my undoing.

I started at the beginning, the first time I'd been tossed into the black prison of metal that sat atop bare ground and reeked of sweat, piss, and shame.

I'd been eight years old.

22

———

GREYSON

Fondled at age eight.

Sucked at nine.

Sodomized at ten—a mere fucking week before I'd met him for the first time.

All ending with Quell's "gift" coating his skin, done in the name of forgiveness and godly love.

I fought to keep from vomiting, my head tipped back against the couch we'd made our way to, Blaine tucked up against my side like the child his voice suggested he was.

Timid and terrified, he trembled against me, and I couldn't begin to imagine the racket in his head. The words continued to pour from him, a torrent of sick filth that had poisoned him for most of his life.

Once the fuck face Quell had his fill, Blaine been gifted to his wife Clara for "aftercare."

The stately, raven-haired, blue-eyed cunt probed and prodded, licked, and sucked to clean Blaine of her husband's seed.

Sick. Fucks.

They deserved an eternity suffering in fire and brimstone, damnation along with the worst of souls burning in hell.

My stomach clenched like granite at the thought of Blaine's sister, the abuse she probably experienced as well.

And her belly swelled from those same *gifts*.

If Blaine learned what the Higgins had found out for me, he would lose his shit. I didn't doubt he would hop on a flight, steal a gun, and break into the compound, bullets flying.

But how could I keep the truth from him? He would hate me if he somehow learned on his own and that I'd known all along—

"I dream about the other kids who didn't escape like I did." Blaine sat quieter, slumped against me as though emotionally drained, the well of nightmares in his soul running dry. I doubted it would stay empty consider the vividness of his memories. "I hadn't ever been close with anyone other than Sarah, my sister."

His voice cut off, his audible swallow harsh in my ears, and I fucking *knew* I had to spill my guts too.

"I left her there, regardless of what awaited her as she grew older." Blaine gulped air into his lungs as though desperate to keep from sobbing. "She was twelve when I took off, and Quell hadn't yet touched her. Anytime I caught him eyeing her, I would misbehave to take his focus off her."

More time in the box, more agony on his knees, I expected.

My eyelids slammed shut, teeth clenched tight to hold back from screaming the curses boiling inside my head.

"She was so beautiful. Gorgeous hazel-green orbs that hadn't hazed over from pain or a conflicted soul." Blaine let out a shuddered sigh and lifted away from me. Palms scrubbed over his face, and I finally caught sight of his red-rimmed eyes.

My hand found his scruffy cheek on its own, and I went with my desire, pulling him closer until our foreheads rested together.

I inhaled an easier breath with the closeness, allowing my love for him to coat the fucked-up mess he'd unleashed.

"What can I do, B?" I whispered, unable to add to his misery in that moment. "Tell me how to make this shit fade inside your head so you can move forward in your life."

His exhale ghosted over my lips, and fuck, how I wanted a taste, but I willed away the blood swelling my dick.

"Anything," I pushed. "Whatever you need."

"It'll never fade," he stated quietly, seeming more settled inside. "But you just being you—listening and acting as my rock makes living easier."

I wished that rock he spoke of allowed for even deeper hardness, one he would accept...

Fucking Quell had ruined Blaine and my hopes of loving him in the way I craved. He would never allow a sexual touch from another man.

Heart heavy and eyes stinging, I sat back, needing a bit of space before I succumbed to the urge to lean in and take his lips regardless of the truth that he would push me away in disgust.

Devastation punched through my chest over his defeated gaze.

Protectiveness rose inside me.

I wanted to insist he see a therapist, someone with the knowledge to help him find some sort of healing. Fuck knew I didn't have the words to guide him.

But if it had taken him over a decade to release that shit

to me, he'd never share it with anyone. Not even a professional bound by patient privacy laws.

"You aren't disgusted by me?" Blaine whispered, glancing down at his palms.

"Never," I rushed to reply. "There's nothing you could say or ever do to change my love for you."

He nodded an acceptance of my declaration and filled his lungs, a shudder ripping through him as though he'd placed a lid back on what he'd let out. "Grey...I-I didn't tell you all this out of...well, manipulation to keep you all to myself."

I frowned at his bowed head. "What?"

"I see how good you and Lily are together. How you fit perfectly in each other's lives. I won't stand in the way if she is the one you're able to let in to fill that hole your mom's passing left inside you."

Fucking Blaine.

Goddamn, did I love him. I grabbed onto him and hugged him tight, my throat attempting to close off. "I won't ever leave you, B," I rasped. "Ever."

Fuck, how I wanted to pour out the rest of my thoughts and feelings, assure him he was it for me—that Lily could be the bridge between us—but enough turmoil had stirred inside his poor mind as it was.

I gave him my affection, stayed steady as that rock he needed me to be. Not that soaking in his tight grip on my back was any hardship.

My stomach growled, and I grimaced at the hunger pains knifing at me, more than ready to set aside the heaviness of serious discussions for awhile. The topics of my unrequited love and his sister could wait another day or so. "Not that you're up for food after that, but I'm fucking starved again."

He pulled back reluctantly and gave me a shy glance. "I could eat."

I needed something sweet to take my mind of the goddamn shit lingering over me and the longing sharp as a blade still bright inside my heart.

"Donuts."

Blaine chuckled. "How the hell you don't have cavities every time you go in for a cleaning is a complete mystery to me."

"Come on." I hopped up and yanked him to his feet. "Shower. Clothes. Frosted donuts for lunch. Then we're going to snuggle on the couch and watch some feel-good movies. Pizza and beer—chardonnay for you—then I'll even let you be the little spoon in my bed if you need me to."

Pink fused Blaine's cheeks at the suggestion we share my bed.

But he didn't say no.

———

Spewing the shit of his past had worn Blaine's ass out. He dragged all day, napping on the couch with his head on my thigh for a couple hours while I ran my fingers through his hair. We'd gorged on donuts, pizza, chips, and then more donuts throughout the day.

Were it not for the other talk we needed to have and Lily's presence in the back of my mind, I'd have been perfectly content.

The cushion on the opposite side of where Blaine lounged against me appeared too damn empty. I wished our girl was there, all those soft curves and the sweet scent of vanilla filling my nose with every inhale, her soft hand in mine soothing the part of me that Blaine couldn't. Wanting didn't begin to describe the stirrings inside me for him tucked in against my left and Lily snuggling on my right.

I clung to the image in my mind, closing my eyes to the fantasy she'd brought on by crashing into my life.

She lusted for us both with hunger I'd seen on countless women's faces, and I couldn't wait to give it to her.

Share Blaine with her.

I wouldn't envy his dick sliding into her when I'd prefer it be my body he breached. I *wanted* her to enjoy his attention in the same way I lusted to watch his face as he found release inside her body.

It would be the closest I would ever come to having my desires fulfilled. No jealousy rose to choke me on either end. Lily would give me a way to live vicariously.

It would have to be enough.

But for how long?

At twenty-four, she had a lot of life to live. Not that Blaine and I didn't, but we'd seen our fair share of wading in the waters around us. I'd partaken ten times as much as Blaine, but with him being an old soul, I expected he'd want to settle down sooner than I ever considered.

Fuck, I couldn't think too long on that shit.

Made my insides twist up tight.

By eleven that night, I'd grown stiff and aching from slouching on the couch with Blaine drooling on my thigh. When I shifted to ease from beneath him, he woke and flopped over.

"Sorry," I muttered over disturbing his slumber, standing and stretching out my back.

"S'okay. Time is it?"

"After eleven."

"Fuck." He rubbed his eyes and rolled to perch on the edge of the couch. Dropping his hands, he peered up at me, shoulders rounded, hunched over.

"Okay?" I asked, my concern overriding the thought of how close his mouth was to my cock.

"Yeah." He cleared his throat and stood, forcing me to take a couple steps away. "Can I...uh..." His motion toward my bedroom door let me know what he couldn't find the words for.

"I meant what I'd said." I laced my fingers through his, clicked off the TV with my free hand, and led him across the living room. "You're welcome in my bed whenever the hell you want, B."

He shuffled into my bathroom while I tossed the throw pillows onto the floor and pulled back the comforter Lily had righted earlier that morning. Usually, I slept in the pitch black, but knowing Blaine's preference for a night-light, I dimmed the overheads as low as they would go—same as I'd done the night before after he and Lily had passed out in my bed.

Blaine stumbled from the bathroom minutes later, bleary-eyed and haggard as hell.

I hurried past him to do my business, wanting to crawl in beside him before sleep claimed him again.

He lay like a lump in the middle of my mattress when I came out of the bathroom, and I slid beneath the blankets, being the big spoon—but keeping my groin well away from his boxer-covered ass while settling my arm over his waist.

A heavy sigh left him lax against me, and I closed my eyes, breathing in the subtleness of his woodsy bodywash and the scent of his skin beneath I would know anywhere. Eyes closed. All Blaine.

Mine.

Fuck, how I wished.

My throat tightened, and I pressed my lips against his hair. "Sleep, baby," I murmured, sure he already did.

23

———

LILY

Haley had been home when I dragged my ass in after the longest shift *ever*. My legs were rubber, my core still ached, but my heart bounced in my chest, same as it'd done earlier that morning when I'd rushed home to change for work.

My cousin hadn't been home to grill me for deets, other-wise, I'd have been late for sure. She'd texted me begging for details about my date with the bossy asshole, but I simply replied with a **Later**.

There was too much to tell, and I didn't even bother ringing her over my break since she worked that afternoon too.

Grey had called me beautiful perfection and Blaine had agreed while snuggling me between the two of them. Warmth tingled through me regardless of how often I reminded myself to not let my feelings get ahead of my thoughts.

Still, giddiness kept me awake all day, but the second I sat with a glass of wine in my hand, Haley peering at me impatiently and waiting for me to spill my guts, exhaustion slammed into me.

"Oh, no you don't." Haley poked me with her toe from where she lounged in the couch's opposite end. I could feel the anticipation radiating off her. "Spill the goods. Details about the details. I want it all. Obviously, that bossy fucker had his way with you..."

"Mind-blowing." I sighed the inadequate description, resting my head against the back of the couch.

"More," she demanded.

"I don't even have the words, Haley."

"Fucking *find* them. I'm dying over here!"

I giggled at her feigned hysterics, finally rolling my head to look at her. "I've found them, Haley."

She blinked. "What?"

"My two lovers. Blaine is Greyson—*Scott's* roommate."

"Wait. What?" Her voice raised to a squeak, eyes popping wide.

"Greyson Scott. Blaine is his roommate. I had no fucking clue—and neither did they when I showed up to find them together at the bar Grey told me to meet him at. Talk about a clusterfuck," I said, grinning at the memory of Blaine's explanation.

"Get. The. Fuck. Out! You're serious right now?"

"Yeah." My throat tightened at the truth my emotions had insisted upon hours earlier but I hadn't given voice to until that moment.

Damnit, I wanted to believe in fairy-tale endings.

So. Damn. Badly.

I choked out a laugh through threatening tears, telling her about how I'd imagined Blaine and Grey together with me before I'd learned the connection between them.

Finding them there at the same table, sure they'd see me as a whore, being assured they didn't, having their attention lavished over every inch of my body...

Not undivided, though.

I remembered the looks exchanged between the two men, the desire I'd seen clear as day, an unpleasant reminder of why I didn't want to put my heart on the line.

"Lily..." Haley's voice trailed off with concern in her tone as I shared that bit of information.

"I know." I closed my eyes again, wanting them both so damn much, but the fear of what might happen snaked in to steal some of my fantasy come to life.

"You need to confront that shit head-on," Haley stated, her tone firm. "Make them face it and figure it out so you aren't left with a broken heart if this all evolves into more than a few bucket list nights."

I'd managed to get over my broken heart once before, and I knew every second of their shared attention would be worth the ache I would be left with once their love came to fruition.

"I could survive it again," I whispered but without conviction.

"Levi didn't shatter you and leave you *completely* jaded, but why allow that kind of pain again if you can keep it from happening in the first place?"

"And if I do point out the obvious, open up Pandora's box for them, I might not get another taste—and I really want it."

"Shit." Haley studied me, her lips pressed tight. The messy bun atop her head sat askew, red tresses and new growth along her temples escaping to frizz around her face.

"Grey's hips are lethal, and Blaine's dick..." Saliva pooled in my mouth, and I swallowed down a groan.

"Then be a selfish bitch, enjoy the hell out of that shit on Friday night, and get them both inside you until you're screaming your pleasure. At least take that much!"

"God." I shifted on the couch at the image of them both sinking into me at the same time, leaving my mouth free for their kisses, inhaling their exhales. "And do what? Blurt out that I recognize they're in love with one another during that postcoital bliss? No thanks."

I'd seen it once before, and I did *not* want to experience it ever again.

Fuckthetwoofthem and fuckmylife.

My throat tightened and eyes welled, hazing the vision of our old TV all but propped up on an end table.

"Then wait until you're ready to leave," Haley suggested. "Give them something to think on and talk about—while you aren't around."

"And spend the next whatever hours waiting to see if they'll want me again or choose to move forward together without me?"

Fuck no.

My heart had already invested—in both of them.

"Goddamnit, Haley, what am I going to do?"

"This sucks." Haley's lips twisted in an annoyed pout.

I didn't bother stating in the worst way possible since my mind could no longer pull words into formation through the emotional exhaustion.

I swallowed down the last of my wine, ready to sleep the tiredness of fucking half the night from my bones.

Hopefully, I would figure out a plan before Friday night.

———

Monday morning's shift started out the same as the week before.

Bitchy people needing their caffeine fix.

At least Cheryl was in a kick-ass mood, her laughter and

big grin rubbing off on me a bit.

"*Someone* got laid over the weekend," I muttered after she hip-bumped me for at least the tenth time and no one stood in line for a change.

"Oh yeah." Cheryl winked, her smirk contagious while filling the final order I'd handed over. "And let me tell you, my girl can use her tongue," she whispered after frothing the milk for a latte.

I blinked. She'd told me about her female partner, but I hadn't considered how they might get it on. "Oh."

"Mmmhmm." Cheryl licked her lower lip. "Nothing better than a woman who knows her way around the female body."

I wasn't sure what to say other than I was recently acquainted with a couple of guys who certainly knew *my* body—

The front door whooshed open, and I turned, my plastic smile put into place.

Blaine.

My lips curled the rest of the way up, warmth rushing through me and somehow setting my jumbled thoughts to rest. "Hey there. I thought you weren't working on this side of town this week?"

Pink flushed his cheeks as his gaze flitted over at Cheryl behind the counter with me. "Yeah—I'm not."

"So you just had to swing by because you missed your coffee girl?" I almost rolled my eyes at myself for the blatant fishing.

He met my focused gaze, his hazel eyes clear and happier than I'd ever seen. "Something like that."

Holy hell and then some, I wanted to swoon at his feet and curl myself around his legs, never letting go.

"Black?" I asked, pleased as hell with my bright world in

that moment and grabbing a cup to put his usual label on.

"Yes."

"Blueberry muffin?"

"Of course."

I rang up his order, feeling Cheryl's stare on the side of my face. She probably wondered if I'd become schizophrenic or if Blaine had become the Lord I found my joy in. A soft snort left me at that thought.

"So...Friday?" I asked quietly when Cheryl stepped away to fill Blaine's order.

He handed over a couple bills, nodding. "If you're still interested."

Need coiled through my core, tight and ready to spring. I could be selfish like Haley had suggested, take what I wanted, then open the doors between Blaine and Grey and leave to let them work it out.

The night of pleasure would be worth it.

I'd make sure.

"Damn right, I'm coming over."

A heavy exhale eased the tension in his shoulders I hadn't noticed. "Good. I'm glad. I mean, we're glad. Grey and I had a really great time Saturday night."

"Same." I handed him his change, heat on my face too.

Our gazes locked for a few seconds, everything falling away like it did in the movies.

Wet panties didn't even begin to describe the state of the cotton pressed against my core. But goddamn it all to hell, the stirring between us was so much more than lust.

"Blaine?" Cheryl stated loudly—from right beside me. She held out his coffee.

He tore his focus off me and offered her a nod. "Thanks."

Our gazes caught again.

"Can't wait," he murmured.

"Same," I barely breathed.

Blaine spun on his work boot's heel and left me releasing a sigh as he ambled toward the exit.

"Someone's got it bad," Cheryl mused, and I nodded as he disappeared out the door, my hands finding my hot cheeks.

"Yeah."

"So, who's Grey, and what was your naughty ass up to on Saturday night?"

I burst into laughter, but sobriety over the situation I found myself in quickly shut it down.

Cheryl got an earful over the rest of our shift, but she insisted with a shake of her head she'd stick to women and the lack of drama, thank you very much.

I told her she could have them. I'd stick to dick—in my case, plural.

For, hopefully, longer than one more night.

24

———

BLAINE

I'd been an absolute mess after laying myself bare to Grey.

And I'd thought exhaustion from being trapped in those steel boxes for hours on end had been horrific.

All my fears about Grey turning away from me knowing how I'd been soiled hadn't come to fruition. He'd done as he always did—held me and loved me regardless of my flaws, wounds, and fucked-up insides.

Relief had sagged me against him, and I'd clung like I'd never done before so damn *thankful* he wasn't going anywhere.

His acceptance soothed, same as usual, and that tug I'd felt, I'd seen, in his eyes while Lily had slept between us intensified. My feelings for him definitely bordered on more than mere friendship.

I hadn't wanted to tear away from his warm skin, the steady thump of his heart against mine.

The idea of Grey touching me in an intimate way didn't turn me off or make me ill when it should have, considering all I'd endured as a child, but I feared crossing a line that would eventually stir up more darkness.

Yes, I had allowed Lily to put her mouth on my dick—I'd been too damn horny, too taken with her big brown eyes peering at me in the back of Grey's car to say no. The second her lips and tongue had caressed my length, I'd been putty in her hands, no thoughts of anyone but my coffee girl.

But I couldn't stomach the thought of that same sickness I felt toward Abraham Quill rising inside me if Grey's hands went from friendship to sexual over my skin. It had been him more than his cunt of a wife who had inflicted the most turmoil in my head.

Allowing such a thing to develop between Grey and I would ruin what we had. I wouldn't ever be able to enjoy his touch—sexual or not—ever again.

And I couldn't lose my anchor.

A few seconds, minutes, of possible release and gratification could never replace what I'd found with him.

Still, I craved more.

In the same way I did for Lily.

The best I could do was roll along with the path in front of me, watching how it weaved. Eventually, a crossroads would appear on the horizon. I just hoped I would see my next steps clearly when the time came to choose.

And contemplating the what-ifs and possible negative outcomes would only make my head hurt worse.

While I woke up somewhat refreshed on Monday morning still wrapped in Grey's arms, I hated leaving the warmth of his bed, losing the presence of his slumbering body against mine.

Even if his morning wood poked against my thigh like it always did whenever I landed in his bed.

The horny little shit couldn't control his body's desires—

but I didn't mind. Not for the first time, goosebumps rose over my skin at the feel of his hardness even though I knew it was just a male's usual good morning gesture.

Slipping out before he woke, I set my mind on moving forward down the path for as long as it lay clear. Living my life to the fullest sat at the front of my mind now that the secrets no longer remained bottled up inside my soul. Diving into the upcoming work week with full determination to do a good job and be worthy of the title my boss Wyatt had gifted me was step one.

We had a meeting with the retirement's board first thing, and I was out the door before Grey even climbed from bed.

He texted me late morning while I still grinned over the responsibilities that had been entrusted to my care. More or less a foreman, I had two new workers assigned to help me with the new account.

No more pavers or grunt work for me.

Most of my day would be spent on the expansive grounds, seeing to grass, hedges, flower beds, and the dozens of blooming posts scattered around the property.

Easy fucking peasy, even though I hadn't minded the more labor-intensive work.

After our meeting, I swung by the cafe to peek in on Lily before heading to the job Wyatt had lined up for me that week to fill in until we took over the grounds keeping starting the following Monday.

Lily's smile had lit me up.

I fucking flew, grinning like an idiot, the anticipation for Friday night about killing me.

Nothing could bring me down.

———

Grey worked late. I'd cooked up a pot of spaghetti and left him a plate, but the second I heard the alarm beep from the front door opening, I hopped off my bed and hurried downstairs.

"Hey."

Shrugging off his suit coat, he gave me a quick once-over, face bland, but I knew he checked to see how I fared after the heaviness of the night before. "You okay?"

"Yeah. You?"

"I always sleep better when you're in my bed." Grey yanked off his tie, and I turned away, the stirring in my groin threatening to tent my sweats.

A first reaction for me in that way toward him.

I liked it. Too damn much.

But it was definitely unwanted since I'd set my mind on keeping us on either side of an invisible line, that barrier that needed to stay fixed firmly in place.

"How was work?" I asked, popping his plate into the microwave.

"Long. Tiring. Think I'm gonna soak in the tub for an hour. Is that spaghetti?"

"Homemade sauce too."

"Fuck, do I love you." Groaning, he sank into a seat at the table. I grabbed a glass and the bottle of Jameson he kept on the counter.

I enjoyed taking care of him in smaller ways around the house. It was the least I could do considering all he'd done for me.

"Why don't you have a glass of wine and join me." Grey didn't ask a question, and his tone hinted at a neediness I'd never heard from him before as I set his dinner in front of him.

Tension rose inside me, but I did as told, a half-glass of

chardonnay in my hand. My stomach soured, so I didn't bother taking a sip, simply watching Grey eat a few bites in silence.

"Grey," I pushed when I couldn't stand not knowing what was up.

He rubbed a hand over his scruffy jawline, weaseling his fingers behind his head to undo the ponytail holding back the top portion of his longer hair. Sun-highlighted golden waves fell around his face, and I tightened my grip on my glass's stem when the sudden desire to touch rushed through me.

Lily had definitely opened something up inside me, a desire to cross barriers I'd never considered before. I should have been disgusted, angry with her...

I just longed for her all the more.

Only three bites put away, and Grey pushed his plate aside, going for his whiskey. He downed it in one shot.

Shit.

I swallowed hard, my insides stilling, the hairs on my nape rising.

"After that news clip sent you spiraling last week, I called a private investigator back east."

My breath held, my mind whirling over his hesitancy, his inability to meet my eyes.

"Why?" I managed to whisper.

"I had him look into the cult's activities." Grey finally lifted his focus off the table, head barely tipped up to peer at me beneath his furrowed brow. "Those boxes are still in the village's center. Still put to use."

"H-how did he..."

"Drones."

I nodded absently, hating confirmation that the cult still survived. "Quill?" I forced the fucker's name out.

"Alive and kicking, unfortunately." Grey leaned onto the table, palm once more upright and beckoning as though he could literally see the goddamn darkness once more pressing upward to drag me down.

I slid my hand into his—gratefully and gladly, the dampness from nervousness wet between our skin. "What else?" I asked, barely any tone to my voice at all.

"It appears his wife has been either banished or passed."

"Good fucking riddance," I muttered with a shudder, hoping she rotted in hell.

"Quell has been seen walking around with another woman." Blue eyes bore into mine, and I knew before he fucking stated the words.

"No." I yanked my arm, but he tightened his hold on my hand, refusing to release me.

"She's pregnant, Blaine."

Fuck, fuck, fuck.

No...no fucking way.

Keening filled the kitchen, and I doubled over in my chair when I realized the agonized sounds came from my chest.

I shook my head, clinging to Grey's hand like a lifeline, my mind too upheaved to deny what he'd stated. Nausea gurgled in my guts, and I swallowed repeatedly.

Why had I left her? I should have stayed. Protected her from that pedophile.

Wetness hazed my eyes when I lifted my head to beg Grey for...something. I didn't know. To make it all go away? Make things better? Say the words and offer me the comfort that always gave my heart rest?

The blurred image of him stood, and he rounded the table without releasing my hand.

"P-please," I choked out, and he pulled me off the chair and into his arms to crush me against him.

For the first time in my life, he didn't ground my emotions or bring in the healing balm my heart needed. I shivered and gasped for breath, eyes wide and unblinking.

"I'm working on having that compound infiltrated and shut down," Grey said in his business tone against my temple as I clung to him, waiting for my rock to settle me. "We're going to get her the hell out of there."

No tears slipped from my eyes, but I couldn't stop fucking *shaking*.

"I'm going to take care of this—I have the money, I have the means. That shit hole will be shut down, I'll see Quell behind bars, and all those innocent lambs being led around will be drinking more than Kool-Aid before summer's end. I *promise*, Blaine."

One thing about Grey's promises...he saw them through.

Every time.

I managed to draw a shuddering breath that completely filled my lungs, and I closed my eyes, willing his warmth to seep into my cold bones. Eventually, I quieted, finding the comfort he always gave me.

Curled up in the cocoon of his comforter and strong arms a couple hours later, I managed to get a bit of rest.

But memories slid into my dreams with inky darkness that left me clinging until morning to the only anchor I had in life.

25

GREYSON

Guilt weighed me down.

I'd done the right thing in telling Blaine what I'd found out. Hell, he'd even thanked me while I'd held him in my bed the next morning, but I hated that I'd hurt him.

For two days, he walked around as though in a haze. His boss Wyatt called me to see if everything was okay since Blaine wouldn't open up to him when he'd asked.

I played it off as family problems and left it at that.

On Thursday night, he didn't come down for dinner, so I climbed the stairs with a roast beef sandwich and chips on a tray. I'd about siphoned the strength well inside me dry, but the man worked too physical of a job to skip a meal. I could give a little bit more and would continue until I collapsed.

I knocked, his quiet call to enter giving me permission to disturb him.

His room sat bare as usual, no sign of personality or keepsakes and pictures to deny the assumption it was a guest room.

Blaine lay curled on his side, his back to the door.

"I brought you some dinner," I told him, my voice loud in the hushed, shrouded atmosphere.

"Not hungry."

I set the tray on the bedside table and settled onto the edge of his mattress, at a loss for what to say or do to ease his pain. My fingers itched to offer comfort, so I stroked his hair since it was what Mom had always done for me when I got sad as a kid. "It's killing me to see you like this," I admitted, my voice as broken as my heart. "I never should have told you—"

"I'm *glad* you did. Given the choice, I would want to know."

"But—"

Blaine rolled, the sight of his red-rimmed eyes stealing my breath. Agony poured from his gorgeous irises, punching me in the gut.

"I hurt you," I choked on the words, my hands fisting in my lap.

"You set me free," he argued, grabbing my hand and holding it tight to his chest. "And not just from that place. In here." He tapped our palms over his heart. "I cracked open the darkness inside me I've been trying to deny and hide from you. Sharing my final secrets left me feeling half-dead but more alive than I've ever experienced, if that makes sense."

His words and heavy exhale lessened but didn't dissolve my remorse.

"But I brought it all back when I reminded you of your sister."

"You didn't." He shook his head vehemently.

"But—"

"No more buts, Grey. I've been a miserable fuck because even though I feel like shit for leaving my sister behind, I would do it all over again without a second thought." He turned his focus on the ceiling. "Could I *be* any more selfish? I should have gone to the authorities. Exposed that fuck face and his followers for what they were. Child rapists. Abusers. Manipulators and thieves."

"You were scared."

"That's no excuse." Blaine sat up against the headboard, our clasped hands falling to his thigh. "Whatever that PI of yours finds, I want it sent on to the authorities. I'll testify to make sure that place gets shut the fuck down."

The idea of him facing Quell, even in a court of law, made me itch to knife someone to death. Preferably the man who'd hurt Blaine physically and emotionally.

"I'll be there beside you through it all," I promised and found myself with his knuckles pressed to my mouth, hoping to somehow find a way to fill up my reserve of strength to share with him.

His lips parted—and I realized what I'd done.

Clearing my throat, I dropped my hold on him and stood. "You should eat."

"Yeah." He placed his other hand atop where I'd kissed. "Yeah. Okay."

Did he hope to seal the press of my lips into his skin or rub it away?

I turned, not giving him a chance to break my needy heart a little more. "I'll be downstairs watching TV if you want to join me."

Letting myself out, I hoped he would take me up on my offer of distraction from his thoughts.

He didn't, and I was left staring at the screen unseeing, still calling into question what I'd done no matter his words on the situation.

I hauled my grumpy ass out of bed the next morning to

find he'd already left for work. At least Meryl took note of my mood and let herself into my office an hour into the workday with a bag of donuts.

Chocolate frosted.

Fuck, did I love that woman.

The sugar made me feel a little better, and after shoving the second into my mouth, I dialed Higgins's phone number.

"I'm tailing her right now," he said in response to my request for a Sarah update.

"What? Where?"

"She's with two other women from the compound. They're headed into town in one of Quell's old vehicles he keeps licensed and insured."

"Think you could get a note to her somehow?" I asked, my mind running like mad.

"I could try." His tone didn't sound hopeful. "It depends on their destination, the reason for leaving the compound, and how close I could get to her without notice. What were you thinking?"

"Blaine's name and number, but if you have a chance to talk to her—"

"Doubtful. The two women with her are the ones who follow her all over the compound. It's like they're glued to her side."

"Do your best," I stated firmly, *needing* that note to get into Sarah's hands.

We chatted for a few more minutes. Higgins filled me in on the people he'd found who had left Quell's flock. He had a meeting set for the following Monday to sit and chat about their time beneath the cult leader's teachings.

"From the things I've recorded with the drones, those fucking boxes and the public whipping that took place on the village green outside the temple, we have enough to bring a case against him—assault and child abuse at minimum."

"It'll take more than that to get his ass locked away for how long he deserves."

"Think your friend would agree to stand as a witness if charges are brought up?"

"I know he will," I said, my tone grim at the reminder of Blaine's steadfast gaze when he'd stated he wanted to help.

"We'll see what I can get from this couple on Monday, and we'll go from there." His voice trailed off but picked up a few seconds later. "Looks like they're going to a medical building...an OB office."

Sarah had a doctor's appointment.

"Let me see what I can do," Higgins said quickly, his voice muffled. "Call you back in a few."

We hung up, and I sat staring at my phone, willing the minutes to tick away, praying for whatever gods existed to allow Higgins to get that note to Blaine's sister.

Close to a half-hour passed, and my guts clenched, making me wish I hadn't eaten those goddamn donuts.

Needing distraction from watching the clock, I checked my email, then shot off a text to Blaine checking in with him.

Within seconds, he replied with a thumbs up.

"Better than not responding at all," I muttered, tapping into the message thread with Lily for a pick-me-up.

I'd texted Lily a few times since she'd left us on Sunday morning, our usual banter and sexual teasing keeping me from spiraling along with Blaine.

Little Minx: **I was just thinking about you.**

I grinned at the text I'd missed earlier that morning and typed out a quick reply. **All good fantasies, I hope.**

Three dots lit up immediately.

Little Minx: **Of course. How are things?**

Things? I shot back.

Little Minx: **You know—life in general. Blaine. You and Blaine.**

A sudden longing to spill everything, to unload the shit I kept taking from my best friend to help carry his burden rolled me beneath the surface like a crashing wave.

I'm exhausted, I typed out that bit of honesty. **Blaine has some family shit going on. I'm not sure what all he's told you, but fuck, I can't make it go away. Can't carry it all on my own shoulders for him.**

Little Minx: **You're a giver until it hurts, aren't you?**

I huffed a laugh even though my throat stayed tight. **Yeah. Got it from my mom.**

Lily knew my dad lived back east, but I hadn't told her about the accident that had ripped Mom from our lives. I hadn't shared the depth of pain I still struggled with when admitting to needs I never got to have filled—and the fear that kept me from trying for more with anyone.

Little Minx: **Are you running dry?**

Fuck, how did she know me so well?

Getting there fast as fuck, I texted more honesty, able to breathe just the slightest bit better.

Little Minx: **What happened to your mom?**

"Fuck." I scrubbed a hand down over my face, so done with the emotional upheavals in my life.

But one had been good.

Lily.

I put through a call, and the second her sweet voice filled my ear, I choked up.

"Grey? Shit. Are you okay?" Real concern laced her tone. "Talk to me. Please."

Swallowing hard, I tried to laugh. "Do you have an hour?"

"I've got two if that's what you need," she promised, and a tear slid down my cheek.

I longed to hold her in my arms—fuck that. I wanted to be in *her* arms, soaking in her sweetness to fill back up the emptiness inside me.

"She was in a car accident when I was ten."

The rest poured from me, Lily's encouraging words when I choked on tears, her own wobbly voice in empathy of my grief bringing a little comfort I clung to for all I was worth.

And that was a fuck ton.

It didn't take more than fifteen minutes before I quieted, feeling more spent than I'd been inside her tight body the weekend before. A shuddered exhale left me sagging in my office chair.

"I can't wait to see you tonight," I told her, my eyes closed and head tipped back.

"Can I give you tons of hugs and kisses? Not that it will make everything better—"

"It will, and yes. I'll take whatever you'll offer me, Lily."

"Blaine's aware of what happened? How you struggle sometimes?"

"Yes. There's nothing Blaine doesn't know."

"Hmm." She made a noise like she didn't believe me. "He loves you, Grey. He's also strong enough to help carry your burdens too. Maybe you should lean on him from time to time. It might open his eyes to the strength he has inside him."

Her words woke me the fuck up, and I stared at my ceiling.

"You don't always have to be the one giving," she continued, her tone quiet. Reflective. "Sometimes we have to be just a little selfish to find what we've been searching for."

Long after we hung up, Lily's words rang in my ears. Everything about her made breathing easier and life just a little bit brighter.

I wondered if Mom would have loved her. I also wondered what Mom would have told me in that moment if I'd been able to call her and ask for advice about loving my best friend and falling for a woman too in such a short time.

Those thoughts brought on more stinging eyes and a tight throat.

Lips in a thin line, I shoved emotions to the back burner and focused on getting my work done for the week so I could get home and ready for my two lovers to join me in my bed.

Higgins called me an hour later. He'd slipped the note into Sarah's sweater pocket while accidentally bumping into her.

All I could do was cross my fingers she found it sooner than later and called her brother.

26

LILY

Both men appeared subdued when I showed up at their front door. They met me in the foyer, grins on both their faces, but something felt...off even after I hugged them hello, lingering more with Grey than Blaine.

And I'd thought Grey and I had made major headway in our...relationship outside sex, but he seemed preoccupied.

We enjoyed a glass of wine, Grey his whiskey, in the living room while chatting a bit, and Blaine wasn't big on eye contact. Not that he ever had been, but he seemed more introspective than I'd seen before. Grey watched him as closely, and I could sense he had the same urge to wrap his best friend up in his arms as I did.

The man loved Blaine. Thoroughly.

I yearned to see Blaine's eyes lighter, free of whatever haunted him, same as my heart ached for the unrequited love Grey held tight to his chest to be revealed and released.

Even though hope lingered inside my heart that the three of us might be able to have something more than a few fucks, I resigned myself to setting aside my desires in order to see both men happy.

I'd done so for Levi and had found peace in that situation too.

I leaned against Grey's chest, my legs stretched across the couch and resting on Blaine's thighs. Both of their free hands caressed my bare skin—one on my forearm, the other on my ankle.

Small circles.

Distracting touches.

But I wanted to know what the hell was going on with the two men. There was no way we could just hop in the sack with whatever hovered like an elephant in the room.

"Are you okay?" I asked Blaine, poking him with my big toe since my sandals had been unbuckled and dropped to the floor a half-hour earlier.

He nodded but wouldn't look at me.

"Blaine."

A heavy sigh left him before he took his focus off my ankle.

"What's going on?" I asked, searching his troubled face, needing more than the tiny bit Grey had shared with me.

"I left my younger sister behind when I escaped the cult," he blurted and shut his eyes.

Empathy lanced through my chest. I could only imagine the guilt he must feel. "Have you kept in touch with her?"

Grey stiffened behind me, but I couldn't tear my focus off Blaine's bowed head as he shook it.

"How old was she?"

"Twelve," he whispered.

"Then you didn't have a choice," I assured him of a truth he couldn't argue.

"No," he finally admitted quietly.

I wondered what had brought his emotions to such a high that even Grey worried with tension behind me.

Setting aside my empty wine glass on the coffee table, I squeezed Grey's knee gently before shifting onto my knees beside Blaine.

Pain-filled eyes lifted, and I held his scruffy cheeks in my hands.

Not having words to ease him, I did the only thing I could.

I kissed him, and he sighed against my lips, his arms wrapping around my waist.

Lust slammed into me where want had simmered in my core for days on end. Moisture coated my pussy from the way he licked into my mouth as though I alone could provide sustenance for his emotions. I whimpered, clinging to his face as he made slow, sensual love to my tongue. Every rumbled moan in his chest was like a wet kiss to my clit.

My core pulsed, and I shifted onto his lap, desperate to ease the ache he caused.

"Touch her, B," Grey said from behind us. "See how wet our girl is."

Our.

A shiver slid over my skin, pebbling every inch of me. Fuck me sideways, I wanted that to be true. Whimpered into Blaine's mouth with a wish upon that star.

Blaine's hand slid up my thigh beneath the sundress I'd worn, his calloused palm perfect on my skin.

He cupped over my bare sex.

A hiss escaped him as I pressed into his touch. "She's not wearing any panties," he groaned, tipping his head back against the couch.

"Fuck," Grey cursed, his exhale hot against the back of my head. I hadn't heard him kneel on the floor between Blaine's spread thighs. "Is she wet?

Blaine's shaking fingertips trailed over and back up my slit while holding my gaze, his eyes hazed with lust.

"Soaked," he choked out and leaned forward as though he couldn't stay away, his lips like butterfly wings over the corner of my mouth.

"Mmm." Grey shifted my hair over my shoulder and tongued my neck, leaving cool wetness behind. His hand slid down my thigh, gathering up the skirt of my dress, and I lifted enough so he could bunch it around my waist.

Hot breath caressed my bare ass cheeks seconds before he lifted my ass toward him and spread me open.

"Oh God." My head tipped back as Grey's tongue slid over my crack.

"Mmm," he hummed his pleasure while rimming my asshole.

My pucker spasmed beneath his lathing, and I arched my back, offering myself to him because goddamn, that man's tongue...

"Greedy little girl." Sexy as fuck, his low tone hardened my nipples. "Fuck her sweet pussy with your fingers, B."

One thick digit slid with ease inside my body, and I gasped.

Blaine took my mouth in a bruising kiss, and I lifted onto my knees, giving both men better access to the ache between my thighs.

Grey backed away, and my whine into Blaine's mouth cut off as a fingertip replaced his tongue.

Yes, oh, please...yes.

I pushed against his probing, and Grey's finger slid into my ass as his mouth latched onto my neck.

Double penetration—but not quite in the way I'd fantasized about and prepared myself for. Cleaned out and stretched a bit while showering earlier, I was *so* damn ready for two dicks at once.

"Want you both," I managed between kisses and moans while their fingers took turns fucking in and out of my holes. "Please."

"Grey." Blaine groaned his friend's name as though he hovered on the edge like I did.

Without a word, Grey stood, yanking my dress off overhead. Cool air slid over my heated skin, but he pulled me from Blaine's lap and into his arms.

My legs wound around his waist, and I met Blaine's gaze over his shoulder as I found myself being carried toward Grey's bedroom.

Blown-out pupils devoured the green/gold of Blaine's eyes, and I held out my hand. He wound his fingers through mine, trailing along behind us. His hungry gaze pulsed need through my core, and I bit back another whimper over the fact I left a wet spot on Grey's T-shirt.

"Strip and lay on the bed," Grey told Blaine while dimming the bedroom's overheads with one hand. His other hand clasped my backside in an owning grip that left me thankful I didn't have to stand.

Clothing rustled.

"You're going to ride Blaine's dick," Grey said, watching Blaine behind me. "Fuck, he's so hard for you. Sheath that thick, juicy cock, B."

A shudder rocked me hard against Grey's torso, and he grinned over what his words did to me, his gaze still plastered on his friend.

Captivated by Grey's blue eyes, I stared as he watched his friend. Lust filled his pale orbs, and he licked his lower lip.

"Tell me what he's doing—what you're seeing," I whispered instead of turning to check for myself, clinging to his broad shoulders, my heart racing.

"His dick is leaking." Grey swallowed hard.

My pussy clenched down on nothing, and I let out another whine of need and frustration.

"He's rolling a rubber down over his length while staring at your ass." Grey squeezed my cheeks, massaging hard enough he gave Blaine a peek at my hole. "But this is mine tonight. He's going to fill your pussy."

Good. Fucking. God.

I gulped.

Grey finally looked at me. "Sit on his cock, Lily. Let him ease the ache in the pussy you're grinding all over my abs." His lips curled upward as heat flooded my cheeks.

I hadn't even realized I'd been doing so.

He set me on my legs but held my waist while spinning me to face the bed.

Blaine lay sprawled on his back in the middle of the mattress, stroking down over his sheathed length. Red flushed his chest and face, and he stared at me with parted lips swollen from our kisses.

Instinctively, I crawled onto the bed, imagining sitting on his dick until he stuffed me full.

"Fuck, that ass." Grey groaned behind me, and I hovered over Blaine, our gazes locked.

"Lily," he murmured my name, his fingers weaving through my hair that blanketed around our heads.

Lowering, I shifted my soaked lower lips over his hot length while my mouth ghosted over his. I yearned for the connection between us—physical and emotional. Diving into his soul, learning him inside and out, became my mission as much as getting his gorgeous dick inside my body. Both of us panted, and the second I shifted to notch the tip of him into me, we both moaned.

Our lips smashed together, and he thrust, filling me to the point I gasped and stiffened at the sudden, stinging fullness.

"Sorry...fuck, Lily, I'm sorry," he whispered harshly against my lips, his upper body curled to keep in contact with my mouth.

I exhaled through my nose and forced myself to relax. He peppered kisses over my cheeks and eyelids, and my body slowly acclimated to his thickness stretching the hell out of me. The sting faded, leaving behind a sweet ache for more.

"Sorry," he murmured again, his dick lodged up against my cervix, hard and pulsing, right where I wanted him.

"I'm good," I whispered my assurance, a swell of longing to hold his heart close to mine stinging my eyes.

Lubed fingers slid down through my crack, and I sagged against Blaine with a groan, all the air in my lungs rushing out as my forehead rested onto his clavicle.

So close...

"Okay?" Blaine whispered against the top of my head.

"Yeah," I managed a strangled whisper.

Grey's finger slid into my ass with ease, pulling another moan from me at the fullness I'd been dreaming about.

Blaine cursed, his shifting hips rubbing my clit over his lower abs.

Tingles raced over my skin that the probe of Grey's finger deep inside me couldn't hinder.

I was going to come.

Hard.

"Grey," I whisper-sobbed, pressing back even though I had no place to go.

He slid his hand down my spine while he stroked over Blaine's dick through my inner wall separating their skin. "He's got you stuffed full, but you want more, don't you?"

"Yes, *please*." I sounded like a needy whore, but standing on the verge of my number one fantasy fulfilled, what woman wouldn't?

"You're going to be a good little girl and take me too, aren't you?" Grey asked, working a second finger into my ass.

I couldn't find my voice as he stroked in and out while Blaine trembled beneath me, without doubt fighting to hold still.

"Your ass is so hot." Grey reached deep, catching my breath. "Goddamn tight. Can't wait to feel you wrapped around my dick, little minx."

His fingers eased out, and I whimpered, my lips trembling against Blaine's chest as I fought to keep from coming over an unmoving dick and sexy-as-fuck words.

The asshole chuckled. "Push out and let me in."

Blunt thickness smeared up over my crack, and I arched my back like a cat in heat. "Please—"

He pressed, and I bit my lip, reminding myself to do as he'd said. I pushed—he pushed—and the head of him breached.

"Fuck!" I stiffened, my breath catching in my throat at the feeling as he ripped me in two.

"Shh." Grey's hands slid up and down my back in a soothing motion that did nothing to ease the tension ramped through every cell in my body. Thank fuck he held still, not trying to take what my body refused to give him.

Blaine lifted my head and kissed my lower lip with gentle nips, his sweet exhales becoming my inhales.

"Too much," I strangled out, trying to shake my head as he held it tight in his hands.

"I've got you," Blaine whispered back. "Relax on me. Let me hold you. He won't push for more unless you want him to."

It took two deep, fortifying breaths, but I managed to do as he said, resting my chest on him as tears rolled down my cheeks.

"There we go." He kissed me gently, his tongue lazily stroking like Grey's fingers did over my back until I finally settled, the pain of having the bulbous head of a dick lodged in my ass easing enough that I could breathe.

"Good girl." Grey's low tone shivered my skin. "Want more?"

My body said no, but I was determined to take them both while I had the chance. I let out a slow exhale. "Yes."

My body gave way as Grey pushed in deeper.

"God," I groaned the word like a curse, my nerve endings firing to life.

Damn near stuffed full—finally—without the pain I'd feared after first being breached. That had been the worst of it.

Grey spread my ass cheeks and pulled out a little bit, the drag of his dick from my ass curling my toes.

So. Damn. Good.

"More," I moaned, trying to arch my back again to take him in.

"Greedy girl," Grey mused, his hands over my back, caressing as he pressed in, burrowing deeper.

"Oh my God." My eyes rolled in my head at the blissful torture of feeling him sink deep inside me, his fingers gliding through the lube around where he penetrated my body.

"Your hole stretching around me is sexy as fuck, Lily."

Goddamn Grey's fingers and his filthy talk.

My climax rushed back to its edge, and I panted over Blaine's chest as Grey's groin rested against my ass.

"Holy fucking shit," I moaned.

Blaine's body went taunt beneath me as I sank into their embrace, ready for the time of my life. "Grey," he bit out the name through clenched teeth as I burrowed my face into his neck, my entire core back on board with climaxing until I passed the fuck out.

Grey had called me beautiful perfection, but the two men had me beat for that title.

They were a lethal combination.

27

BLAINE

Grey and I had spit-roasted plenty of women, but I'd never ridden such an edge, ready for my body and emotions to erupt at the feel of him stroking a mere membrane of skin away. Maybe it was Lily between us, the fact we'd never penetrated a woman like that at the same time, or that I found myself drawn to him in a different way, I wasn't sure.

Probably all three.

Our gazes clashed, and he pushed fully into Lily's ass, stilling as his balls rested against mine.

"Holy fucking shit." Lily moaned between us, her body trembling even as she went lax against my chest.

Every muscle in my body tensed, and I clenched my teeth. "Grey." I needed...

The blue of his eyes shrunk to a thin circle, the black of his pupils overtaking and holding me captive. Was the cause of it how I'd said his name, desperate as fuck for...I didn't know what?

He planked over us, his hands resting beside my shoulders. A grind of his hips moved Lily's wet clasp over my dick, and I groaned, my jaw aching.

I'd seen the way he gyrated his hips, and the imagery of him fucking into Lily's ass, every brush of his balls over me, heightened my need to erupt.

Lily moaned, shifting her head so her cheek rested on my chest. "Oh my *God*..."

Sweat lined Grey's brow, and my tongue salivated to lick it off.

I blinked at the thought.

He grinned down at me. "*Move*."

Lips parted to suck in oxygen, I pulled out as he thrust in.

"Fucking hell!" Lily writhed between us as we took turns gently fucking into her tight body. "Oh my fucking...Jesus... holy shit." She whined and choked on her curses, the cream of her pussy hot and slick around my length.

I once more had to clench my teeth to keep from rutting up into her like a damn animal hellbent on filling her up with my cum.

"You like having both our cocks inside your body, little minx?" Grey asked, still holding my gaze which only made my need to blow worse.

"Fuck, yes." A guttural groan rushed hot air over my chest as she tried to arch toward him. "Oh God...better than...oh *fuuuck*."

Grey had swiveled his hips in the way that made women crazy, sliding his hot balls over mine.

Fuck. My teeth were going to crack for sure. "Grey," I begged again, not sure what I asked for or if my eyes gave away the swirling lust coursing through me. His dick all but stroked mine, his balls slapping me—but I needed more...

Lily propped up onto her elbow, lust-blazed eyes ensnaring mine.

I lost myself to the dark haze of her orbs, like she'd sucked my soul inside and cradled it close to her heart.

Her whimpers soaked into my ears, Grey's groans heightening my urge to release as we took turns filling her in steady rhythm.

"You both feel so fucking good," Grey's ragged words drew my focus from Lily.

The desire burning in his pale eyes pulled my balls up tight against my body, catching my breath.

Lost...fuck, could I get lost inside him. My anchor, my—

"Kiss him." Lily's whisper tore my attention off his face.

Both Grey and I stilled, him buried, only the tip of my shaft squeezed by her tight pussy.

I blinked. "Wh-what?"

She settled her chest onto mine, arms sliding up around my head, palms cradling my ears. "I want you to *kiss* him."

My dick throbbed, and I pressed back into her body on instinct, my balls ready to let loose.

I should have felt sick at the thought of touching my lips to another man's, but my entire body thrummed, climbing aboard with her demand.

I forced my eyes to Grey.

He'd shuttered his gaze, leaving me floundering over the decision to give Lily what she wanted.

"Grey?" I heard myself ask, needing him to lead the way.

His dick jerked against the back of mine, a hint of direction. "Tell me what *you* want, B."

His lips on mine—a kiss with burning desire that I knew would sear my skin like flame.

Lily lay still between us but hardly forgotten. The sweet scent of vanilla filled my nose, her hair tickling my side where it rippled over my body. Her hot breath teased at my nipple, her heart pounding against my chest. Longing to please her flooded through me as much as my desire to taste Grey's mouth.

"Yes," I whispered.

Grey lowered himself onto Lily's back, pressing her tightly against me where she'd shifted more to the side to give us access to one another.

She whimpered as Grey wound his fingers through hers beside my head. He paused, inches from my mouth.

"I'm not him," he murmured, his eyes boring into mine with an intensity that felt like he read the turmoil, the darkness trying to push to the forefront of my mind like he always did. "You're not submitting to me…"

I let out a slow breath and jerked my head in a nod.

"Keep your eyes on me, B." Grey closed the distance, his exhale hot over my mouth.

I blinked, lost in the black of his swelled pupils.

A mere brush of his soft lips across mine roused hunger inside me I hadn't known before. Jacked endorphins like a bursting rocket, jerking my dick inside Lily's wet heat.

She released a whimper that matched mine, her palms trapped against my ears as Grey's larger hand cradled my head, holding me still.

Eyelids fluttering shut, I rode a mind-altering high as Grey continued the most gentle of kisses over my lips. He licked along my seam, and I opened at his coaxing, both of us groaning at the first brush of our tongues.

He tasted like whiskey and masculinity—all Grey. Home and comfort even though every cell in my body ached for release.

"Blaine." His whisper ghosted over my senses like a

prayer, and he ground his hips against Lily's ass, our balls once more rubbing until mine drew up tight.

Fucking hell.

My back arched up off the mattress in desperation for more. He dragged his dick out, and I grabbed hold of his shoulders with a harsh whimper, thinking he pulled away from our kiss.

Grey thrusted in with a grunt, jolting Lily over my chest and slamming me back down.

She cursed and tried to move between us. "Please...*please* fuck me."

Lust ignited, clenching every goddamn inch of my abs, and the kiss between Grey and I grew frantic, tongues fucking in time with our thrusts into the woman trapped and panting between us, begging for more.

Sweat slickened our bodies, every drive of Grey's hips sliding her softness against me. Our mouths stayed fused as though the passion between us gave us breath. Life.

My arm wrapped around Lily for Grey, my hands finding the muscles along his spine. They flexed beneath my hold, hot and hard, and I clung to him, my desperation at the point where my moaned whimpers filled his mouth.

I tensed, my balls tingling.

Grey tore his lips off mine and planked.

Trying to pull him back to my panting mouth proved fruitless against his strength. His body rocked, fucking into Lily's ass hard enough he moved my back along the mattress. "Touch her clit, B. Make her come around us." Ragged, his command took me to the edge of sanity.

I shoved a hand beneath Lily's belly, easily sliding through the sweat smeared between us to find her clit.

"Oh God," she groaned, her forehead once more tilting on my chest.

Her cream smeared over our groins, the wet sounds of our fucking as loud as all three of us vocalizing and panting our need.

She shuddered as I slid my fingers along her nub, Grey's thrusts rubbing her off on my hand.

"Yes. Oh, *fuck*, I'm going to come so hard."

I pressed my fingers together, her slick clit between them.

She released with a shriek, arching, her head tipping back up toward Grey where he planked and fucked into her with abandon, slamming her against me.

"B..." he gasped out as we both buried deep.

Cum shot up through my length, ripping a grunt from my chest. Euphoria swelled in like a crashing wave, and I yanked him back down, the three of us a writhing mess of sweat and tangled limbs.

Grey waited for me to release, same as he always did.

He thrust twice more along my length while I filled the condom, the push and pull of both their bodies milking me dry and leaving me light-headed and gasping for breath.

A heady, spine-tingling moan, and Grey came, shuddering beneath my hands grasping at his back.

My ears rang as reality slowly settled over us.

Lily lay lax, trapped between two walls of hot, sweaty muscle. She let out a shuddered sigh. "I'm wrecked," she murmured then giggled. "Seriously."

Sated blue eyes found mine, the question clear as day in Grey's gaze.

I smiled, letting him know it was all good. Unable to move and riding the highest of all highs.

Better than good.

"Thank fuck." He tipped his forehead against my

shoulder for the span of three heartbeats before pulling out and leaving Lily shivering in my arms.

She whimpered at the loss of him, and I soothed my hands down over her damp back, holding her close.

Grey headed to the bathroom, and I closed my eyes and exhaled slowly, my mind blown over what we'd done. Line thoroughly crossed. Not one ounce of regret or tendril of past shit pushing upward to steal my joy.

Lily released a shuddered sigh, shivering again, and I wrapped my arms tight around her realizing we hadn't exactly taken it easy on her the first time being stuffed with two dicks. I'd been lost in the passion, same as Grey had seemed to be—bastards, both of us, for not thinking of her comfort. "Are you okay?" I murmured, my lips against her hair.

"Yep." She popped the P, making both of us chuckle enough that my spent dick slid from her body. "That was the single hottest moment of my life." Lifting her head from my chest, she held my gaze with a steady inquisitive one. "He's a good kisser."

Hell yes, he was.

My lips tingled, and I pressed them together, trying to hang onto the feeling of having his mouth on mine. Had I been standing, I felt sure just the touch of his mouth minus the hunger we'd gotten caught up in would have been enough to weaken my knees. All that talk about fireworks and the world falling away didn't compare to how Grey's mouth made me feel.

She clasped her hands over my pecs, resting her chin atop them. "Did you like it?"

"Yeah," I admitted, my voice barely audible.

"Do you think he did?"

I glanced toward the bathroom door, watching Grey's

flexing ass as he moved to the sink to wet a towel to clean Lily up. "Maybe?" I offered.

"Please." I could hear her eye roll. "Couldn't you feel how he fucked me while eating at your mouth?"

Lust shot through me again, and I bit back a moan.

"Yeah." Her smile seemed...fixed in place, tickling unease in the back of my mind. "That's what I figured."

Our gazes held as Grey joined us. He rolled Lily off me, breaking the moment between us. I looked at him for another confirmation he was all right with what we'd done, but he'd locked his gaze with hers in their own little cocoon while gently wiping between her splayed thighs.

I rolled from the bed with a groan, ready to rid myself of the full condom hanging from my dick.

"Shower?" Lily suggested as I headed to the bathroom.

"B?" Grey called after me.

I tied off the condom and trashed it before turning on the water.

I stayed settled, calm. What Lily had initiated between Grey and I had felt good...right. Nothing inside me had wanted to turn away or curl up inside myself.

The darkness I'd expected on choking levels lay beneath a heavy blanket of ball-tingling euphoria.

I wanted to kiss my best friend again.

28

———————

GREYSON

Was it possible to fall in love with a girl just because she broke down walls you'd been wanting to scale for over a decade? She'd seemed so damn set on her lovers not touching, so her suggestion had blown me away and made me happier than I'd ever been. Her body's desire had overridden her mindset, and Blaine had given me permission to taste his lips.

Fuck, what a mouth...

My dick stayed half-hard while carrying Lily into the bathroom after she claimed she couldn't walk. It got even harder once we stood beneath the spray and she leaned against me while Blaine used his hands to wash over her front.

He gave me his eyes a few times, and the relief, the interest I found there, eased the tension that had wanted to rise inside me.

No regret, his gorgeous hazel eyes promised.

I need more, I hoped he could read in mine.

"The way you were plowing into me, Grey, you had to be bumping balls back there with Blaine."

A barked laugh ripped from me at Lily's blunt statement.

"Oh my God," Blaine said, shaking his head and smirking while kneeling to rub soap over her calves.

"I gotta admit," she murmured, "I've fantasized about being fucked like that for years, and the two of you together...yeah. It hurt in the beginning, but it turned out better than I imagined, that's for damned sure."

I slid my lips over her neck. "Does that mean you hope to do it again?"

She sighed, tilting her head to give me better access to her delicious skin. "And again and again and again..."

Blaine stood, our gazes locking while I tongued up to Lily's ear.

She shuddered in my arms I had wrapped around her body to keep her upright.

"I think we'd both be up to the task," I told her.

Sliding my dick along Blaine's with a bare hint of latex and skin between us had been fucking heaven, and Lily's ass had been tight and hot.

I wanted to feel her with nothing between us, fuck my load into her ass and watch it drip out.

I wanted to see Blaine's do the same from her pussy.

Even more, I wanted both of us in her tight sheath together, our cum spurting and mixing together, slick skin rubbing—

"Someone's ready for round two," Lily said, grinding her backside against my stiff dick.

Chuckling, I spun her around into Blaine's arms.

"Mmm." She wiggled her ass against his groin, smirking up at me. "You aren't the only one."

Blaine's cheeks flushed, but he shook his head. "You're not taking us again tonight," he told Lily, "or you won't be able to walk tomorrow."

She pouted, her gorgeous lips calling out to me.

I traced a finger over the lower.

"Grey."

I lifted my focus to her eyes to find hesitancy—a questioning gaze. She'd asked us to cross a line she'd laid in what I'd thought had been stone. Did she regret doing so? Fear being set aside?

She'd weaseled her way into my heart so fucking fast that I was so damn sure no such thing would ever happen.

"Kiss me," she demanded, those dark of eyes telling me she wanted to see if the same passion Blaine and I had shared simmered between the two of us.

"Needy little girl," I said, still smiling because I *knew* it did.

"Yep." She popped the P, but the usual confidence wasn't behind her action.

I gave her what she demanded but lazed my mouth over hers, a hint of tongue teasing me with a taste of her sweetness, a deep groan rumbling in my chest.

Lily wound her fingers in my hair, pulling me closer as though desperate to get inside my body and know my mind.

Unleashing the intense desire to assure her of my feelings, I pressed against her, my hands grasping her hips and eating at her mouth until she went lax, her fingers soothing through my hair rather than tugging.

She shuddered. Sighed.

I eased up, peppering small kisses to the corners of her smiling lips.

"Love me a Lily and hot hunks sandwich," she murmured, seemingly set at ease over what had transpired between the three of us.

I laughed again, resting my forehead against hers, the

passionate kiss broken but lust still radiating between us. "You're one of a kind."

And fuck, could I fall in love with her over that fact. I felt like I was already halfway there.

She wiggled again, her belly rubbing against my hard-on. "Watching the two of you kiss was hot as fuck."

My dick jerked against her soft flesh.

"Mmm," she murmured. "I think you enjoyed kissing your best friend."

Thank you, I wanted to shout out but bit my tongue. She seemed okay with it, but was Blaine now that the sexually charged moment was over?

I lifted my head to find him studying me.

Heat lay in his gaze, but was it only for the woman smooshed between us?

Admission time and take another step? Cross my fingers the shit she had started didn't backfire?

Lily shuddered as he and I continued to stare at one another, the only sound the spray of water against his back as I tried to get a read on his thoughts and feelings.

His tongue had slid along mine with a hunger that had curled my toes and made my heart stutter. Panted breaths, the moans I'd swallowed down while eating at his mouth, told me he'd enjoyed our kiss.

Hot as fuck kiss.

Those greenish-gold orbs stayed locked on me, and I saw the desire swirling inside his brain as easily as I could read a book.

"You're doing that silent communication thing, aren't you?" Lily murmured.

"Yeah," I rasped out, knowing without doubt Blaine wanted the same as I did. To explore what she'd started.

"What do you think, Blaine?" Lily asked. "Is that thick and juicy cock pressing against my back all for me?"

He swallowed audibly and shook his head before whispering, "No."

My balls seized right the fuck up, but I held still, every cell in my body lusting to lean in and capture his mouth again. "Blaine…" I choked out his name, desperation evident in my tone.

He grasped the back of my neck and yanked me in, his mouth slamming onto mine.

All three of us moaned, and I sank into his initiation, the hunger in his hands wrapping once more around my back.

"My God," Lily whispered. "I could come from just watching the two of you. So sexy. So fucking hot…you're both hard as hell. Shit, I wish I could take you again."

I groaned, grinding my dick into her belly, thinking about plunging deep into her sweet warmth.

"Why am I loving this so damn much?" she whined, her tiny body wiggling between us. She'd expected to hate it, I didn't doubt, and fuck how I wanted to give her assurance she'd made the right choice—for all of us.

Cursing over the knowledge she had to be sore from the way we'd fucked her, I tore my mouth off Blaine's. "Play with her tits," I told him and dropped to my knees to shove my face between her thighs.

"Oh…shit, yes." She widened her stance, allowing me better access to her musky core.

Tongue lathing through her slit and up over her clit, I peered up. She tipped her head back against Blaine's chest, and he watched me eat her out with lust-blown eyes, his hands wrapped around her breasts, thumbing her tight nipples.

Sweet and tangy arousal coated my tongue, and I lapped that shit up, pre-cum welling and sliding down my length.

"You taste so damn fine." I licked again, adding a finger to my exploration. Latching onto her clit with my lips, I dipped a fingertip into her pussy.

She let out a hiss.

"Sore?"

"Yeah," she moaned, shoving her hips forward at me.

Chuckling, I gave the needy girl what she wanted, nuzzling and licking, kissing on her hard nub like I would her mouth.

"Make her come," Blaine whispered, his words half-slurred as though sex-drunk.

He never demanded things from me with a woman between us...I liked it.

I glanced up at him again. Those goddamn eyes of his had gone near black with lust, but gentleness resided there too—a yearning bordering on desperate to please her, the same way I wished to do.

Suckling her clit between my lips, I nipped with my teeth. He pinched her nipples.

"Just like that..." She grabbed hold of my head and fucked her pussy against my mouth, chasing her orgasm. "Just like that. Fu—" Her curse was cut off by a cry of release, and a burst of cum dripped down my chin.

"Fuck, Lily," Blaine bit out, cradling her tight against his torso as she shuddered.

I spread her labia and licked her cream, swallowing it down with a deep groan.

So. Damn. Delicious.

She went lax in Blaine's arms, and I stood, shoving my hard dick between her thighs and grasping her legs to shut them against my length.

"I'm gonna get off between your legs," I told her, biting along her jawline, tension stringing my body tight.

"Mmm." She sagged against Blaine, and I caught his gaze.

Do it with me.

She reached back between their bodies, and my breath left in a rush as his hard length slid along mine between her wet thighs.

Flames ignited inside me.

She'd read my goddamn mind and put his dick right where I wanted it. Against mine. A complete crossing of swords I'd thought she'd been dead set against.

"Lily." Her name tore from my lungs as his hot skin slid along mine.

She wrapped her arms around my back and yanked me in close, once more trapping her form between us. "I want it." Her whisper against my chest unleased the fire fighting to burst through my skin.

I took his mouth without request or consent, but he gave as good as he got. Teeth, tongues, lips—nothing stayed passive in our passion. Lily's soft noises, as erotic as her shivers, egged me on, drawing my balls up faster than normal.

Hot flesh, hard as steel stroked mine, welling euphoric waves through my heart.

No latex barrier, no layer of skin stretched between us.

Bare and raw, frotting against Blaine's thick dick was the best sexual experience of my goddamn life.

I'd never felt so close to him, and it was all because of Lily...

"Gonna come all over your cock, B." I said against his mouth and chased his tongue, trembling in my need for release.

He moaned—and erupted, wet heat hitting my balls.

"Fuck!" I squeezed the two of them to me, rutting as spunk shot from my dick to return the favor.

Gone.

There was no other word for what I felt.

Simply wrecked, exactly as Lily had said—and I loved it.

———

Sunday morning, I dragged my exhausted eyelids open to find Lily watching me sleep.

Blaine snuggled up against her backside, his face in her neck.

"Morning," I whispered, smiling and tucking hair behind her ear, my mind rushing through the many hours we'd spent satisfying her sweet body.

"Hey." She blinked, pressing into me.

"Tea?" I offered even though I'd rather have spent the entire rest of the day with Blaine and Lily in my bed.

"Yeah...then I've got to get my ass to work."

I pouted, and she quietly giggled, lifting her head to kiss my lips.

"Come on." I rolled out of bed, and she followed gently enough she left Blaine sleeping.

We both stood beside the bed watching him sleep, our hands somehow clasped before I realized we'd done so. Like we'd been drawn to do so, instinctive in our desire for each other—for Blaine.

Not for the first time since she'd come over for the weekend, my heart swelled up to bursting.

I had no words to express my gratitude to her or the growing emotions inside me.

I'd have loved to climb back in beside Blaine and snuggle against his body as he'd done with Lily's with her on the other side, but I'd promised our girl caffeine. Squeezing her hand, I motioned toward her clothes on the chair.

She let out a sigh as though her mind rested where mine did and nodded.

I pulled on a pair of shorts over my morning semi while she quietly dressed.

"I don't have time for tea—I'll grab some at work," she whispered while trailing behind me into the kitchen.

I'd hoped for a few minutes alone with her to work through the thoughts in my head, to put them into words she needed to hear, but nodded.

I stood by the front door and held out my arms.

She didn't hesitate to walk into them, squeezing me tight.

A heavy sigh left me, and I kissed the top of her head.

Lily tipped her torso away from me, a soft curve on her lips assuring me I was sending her off happy and sated.

"Thank you," I said, not expanding on the reason, but at the fade of her smile, I realized maybe she wasn't as okay with the situation as I'd assumed.

"Remember my ex?"

"Yeah." I pulled her tighter against my chest, needing her to know that shit wouldn't happen with the three of us.

It wasn't regret but fear in her big brown eyes as she stared up at me. Such a thing wouldn't be on her mind unless...

Fuck, this woman.

I squeezed her tighter, my lips curling upward at the renewed euphoria flooding my chest.

"Are you saying you like us, Lily?" I asked, my hands sliding down to cup her fine backside.

"Yep." She popped the P, so I didn't think she wasn't too upset...until she spoke again, that unease lingering in her gaze. "And it scares the hell out of me."

The truth lay clear in her dark eyes, and I wanted to wrap her even tighter against me, take away the obvious dread inside her.

"As much as I'm in love with Blaine," I admitted, "I would never kick you to the curb. You do funny— extraordinary things to my insides, and I'm completely enamored with you."

She giggled, making a rushed exhale of tension relax my shoulders. "Who even uses that word anymore?"

"A man helplessly falling for you," I offered with a small smile, smoothing her hair back from her face. I hoped she recognized the truth that she wasn't the only one traversing the path we'd set upon.

"Well damn." She let out huff, her smile fixed firmly in place again, her eyes brighter than I'd seen since waking. "Now I'm all warm and tingly inside."

"Ditto, little minx." I kissed her on the nose as said tingles swept to my extremities, dick included. "You're welcome to come back here anytime you want, and we'll take care of that problem for you."

Please. Sooner than later.

I wasn't beyond begging. She'd given me so much more than I'd ever expected, beyond opening the door between Blaine and me—she'd begun to fill the emptiness inside me for a soft, feminine touch. Affection and gentleness.

She'd created a longing that I needed her and her alone to satisfy.

Lily stood on her tiptoes, brushing her lips over mine in

a sweet kiss that stuttered my heartbeat. "Oh, it's no problem. More like an absolute pleasure." One firm press of our mouths, minus the tongue, and she stepped back. "Text me all the naughty stuff this week?"

My dick thickened further at the idea of teasing her with words and videos and what I might get in reply. "Count on it." I allowed heat to fill my gaze, and the pink spreading over her cheeks brought satisfaction crashing into my chest.

She was good.

We were good, thank fuck.

With a flutter of her fingers, she was gone, and I locked up behind her, grinning like an idiot at the door.

The back of my neck tingled, and I turned to find the kitchen empty even though I could feel him. Tension lifted those hairs, and I drew a breath to steady myself.

"Come on out, B."

Blaine sauntered around the corner, gray sweats hanging low on his hips.

For the first time, I allowed myself to check him out from the tips of his bare toes, up over his delicious bulge, all the way to his sleepy eyes that peered at me with a million and one questions.

Stifling silence thickened the air between us, and I needed to know his thoughts more than oxygen in my lungs.

"How much did you hear?" I asked, my voice surprisingly calm.

"Every word." Blaine was quiet in answering, his eyes unwavering on mine. "Is it true?"

Nerves woke inside me, teetering me on the edge of what could be the end—or the beginning. "Which part?"

He held himself in check, eyes shadowed, his focus dropping to my mouth. "How long?" he whispered.

So that was his focus...

"I've been in love with you since forever, B," I admitted, praying like fuck he wouldn't abandon me in my most vulnerable. "There was no one moment for me, and…"

"And?" he pressed when I didn't know how to explain the desire and fear all mingling together in my guts.

I released an unsteady exhale, my hands clenched at my sides. "The thought of you falling in love with Lily and leaving me has me twisted up tight inside."

"I would never leave you," Blaine stated as though it was a given, his brow furrowed as he once more gave me his eyes.

He hadn't told me he loved me in return, not that I'd expected him to, but I would be content with whatever he did have to give. First, though, I needed to make sure he remained steady.

"What we did—"

"It's fine," he said, cutting me off. "Don't worry about it."

Red flooded his cheeks, settling my insides the slightest bit.

"Just fine?" I pushed, needing clarity of what his flush suggested in my brain.

He swallowed hard, his shoulders tensing, but he didn't shift his attention off my face.

Nor did he speak.

My gaze dropped to his sweats. A defined outline of his hardening dick pressed on the cotton material, causing my own length to swell back up.

More than fine, his thickness all but spoke his desires out loud.

"Christ, B." Throat tightening, I met his stare, energy rising to crackle between us like a livewire.

I took one step…two…Blaine didn't back away as I slowly advanced into his personal space. No hesitancy filled his eyes over darkness that ought to be rising in his mind.

He'd shared it all, and the fact he allowed me that close with sexual intent flooded me with unfathomable thankfulness for his trust.

It was as though he'd fixed in his heart and mind that he wasn't submitting to me but rather giving freely, same as he'd done with his kisses in Lily's presence.

"B?" I whispered, the distance between us less than two feet, the hunger in the air palpable, but I needed words. Assurance that what I desired wouldn't send him spiraling.

"Yes."

Pure consent rested in his answer, no question.

I cradled his face in my hands, the scratch of his scruff on my palms welcome and arousing as fuck. A shudder ripped through me, and I struggled to fill my lungs. "You have no idea how long I've wanted this," I rasped the words and moved closer, my pulse pounding in my ears.

The chaste swipe of lips quickly turned into a blaze of passion, tongues twining regardless of morning breath. I swallowed down his moans and pressed his back against the counter, our groins tight, hands grasping at each other's naked torsos and hair.

His thick length slid along mine as we ground against each other, the motion taking me to the point of coming in a matter of seconds.

"Can I touch you?" I asked between kisses, so damn desperate my dick jerked at the thought of finally feeling his hard flesh against my palm.

"Yes."

There was no teasing of fingers at the waistband of his sweats—I shoved my hand inside, wrapping around his cock.

And damn near came from his guttural groan.

"Okay?" I forced through gritted teeth, grinding my dick all over his tensed thigh.

He let out a hiss, leaning back to watch me stroke him, lips parted as he panted. "Fuck. Yes."

I yanked his sweats to his knees with my free hand before doing the same with my shorts. Closing the distance, I added my dick to the jerk off session.

"Oh...*fuck*, that feels good."

I groaned in agreement to Blaine's moaned words, smearing our pre-cum all over my palm and fingers. Slick and hard, we rutted into my hand, the sounds of wet schlicking soon rising along with our heightened breaths.

"Gonna come," Blaine rasped, arching his hips toward me.

Our mouths crushed together, and Blaine grasped at my back as he'd done with Lily between us, his fingers digging into my muscles as though desperate to pull me inside him.

Fuck, yes, what I wouldn't give—

Wet heat erupted on my hand, and I soaked his groan into my memory before allowing myself release. Elation crashed over me like a storm's swell, dragging me under, leaving me breathless, adrenaline coursing.

I lusted to drop to my knees and clean him with my tongue, to swallow his essence down so he would always be a part of me.

He'd allowed himself to cross lines I'd never in a million years expected, hadn't hoped for, so I made myself content in what Blaine had gifted me. Kissing and frotting, loving on Lily between us would have to be enough.

We panted for breath, our foreheads tilted together as the ocean of lust settled along the shore in quietness.

"Okay?" I finally checked in with him again, winding my

non-sticky hand around the back of his neck to keep him close.

"Yeah." He blew out an exhale that I dragged into my lungs. "Better than."

A grin spread over my face, and I pulled back, needing his eyes.

Our slick chubs still rested in my hand, and I gave him one last squeeze as our gazes connected.

He smiled rather than turned away. Bashfully, pink staining his cheeks instead of bone-white paleness.

Unrequited love uncovered...and he hadn't turned away from me. I swallowed hard, warmth rushing to every nerve ending in my body. A deep longing for Lily intensified the feelings coursing through me.

Blaine tore his gaze away first, glancing down to where I still held him. "Too bad Lily isn't here to clean us up."

"I was thinking the same thing."

He let out a shaky laugh, and I gave him one last peck on his soft lips, lingering to savor the moment, loving how we were of the same mind.

"Got any plans for today?"

"Sleep."

I nodded, my heart falling a little over the fact he didn't want to spend his time with me. Forcing myself to step back, I pulled up my shorts, giving him some space I expected he needed.

"In your bed," he added as though he read where my thoughts had gone.

A grin took over my face, my heart once more light as a goddamn feather. "I could go for a snuggle fest," I said, grabbing a towel to wipe my hand free of our spunk.

His smile felt better than cool salt water on sunburned toes.

Thank you, Lily.

I followed his firm, flexing ass back into my bedroom, and after cleaning up, he became my little spoon—and for the first time ever, I didn't bother shifting my groin away from his gorgeous ass. I rested my flaccid cock against his crack and closed my eyes, finding the kind of rest I hadn't known was possible.

29

LILY

We'd spent the weekend in a tangle of limbs covered in sweat and cum, but my wrecked ass wouldn't be taking another dick for at least a week or two. My pussy and mouth had gotten one hell of a workout too though, and I'd never been so jelly-legged in all my life.

Grey and Blaine had often become caught up in the lust among the three of us, their mouths finding each other's, but not once had I felt left out or on the sidelines. Same as in the shower Friday night, they took care of me before getting off.

There was no frotting, no man-on-man blow jobs, and no fucking that didn't include me.

But I wondered what would happen with the two of them being alone. Would the men explore the door I'd pushed open between them sooner than I'd planned on? Would they realize they didn't need a feminine counterpart to find contentment in Grey's bed?

I rushed through the café's door to get my ass on the clock. A niggling of fear wound around me like a python like it'd done often through our weekend together, worrisome enough that I twisted my own stomach into knots.

I almost *wanted* them to interact on their own even though I dreaded it. Grey and Blaine deserved happiness just as much as the next guy.

I just really wished it could be with me.

Yes, my determination to keep emotions out of our hookups had fled my heart. I was truly caught up, captured, in the fantasy of a happily ever after with my two lovers.

And it scared the fuck out of me even while memories of their touches heated my face and dampened my panties.

Cheryl watched me with a raised eyebrow as though she felt my conflicting emotions that caused grins then frowns to morph back and forth like shifting shadows. I eventually spewed the delicious details of my weekend between serving customers.

Seeing as how she preferred pussy, she didn't catch on with my swooning excitement, but she did offer her congratulations on finding what I'd set my heart upon.

If only it would last...

When the second break rolled around, I hurried outside into the sun, my cell in hand. My fingers shook, and I swallowed hard as I swiped my screen to life.

Blaine had texted first. **Miss you.**

My exhale quickly deflated my lungs.

So even if they *had* gotten it on after I'd left, he still thought of me.

Miss you too, I typed out a reply, breathing a tiny bit easier.

I swiped over to Grey's number and shot off a text, my words thoroughly fishing. **What are you up to?**

Wishing you were here between us, he texted back before I had a chance to chew on a fingernail.

Lower lip between my teeth, my fingers flew over the screen before I considered the words that rushed to mind, knowing it would be better if they figured it out and broke my heart sooner than later. **You can always pretend I am.**

I tossed in a wink and the devil emoji to drive the point home.

And fish for yet more information.

Grey: **I got us both off with my hand after you left.**

Heat rushed through me instead of the fear I'd expected. He'd been blatantly honest, no sneaking around like Levi and Zeke had done behind my back. Biting back a smile, I sent off another text: **I want evidence.**

Grey shot back a lol emoji along with, **Already cleaned up.**

A thought flitted through my head, so I asked the question because I couldn't *not* know. **Is that why Blaine texted he missed me—because he felt guilty for what the two of you did without my being there?**

Grey: **No. He texted because we both said we wished you were there to lick us clean.**

"Oh, God." My fingers shook while searching out letters on the screen. **You can't say shit like THAT when I'm at work!**

Grey: **Go to the bathroom and get yourself off.**

Me: **No!**

Grey: **Yes. I want evidence.**

The damn man echoed my words.

Mr. Yummy: **Do it.**

Furrowing my brow, I texted back to Blaine. **You're together right now, aren't you?**

They both replied an affirmative at the same damn time.

I started a group chat including all three of us, grinning as I did so, my heart so damn light in my chest that I swore it skipped a few beats. **I want proof first**, I texted. **Of the kissing sort.**

Breath held and pulse thrumming, I waited. A pic came through of scruffy jaws and locked lips, Grey cradling Blaine's face with one hand.

I throbbed between my thighs and bit back a groan at how beautiful they were together. I wanted in on that— needed it.

Three minutes later, a definite record for me, the boys got their requested *evidence*. Creamy fingers from my sopping pussy.

Now where's mine? I texted.

Mr. Yummy: **I got nothing left.**

I snorted, well aware of how many times he'd drained his balls into condoms and my mouth over the previous two nights. Add in one last one from Grey he'd mentioned...or had it happened more than once since I'd left them?

The inside of my lip became well acquainted with my teeth as I worried over my thoughts. Goddamnit, would I always question everything? Would my emotions always rollercoaster with suspicion?

Grey: **Come over tonight.**

The threatening tension twisting up my stomach again eased.

Me: **Bossy.**

Grey: **You love it.**

I considered doing what he wanted since I *did* kind of like when he made demands, but while my body was warmed and ready for another romp in his bed, I needed to take it easy on my heart.

They needed to thoroughly work things out between the two of them too before I allowed myself another fantasy to be fulfilled.

Me: **I'm staying home tonight.**

Blaine dropped a sad face, but I forced myself to stick to my guns and text what needed said—for all our sakes.

Me: **You boys enjoy a guy's night, and just so you know, I'm not against dick pics with…evidence. Just sayin'.**

Grey: **We'll miss you.**

Blaine didn't send another reply as I rushed back to the counter, but Grey's response had been more than enough. He was the one in love with his best friend, had admitted that fact to me earlier before I'd left their house. For him to assure me that he wouldn't kick me to the curb because he was enamored with me too, I told myself I had no choice but to believe him.

Trust just came so damn hard to someone who'd had their heart broken.

———

Grey: **How far is too far?**

He'd sent it to me directly while I sat sucking down wine and waiting for Haley to get home from her dinner date with some guy she'd met online. I studied the words a few times, my buzzed brain not really sure what he was asking.

Grey: **Lily?**

Needing to go with my desires for the two of them over my fears, I replied, **There's no such thing. I WANT you to explore whatever woke up over the last two days—if that's what you're asking.**

Grey: **I really wish you were here to love on him with me.**

That damn python I hadn't realized had gripped my stomach again relaxed. He was well aware of my past and what the possible outcome of knowing they were together would do to me.

And he cared enough that he reached out rather than jumping his best friend because walls had finally torn down between them.

Me: **I'm enjoying a glass of chardonnay. A little too much to drive—or appreciate dick. You go enjoy Blaine for me. Love him, Grey.**

Grey: **Already do and always will.**

I smiled, my eyes stinging even though I didn't know why. Happiness for him? Excitement for Blaine to have the love he deserved? Or just exhaustion from a weekend of fucking like rabbits and a too-long shift on my feet?

Me: **Send me some pics so I have something to look at tonight when I'm horny from thinking about the two of you together in that big bed.**

Grey: **We're going to want evidence of that.**

I snorted a laugh, starting to get annoyed with that damn word even though it turned me on. **It'll be my pleasure if I don't pass out from drinking on an empty stomach.**

My phone rang a few seconds later.

"I had to hear your voice." Grey sounded muffled and lazy, like he already sprawled in his bed.

Warmth tingled through me, and I settled back into the corner of the couch with my nearly empty glass, surprised by how happy I was he'd called.

"Did you need my assistance in getting it up for him or something?" I asked with a snicker, sticking to silliness rather than focusing on how damn good Grey made me feel.

"Nope." He popped the P like I usually did, making me outright laugh.

Grey could get hard for his best friend without my help.

My grin faded, and I wondered where his mind was with all that had unveiled in the previous two days.

We quieted, the silence allowing my mind to float back and forth for too long from insecurities to hopes I desperately wanted to dream about.

"Does he know how you feel about him?" I asked while staring at the last swallow of white in the bottom of my glass, my tone much quieter, all trace of silliness gone.

"He overheard what I told you this morning, so yeah."

"He feels the same," I stated, closing my eyes as memories flashed through my mind. "He stares at you like you hung the moon and stars in the night sky."

Exactly as Levi had with Zeke.

"That's thankfulness. Gratefulness for all I've done for him."

"Hmm." My lips thinned at the bullshit he spouted, but I tipped back my glass, emptying it rather than arguing. I could lead the man to water, but I couldn't force him to drink.

"He'll only ever look at *you* like that," Grey said.

My forehead dented in a quick furrow as I swallowed. "Like what?"

"You're the sunshine in the garden of his soul," he stated as though sold on the idea but without a hint of jealousy in his tone.

I almost snorted a huff. *If only.*

But I remembered the flush on Blaine's face when around me, the way he kissed and touched my body as though in reverent worship...

Damn emotional roller coaster—damn wine—laughter bubbled up on the heels of my frown. "I am not. He's only known me for a couple weeks."

"The first day I met Blaine, I was sure I wanted him in my life until I died."

Shit, I was aware Grey had it bad for his best friend, but still. "How old were you?"

"Ten."

"Did you know you were bi?" I closed my eyes, head tipped back against the couch, empty glass cradled to my chest.

The spins...shit.

I popped my eyelids back open and slid a foot onto the floor to ground me.

"Not right then, but the first time I thought about kissing it was because of Blaine's mouth. And the first time I realized I wanted to touch another dick, it was his."

Blaine had been Grey's first crush, his first love. Envy sneaked into my mind, but what woman wouldn't be jealous or anxious about losing what she'd always wanted and thought she might have found?

"He's it for you," I spoke truth both of us knew deep inside our souls, needing confirmation one way or the other. The teeter-totter of emotions was doing my buzzed brain in.

"I'd like nothing more," Grey admitted without hesitation, "but if I'm being honest, there would still be something missing. Is it greedy to need him and crave a soft, loving woman's touch too?"

My heart beat heavy in my chest at the suggestion in his deep voice and the words caressing my ears. "No." I swallowed hard. "Why else would Missing Link be in existence? A triad is probably tough as hell, but it's doable. It can work if the connection, the dedication, and the honesty is there."

But was that what he suggested he wanted for the long haul?

He made an agreement in his throat. "And what do *you* desire, Lily?"

"I'm greedy like you," I whispered the truth in my heart, for as long as I could hold onto them.

"And what if that isn't what Blaine wants?" Grey sounded concern as though our hearts longed for the same thing.

My chin lifted. "Then we show him it's what he *needs*."

"Fuck, woman, you fill me up with all kinds of emotion..."

My throat tightened, and I waited, desperate for more affirmation.

"I don't even know what to think or how to handle my head right now," Grey whispered, his tone ragged. "Next time I see you, I'm bringing you an entire shipping box full of Andes candies."

Aaaaand, my heart melted.

"Go lose yourself in him," I said with a soft laugh even while my eyes burned. "And think of me while you're doing it."

His promise to do so rang in my ears long after he hung up.

30

———

BLAINE

Either Grey ignored my presence, or he had been too wrapped up in his conversation with Lily that he didn't notice me standing in his home office's open doorway.

He'd had her on speakerphone while he tipped back in his chair, hands clasped behind his head—facing the far wall.

And I'd heard every word.

I wanted what both of them did—my damn heart settled on it.

Quietly, I crept back upstairs to my bedroom, bypassing the bathroom I'd occupied up until ten minutes earlier.

I'd gone downstairs wrapped in my towel, needing food —and maybe a bit more.

Grey and I had slept most of the day, but he'd been up and out of the bed before I woke. We ate dinner together, no weirdness occurred between us except for a few heated glances. Unsure how to make a move or if he would even want a repeat of what we'd done earlier that morning, I'd escaped to my bathroom for a long, hot shower.

I hadn't gotten myself off.

Just in case.

Then I'd set my mind on having him, gone looking, only to be blown away by his and Lily's short conversation.

Sprawling on my back atop my mattress, every inch of my naked body lay in unrest. Itchy skin. Shivers and goosebumps.

Would he come to me like Lily told him to do? Love me like she suggested?

My dick strained, and I pulled down on my balls, needing to calm the fuck down.

Like my anchor had become a key, he'd locked up the darkness in a deep cave, one that couldn't touch me when were together.

He'd been right about my thankfulness, my gratefulness for his life.

And Lily had been right too. In my mind, he hung the moon and stars, but they shone down on the precious garden she'd planted inside me.

I loved him—and was well on my way toward those feelings with her too.

I stared at my ceiling, my heart light, excitement for the future ready to whisk me away to another plane. Perhaps Grey's arrival would take me there—

My cell rang, and I grabbed it off my bedside table, grinning at the fact she would want to hear my voice after speaking to Grey.

A number I didn't recognize flashed at me—New Hampshire area code.

Adrenaline shot through me like a carefully aimed bullet, striking me directly in the heart.

All thoughts of Grey, of Lily, fled as my past crashed into me with the force of a tidal wave, jackknifing my heartbeat.

Stop ringing...stop ringing...

My cell went silent, and I sucked oxygen into my lungs I hadn't realized I'd starved, my temples throbbing from my rapid pulse.

"Goddammnit." I rubbed at my chest and gasped as my cell rang again.

Same. Fucking. Number.

I'd gone from the highest peak of a mountaintop to the valley in seconds, and anger over having that feeling ripped away from me roused inside.

Fuck it.

"Hello?" I answered, my tone surprisingly calm considering how my insides quaked.

"Blaine?" A timid voice whispered.

"Who's this?"

"It's Sarah."

Sarah—

A sob rolled over me, choking and debilitating, devastating all other emotions into rubble, and I tensed, every muscle in my body ready to move. Run. Escape. Hold her. Beg for her forgiveness.

"Blaine?"

"Yeah," I gasped, clutching the cell to my ear harshly enough the tiny device should have shattered in my palm. Fearing doing so and ending our call, I forced the phone from my ear, tapped on speaker, and set the device on the bed between my legs. "H-how..." I swallowed hard, tears coursing down my face to drip onto the mattress.

"Your name and this number were on a piece of paper I found in my sweater pocket this morning." She sounded muffled, and I wondered if the compound still only had the community phones scattered throughout the common areas.

Grey and his PI had slipped that note into her pocket.

No fucking doubt.

My chest ached, and I covered my eyes with my hand, trying like fuck to calm myself. "Are you okay?" My voice hardly held tone. "I heard you're pregnant."

"Yes." Her voice broke too, and longing to hold her and wipe her tears away tore through me.

"Do you love Quell?" I choked on the question, desperate for her to deny it.

"Never. No." She swore with vehemence in her tone. "He's a sick man, Blaine. So. Sick."

"I know." I swallowed down bile even though her pregnancy meant she'd experienced his aftercare and supposed love like I had. "It's why I fled," I spilled out, needing her to understand.

"He...did those awful things to you too?"

I knew what she'd experienced...what all the rebellious teenagers did beneath Quell's teachings. "Yeah," I managed to whisper.

"I'm so sorry." More tears laced her voice.

"I should have taken you with me when I left—fuck your young age."

"Dad would have hunted us down to the ends of the earth." Sarah's voice soothed but didn't take away my regret. "I'm glad you escaped, Blaine. Don't ever feel bad for running away. Please."

"You need to get out of there. I'm going to help you."

"I-I can't...don't want to." The hesitation in her voice furrowed my brow.

"What?" I sat upright, catching sight of Grey in my doorway.

Hands fisted at his sides, he stared at me, his eyes full of pain and love. Some of my anxiety eased as my gaze locked on my anchor. As always, his presence brought me peace, and I inhaled a shuddered breath.

"I *am* pregnant with Abraham's child," Sarah said, "but I'm in love with someone else."

"Are you married to Quell?" I asked, remembering how Grey had told me she was seen walking around holding that fucker's hand whenever together with him on the compound's grounds.

"I was forced into marriage after his wife disappeared. Dad made me. Literally threatened Mom's life if I didn't do as told."

Grey muttered a curse, his frown deepening.

"Now, they're both gone, and I'm stuck with that asshole and the two bitches he sewed to my side to keep me in line."

"What do you mean they're gone?"

"Dad and Abraham got into an argument. Mom sided with Dad, surprisingly. They were banished. There for breakfast the next morning and disappeared without a word to me by lunch."

"Where the hell are they?"

"I don't know, Blaine." Sarah's voice broke. "But they took off without me. They left me here with him."

The whereabouts of Mom and Dad would have to wait. "Where are you? How are you calling me without your two shadows?"

"I stole one of their cell phones and took it with me into the bathroom."

"Shit." I scrubbed a hand down over my face, my heart rate jacking back up. "They'll toss you in the box for sure if you get caught."

"Abraham is mad in lust with me." Sarah huffed a snort. "He says I'm carrying the promised child that will rise to conquer sin in this world."

"The fuck?" Grey muttered from my doorway.

I met his gaze, his pale eyes piercing straight through to my heart with yearning. Fuck, I needed his arms around me. My own wrapped around my core, but it wasn't nearly enough. "You said you're in love with someone else?" I asked Sarah, knowing we couldn't draw out the call too long and risk her safety.

"Franklin."

Franklin...Franklin...

"That boy that followed on your heels wherever you went?" I asked, finally remembering the towheaded kid a year younger than my sister.

"I love him, and we're going to find a way to leave this place—regardless of this child Abraham planted inside me without my consent." Her tone suggested she'd straightened her spine and lifted her chin.

Her rebellion would be the death of her if Grey and I didn't make shit happen.

"How far along are you?"

"Just shy of five months, but I look like I'm ready to pop already. I'm so tired. I-I need you," she broke down again, slamming the guilt back into the forefront of my mind and doubling me over. "Please, Blaine, you have to help free us— I have to get Franklin out of here too. We want to run away together, but I'm never alone anymore!"

I sucked in a shaking inhale, forcing myself to keep my tone level. "My friend Grey has already set something in motion, but I need you to hang in there. Be patient. Be strong—and stay away from Franklin until we can make a move, okay?"

"He's the only thing that makes life worth living. I can't imagine...please hurry. I'm so scared."

I offered dozens of assurances I doubted I could fulfill, solidifying one thing in my heart.

Abraham Quell would stand before a jury, and I would face him down and spill every last bit of shit he'd heaped on me as a child in order to land his ass in jail where it belonged.

I forced a promise from Sarah to be careful, to not reach out to me again unless there was an emergency.

Tears rolled down my cheeks through our dozens of I miss yous and love yous. The second I forced myself to hit the end button, I sank into the bed, sobbing, my heart shattered.

Strong arms wrapped around me where I lay curled up in a fetal position, and I turned to press my face into Grey's neck. His clean scent surrounded me, filled my lungs, and I clung to him in desperation.

"Grey." I choked out his name, my eyelids clenched shut, unable to ask him for what my entire body craved.

Him.

My anchor.

He was the only one in that moment who could set me free and stitch my heart back together.

Grey held my face in his hands, wiping my tears with his thumbs even when I couldn't meet his gaze. "Let me help carry the burden, baby."

A warm exhale ghosted over my lips before he pressed his mouth to mine.

Voracious hunger woke, swirling along with my sadness like oil and water while I struggled to swim to the surface of choking emotions.

His tongue stroked along mine in lazy licks, but I wasn't having any of that nice and easy bullshit.

I *needed*, Goddamnit.

Escape.

Mind-numbing release from the anger, remorse, and fear entwining itself in my soul.

I tore my mouth off his and ripped at Grey's T-shirt.

Our eyes locked, the love in his eyes catching my breath. "Save me," I managed to spew while fumbling to rid him of his shorts.

"Always." Grey's rumbled word slid over me like a warm caress, allowing me to breathe easier.

Trust flooded through me, separating the pain from the pleasure.

I allowed him roll me onto my back, and he sank between my spread thighs after ripping off his sweats, his hot, hard body touching mine from chest to toes.

Blue eyes, blown nearly black by swelled pupils, peered into mine, and a shuddered sigh escaped me.

He rubbed his dick over my groin, and my semi thickened.

"Grey..." I thrust my hips up into him.

"I want you," he murmured, lowering so his lips barely brushed over mine. "I have from the first time I saw you."

"I'm yours," I rushed to say in my need to clear up any doubts, any restrictions that had been erected between us.

He took my mouth with a groan, a culmination of years' worth of longing releasing in a torrent of lust.

There wasn't anything I wouldn't give him. He already owned most of my heart, and even though I recognized in that moment a piece of us was absent, I needed him too much to wait for Lily. "Please, Grey."

"What do you need, B? Tell me. Anything—it's yours."

"You...inside me."

"Fuck." Grey stilled, his forehead on mine, and we panted for breath, both of us trembling. "As much as I've dreamed about owning you in that way, B, I-I can't. I'm afraid it'll be too much after…" He trailed off as though reluctant to speak about what had upheaved my life in a matter of minutes.

"I *want* you," I argued even though a part of me feared he might be right.

He rolled us, putting him on his back and leaving me peering down at him. "Lose yourself in me. Take whatever you need from me to forget."

"Grey…"

He shifted his knees higher alongside my chest. "Please."

"Fucking hell." I lifted into a plank and glanced between us at a sight I'd never expected to see. Two dicks leaking pre-cum pressed tightly together—Grey hard because of me. Flutters erupted inside my stomach like butterflies, and I swallowed audibly as arousal jerked my length against his.

But it wasn't damn near enough.

I wanted to lose myself to the quiet intimacy between us, fill my eyes with every inch of him.

Moving back onto my heels offered me a full view of what I'd never seen with such blatant honesty before.

Grey's hairless hole…pink and puckered.

My finger caressed over the sensitive skin before I realized I'd made a conscious decision to touch. Drool pooled on my tongue.

"Yes." He moaned and grabbed the back of his knees, lifting his ass higher—thighs wider.

"God, Grey…I never…" I stared, touching him again with a gentle feather of my fingertips over the softest skin.

"B—please." His hole contracted, breaking me out of whatever trance I'd fallen into.

Desperation returned like a tsunami, sweeping me up in its madness. I scrambled to the bedside table, yanked open the drawer, and grabbed the lube and condoms I kept stashed there in the rare event we fucked a woman in my room.

"No condom."

My head jerked toward Grey, my heartrate jacked and hands shaking.

"I'm finally going to have you balls deep inside my body," he said, holding my stare. "The last thing I want is something between us."

I didn't argue, simply focused on his face and the desire in his beautiful blue eyes.

We never fucked women without condoms, and we both tested regularly. He was also on PrEP seeing as how he enjoyed dick occasionally on the side.

He nodded, our silent communication over the thoughts in my head settling the issue.

I sat on my heels once more, unable to keep from eyeing his tight hole while snapping open the cap of the lube. Never had I imagined readying myself to fuck my best friend—the act hadn't ever crossed my mind.

But faced with his offering of love, of submission to the desire between us, there was nothing I wanted more.

"Fuck, Grey...need you so damn bad. Can't even..." The words dragged from my throat like a ragged whisper, and Grey groaned his agreement.

My teeth gritted as I covered my length, squeezing the base after two slow jacks.

"Touch me, baby."

Even on his back, Grey gave direction.

I slid lubed fingers over his hole, sending a shot of lust twitching through my balls, drawing them tight against my body.

"Mmm," Grey moaned, pushing against my touch. "Put them in me."

"Fuck, Grey," I forced through my clenched jaw and eased the tip of my index inside his ass. Tight heat clamped around my digit, and I cursed a half-dozen times while pressing in further.

"Christ, B."

I cursed again.

"Give me another."

The bossy fucker got what he asked for as I worked a second finger in along with the first. My gaze dragged up over his tight balls, over his hard length, to the drip of pre-cum dangling from his slit to land in the small puddle collecting on his rippled abs.

An image of Lily slurping it up and closing her mouth over his bulbous head kicked up my need to a ridiculous high. I scissored my fingers like I'd seen Grey do to our hookups, readying him to take me because nothing would stop the rushing train we'd climbed aboard.

Grey reached down and jacked himself while I fucked into his tight hole. "Jesus, that feels good, B. Better than I imagined. Curl your fingers up...more...deeper..."

I did as told, and he hissed a curse, hips snapping upward when I hit his intended target.

"Bingo." He groaned, his head tipping back. "Jesus fuck..."

I caressed his prostate a few times, but he tapped my wrist and squeezed the base of his dick. "Shove that cock of yours inside me before I erupt," he begged, breathless and panting.

"You're sure?" I shifted closer, once more eyeing the small hole my dick would never fit inside.

"Never been surer of anything in my life."

I held the tip of my dick to his pucker, smearing my pre-cum into the lube my fingers had left behind. So slick and soft, like a wet kiss—

"Give me your eyes, B."

My focus snapped up to his face, our gazes latching. Energy zapped between us, all the goddamn feels crowding together in my heart.

"Do it," he whispered.

Breath held like I'd reached the peak of a roller coaster's heights, I pressed forward, watching his pupils swell fully.

"Yesss," he hissed and bore down—allowing me to breach his body.

"Oh fucking hell." I strained my head back, my focus torn from his face and teeth gritted as a rush of *fuck yes* whipped through my body.

So. Fucking. Hot.

Tight.

"Grey—fucking...I can't—" I gasped between words, every muscle in my body trembling.

"Take, baby. I'm all yours." He wrapped his heels around my ass and pulled.

"Fuck!" I shoved in, one ball-tingling glorious slide that surged arousal and love through my blood.

Grey's body surrounded my throbbing length, and I held still, head hanging, panting for breath in a plank over him.

I shook my head, unable to explain the insistent craving coursing through me. "Need..."

...emotional grounding.

He grabbed hold of my neck and yanked me down, taking my mouth and setting me free.

31

GREYSON

Holy fucking shit, my love had girth. Was it any wonder women moaned about his dick? I'd seen it dozens of times in action, but to be on the receiving end? Goddamn delicious.

I'd had my fair share of cocks shoved up my backside, but no one stretched me like Blaine. No one filled up every inch inside my hole with such perfection to the point I could almost feel him stabbing into my heart.

Or perhaps that was my thrumming elation from finally having him inside me.

And to taste his mouth as he buried deep...

I had no words to express my happiness, my emotions toward him.

Spine-tingling energy amped my feelings by tenfold, making me desperate for him. More. Deeper. Lodged in my body as integrally as he was in my head and my heart.

He pulled out and thrust back in with a groan, shuddering against me.

I grasped at the muscles along his spine like he'd

enjoyed doing to mine all weekend while Lily lay between us, my legs wrapped around his waist.

His fingers tangled in my hair as he ate at my mouth, allowing me to swallow down his every moan and whimper as he glided into my body over and over again.

"Grey," he gasped against my mouth as I squeezed my ass around his thickness.

"I have you," I promised, lifting my hips to meet him on the next thrust—and the next, encouraging him to let loose.

"Fuck. Fuck. Fuck." He lost himself in me, cursing every time my loosened hole welcomed his rigid length. Face buried in my neck, he stopped holding back his body's chase for orgasm, thrusting into me hard enough I knew I wouldn't sit right for a week.

I hoped I wouldn't.

Lusted for the painful yet pleasurable reminder he'd been in my body to the point I urged him to go harder, faster.

"Grey." He planked on shaking arms, and I jacked my dick, our eyes ensnared in the lust and love radiating in one another's as he pounded into my ass. "Want. You. To. Come." He gasped out with each slam of his hips against the backs of my thighs.

His hair stuck out from my fingers running through the strands, his cheeks pink and lips parted. The black of his pupils had overtaken the golden-green, and although I didn't recognize him fully in that moment, he was my Blaine. My love.

"Fill my ass up, B," I begged, my voice breaking. "I need to feel your cum deep inside me."

"Can't...fuck..."

I clenched my ass around his cock. Once. Twice.

His eyelids fluttered, he gasped— "Grey!"

He shoved in deep, and heat erupted inside me.

My own spunk shot from my throbbing length clear up to my goddamn chin. His name hissed from my lips amidst curses with every rope of white flying up over my chest.

Watching Blaine find his release had always been the sexiest thing I'd seen, but hearing him shout my name while losing himself to passion flooded my heart with the kind of euphoria that buzzed better than any bottle of Jameson. Twitches and shudders and rushed exhales and grunts accompanied every pulse of cum from both of us.

I fucking whimpered toward the end of my climax, tears hazing my vision of him still wrapped up in rapture. Overwhelmed, I grabbed hold of his face, caressing his scruff with my thumbs.

I squeezed around his girth, hoping to draw out his climax, if only to keep him inside me for just a bit longer because I'd never felt so complete.

"Grey," he whispered, one last ripple of release shivering over his skin, leaving goosebumps behind. His arms trembled, fighting to hold his weight off me.

His eyelids fluttered open, and I once more pulled him down to rest on me.

Brushes of lips peppered between our pants for oxygen, sweat and cum smearing over our abs and chests.

I wrapped him fully in my legs and arms, wishing we could stay that way forever.

My heart soared on the high of endorphins, of my dreams coming true. The word love hadn't held meaning until that moment of giving myself to him. No longer were we merely bound by experience and daily living.

We'd become one body, one soul, and there would be no tearing us apart. Ever.

"Love you so damn much, B," I whispered, my throat tight.

He coaxed his face from my neck where he'd been buried, his sated and sleepy eyes making my chest ache. "I love you."

Commence the flowing of tears.

"Shh." He kissed my trembling mouth and licked the salty tracks from my cheeks. "You're everything to me. My stars, my moon."

I grasped his face, recognizing parts of my conversation with Lily. "Everything?" I asked, searching his face, hoping like hell he would be on board with the greediness in my heart.

"Almost."

"Lily." I didn't ask a question, but he nodded in answer.

"Is...that's okay, right? It's what you want? What she wants, right? That's what I overheard you talking about on the phone. Sorry."

My breath left in a rush, and I almost started crying again. Blaine and Lily...we could have a future together. "Yes—and you can listen in on any conversation for the rest of my life, B. I have nothing to hide from you."

His slow smirk and the pink once more rising to his cheeks tempted my blood to rush back to my spent dick crushed between us.

Silence settled, but neither of us moved. We simply stared at one another, enjoying the coming down from our climax, the closeness and warmth of being where one belonged.

Eventually, reality settled back in, and the bliss faded from Blaine's eyes. He gently backed out, leaving my hole sore and gaping.

"Fuck, that's hot." He trailed a fingertip through the

wetness seeping out of my ass, and I hissed in discomfort as he pushed it back in. "Sloppy and relaxed like this." He stroked a few times, a groan deep in his chest every time I twitched from him rubbing over my sensitive prostate. "Almost as sexy as when it's pink, puckered, and desperate for more."

"Christ, B." I gritted my teeth, and he finally stopped with the torture, gently pulling his fingers from my sore-as-hell ass.

"How easily you make me forget the real world." Blaine sat back on his haunches, and I stretched out my legs beside him, not caring that his cum would puddle on the comforter beneath my ass.

I couldn't fucking move, and the ache in my backside... Christ, so good.

His gaze rolled slowly up over my sprawled form, pausing on my mouth briefly before lifting to my eyes. "Shower?"

"You might have to carry me."

A huff of laughter left him, pulling my lips up, but both our mouths flatlined in a matter of seconds.

I'd managed to distract him for a time, but the darkness rose through the pleasure in his eyes. "We need to get Sarah out of there, Grey."

"We're will," I stated firmly, conviction in my heart.

Grim determination glinted in his eyes and lined his lips. I'd seen that stubbornness before—it'd been in his decision to leave with me when I hightailed it for the West Coast and sunshine.

I held out my hand, and he twined his fingers through mine even though we'd already silently agreed. "We're going to see this through to the end."

"Together," he vowed, his tone as firm and unyielding as my mind.

32

LILY

A door squeaked open, waking me from my drunken stupor on the couch. I blinked as light flooded the living room from the kitchen behind me.

Sitting up, I peered over the back of the couch, eyes narrowed against the bright overheads. My buzz kept me from focusing for a few seconds.

Haley dropped her bag onto the table, tossing her keys to land beside them.

"How was your date?" I asked even though her scowl stated it hadn't been good.

"Another asshole narcissist. It's like I'm a goddamn magnet for the fuckers!" She grabbed a bottle of wine from the fridge and uncorked it while I considered her sour mood.

Haley seriously couldn't catch a break. Every time she finally gave into the need to find a real date rather than mere hookup, shitheads came out of the woodwork.

She shuffled into the living area of our open-concept apartment, her hold on the bottle's neck letting me know we were in for one hell of a night.

"Come here." I sat and held out an arm, and she sank against my side.

She smelled like lavender, soothing when she tended toward prickliness.

Bottle tipped upward, she guzzled, and I closed my eyes again.

At least the spins had left, so I would be able to focus on her.

"It started off perfect," she began. "He asked about me, got me talking—and you know I don't open up easily—then after his third or fourth shot, he turned everything we discussed back toward him. How successful he was, how he had no issues getting hookups... Fuck." Haley guzzled again, and I ran my fingers through the straightened strands of her hair falling over her shoulder.

"And don't get me *started* on his sense of entitlement."

"That bad, huh?" I asked, wishing that just once Haley would find a guy whose personality didn't take her back to the abusive childhood she'd endured beneath her psycho mother's care.

"He got pissed when I wouldn't fuck him. Just because I agreed to dinner, he felt that I had to put out. Like paying the bill made it his right to what's between my thighs."

My forehead dented in a deep scowl. "Did he? Touch you without your consent, I mean?"

"The fucker tried. I kneed him in the balls and called an Uber."

"Go you." We knuckle bumped.

Haley sank against me, letting out a heavy sigh. "I don't even know why I bother anymore."

"There are good men out there," I stated quietly, thinking about Grey and Blaine. A swipe over my cell screen showed it'd been two hours since I'd talked to Grey. Had he done what I'd told him to? Were they still in a fuck-fest for the ages?

I shifted against Haley, aroused by the thought and fearful at the same time regardless of Grey's assurance he wanted me in his life.

"What's up?"

"Nothing," I muttered. "Talk to me about *you*."

Haley pulled away, eyeing me while going in for another swig of wine. Her gaze narrowed as the bottle once more rested on her lap. "You're like an open book, Lily. Don't bull-shit me."

A pitbull, I knew she wouldn't let my mood go until I relented and spilled my guts.

"Fine," I huffed. "I did what we decided I should do and all but told Grey to fuck Blaine so I could get my broken heart over with already. Now I'm wishing I hadn't. Kind of. I think."

"Shit." It was Haley's turn to pull me into her side, and I snuggled in tight.

"I'm a selfish bitch—tell me more about your date," I begged, needing to take my mind off Grey's bed. "Please."

"It's in my past, and I have zero more fucks to give about it." Her firm tone stated truth, but I heard the hurt lingering in the back of her words.

"I didn't mean to move the conversation toward me," I muttered, hating myself in that moment because it's something her mom would have done.

Make everything about her, causing Haley to feel as though she didn't matter.

"You're the furthest thing from a narcissist, Lily," Haley argued. "You're empathetic, kind, and sweet—all the things my mom wasn't. *Isn't*." Another long pull on the bottle tipped her head back.

I knew she hadn't spoken to her mom for years, but childhood trauma like she'd endured didn't fade easily even with talking to a therapist once a week.

"You're going to end up dead drunk on the floor," I warned her.

"Good," she snipped. "I'm in the mood."

Silence settled over us for a little while as she continued to drink, the clock's ticking in the kitchen behind us loud in the stillness. A horn honked outside from our narrow street, and another car rolled by with deep bass thumping hard enough a few trinkets on Haley's bookshelf rattled.

My cell dinged, sending a shot of adrenaline through me.

"Is it Grey?" Haley asked as I sat up quickly, reaching for my phone on the cushion beside me.

"Yeah." My grin flashed automatically—then my excitement hit a wall, my lips flatlining as my chest squeezed. "I'm scared to read it," I whispered.

"Oh, for fuck's sake, Lily." I could hear her eye roll.

"Fine." I huffed, held my breath, and tapped on his message.

A pic of Blaine sleeping—drooling on Grey's chest—filled my screen. Grey must have taken it while holding this phone above his head because I could make out his other arm holding Blaine tight against his side and the navy of his silk sheets covering them from the waist down.

My throat thickened, and I couldn't decide if it was from happiness or sadness.

Shouldn't have drunk all that damn wine.

"He wouldn't have sent that to you if he wasn't wishing you were there," Haley murmured, leaning close to check out the image. "If they had gotten it on and Grey decided he wanted Blaine all to himself for the rest of his life, he'd ghost you just like all the other assholes who lose interest after a weekend of free pussy and ass."

I squeezed above her knee at the jaded tone, and another message popped up.

Grey: **His sister called right after I got off the phone with you…long story. Missed you tonight while I helped distract him. Major walls came down between us, but you were never far from our thoughts. When can we see you again?**

"Oh God." I swallowed against a torrent of tears that wanted to pour down my face, my insides going all gooey. I damn near swooned at the relief that flooded through me.

Haley let out a sigh at the same time I did. "I'm so jelly right now, I can't even."

"Hal…"

"It's okay, really," my cousin murmured. "I'm happy for you. Truly." Wetness coated her dark eyes, making them appear like melting chocolate.

My heart yearned to head over to Grey's immediately, but between my still-buzzed brain and Haley's depression I could feel ramping up from a mile away, I wasn't about to leave her alone.

I texted Grey a smiley face to let him know my lips curved upward, a hearts-for-eyes emoji since I was falling hard and fast, and a promise for the following weekend. Usually, I had trouble seeing through my promises, but nothing would keep me from my boys come Friday night.

When Haley spiraled, I feared her falling in deep enough she would end up in a psych ward like her mom even though my cousin had always been more focused and mentally healthy like her father.

Tucking my phone away, I pulled my closest friend back

against my side and continued to play with her hair even though my thoughts and heart wished to be far away.

Haley had never gotten physical attention as a child, the kind of touch that offered affirmation and appreciation. Her dad had been a chickenshit, bowing to his tyrant wife's every whim and mood.

Haley had been left alone in her own emotions with no one to guide her.

Every time I squeezed her or petted her like a cat, she went all limp. *Soaking that shit up*, she'd say, oftentimes laughing because she owned how starved she was for affection.

"What's going to happen when they ask you to move in?" she asked, her tone resigned and quiet.

I opened my mouth to assure her I wasn't even thinking that far ahead, but she cut me off.

"It's going to be in the next couple of weeks. I can feel it. And you'd be crazy to say no. From all you've told me, from the texts from both men, they're so far gone on you, you could wrap them both up around your pinkies."

"It's too soon."

"Is it?" She slurred and snuggled in closer, the near-empty bottle tipping almost sideways across the couch.

I took it from her light grasp and set it on the end table.

"Life is fucking short," she muttered, well on her way toward that drunken stupor she'd been chasing. "Grab it by the balls, Lily. Ride that damn roller coaster with your arms held high, screaming at the top of your lungs. Nothing holding you back. Speed forward and enjoy every second."

"I'm not leaving you alone."

"I'll be fine. There are always people looking for rooms to rent."

"Why the hell are we even talking about this?" I groaned,

tipping my head back against the couch. "I've fucked them all of twice—"

"Thought it was three in thirty-six hours and once before that?"

"—way too fast for that option to be set on the table."

"It will be. I'd bet money on it." Haley sounded so damn sure of herself that a selfish flutter of hope spun through my veins.

33

BLAINE

By the time Wednesday rolled around, I'd been jacked and sucked off so many damn times I'd lost count, and not once did darkness stir vomit up my throat.

It was like the floodgates of Grey's love had been bashed open, and he poured physical expression of his feelings all the fuck over me.

Left my dick chafed.

Satisfied as fuck in ways I'd never expected to enjoy.

But my heart continued to ache.

Lily had put us off until the weekend because her cousin was having a bout of depression, and I couldn't stop worrying over my sister.

Higgins, Grey's PI, continued to monitor the compound with stealthy as fuck drones, letting me know Sarah was alive and well. No appearances of bruising, no limping while walking around holding Quell's hand in her usual display of servitude made me believe our phone call and the "borrowed" cell phone had gone unnoticed.

I couldn't begin to imagine her fear. The anxiety she

dealt with every day couldn't be healthy for the child swelling her belly.

Higgins had sent pictures, and I'd cried over every damn one.

Petite like Mom and just as beautiful, Sarah deserved to be held and coddled by the man she loved rather than forced into sexual slavery to an asshole who ought to be buried six feet under—alive.

Preferably in a box full of spiders, snakes, and scorpions.

By Thursday, we learned the couple Higgins had met with agreed to testify about the abuse they'd endured while indoctrinated and living on the compound. He'd gathered his evidence over the week and had gotten in touch with a buddy of his in the FBI.

It turned out Quell was already being watched, but Higgins hadn't been able to gather any further information. He handed over what he'd compiled, much to his friend's excitement.

The process of ruining Quell's so-called utopia had begun, and I dove into work with vigor to keep my brain and body occupied.

I dug posts in the hot California sun for a new fence at Sunrise Condos, Wyatt laboring alongside me. He'd spent the week at the new jobsite, helping me settle into my new role while interviewing for a couple guys for me to boss around.

I'd never opened up to him, never shared the shit of my past or why I'd left the mountains of the east for California, but after two days of him seeing me bow beneath my anxiety I didn't do a good enough job of hiding, I fucking caved.

Over lunch on Wednesday, I spewed everything but the sexual assault only Grey knew about.

The compound, the cult my parents allowed to brain-wash me and my sister—all that shit and more. My escape with Grey, the guilt over leaving Sarah behind. The physical abuse given in the name of following God's will, Sarah's pregnancy, the case we'd built to take Quell down...

He'd listened without interruption, without a hint of pity on his face.

A simple clasp to my shoulder, a *that fucking sucks,* and a promise to help out in whatever he could...yeah. Wyatt offered me the support I'd needed and trusted me with his family business.

I couldn't ask for a better boss.

And once I'd started talking? I couldn't stop.

I told him about Lily.

And Grey.

He'd smirked at the last bit while my chin had raised, waiting for some homophobic bullshit to spout from his mouth. "You're one lucky fucker."

My jaw dropped, but I didn't know how to push him to open up and share like I'd done. I let him have his few words and left it at that.

"I could use some iced coffee."

I glanced at Wyatt to find him wiping his forearm across his sweaty brow.

"Is coffee girl over at Carla's Cafe today?" he asked.

"Yeah, she works every Thursday morning."

"Why don't you make a muffin and coffee run. Ask her out on a date."

"She's spending the weekend with us," I said, brushing my hands together to rid them of dirt.

"So. Doesn't mean you can't wine and dine her on your own, right?" Wyatt peered at me, his dark blue eyes curious.

"Or are there rules in place for your...threesome thing you've got going on?"

"No rules." I shrugged. At least, we hadn't discussed any. Hell, we hadn't even talked about *being* a threesome outside the amazing sex we'd had the weekend before.

"Think your buddy would mind if you had Lily all to yourself one night?"

I didn't even have to consider my answer. "No."

"Would you be jealous if he took her out and left you at home alone?"

"No." I knew Grey's love for me was an unbreakable bond. "I trust him. Fully."

"It's a rare thing to find that with another person." Wyatt pulled a twenty from his pocket and handed it over, his brow furrowed. "For break."

I nodded and took the bill, trying to read his face he kept pretty closed off. I wondered if he was bi—and envious of the potential me and my two lovers had to create something special.

"Go ask your woman out and bring me back an iced black coffee and one of those blueberry muffins you were going on about the other week." He picked back up the post hole digger and went to work, effectively keeping my questions in my head. "And it's okay if you take your time."

After a quick brush of dirt off my pants and shirt, I climbed into the business truck and headed across town. Working in the sun all morning had resulted in my not smelling the best, but considering how sticky and sweaty the three of us had been in Grey's bed, I didn't think Lily would mind all that much.

The cafe sat quiet, only a couple of the tables occupied with couples chatting and two people staring at their laptops.

Cheryl stood behind the counter, grinning as I walked into the air-conditioned building. The cool air slid over my sweat, creating a groan in my chest. "Hey there, Mr. Yummy."

Heat flooded my face.

With how silly and talkative Lily got sometimes, I feared what all she had told her manager. At least she'd shared that nickname for me rather than the other one.

"Lily around?" I croaked out, not as confident as I'd been a few seconds earlier.

"She's on break." Cheryl glanced down over my filthy clothes. "It looks like you've been hard at work."

I cast a quick glance over my attire, grimacing over the dirt caking my boots. "Yeah...sorry if I make a mess of your cafe."

"Don't worry about it. What can I get for you?"

I gave her my order, and she handed it over to the barista. "I'll let Lily know you're here."

She disappeared into the side room, and seconds later, my coffee girl came rushing out, eyes sparkling and cheeks the prettiest shade of pink, her ponytail swinging behind her.

Warmth once more flushed my face.

"What are you doing here?" she asked, rushing around the counter to throw herself into my arms.

I caught her with an *oomph*, quickly pushing her to arm's length even though she smelled sweet and delicious.

She pouted.

"I'm filthy," I muttered an explanation.

A slow smirk lifted her lips, and she lowered her eyelashes even while keeping her head tipped back to see me.

That heat in my face rushed southward. "I'm here

because Wyatt wanted coffee," I finally answered, "and I missed you."

"I missed you too," she said with a quiet sigh, threading her fingers through mine. "It feels like it's been *forever*!"

"Blaine," the barista called out my name, and I retrieved my order, able to grab the carry tray with one hand since Lily clasped my other tight to hers. Damn butterflies tickled my insides at the thought she clung to me—didn't want to let me go—uncaring it was in front of her coworkers.

Complete acceptance of me regardless of my messy state and sweat stink.

"How long do you have until break is over?" I asked as she tugged me toward the exit as though anxious to get me alone.

"About five more minutes. Enough time to climb in that truck and kiss you senseless."

I chuckled and stumbled after her in her haste.

"Holy hell, it's hot out here," she grumbled as the sun hit the tops of our heads.

The second we climbed into the parked truck, I turned the AC on full blast.

Lily angled to face me in the passenger seat, scowling at the console and its pile of miscellaneous shit atop it. "Hmph."

I held the coffees up near my left shoulder, safe out of harm's way in case she came scrambling over like she appeared ready to do.

"Dash." She pointed, and I did as told, setting the holding tray down.

A quick shuffle, and she *did* land on my lap facing me. Her bright smile lit my insides and woke my tired dick. "Hey." She wound her hands around my neck, pressing her chest against mine.

"Hey back—I'm filthy."

"And I don't give a shit," she snipped.

Well, in that case...

I gripped her ass, tugging her closer so her core pressed against my groin.

"Mmm." She licked over my lips, a mere tease, pulling back when I leaned in for more. "So, you and Grey, huh?"

Heat rushed through me, without doubt turning my face red, but I held her gaze and nodded.

He'd told her.

I'd let her know by text too the next morning.

I just hadn't discussed anything in detail over the phone with her.

"Things are...okay?" Hesitancy replaced the happiness in her eyes.

The sudden need to soothe her anxiety had my arms wrapping around her and hugging her tight. I breathed in the scent of vanilla and coffee beans. "Better than okay, but having to wait for you to join us is killing me."

"Grey's not enough, huh?" she murmured against my damp neck and took a quick taste with her tongue. "Mmm. Salty."

Chuckling, I set her back a bit and cocked my head, studying her. Lily usually wasn't so...indirect. "Are you fishing?"

She shrugged, but none of her usually silliness twinkled her eyes. "Maybe?"

"He loves me. I love him," I stated what she already knew, "and we're both falling for you. Like you two discussed over the phone Sunday night, we're all a bunch of greedy lovers. Being with him is...fuck, it's magic, but there's always something missing. That's you, Lily."

I cradled her face in my hands, hating that wetness

welled in her eyes, the insecurity that still hounded her even though both Grey and I assured her we wanted her in our lives.

"I'm not Levi. He's not Zeke."

She nodded, a tear sliding down her cheek.

I kissed it away, and she allowed me the gift of her soft lips. So damn sweet, she opened to me, sagging against my chest.

My dick went from chub to achingly hard within seconds. "Fuck, I want to eat you alive."

"Haley is doing better, so..." she murmured over my mouth, her hint so damn obvious butterflies swirled in my stomach again.

I once more shifted her face away from mine so I could see her eyes. Dry and darkened by lust. Fuck, was our Lily beautiful. "Can I take you to dinner tonight?"

"Mmmhmm," she hummed her agreement, her focus on my mouth as I tucked wayward golden strands of hair behind her ear.

"I can get you caught up on the whole case."

"Shit." She blinked and sat back, her gaze flitting from one of my eyes to the other. "I forgot about your sister."

"It's okay."

"The fuck it is! I'm such a self-centered bitch caught up in hoping Haley will get out of her slump so I can move on with my life. How is your sister? Have you talked to her since Sunday?"

"You're hardly self-centered. Just horny for my thick and juicy cock."

She stared for a second, then laughed, the tension over being pissed at herself easing. "Blaine, fucking around with Grey has totally corrupted your mouth. You aren't even blushing."

I pressed my lips to hers, making a noise of appreciation in my chest. "Falling in love has brought out my naughty side."

She pulled away from my grasping hands and studied me, her gaze intense. "Should I read into that statement?"

She fished again, but rather than answering, I shrugged and fought to hold her stare since I wasn't sure either of us were ready for those words.

Too soon...right?

Lily let out a sigh and ran her fingertips over my lips while snuggling her pert breasts against my chest. "So. Dinner."

"Tonight?" I suggested, running my hands down her back to cup her ass cheeks resting on my thighs.

"I'd love to. And afterward?"

"I could take you home to check on my roommate. I expect he might be a little lonely. Perhaps sulky. You could kiss him and make it all better."

"Or—" Her eyes lit again with that sunshine I adored "—you could kiss it to make it all better while I watched."

My dick swelled, and I shifted beneath her with a low groan.

"Is our boy an exhibitionist at heart?" she asked with a smirk, giving me a flirty look through her eye lashes.

Our boy...

Fuck, did I want that to be true.

"Anything for you, Lily," I told her with a ragged tone, serious as hell.

"Anything, huh?"

The glint in her gaze made me pause. "Um...*almost* anything?"

She smiled and pressed her lips chastely against mine.

"Everyone has limits, Blaine, and that's okay. If I do ever push too hard, no means no. I'll listen. Always."

I love you.

I bit the words back, sure it was too damn early to voice them, so I kissed her instead, hoping she could feel the emotions I did, the trust I was willing to offer her along with my heart.

34

GREYSON

I wasn't jealous Blaine took Lily out to dinner, but that didn't stop me from behaving like a creep and stalking after my two lovers. Luckily, the hostess led them to a table near a window at the small bistro they'd gone to, so I was able to keep watch on them from where I sat in my car along the street.

My dick grew half-hard from just looking at the two of them. I stared at how their mouths moved while talking, how they leaned toward one another over the table as though drawn like magnets to the other's energy.

I knew he planned to share with her all we'd learned about the compound and Sarah, but even from the distance between them and me, I could tell that a lot of Blaine's anxiety over the entire situation had eased.

For the moment, anyway.

Lily had given him that. She'd brought sunshine when I'd offered emotional support, but we were both excellent distractions to help him ignore the darkness that had been eating at his insides since childhood. She and I made a good team, I knew, complementing each other in our love for Blaine.

I wondered over the full extent of her emotions toward him.

Toward me.

Yeah, she claimed to be greedy, but at twenty-four and sowing her wild oats due to her upbringing, was she ready to settle down? Would she give up the freedom to fuck around and commit to the two of us?

Or would she eventually grow bored?

My love for Blaine had been unwavering since almost day one.

I wanted her to feel the same for him.

For me.

Yearning engulfed my heart, tugging like a riptide, attempting to drag me under and drown me in who they were. My lovers, my goddamn everything.

"Please let it stay that way," I murmured to the still interior of my car since I couldn't imagine living without the woman who filled me up when my well ran dry.

Releasing a slow exhale, I forced myself to leave. Driving through the darkness, windows down and wind whipping at my unbound hair, I imagined a future with both Blaine and Lily. I saw us snuggling on the couch together in a tangle of limbs. I envisioned a sleeping Lily wrapped around Blaine's front while I big-spooned his back.

I wanted them together with me always. Felt that yearning deep inside me, same as the summer I'd lost my mom and had first laid eyes on Blaine.

The TV and couch didn't call my name when I got home. I bypassed my usual haunt for crashing after a long day and made for my bedroom.

I left the door open, stripped off my T-shirt, and traded

my jeans for comfy cotton sleep pants. Alexa turned on some quiet background music at my request, and I laid in bed, hands behind my head, my heart...resting.

No anxiety over their date, no excitement that they might come back to our place, no worry. Even the whole cult and Quell affair sat peaceful in my head. I trusted Higgins, and I trusted the FBI to make things right.

It was like peace settled in my heart, and I decided I would be good with whatever the future held. If I had two lovers for a short time, I would enjoy the fuck out of our moments together. If it ended up being a long-term investment on all three of our parts, I would die a happy man.

Another hour of near-silence passed while my eyelids remained closed.

The front door's lock sounded, alerting me to the fact I was no longer alone.

Energy lapped at my skin like the ocean on shore, a rejuvenation of wakefulness. My senses came alert, my ears easily picking up the murmur of voices...

Plural.

Blaine had brought our girl home.

My pulse picked up pace, my muscles tightening in readiness...

But would they seek me out or climb the stairs for a bit of privacy? We hadn't discussed parameters, hadn't talked about any boundaries we might have in going forward.

Not that I had a damn one when it came to either of them—as long as no outside party got involved.

Feet tread across the living area, headed my way.

A slow smirk lifted my lips, but I kept my eyes closed, focusing on the adrenaline in my blood rushing to my groin.

I could feel eyes on me, soaking up the near-naked image of me on the bed.

"I want to watch." Lily's husky whisper jolted lust through my balls, stiffening me fully.

"Fuck," I groaned the word, my hips lifting the slightest bit.

"That would be a yes," Blaine explained a word and sound he'd heard often enough from my mouth to decipher its meaning.

"Mmm." Lily's hum of approval finally had me peeking through my eyelashes.

She wore a cute skirt that fell to mid-thigh, every step she took toward my chair swishing the material around her tanned legs. Red heels.

"Fuck me," I muttered with a groan as my dick jerked inside my pants.

"Is that what you're hoping for?" Blaine asked, the lust in his voice enough to rip my focus off Lily.

"Whatever our girl says," I told him, holding his gaze.

"Yes, please."

Blaine and I both turned our attention toward Lily where she sat, facing our way. Too fucking far away—like she intentionally put distance between us.

My brow furrowed, but the reasons of why she'd placed herself there flitted through my brain.

Levi.

It was on the tip of my tongue to demand she set her pretty little ass on my face for me feast on, but perhaps she needed to watch us for her own peace of mind. "Are you sure?" I asked instead.

"Lily..." Blaine murmured at almost the same time as though he too worried over shit from her past that might ruin what we'd just begun.

She nodded. "Please." Her big brown eyes luminous in the dimmed overheads revealed arousal in the widened pupils. A flick of her tongue over her lower lip, and I knew whatever panties she wore creamed at the idea of Blaine giving me his dick.

Perhaps there was a different reason she'd put space between us after all.

"If it's too much, just say stop and we will, okay?" I stated just in case.

"And feel free to jump in whenever you're ready," Blaine added while pulling his shirt off overhead.

"M'kay."

"How should I take him, Lily?" I asked, shoving off my pants. "On my knees? Back?"

"I want..." She swallowed hard as though gathering her courage to speak what went through her brain. "I want you to fuck face-to-face. See you together, kissing. Lost in the lust between the two of you."

"Fuck," Blaine groaned, but I bit mine back.

She did fear seeing the connection between Blaine and I, needed an answer to the question in her head thanks to her ex.

Fuck, if she could read our minds...

I rolled for my bedside table to grab lube while Blaine finished stripping.

She wanted a show, she'd get one—but it wouldn't be the heartbreaking type I felt sure she expected.

Gaze on my face, Blaine crawled onto the foot of my bed, not stopping until he lay atop me. Lily must have gotten him worked up over their dinner, because his dick was hard as hell pressing against mine.

A gentle smile curved his lips, and I cupped his scruffy cheek.

Fuck the lovemaking, B. Let's give our girl a good memory, something she'll never forget.

He grinned—and dove for my mouth with voracious hunger.

Tongues tangled and teeth nipped as passion ignited between us regardless or perhaps intensified by the warmth singeing us from Lily's gaze.

The two of us had been tangled up countless times since she'd left us, but he roused my body to life with flaring passion I would never be too tired to ignore. I clung to Blaine with all four of my limbs even while wanting to push him away and beg him to sheath up and claim my ass already.

We frotted together in a slickening, sticky mess, eating each other's moans.

"Oh God." Lily let out a whimper, and knowing the sight of us turned her on rather than off ramped up the need swelling over me like a wave.

She'd wanted a show, but I was already near the edge. "B."

He backed off and grabbed the lube but glanced at Lily. "Okay?"

"Oh yeah." Pupils blown, she stared at Blaine between my splayed thighs.

I grabbed the backs of my knees and pulled them higher, opening myself up.

A squeak left her, and she shifted on the chair.

"Take off your clothes," I told her, needing her to participate even if she'd put that fucking distance between us. "Touch your wet pussy while you're watching our boy own my ass."

Heat flushed her face, and she hopped up to do as told, going for her heels first.

"Leave them."

She blinked at me before a sexy-as-fuck smirk curled her lips upward. "Bossy."

"You love it."

The snap of the lube cap sounded, but I watched Lily put on a tiny striptease for me, every inch of delicious skin she revealed making pre-cum ooze from my slit to drip onto my abs.

"Fuck yeah," I muttered when she revealed red lacy panties. "Fucking gorgeous—but take them off. Put your bare ass on my chair. I want to see your arousal smeared all over the leather."

"Shit." Blaine fumbled with the lube, and I turned a grin toward him.

"Don't empty those balls until you're deep inside my ass."

"Fuck, you can't...not while I'm..." He stroked lube over his length, his lips parting, his face a luscious pink.

I spread my thighs wider, still grinning like an idiot and dripping pre-cum. "Stretch me out good, B, then let's give our girl what she wants."

35

LILY

Filthy, filthy mouth.

Grey made me wet, and considering Blaine's invitation to go home with him had already dampened my panties to an uncomfortable level, that mess Grey wanted on his chair happened.

Before Blaine even got his dick inside Grey's ass.

But the working of Blaine's thick, calloused fingers to stretch Grey...I bit my lip to keep from matching the groans leaving Grey's mouth.

I clutched at the chair's arms in my determination to not touch where I throbbed until Blaine sank into heaven.

"Right there." Grey's head tipped back, tendons in his neck straining. "Fuck yeah. So good."

Blaine watched him, leaning forward on one hand by his shoulder, the other stroking between Grey's legs. I didn't have the best view in the house. That would be right there beside Blaine, up close and personal with lubed fingers sinking into Grey's hole.

But I held my seat for a reason.

Even though my body ached to join them, I wanted to

see the two of them together in action, far enough away that I could take them in as a whole. I needed to observe their eye contact, witness how they loved each other without me close enough to distract them—or if I would even *be* a distraction.

Seeing Levi and Zeke together in the same way had let me know where I stood in that relationship, and before the night's end, I expected my fears to either be recognized or set to rest. Nervousness kept my stomach in knots even though both men had tried to assure me I belonged with them. Having them lose their minds to passion would reveal the truth.

I prayed fate allowed me my happily ever after, that I'd found my two lovers for real.

"I'm ready," Grey said on a gasp, and Blaine shifted his hips.

Their gazes remained locked.

I held my breath at the intense energy radiating off them —between them—like erotic, pulsing waves that simmered my blood and pulsed my core.

Grey's jaw clenched, his teeth locked. A slow hiss leaked between his lips, and my pussy spasmed at the image in my mind of Blaine slowly sinking into his body.

Fuck—I wanted a better view.

I was desperate to slide my fingers down over my labia, finding the wetness I knew smeared over my slit, but didn't twitch a muscle, couldn't do a damn thing to interrupt the moment.

Blaine groaned, his head hanging low as he slowly pushed forward until stopping. He fully filled Grey's ass, I realized, bonding the two of them in a way I would never be part of.

I'd expected heartache, but flutters inside my belly and

chest kept my gaze focused, sharp and ready to read every emotion I could pick up from both of them.

"Okay?" Blaine murmured, his voice strained.

"Fuck me, baby."

Blaine began to rock in and out of him.

So. Damn. Sexy.

I soaked the sight up, my focus flitting from one face to another, from Blaine's flexing ass cheeks to the thundering pulse in Grey's neck as he clung to Blaine's body planked over him.

Their eyes remained locked together, their love for one another thick in the air, as known to my heart as the sounds of wet fucking and balls smacking flesh in my ears.

My boys were beautiful...but *were* they mine?

They moved together like they'd escaped into a world of their own, cut off from reality, from everyone but each other.

Grip still tight on the chair's arms, I swallowed hard, every passing second making me believe I didn't stand a chance to be a part of the beauty they created, the connection they experienced.

Heaviness descended over my shoulders, my heart, but I lifted my chin, refusing to let tears ruin the sight in front of me.

I wondered over their silent communication, if their minds were as lost to the other as their bodies were. What they thought, how they felt being so deeply connected.

Had they forgotten I existed, that a woman watched them? Because their movements transcended mere fucking. Cliche, but Blaine and Grey were poetry in motion. Sweat-glistened tanned skin, rippling muscle, and guttural noises that kept my pussy juices flowing regardless of my tumbling emotions.

They don't need me...

I bit my tongue to keep from sobbing, and without a shared word, they both turned their heads my way like they'd heard the words drifting through my head. Their faces filled with lust, eyes burning with intent.

Blaine shifted back on his haunches, grabbing hold of Grey's thighs as though they'd agreed upon the action before he'd taken it.

"Sit on my face," Gray demanded, his voice a low rasp.

Holyfuckingshitandallthingsholy...

I gulped, and he crooked a finger at me even as Blaine continued to thrust into his body.

Grey wanted me.

Blaine had made room for me.

They'd reached a conclusion without a vocalized agreement between them, as though they were of one mind.

Wetness hazed my vision as my chest squeezed. Biting harder on my tongue, I stumbled toward the bed on shaking, desperate legs, damn the heels Grey had wanted me to keep on. I climbed over the mattress toward him, the scent of musk and sweat flooding my nose.

"Come here, little minx." Grey grabbed hold of my waist and easily settled me right where he wanted me. Facing Blaine, my sopping pussy against his hungry mouth.

There were no tender kisses to my clit, no long, lingering licks up my slit like the ones that had driven me mad the weekend before.

Grey shoved his face against my core, tongue and lips devouring the arousal the two of them had brought to life between my thighs.

My heart soared, and my breath caught as my gaze land on Blaine. Black ate at the golden-green of his eyes that seemed to pierce deep inside me. Lips parted, he continued to thrust into Grey, his slack, panting mouth mere feet from mine.

"Lily," he groaned, and we leaned toward one another as though magnetized. "Need you."

I grabbed hold of his neck and pulled him closer, and we ate at each other's mouths as hungrily as Grey did my pussy. Whimpers rolled from me, both men's moans and gasps the most gorgeous symphony I'd ever heard.

No way in hell was I going to last.

"Gonna come," I panted against Blaine's lips—and did so with a shriek, grinding my core all over Grey's face.

He made appreciative noises, slurping and sucking as I trembled and spasmed while I suspended over his body. I panted against Blaine's mouth, my hands grasping at his head to keep my balance, Grey's wide hands spanning my waist holding me steady.

"Beautiful," Blaine murmured, licking over my lips without losing rhythm with his hips.

Halfway down from my high, I eased back and caught Blaine's eyes with mine again.

"Suck him?" He rasped out the request, shifting back on his heels enough that Grey no longer bent damn near in half.

Grey's tongue flicked over my clit, and I shied away. He held me firmly in place, returning to my tightened hole.

His dick strained, pre-cum smeared up over his contracting abs.

My mouth watered, and I grabbed his base, lifting him toward me, pre-cum sliding down to my fingertips.

A flick of my tongue and Blaine thrust hard, jacking Grey's length clear through to my throat.

I gagged, never more turned on in my life, and Grey groaned. His fingertips dug into my ass cheeks. "Fucking *hell.* Shit, I'm gonna blow." The lust in his tone caused my pussy to pulse again.

"Not yet." Blaine spoke as though through clenched teeth while I worked my tongue and lips over Grey's hardness, desperate for his cum on my tongue. "I want to watch her suck you while I fuck your tight ass."

Fuck, fuck, fuck...

Could they be any hotter?

My arousal vamped back up to full-on *shovesomethingupmypussyrightthefucknow*, every lathe of Grey's tongue over my slit and asshole bringing another climax to tingling in my spine. I'd never given such a sloppy blow job, but with Blaine's groin right in front of my face, the sight of his slickened dick stretching Grey's hole with every thrust...

Best seat in the damn house.

Drool and pre-cum leaked around my mouth, soaking Grey's base and trimmed pubes. Wetness smeared at the corners of my eyes every time I gagged due to Blaine's deep thrusts.

Moans, curses, slurps, and grunts filled the air along with the musky scent of sex, and Grey's mouth brought me back to the edge again.

I decided in that moment I *did* believe in heaven—on earth, one of our own making.

"Gonna come," Grey gasped against my clit—the same thought I had.

Spunk shot into my throat, and I swallowed quickly, whining over the tingles racing to my pussy. My climax hit me a heartbeat later, and I struggled to keep my mouth around Grey while he continued to ejaculate bitterness onto my tongue.

"Oh fuck. You're pulsing around my dick." Blaine

panted, thrusting harder, gagging me over and over while I trembled from my release.

Absolutely. Fucking. Delicious.

"Grey." Blaine groaned his name and buried deep, stilling. His abs rippled, and I licked every trace of cum from Grey while his friend unloaded in his ass in short thrusts, his deep moan of release in my ears.

"Fuck, yes." Grey ran his hands over my backside in absent caresses. Murmured praises for his good little girl and boy swelled through my heart.

I'd gotten the answer I'd asked for.

Had barely hoped for.

I'd found the two lovers I'd been seeking.

36

BLAINE

My cell rang, but I ignored it for the warm, vanilla-scented woman I cradled in my arms. A grin lit on my face as I took stock of the fact it was early morning and I lay in bed with my two favorite people.

Grey at my back, his groin tucked tight against my ass, and Lily snuggled into my chest.

She huffed with annoyance. "Who the fuck is calling before the sun is up?" she grumbled, her breath hot on my neck.

I rubbed a hand down over her spine to cup one of her ass cheeks. "Don't care," I muttered back.

The ringing stopped, and I sighed, sinking into warmth and comfort.

The damn cell started back up again.

"Better answer," Grey stated quietly against my hair.

I opened my eyes as reality settled in, dissolving the cocoon of Elysium we'd found in each other's arms. No one would be reaching out to me in the pre-dawn hours, not even Wyatt my boss.

"Shit." I shifted and half-rolled over Lily to reach my cell on the bedside table.

The New Hampshire number glowing like neon in Grey's dimmed room jacked my heart rate to top speed.

"Hello?" I asked, adrenaline rushing straight to my heart.

"B-Blaine?" My sister broke into sobs, and my gut clenched up tight.

"Sarah! What happened? Are you okay?"

She cried in my ear as I hopped off the bed, my mind racing over what could have prompted the call and her harsh tears.

Grey's lamp clicked to life behind me, and I turned, needing his eyes to keep me anchored.

Pale blue, sleepy and yet alert, his orbs captured mine, releasing some of the tightening of my chest.

"Sarah?" I asked again.

Lily scooted close to the bed's edge and reached for me.

I gave her my hand, clinging tight to the comfort her soft touch offered. My sister sniffled in my ear, but I could breathe easier. "Tell me you're alright. Please. What's going on?"

"H-He hurt me. Bad." Her whispers barely made it through the line.

"Where are you?" I barked the question as the darkness deep inside me began to rise like oozing sewage.

Grey hopped off the bed, moving quickly toward me.

"H-hospital."

"What happened, Sarah?" I choked out as Grey's arms slid around my waist from behind, his firm, warm chest giving me something to lean against.

More whimpers and sobs broke in my ears, and I barely

contained the angry demands that wanted to escape from my lungs.

I couldn't fist either hand, couldn't smash my foot through a wall—because my lovers held me tight, offering shelter from the storm raging inside me.

Muffled noises, then a new voice came over the line. "Is this Blaine Mitchell?"

I swallowed hard at the calm tone in my ear. "Who's asking?"

"I'm Nina Delmsford, Sarah's nurse."

Not a name I recognized from the compound—I had no option but to trust her. "What happened to my sister?" I demanded, my entire body trembling in Grey's hold.

"She arrived at the ER badly beaten—she miscarried late last evening."

Fuck.

My eyelids slammed shut, and I slumped into Grey.

Lily's soft warmth pressed along my front, her cheek atop my pounding heart.

"I-Is she okay?" I rasped around my tight throat.

"Yes, she's going to be fine," the nurse assured me. "She said that you're her next of kin."

"Yes. Is there anyone else with her?" I asked, thinking of Franklin, the only person she had besides me who cared for her wellbeing.

"No. She arrived alone after eleven last night, and we just settled her into a room a little bit ago."

A shuddering exhale caved my chest in. "Can I talk to her again, please?"

"Sure thing."

More muffled fumbling, and sniffles met my ears.

"I'm coming to get you, Sarah."

"No! No. Please. I-I don't want you anywhere near here, Blaine. Please. You can't."

"What happened," I finally demanded, my tone firm since she'd calmed down. But I felt anything but stable inside. Were it not for Grey and Lily holding me up, I'd have sunk to the floor and curled into a fetal position.

"He—He caught us together." Her voice broke, but I waited. "Franklin..."

I scrubbed a hand down over my face, my chest aching from the devastation I heard in her voice, knowing I was powerless to help her from afar.

"Abraham beat him with his fists until he could barely move."

Fucking monster.

Grey's hands on my lower belly kept me still, Lily's kiss over my heart and her clutch on my free hand soothing the emotions wanting to explode from me.

"Then he hit me. Called me names. Told me I would pay for my sins." My sister's breath shook, but she pressed on. "I started bleeding down there, and—and he said it was my fault, that God would never allow a harlot like me to carry the promised child."

I should have felt bad for my sister's loss, but I couldn't rouse an ounce of sympathy over the miscarriage. I would offer condolences if she needed, but beyond that? A sense of sick satisfaction rolled through me over the fact Quell wouldn't get what he'd wanted from my sister.

"How did you escape?" I asked, turning our conversation away from what might cause even more pain for Sarah.

"Franklin came to enough to help me climbed over the fence where you always used to go to meet Greyson when you were a kid. Then I hitched a ride to the hospital."

It was a good two-mile walk from the compound's fence

to the main road leading to the Scotts' vacation home. The fact she'd traveled that far beaten and bleeding...

Rage tightened every muscle in my body again, and I fought to keep my breaths even.

"Franklin went back, Blaine. He saw me to safety—then told me to stay away and never return no matter what happened to the baby. He made me promise I would move to California to be with you."

"You're going to be okay, Sarah," I promised, my voice barely contained. What if the reassurance I offered was a pile of bullshit? What if Quell changed his mind and went looking for Sarah...took even greater revenge? "Let me talk to the nurse again."

A shuffling, then Nina got on the line.

"How long will Sarah have to stay in the hospital?" The second adrenaline rush had come to an end, and I began to sag, my energy quickly dissolving.

"Her vitals are fine. She's been patched up, X-rayed... nothing is broken, and there's no internal or permanent damage from the miscarriage or the beating." Nina's tone took on more anger than professional. "I expect she'll be released in the next twenty-four hours if she's feeling up to it."

She would be fine...no permanent damage.

My breath left in a shuddered exhale. "Can you help her? Keep her safe—I'm too far away—"

Grey took the phone from my hand, and I gave over control, trusting him to make things better. He settled me on the edge of the bed where Lily wrapped her arms around me.

"Hi, Nina, this is Blaine's partner, Greyson Scott." His business voice faded as he walked off.

Silent tears poured from my eyes as Lily and I lay back. I

clung to her, my face buried in her hair, and took what comfort I could find. Soaking in her sweetness, her soft hands caressing me, the quiet words of affirmation she poured over me, I forced myself to breathe through the quiet sobs ripping from my lungs.

I would never forgive myself if Quell got his hands on Sarah again. If he so much as harmed another hair on her head, I would rip him limb from limb with my bare hands or see him crucified with spikes in his hands and feet.

Imagining Sarah's anguish over leaving her heart behind with Franklin intensified the agony in my chest. He loved her enough to make her leave, wanted my sister's safety more than his own.

My entire body ached with deep-rooted exhaustion, physically, mentally, and emotionally.

Hard muscle and warm skin once more cradled my back, and Grey wound his arms around both me and Lily, sandwiching me in their love.

"I'm going to take care of everything, B," Grey stated firmly against my ear. "Physically, she's going to be fine." He kissed the back of my neck.

Losing her lover and a child she'd become somewhat attached to no matter who'd planted it in her belly...I knew it would be a long time, if ever, before emotional healing occurred.

My heart broke all over again, and I clung to my two lovers, barely keeping the darkness inside me from over-shadowing all the good I'd finally found in my life.

37

GREYSON

I'd overheard every word Sarah and the nurse, Nina, had spoken to Blaine.

Teeth clenched, I had to stay still and offer comfort when I wanted to charge forward and wear a path pacing my bedroom until I resolved the situation.

The second Blaine's anger flagged the second time, I'd taken the phone from his limp grasp and did what I did best.

I handled the reins he'd given me allowance to control, and I learned all I could from the nurse before setting a plan in motion.

I named the man who had beaten Sarah, offered detailed descriptions of him and a few of his men I'd studied countless pictures of from Higgins. I also demanded Sarah be moved to a secure room, her information given to no one without my consent.

Sarah refused to press charges, but that didn't mean we couldn't protect her. She just wanted to leave New England and never look back. While I would have loved for her to do the opposite—tell her story to the authorities and stick around until that fucker locked up—she had no one there to support her.

No parents. No siblings. No friends outside the compound.

And she refused to allow Blaine to go anywhere near the place that had caused him so much pain.

With no police report being filed, she would be free to leave once released from the hospital. I promised someone would be there to collect her and see her to the airport.

The first phone call I made when I finished with Sarah and Nina was to my father.

He knew some of what had happened to Blaine as a child and didn't hesitate to agree to help Sarah. My dad was well aware of what I'd set in motion with Higgins, and he promised to do everything he could to speed up the process.

Dad gathered some clothing, since Sarah had fled with only the dress on her back, and promised to put through the call to ready the family jet the moment she was released.

A bit of back and forth, a long chat with Higgins to let him know the latest, and the plan was set in stone.

Higgins would visit Sarah in the hospital, take pictures of her injuries, and document what had happened.

Dad would get Sarah to the plane once she was released from the hospital.

She would arrive in California later that evening.

With the ball rolling, I'd crawled back into my bed and offered silent, physical support to Blaine who lay there like a dead man.

"My dad is going to pick Sarah up and take her to the airport," I said even though I'd carried on the bulk of the phone conversations right there in my room where they both must have heard every word I'd spoken. "He's going to see her safely onto the family jet, and we'll pick her up tonight."

I tugged on Blaine until he rolled onto his back, and he pulled his and Lily's clasped hands atop his belly.

Propped up on an elbow, I peered at his pale face and into the shadowed darkness in his eyes.

"She's safe. Healthy. Yes, she's going to have some serious emotional shit to heal from, but if she's half as strong as you, she'll be fine." I smiled, cupping his cheek.

He nodded, not making a noise even as tears began to fill his eyes again.

"I love you, Blaine." I softly kissed his lips. "You've come so far since we moved out here, and Sarah is going to find the same healing as you have. I'll make sure of it."

Lily snuggled into his side, and I focused on her dark eyes. "Thank you for being with him while I took care of everything."

"There's no place I'd rather be." Her smile trembled, and I leaned over Blaine to kiss her mouth too.

"You both look really good in my bed," I said, glancing between them. "I think I want to keep you."

"Not going anywhere," Blaine muttered, grasping at my hand I'd laid top their clasped ones. His fingers thread through mine, holding on tight in a four-hand sandwich.

I kissed the back of his knuckles, my eyes on Lily.

Hers had welled also.

"Bikini girl?"

"Hmm?" Her smile lit her face even as a tear slid over her cheek.

"Are you gonna stick around?" I asked, feeling as though I'd stepped to the edge of a cliff where who the fuck knew what laid below. My stomach cramped more in hope of her reply than it had over the entire conversation with my dad.

Please say yes...please complete me. Us.

"Yep." Lily popped the P.

"Thank fuck." I kissed her again and laid back down beside Blaine and closed my eyes, a slow exhale sagging me into the mattress.

Content—for the time being.

Once I got Sarah safely in Blaine's arms, all I had left was to watch Quell's kingdom crumble to the ground.

Which I would do with the utmost satisfaction.

Lily called off work, and I had Meryl cancel all my meetings for the day. The three of us made breakfast together—pancakes, bacon, and home fries. Like the perfect picture of domesticity, we worked well together, only bumping into each other on occasion. I'd gotten a handful of Lily's ass intentionally and caught Blaine doing the same out of the corner of my eye.

A few stolen kisses, brushes of hands, caresses on shoulders...were it not for the elephant in the room of our impending guest and the reasons behind it, I'd have been in heaven.

Between the meal and a few cups of coffee and tea, we didn't much feel like moving after finishing. We left the dishes for later and curled up on the couch together, Blaine once more being loved on in the middle. His head lay on Lily's thigh, his feet in my lap where I kneaded and rubbed the soles exactly as he liked.

The TV ran through the news—my decision—on the quiet side while I only paid attention to the stock market numbers scrolling by rather than the day's headlines.

"Where is Sarah going to stay?" Blaine asked, taking the quiet haven we'd created around us to the situation I felt sure loomed in the back of their minds as well.

"Here." There was no other answer as far as I was concerned.

"Do we have time to get furniture for the other bedroom upstairs?" Blaine asked me.

I paused in my massage of his feet and focused on his face. He peered at me while Lily ran her fingers through his hair. "She'll stay in your room. You're moving into mine."

"I don't want to impose."

A soft snort escaped me. "I've finally gotten you into my bed, so don't think for one minute I'm going to let you out."

"Okay," he murmured, his eyelids falling shut again.

Too exhausted to argue or perfectly content to let me lead?

Lily studied his face, and I wondered if she felt a little left out. I knew I would in her shoes. While I would have loved to tell her to look at me so I could demand she stay with us too, it was a bit soon considering we would have another house guest within a matter of hours. Blaine, I expected, was going to need some alone time with his sister anyway.

If that meant my desires taking a back seat for a short while, I would do it. Rest in my heart came easy knowing Blaine loved me, and a relieved and happy best friend meant I would feel the same.

I stretched one arm over the back of the couch, barely able to reach Lily's hair that fell in tangled strands over her shoulder, but I needed the connection between the three of us. Perhaps it would better boost her spirits as well.

She and I would have to content ourselves with what little crumbs we could get. At least I would have him in bed with me every night.

"She's going to need clothes. Toiletries," Lily stated quietly, leaning into my hand, eyelids fluttering shut as I gave her what affection I could from the distance between us.

"We ought to buy everything before she gets here," Blaine suggested without stirring or opening his eyes, but his ass was worn out from the emotional upheaval the phone call had brought on.

"Lily?" I asked.

She finally gave me her eyes, and while she tried to keep me shuttered out, she failed. A bit of fear, perhaps hesitancy, over the situation had definitely taken root in her mind, exactly as I'd expected even though we'd had mind-blowing sex the night before. "Are you up for a shopping spree?" I asked rather than opening a can of worms over our exhausted boy.

"I'll do whatever Blaine needs me to do."

I nodded and gave her a reassuring smile, her words just what I'd hoped to hear. "Let's make this happen."

38

LILY

Haley took the day off to accompany me on one hell of a shopping trip. Grey's credit card in hand and his command to not worry about costs, we set out to get everything Sarah might need to begin her life over again.

At least my cousin seemed more settled, a little light in her eyes that had been missing since the weekend.

"So, I guess this means you won't be leaving me anytime soon," she said when I explained what had gone down since earlier that morning.

I'd gotten Blaine's permission to share a bit about his childhood, and Haley had sat in stunned silence while I drove toward the mall through traffic, talking nonstop.

"Guess so." I couldn't keep the disappointment from my tone or the whispers of fear that had come to life in my mind when Grey told Blaine he would move into his room.

My emotions were like a damn roller coaster, going from one high to a dropped-stomach low in a matter of hours. Grey wanted to keep me, but having Blaine at his fingertips whenever they were home together meant a higher possibility I might eventually be forgotten in the stressful days ahead.

My heart ached, but for so much more than my own fragile existence in the relationship I'd felt sure had begun the night before.

Blaine would be wrapped up in having his sister in his life again, and Grey would be close by for comfort whenever his own well of empathy drained.

God, how I wanted to be there for him too rather than waiting on the outskirts.

I could trust Grey to give Blaine what he needed—but I desired to be someone Blaine would reach for too. With how devastated he'd been after speaking to Sarah and learning the horrors of what she'd faced and endured in the previous twenty-four or so hours, I expected he and she both would stay shut up in their home.

And I doubted they would want company of any sort—perhaps even Grey.

"Your thoughts are getting heavy."

I smiled even though it didn't feel genuine. "Yep," I stated quietly without popping the P.

"Nothing we can do except continue down the path in front of us and hope for the best."

"Sometimes it's hard to keep your eyes on the prize," I muttered, wishing I wasn't so damn insecure about them seeking solace in each other over a situation that affected them ten times more than it did me.

"You got that right." Haley let out a huff, her arms crossing beneath her breasts. "But I know if I don't, I'll spiral —and I'm over the depression from this past week, thank you very much."

"Why don't you pull out the list Grey made from my purse?" I suggested, wanting to change the conversation since I'd had enough of my heavy heart threatening to give out. "With him being a guy, I'm sure it isn't inclusive."

I changed lanes for my exit, which lay a mile up the highway. Haley rifled through my bag and found the printed paper I'd folded into fours after Grey had handed it to me before we'd left.

"Shit." She snickered. "He is one organized dude."

"Right?" My smile came easy. "I love it."

"I'm wondering if you don't love *him*," Haley murmured while reading over the pile of items Grey had typed up by category.

Warm fuzzies rose to life in my belly. I wondered myself. How soon was too soon to fall in love? The connection was definitely there, the shared love for Blaine...and the sexual chemistry was off-the-charts smokin' hot.

Time would bring the path ahead of me into focus, and I needed to be patient and allow the puzzle pieces of my life to click into place.

Hopefully in the way I wanted.

"She just had a miscarriage, so I'm sure she's going to be bleeding for awhile," Haley said, digging through my purse again. She grabbed a pen and began writing on Grey's list. "The hospital might have given her some meds, and while Grey might have over-the-counter ones at his house, I don't think we should take the chance."

"Agreed."

"He's got leggings written down, but she's probably not going to want any restrictive clothing."

I nodded. "We can pick out a few loose-fitting sundresses. Oh, a warm robe too, and slippers if they're not on there."

"Hair dryer."

"Journal and some really nice pens."

"I'm thinking the girl is going to need an e-reader."

"Oh, great idea! He said no cap?"

"Right."

"Must be nice to not have to worry about money," she muttered.

We went back and forth, filling up the next ten minutes it took to get to the mall.

Within a matter of two hours, we'd taken three trips out to the car to unload our arms. On the fourth and final trip, my cell buzzed in my jeans' back pocket.

Haley had a free hand and pulled it out for me. "It's Mr. Yummy."

A smile erupted on my face. "Answer it?"

"Hey, there, Mr. Yummy," Haley said with a singsong voice. "How are you holding up?"

Blaine spoke to her while I dropped one arm load of bags to dig my keys from my purse.

"Mmm. Yeah, I hear ya," Haley said, no longer as chipper.

I hit unlock and popped the trunk.

"Well, I want you to know that I'm available to help out in whatever way I can," I heard Haley tell him. "If your sister decides she wants to stay out here in the Golden State, I'm thinking I'll be looking for a roommate around the same time I lose my current one."

Heat flooded my face. "Haley!" I hissed.

She winked. "Oh, I hear that too," she told Blaine then blew me a kiss. "Yep. Hold on a sec..." My intrusive cousin handed over my cell.

"I'm going to kill you!" I whispered furiously, my palm covering my cell's mic.

The bitch laughed while putting her bags into the trunk.

"Hey," I said into my phone, my heart in my throat.

"Hey," Blaine murmured, sounding a little more upbeat than when I'd left him earlier. "Would you mind coming with me to pick up Sarah at the airport?"

My chest squeezed up tight with delicious threads of happiness over the fact that he wanted me with him for such an intimate reunion. "Of course!"

"Grey had to go into work for an emergency meeting with one of his pain-in-the-ass customers."

Second choice...

The bright smile on my face faded, and I climbed into the hot car, stabbing my keys at the ignition in my piece-of-shit car. "What time is her flight coming in?"

"Seven forty-five."

Swallowing hard, I nodded and roared the engine to life. I tucked my cell between my ear and shoulder, cranking down the window to let some fresh air into the stifling interior.

"We'll be there in a half-hour with all of Sarah's stuff."

"I'll be here to help you unload. I got the sheets laundered and the bed all ready for her, so there really isn't much more to do."

We said our goodbyes, and I fought to keep my tone light and encouraging.

"What?" Haley asked the second I hung up.

I clicked my cell onto the magnetic holder I'd mounted onto the dashboard. "He asked me to go with him to get Sarah—but only because Grey got called into work."

"You're sure that's the reason?"

I shrugged, but the thought had processed thoroughly in my head, and there was no escaping it.

"Don't think too hard on it, Lily. He wanted you there enough to ask you."

Throat tight, those damn roller-coaster emotions going wild, I nodded.

Focus on the now...

I released a slow exhale, determined to stay positive regardless of my Debbie Downer mind.

"Let's hit the drug store up the road to get all the toiletries before heading to their place, okay?" I said, trying for an upbeat tone. "We're going to help Blaine ready his bedroom he emptied for his sister, then order some food because I'm fucking starved."

His bedroom—no more.

Grey's had become his overnight, and no matter how hard I tried to assure myself I still stood a chance to enjoy a future with them, the fears of my past didn't allow my mind or emotions rest.

39

BLAINE

Lily held my hand the entire way to the airport. I clutched to her like the lifeline that she was, thankful she'd come into my life when she did. How I had managed without her sunshine, the happiness she'd brought to my heart, I had no fucking clue.

Between her and Grey, I'd found my place. Contentment. Rest from all that had happened to me.

I couldn't wish my childhood had been different, otherwise I'd never would have found my best friend, moved west, and met the one who brought light to the darkness inside me.

"Thank you," I said, not for the first time, squeezing Lily's fingers. "I—I couldn't do this without you."

"Grey would have been in my place if he'd been able to," she reasoned quietly.

I shot a glance her way, frowning at her tone of voice. Was she still feeling insecure about what the three of us had together? I had to focus on the road before I ran off it. "I didn't want him, Lily. I wanted *you*."

Her head jerked toward me in my periphery, and I glanced over to find her eyes wide. "What?"

"I didn't need Grey to come with me for this," I repeated, once more turning to face forward. "Just you."

"Why?" Her whisper sounded more rasped than her usual husky tone.

I rubbed small circles over the back of her hand with my thumb. "Because while he's my anchor in this world, you're my happy place. The softness to his hardness. He's the moon in the night sky, but you're my sunshine."

"Ohgoodlordandallthingsholly." She let out a breathy laugh. "Are you serious right now?"

Heat rushed up to my cheeks.

"I didn't know you were such a romantic." Wonder still laced her tone.

I shrugged. "I surprised Grey too, but the two of you... bring out a lot of emotions inside me I didn't realize I was capable of."

Lily leaned over the console and kissed my cheek. "Thank you," she whispered against my ear and kissed me again. "You have no idea how badly I needed to hear that today."

A quick glance over revealed her eyes filled with tears. Empathy welled inside me, tightening my own throat. Just as I'd thought. "You did?" I asked to be sure of how I could make her understand how desperate I was for her—inside our bed and out.

She nodded and laughed while running a finger beneath one of her eyes where a droplet had escaped. "All I can think about is you sleeping in Grey's bed every night without me, and I'm so afraid..."

I squeezed her hand. "That won't ever happen with me and Grey."

"How can you be sure?" she asked, quiet and more meek than I'd ever heard.

"Because every single time he and I messed around this week, every moment he held me in his arms, we both mentioned missing you. Needing you. Falling for you."

Her stare heated the side of my face, and I squeezed her hand again.

"I don't understand how, but Grey is it for me—and so are you, Lily. I-I realize it's fast, and most people don't believe in love at first sight, but the second I saw you behind that counter, your smile bright as the summer sun..." I shrugged, having run out of words.

"I've fallen hard and fast too, Blaine," she admitted. "For both of you—so damn fast it scares the shit out of me—and you know why."

"Understandable." I lifted our clasped hands and kissed the back of hers. "The last thing either of us wants is to hurt you. If I had it my way, you'd be in our bed every night from here on out for the rest of our lives."

Lily released a shuddered sigh, and I exited the highway, wondering if she felt the same or if that darkness thanks to her old fiancé would make her draw away from us out of self-preservation.

"Please don't leave me," I whispered the thought as it flitted through my mind.

"Never," Lily vowed, the words fixing like a brand on my heart.

"There's a lot of shit from my past that I haven't told you about," I said, recognizing that if I wanted to move forward with her, she needed to hear everything, just like Grey had.

"You don't have to tell me anything that will bring that haunted look back to your eyes," she murmured, squeezing my hand.

"You see the darkness inside me, huh?"

"A bit, but I don't want you dragging it to the surface right now."

I glanced over to find a soft smile that soothed the darkness back down.

Do it.

My focus on the road, I took a deep breath and slowly let it leak out. "Quell abused me in every way imaginable."

Lily didn't speak right away, and the fear she might find me repulsive started to twist my guts up tight.

"I'm sorry," she finally whispered, tears in her voice.

My eyes stung.

She lifted our clasped hands and kissed the back of mine. "I'm here and not going anywhere for as long as you'll have me."

Forever, I almost blurted but bit my tongue.

"You and Grey are the only two who know," I whispered, surprised by how much relief swept through me over sharing a few little words.

"Thank you for trusting me, Blaine."

"Always." I could at least say that.

"So do you think we have everything Sarah will need?"

I swallowed hard at Lily's sensitivity in not pushing for details and changing the topic to things ahead rather than behind us.

Signs for the airport led us off the main road, and my focus slipped fully back to my sister at Lily's request. Sweet anticipation rose when I'd expected anxiety over how much shit would stir up in my brain from finally seeing her after nine years apart.

Ten minutes later, I still clutched Lily's hand as we walked toward the arrivals area which flooded with people and made my skin itch. We sat on plastic seats and huddled close, waiting and watching the board for Sarah's flight to land.

Everything had been prepared at home for my sister. After moving my clothing and the few personal items I had into Grey's room on the first floor, I had stripped down my bed and washed all the linens. I even wiped down the bathroom across the hall, setting out fresh towels for Sarah's use while Lily and Haley had gone shopping.

My coffee girl had laundered some of the new clothing Grey had paid for, and after everything sat in drawers, atop the dresser, and ready for use, I'd been exhausted.

Emotional weariness weighed heavy on my shoulders, and I bent beneath its weight.

Same with the feelings of thankfulness and gratefulness to both Grey and Lily. They had made the day easier. Brighter.

But it had been a trial regardless of their support—and a few hours lay ahead before I could crash and pass out.

I rubbed my thumb over the back of Lily's hand. She rested her head against my arm, and we sat in comfortable silence while my mind continued to race over how I would react at seeing Sarah. How she might appear after the beating Quell had "gifted" her with.

My jaw clenched, tension once more stringing me tight and making me want to punch something.

The board I stared at to take my mind off the crowd around us updated with arriving flights.

"She's here," I murmured, my anger dissolving as that excitement to see my sister returned.

Adrenaline leaked into my bloodstream, and I hopped to my feet, my heart racing. I rubbed my damp palms down my jeans and started forward regardless of the dozens of people.

I needed to move, when seconds earlier, I'd been ready to sink into the floor and sleep for three days straight.

Lily came up beside me and took my hand again, the contact immediately settling my insides enough that I could breathe steady rather than in the pants I hadn't realized I'd been attempting to fill my lungs with.

"It's going to be okay," she stated firmly as we came to a stop just beyond the roped-off area Sarah would appear behind. "Grey took care of everything. I'm here for you, and your sister needs you. You're strong enough to help carry her burdens, Blaine, and Grey and I will be here for you when you need the same."

I nodded, unable to move my attention off the hallway ahead.

"I believe in you, Blaine. You're a good man—one of the best I've ever met."

"And Grey?" I asked, desperate to occupy my mind for the final moments before Sarah's arrival.

"Top-tier, just like you." Lily's slender fingers gave a few pulsed squeezes around mine, and I tore my focus off the hallway to glance down at her. "You're pretty special, you know," she murmured, smiling up at me.

The light in her eyes filled me up, and I found my lips responding to her smile even though anxiety still riddled me clear through. "I think I love you, Lilliane Astbury."

"Ugh." She made a gagging noise, then giggled. "Not the full name! Please!"

We both broke out into real laughter, and I hauled her up into my arms, burying my face into her neck.

"I'm falling in love with you too, Blaine Mitchell," she whispered, her small hands cradling my face.

I pulled back, and our gazes held. Tears once more flooded her eyes.

Desire rushed up to choke out all negativity, and all I yearned for in that moment was to lose myself in her. Soak up her sunshine. Bask in the joy she brought to my life. Kiss all her tears away until she smiled in satiated bliss.

I wanted to tell her over and over how much she meant to me so she would never fear again—

"Blaine?"

My focus ripped off Lily.

Sarah.

My baby sister...less than ten feet away. She appeared pale, bruises littering her face, one eye an ugly shade of purple and swollen shut.

Wetness hazed my vision of her, and I set Lily to her feet, turning fully to face the tiny girl—woman—I hadn't seen in almost a decade.

"Sarah," I choked out her name.

She bit her lip, but a sob broke through.

We both rushed forward at the same time, and she threw her arms around my waist, burying her poor battered face against my chest. I cradled her gently, afraid to hurt her any more than she'd already endured.

Home—Sarah smelled like home, I realized while breathing her in.

My tears soaked her hair.

———

Grey was already at the house when we finally returned, my emotions feeling ragged and run dry. He had coffee waiting, his Jameson, and a few bottles of chardonnay since he wasn't sure which we would all be in the mood for. A snack tray with cheese, crackers, and red grapes sat waiting for us on the island too—Meryl's doing.

I'd talked Lily into coming home with us rather than dropping her off at her place like she'd insisted on since Haley had taken the car back home earlier in the afternoon. She kept busy tidying the kitchen and puttering around while Sarah, Grey, and I perched at high barstools. My coffee girl wore a pair of tight jeans that cradled her ass perfectly, and every move she made had her hips swaying and tempting my mind off the exhaustion settling into my bones and the many unanswered questions for my sister I still held quiet in my head.

Since her arrival, we hadn't discussed what Sarah had gone through.

I figured she would share when she was ready. Instead, we had focused on the "now"—her room, all of the things Lily and Haley had gone out shopping for, and the promise of a job at the boutique Pieces where Lily's cousin managed whenever Sarah was ready to spread her wings a bit.

"Shit," Lily muttered, bending over to pick up the hand towel she'd dropped.

That denim...fuck.

Sarah elbowed me like she had always done when wanting attention as a kid, and I jerked my focus off that perfect backside to find my sister staring at me. A small smirk lifted the corner of her lips, the first appearance of happiness I'd seen since she'd hugged me.

"You found your woman," she whispered.

"I found a lot more than that," I replied without hesitation, glancing over at Grey who sat on her other side.

Sarah shifted her focus between the two of us a few times. Blinking, her eyes widened. "No. Way." She giggled.

She. Fucking. Giggled.

Goddamn emotions I'd thought drained erupted inside

me again, and I stared at her smiling face, so damn thankful I wanted to sob.

My baby sister was going to be okay.

"The three of you, huh? That's *so* hot." She waved her hand like a fan over her face.

"Y-you don't think it's an abomination?"

Sarah snorted. "I might have been stuck beneath those bullshit beliefs of Abraham's, but I never took them on as my own."

"Thank fuck," I grunted the curse, a shit ton of heaviness I'd had lingering over my head concerning my sister dissolving.

Her smile faded, but our gazes stayed locked.

"It's going to be okay," I told her what I'd already said a dozen times. "The FBI is going to shut that place down, and Grey said he would fly Franklin out here to be with you."

Sarah glanced at the empty coffee cup in front of her and the small plate that held nothing but cracker crumbs. "He won't leave his family."

"I thought he loved you?"

"He does, but he's got four younger siblings, and his parents are two of Abraham's closest confidants."

"You think they'll be found guilty of something or another when Quell is?"

"Without a doubt. I have so much stored up in my brain —" Sarah tapped her temple "—the things I saw as his supposed wife..."

"Is the marriage between you and Abraham Quell legal?" Grey asked.

Sarah snorted again, and I got a kick out of the hint of rebellion she portrayed. "He wishes—or *wished* before he caught me kissing Franklin—but a claiming before his flock and God on the village green doesn't mean squat."

I snickered at the term she used instead of shit—one our father had been fond of since cursing meant time in the box.

She shrugged as though unaffected, but the haunted look taking back over her eyes claimed otherwise. "Knowing him, he'll denounce me in the same way he claimed me, and that will be that."

Lily finished cleaning up, and Grey pushed back his chair, patting his knee. She perched there, wrapping one arm around him and resting her head on his shoulder.

"I think we're all pretty exhausted," I said as I once more realized I had close to zero energy left inside me. "It's not even ten, but I'm ready to crash."

"I can have Haley come pick me up," Lily said, sliding off Grey's lap.

He grabbed her hand and tugged her back against his side, shooting me a quick glance, a question in his eyes.

I nodded without hesitation, thankful as fuck he knew what I needed—and what I felt sure he'd seen in Lily's eyes as well. "You're staying with us tonight," I told her, sounding bossy just like Grey.

Lily glanced between us, but her gaze flitted toward Sarah and stayed put as though asking *her* permission before agreeing to my declaration.

"Stay," Sarah suggested quietly, and I let out an exhale I hadn't realized I'd held.

So did Lily.

40

GREYSON

We crashed.

Hard.

Even naked and in a tangle of limbs, not a single one of us turned frisky.

I woke wrapped around Lily's backside, and she clung to Blaine who'd burrowed his face in her hair.

Quietness lay over my bedroom, but my mind refused further rest.

Sarah looked a hell of a lot worse than I'd expected. I couldn't believe the doctors back east had allowed her to leave less than twelve hours after arriving in the emergency room, beaten half to death and miscarrying.

But she'd insisted and had been stable enough for the doctors to allow her freedom.

She had assured us right before heading to bed that the loss of the fetus hadn't caused any internal harm, bluntly telling us she was thankful her body had aborted that monster's spawn and that the leftover bleeding from the D&C was no more than a light period.

There was no need to check on her during the night, she'd told us with a wink.

But her face...the bruising on her arms clearly defined fingers...

Fuck.

I saw red, and the girl wasn't even my own blood.

Lily had told me while Blaine showed Sarah to her room that our boy had broken down pretty hard when he finally saw his sister. She'd said it had torn her own heart in two and made her even more determined to help both Blaine and Sarah find happier, healthier lives.

I'd assured her with a quick hug and lingering kiss that she'd given Blaine that and so much more. I'd also claimed she'd done the same for me, which earned me another kiss, one that had a bit of spine-tingling heat behind it.

But we'd fallen into bed minutes later, my chub ignored by her and myself.

The sleep had been unbroken, and I hadn't felt that rested in weeks.

Like usual, I ran through my daily to-do list for the day in my head but within minutes decided to fuck it all off into the wind.

I wanted to be home with my two lovers and help in whatever way they needed.

A cell beeped quietly.

Lily stirred and groaned while rolling onto her back, blindly reaching for the phone on the bedside table. She turned the alarm off and rubbed her eyes. "Shit." She sat and grabbed her clothes off the floor where she had dropped them the night before.

"Lily?" I questioned quietly.

"Gotta work." She pouted over her shoulder while pulling her bra into place.

She'd called off the day before to help us get ready for Sarah, and I'd never been so grateful for a woman. Since I hadn't been able to drive Blaine to the airport due to Mr. Joseph I. Devonshire III demanding an in-person meeting at my office, she'd been by his side.

And I'd found myself fully trusting in her to see to whatever Blaine might need emotionally to make it through the day.

To have to sit and listen to that rich asshole feign politeness—it had sickened me. I hadn't been able to wait to get home to my lovers who held no such pretenses or bullshit and would soothe rather than aggravate me.

"Will you come back tonight?" I asked Lily, Blaine still dead to the world between us.

"I...I think I'll stay home with Haley." Lily stood and pulled her jeans on. "He and his sister are going to need some alone time, and I'm not going to impose."

"Maybe we could all go down to the beach behind the house tomorrow?" I suggested, not ready for her to just disappear for a few days while Sarah settled in. I had needs too, damnit.

Fuck, I can be a real selfish asshole sometimes.

"Would you mind if I bring Haley along?" Lily asked while slipping her sandals on.

"Of course not."

She rounded the bed and dropped a kiss on my lips. "I'll call an Uber and see myself out."

"I'll get up and make you some tea at least."

Lily pressed on my shoulder to keep me in place. "You stay right there and keep our boy warm and happy, okay?"

"My *pleasure.*" I winked while relaxing once more, and pink flushed her cheeks. "Do you require evidence of him being fully sated and resting this evening?"

"Is that a trick question?" Her dark eyes twinkled down at me, her golden hair cascading around my head. Another quick kiss, and she pulled back. "Tomorrow?"

I nodded, afraid if I opened my mouth that I would blurt out those three little words that shouldn't be said after a few weeks of meeting someone.

Lily fluttered her fingers once at our bedroom door, disappearing a second later.

A heavy sigh settled me back onto my pillow, and I gently tucked an arm around Blaine who didn't so much as twitch.

———

I sat in my home office later that afternoon, Blaine and Sarah ensconced in her bedroom. Neither of them had woken until close to lunchtime, and after I fed them and shooed them off together, I'd gotten some work done since I'd missed most of Friday at the office.

Once I combed through my emails and took care of shit that couldn't wait for Monday, I called up Higgins.

We spoke briefly about Sarah's safe arrival, but he got straight to business afterward. I'd told Sarah that even though she had no wishes to press charges, I was sending my PI to her hospital room to document what had happened.

She hadn't been averse to my suggestion of simply speaking with Higgins, thank fuck.

"I snapped dozens of pictures and eventually got her to talk about the attack," he told me. "Quell is one sick fuck, and I'm going to enjoy watching him get taken down."

"What's the latest?" I stood at my home office's window overlooking the Pacific while Higgins filled me in.

The FBI agent he'd been in close contact with had wanted to talk to Sarah—and wasn't too pleased she'd fled across the country. But she'd given her agreement to Higgins to stand as witness when the time came.

The case against Quell and the cult sped forward at a vicious pace. While there was more than enough evidence for a peaceful search warrant of the compound, there had been other intel coming in for months about Quell prepping for an apocalypse that would bring a "new dawn."

Higgins had spoken with the couple who had escaped earlier in the week and then he'd contacted his FBI friend about them as well.

It seemed Quell's teachings the previous couple of years had tended toward suspicion of government, and it had been rumored he'd built a supply of weaponry—which the couple confirmed.

With another possible Waco situation in its infancy stage, I expected the FBI wouldn't waste their time—hoped —they would go sneaking in like a thief in the night, shutting the cult down and hauling Quell off in cuffs before anyone knew what happened.

Higgins's contact hadn't shared details about the when, but he did promise sooner than later.

Blaine and Sarah eventually joined me in the living room, and they both once more appeared exhausted, eyes red-rimmed and faces haggard.

We ordered Chinese for dinner at Sarah's request and stuffed ourselves full.

Sarah crawled back into bed within an hour, agreeing to spend the following day at the beach to relax and soak up some sunshine in her newfound freedom.

Blaine slumped against me on the couch, and I wrapped an arm around him, holding him close.

I wasn't about to share Higgins's update with Blaine. Fuck knew he had enough to think about.

"Want to talk?" I asked, and he let out a sigh.

"Not really."

"Okay." I kissed the top of his head. "Want to just cuddle in bed?"

"I'll probably pass out the second I lay down."

"Do you mind if I snuggle your sexy backside while you sleep?"

He let out a soft chuckle. "Nope." He popped the P like Lily, and an ache spread over my chest.

I hated that she wasn't there with us.

"Come on." I stood and tugged Blaine to his feet.

He shuffled along after me toward our bedroom, and I dimmed the lights for him. We brushed our teeth at the double sink and stripped down to skin before crawling into bed. My pillow smelled like vanilla, and I filled my lungs.

Blaine buried his face in his pillow and did the same.

"Lily," we both murmured at the same time—and grinned like couple of idiots while scooting close to each other.

"I love her," Blaine said, watching my eyes carefully in the dimmed lights as he rested in my arms.

"I do too," I easily admitted.

"Have you told her?"

I shook my head, soothing my hand down his back. "Have you?"

"Yeah. Right before Sarah showed up. I was just so thankful for her being with me. Filled up with emotion and ready to explode."

"Did she say it back?"

"Yeah." He smiled lazily, a slow blink of his eyes letting me know he was ready to pass the fuck out.

Seconds later, he snored, and not one ounce of jealousy burned in my gut. I *wanted* them to love each other. Nothing would make me happier.

Except perhaps hearing Lily tell me the same.

Any harsh grief I'd held onto from Mom's passing had faded, I realized. Lily had given me help in healing—and I hadn't even been aware of her weaseling into my heart. I expected some days would be tougher than others, like Mom's birthday or the anniversary of the accident, but I no longer felt anxious in my bones of their arrival.

Lily would be there with her soft, gentle touch, the light in her eyes, and the soothing affection I craved from a nurturing hand.

I would tell her the truth of my feelings, I decided, since Blaine had taken that leap in vulnerability first.

He'd gotten what he'd wanted in return.

I hoped I would too.

41

LILY

Our outing to the beach below Grey and Blaine's got cancelled thanks to the FBI showing up at their house on Sunday morning.

The better part of the day had been spent answering questions—or so Grey told me.

I hadn't spoken to Blaine at all other than a goodnight text on Saturday, then one on Sunday.

Even Grey hadn't reached out with an actual call, simply texted to give me updates throughout the day.

While I understood the upheaval in the household and the stress and anxiety Sarah had brought into Blaine's life, I still felt hurt. Ignored. Selfish, perhaps, but I couldn't talk myself out of my feelings.

Maybe it was just damn PMS creating a worrywart bitch in my head, but I battled negative thoughts non-fucking-stop.

I wasn't about to poke and intrude into who the hell knew what kind of emotions ran through the house after the FBI dug into Blaine and Sarah's lives though. I couldn't even begin to imagine what either of them experienced from having to dredge up shitty memories and recount details they would both rather have burned from their minds.

I told myself to rest in the fact that Blaine had his anchor.

I just wished he'd reached for his sunshine too.

"Quit pouting."

I flipped Haley off even though I laid on the couch, my head on her thigh for the previous hour of our movie marathon night we'd spent downing Andes candies and chardonnay. "Can't help it," I muttered, only slightly buzzed and still tasting chocolate and mint on my tongue. "I hate not knowing what's going on over there."

"Probably a lot of stuff that they would rather you not hear about."

Haley had a point, but it didn't make me feel any better.

"Once this shit with the cult and its leader calms down, the three of you will be smooth sailing into the sunset."

I snorted at the strange wording my cousin *never* used. "Since when, Haley?"

"Just because I'm a jaded bitch doesn't mean I can't still be a dreamer at heart."

I rolled from facing the TV to my back so I could see her face. "It'll work out for you too."

She sighed, her focus flitting to the dark sky beyond the curtained window. "A girl can hope."

A news bulletin cut off the show we'd been watching, and at the mention of Abraham Quell and the cult he led in New Hampshire, I jolted upright.

Fires raged in the background of the rolling video, lighting the night sky.

The FBI had gone in with a warrant.

A short showdown had ended with a few gun wound

injuries, but Abraham Quell had been arrested and hauled off.

Uninjured, the fucker.

"Holy shit...holy shit." My pulse raced, my eyes wide and unblinking on the TV.

While a short list of charges had leaked out to the press, rumors led them to believe much more would come to light in the days ahead.

My hands shook as I grabbed my cell and shot off a text to Grey. **Did you know they were raiding the compound tonight?**

I chewed the inside of my lip, perched on the edge of the couch while waiting for a reply. It took a long as fuck ten minutes before he got back to me.

Grey: **No. Higgins didn't either.**

My fingers flew over the screen. **How's Blaine? Sarah?**

Grey: **Shocked. Staring at the TV.**

I wanted to head over there, be by Blaine's side if he needed me. Grey didn't suggest it. In fact, he didn't text again while I took to pacing across our living room.

"What the fuck should I do?" I asked Haley, swiping my screen to life every time it blackened out while I strode one way then the other, chewing on my fingernails.

She'd turned on a new station and watched the same video recording over and over while the broadcasters speculated on what went down and why.

There were reports of Quell's second wife being treated for a miscarriage at the hospital. Rumors she'd disappeared in a private jet. Guns had supposedly been stockpiled. Over a dozen people had been taken into custody.

"If Blaine wants you there, he'll call you."

I took to nibbling on the inside of my lip. "What if he

doesn't?" I whispered, swiping my finger over the cell's black screen.

Nothing.

Swallowing hard didn't ease the tightness in my throat and chest.

"Imagine what he's going through right now. How badly his sister's mental health is occupying his mind."

I *had* told him to be strong for her... He would put his needs aside to comfort her without doubt.

I sank onto the edge of the couch, my knee bouncing. "I'm going to text him."

Me: **I know you're being brave for Sarah right now, and I just wanted you to know that I'm here for you. Tonight, tomorrow, next week...whenever you need me.**

His reply came through almost immediately.

Mr. Yummy: **I love you.**

A sob choked out of me. **Love you too—so damn much.**

Mr. Yummy: **The emotions over here right now are out of control. While I want you here with me so much it hurts, Sarah's my focus right now.**

Exactly as Haley had stated, the smart-assed bitch.

Me: **Please allow Grey to help carry your burdens. Don't feel as though you have to handle everything on your own. Emotions included.**

Mr. Yummy: **I will. Promise.**

A shuddered sigh fled my lungs, and I sank back into the couch, handing over my cell to Haley to catch up so I wouldn't have to speak.

She didn't say anything, and I took back up my station on her thigh, staring at the TV, desperate for any bit of news I could get.

Three agonizing days passed.

Work sucked.

I didn't get to see my two lovers, but we'd been texting on and off throughout our time apart—always in the group chat.

Both Blaine and Sarah had been sat down and questioned again by the FBI, dealt with follow-up and more bullshit.

I was clueless, but the media gained additional insight every hour that passed, it seemed.

Illegal guns had been found on the compound—thanks to Quell's right hand man spilling his guts in hopes of leniency. An inside leak had informed the press, and the shit hit the fan.

Child molestation and rape.

Physical abuse.

Murder.

Bodies dug up from a corner of the property, autopsies on order to identify who they were.

But Quell's man? He claimed he knew each and every one—by name, and he spilled that shit too.

Again, I clutched my cell in my hand, desperate to talk to Blaine. His parents had disappeared without warning, without a word to Sarah all because there had been an altercation with Quell, and I feared the worst.

The phone rang a heartbeat before I could put through the call.

Grey.

"What the fuck?" I whispered in greeting, hoping up to paced behind my couch while Haley sat on its edge. Both our gazes glued to the TV.

I could hear sobs in the background.

"He killed them," Grey bit out.

I clenched my teeth as my eyelids slammed shut. My feet stumbled to a stop.

Oh God.

Imagining Blaine and his sister's heartache, hearing their sorrow beyond Grey ripped grief through my chest. Grey knew their emotions to some extent, and I couldn't begin to wonder over how he held up.

"It'll take some time to identify the remains of the bodies they exhumed, but I have no fucking doubt." He stated each word like a curse with barely controlled rage. "I'm going to fucking rip his goddamn guts out!"

So anger, not reliving his own grief.

"Grey." I swallowed hard, seeing him in my mind, pacing as I'd been doing, his heart broken and bleeding for Blaine. "You have to stay calm. He needs his anchor. Breathe. Count to a hundred if it'll help, but you've *got* to cool down."

"Fuck, Lily." His voice broke. "I can't even right now."

"Yes, you can." I straightened, stiffening my spine for him even as tears of empathy stung my eyes. "You can't lose your shit when you're his rock. You and I can break down together later then kiss and make everything better, okay?"

"I love you," Grey choked out the words, and my eyes welled at the pain and longing in his voice.

"I love you too," I barely managed to whisper through a happy sob that wanted to release coursing tears down my cheeks. What a fucked-up time for exchanging those three words, but when had anything in my life come to pass by conventional means?

"I-I needed you. That's why I called."

Aaaaand the dam broke, wetness dripping from my chin.

"I'm his anchor," Grey continued when I couldn't speak, "but I'm starting to feel like you're my emotional gas tank, my GPS to navigate the softer side of me I've denied myself for too damn long."

I laughed through my tears, and Grey even chuckled. "It's okay to be needy," I said through my tears, feeling a shit ton better since he'd called.

"You've got it down to an art."

A huff escaped me as I wiped my arm across my eyes. "You *love* when I'm begging for all your attention."

"Fuck yeah, I do."

My smile faded as I once more focused on the quiet sobs beyond Grey. "Go hold them," I told him, my emotional turmoil over *us* locked in a casket and buried. "Let them rest against you. You're strong enough for the both of them."

"Okay," he whispered. "I miss you."

I smiled so damn hard my cheeks hurt. "I miss you more."

"Soon."

I nodded, my heart soaring. "Soon."

42

BLAINE

Sarah had officially been with us for a week when Franklin finally got in touch with her. I hadn't recognized the New Hampshire number calling my cell but had answered anyway. A quiet, hesitant voice had introduced himself, and I'd promptly handed my phone over to Sarah who'd been sitting eating dinner with me and Grey.

Cheeks pink and tears in her eyes, she'd scampered up the stairs, leaving me alone with Grey for the first time outside our bed in seven long as fuck days. We hadn't done more than cuddle and kiss in that week. Sex of any sort had been the last thing on my mind, which wasn't surprising considering what Sarah and I had gone through since her arrival.

Countless questions and hours upon hours of having to wade through the darkness I could no longer keep under lock and key. That shit was needed to build the case against Quell.

Turmoil no human being ought to experience raged in our hearts regardless of our attempts to think on other aspects of our lives. Exhaustion didn't begin to describe both my and Sarah's bodies and minds.

Physically drained, emotionally spent, we both needed a long-as-hell vacation far away from everything and just about everyone.

While I felt all kinds of satisfaction in seeing Quell hauled off in cuffs, the cult disbanded and a few of the buildings razed to the ground, I knew I would never be able to forget what had taken place inside the cult's fence.

Sarah fared a little better than I did. The bruises had begun to fade, and she'd lost the pale face and frightened eyes. Watching the aftereffects of the raid on the compound, finally having answers of where our parents had gotten to—even if it hadn't been confirmed yet—had settled something in her.

My head still floundered like a damn hot mess.

Grey and I finished eating, not talking a whole lot, and cleaned up. He'd been quiet throughout week but always there if I needed him. The man I could count on.

The man I loved desperately.

Pain lanced through my chest, and I set aside the towel I'd been using to dry the dishes he washed and tugged his forearm.

Suds up to his elbows from the dish water, he turned toward me, his brow furrowed. "Are you okay?"

Throat tight, I nodded and moved in close, resting my forehead on his shoulder to soak in his warmth and the sure peace being in his arms always brought.

He hugged me to him, wet hands soaking through my thin T-shirt as he rubbed up and down my spine, soothing my mind as I knew he would.

I sagged against him, tucking my face into his neck, my fingers digging into the muscles along his spine. He smelled like soap and masculinity—my Grey. Emotions rose up in my chest but with sweet longing rather than sorrow.

Trailing my lips over his neck, up over his jaw, I attempted to give him something in return for all he'd sacrificed for me.

"Grey," I murmured against the corner of his mouth, and he turned toward me, brushing his lips over mine. The chaste touch of lips we'd shared over the previous seven days gave way to rising hunger from a mere flick of my tongue along his seam.

His hold on me tightened, and he groaned, his tongue lashing against mine.

Life returned to my groin for the first time in over a week, and I leaked pre-cum like a goddamn broken faucet.

"Grey," I whispered once more over his lips.

"I know, baby...I know." He squeezed my ass and kissed along my scruffy jaw. "Fuck, have I missed you."

"Mmm." I swallowed hard as he closed his lips over my earlobe.

Footsteps sounded, and we both stepped away from each other, panting. Gazes locked, we adjusted the obvious bulges in our pants. He smirked and winked, the lightness in the moment curving my lips into a soft smile.

I slid onto the barstool I'd vacated to clean up while he turned to finish the dishes. Hard-ons officially hidden.

Sarah breezed into the kitchen, face flushed and eyes more alight than I'd seen since she'd landed in California.

"He's good, I'm guessing?" I asked, my tone steadier than I'd expected considering how my pulse still raced and desire for my man still coursed through my blood.

"A-Mazing!" She plopped onto the stool beside me, handing over my cell. "So, he found out he has grandparents he never knew about, and he and the other four kids moved in with them. They have a farm in Maine, a big one, with plenty of room for all of them. Franklin won't be responsible for his siblings like he'd feared—he wants me to come home so we can be together."

Her words rushed out, leaving me stunned and silent, dick officially checked out.

My face must have betrayed my disappointment in her announcement, because her smile faded.

"What?" she whispered.

"You seem...like you want to go back."

Leave me, I couldn't choke out.

"I do." She smiled again, but her mouth wobbled. Taking my hand, she glanced at Grey. "I'm thankful for everything you've done for me, but I...I can't stay out here, Blaine. I love my Frankie baby so much, and being away from him has been half of my depression."

I'd figured it had been the hormones of the lost pregnancy and all the shit we'd endured that had kept her in tears.

What an asshole I'd been, not even considering how she would feel being separated from the man she loved. I couldn't imagine those miles keeping me from Grey—or Lily which had been agony enough with one town between us.

"He asked his grandparents if I could move in too, and they agreed. I know I just got here, Blaine, but I really miss him."

I nodded, hating that wetness filled her eyes for what seemed like the hundredth time in seven days.

"And with the upcoming trial, it would be best for me to be nearby," she added.

As Quell's supposed wife, Sarah had indeed been privy to a shit ton of information. While the graves had been a surprise to her, the fact they existed didn't. Too many people had pissed off Quell over the years and disappeared.

Including his first wife.

"I want you to be happy, little sis, and if that's being with Franklin, then I won't stand in your way," I managed to get out past the lump in my throat. Complicated emotions once more took over my brain. Longing for a renewed relationship with my little sister I'd just gotten back in my life and want for her to find her fairy tale ending like I'd done with Grey and Lily.

"Frankie does make me happy. I miss him so damn much—just like you miss Lily."

My brow furrowed, and Sarah let out a soft laugh while drying her eyes. "Seriously, Blaine? You and Grey have been miserable since she left. Neither of you have said a damn word about her absence, but I'm calling bullshit if you even think about denying the truth in front of me."

Grey turned to lean against the sink, drying his hands. He eyed my sister. "I didn't want to overcrowd you."

"As if one more person here in this massive house would make a difference," Sarah huffed out her opinion.

Grey gave me his full attention. "I didn't ask her to visit because I thought you would need time."

"Well, maybe you should have opened your mouth and communicated instead of assuming," Sarah told him with a saucy tilt to her head.

Lips tight, I grabbed up my cell and swiped the screen to life.

"What are you doing?" Sarah asked me with a teasing tone.

"Telling our girlfriend to get her fine ass over here where she belongs."

"Thank God!" Sarah slapped her palms onto the table. "You two men have been miserable messes without her."

Lily immediately texted back a heart-eyed emoji and **Be there in an hour!**

I grinned, feeling as though oxygen freely filled my lungs for the first time all week.

"Soooo..."

I gave Sarah my attention at her drawn-out word. Pink once more flushed her face.

"I'm going to be taking a nice long bubble bath tonight with a glass of that white wine you introduced me to and enjoying those chocolate mint candies Lily had stockpiled for me. And did I gush about that new, delicious book I started this morning? Don't plan on laying eyes on me the rest of the night." She slid off her stool and ambled toward the stairs. "Tell Lily I said hello, and I'll see you all in the morning!"

Grey and I caught each other's gazes.

"Shower?" he suggested, his tone raw.

My dick swelled back to full mast at the drop of a damn hat. "Together?"

"Fuck, yes."

He palmed my ass the entire way into our bathroom.

———

Grey let Lily into the house and swept her into the foyer, devouring her mouth before the door even slammed shut. I slid in behind her tight little body covered by a flowing sundress, flipped the lock, set the alarm, and crowded in close to get my mouth on her neck.

Sweet, delicious vanilla filled my nose.

She moaned and squirmed, turning to face me. Her soft

hands found my face, and she peered up at me. Her big brown eyes revealed her worry, but for once, she didn't seem to be able to find words.

"I'm going to be fine," I assured her, pressing in close along her body.

A heavy sigh shuddered through her, sagging her shoulders. "I love you."

"Love you too." I took her lips, feasted on the heaven I'd been missing for too damn long. She tasted of mint—chocolate—and I couldn't get enough.

If burrowing into a person's skin and taking up permanent residency was a possibility with science, I'd have been first in line to offer my body up for testing.

As long as Grey agreed to do the same along with me.

His hands found my ass around her body, and even though we'd jerked each other off in a matter of seconds earlier in the shower, my dick thickened against Lily's belly.

"Missed you," I said, lifting her into my arms. "So damn much—I don't know why I didn't just tell you to stay with us the whole week. I needed you. Wanted you."

She slid her palms along my jawline, her smile like sunshine and dew drops. "It's okay. I'm fine—we're fine. I'm here now, and that's all I care about."

Her legs wrapped around my waist, and Grey went for her ass instead of mine, yanking on material to get at her skin.

"No panties. You naughty little minx." He dropped to his knees, and Lily let out a breathy moan that went straight to my dick.

"Is he eating your ass?" I asked even though I palmed her cheeks, opening her even wider for him.

"God, yes," she hissed, her forehead tipping onto my shoulder.

"Grey," I bit out his name.

"Hmm?" His voice was muffled by flesh, a slurp following the moaned response.

"Bedroom. Now."

He stood and nuzzled Lily's ear. "You're so damn delicious. I could lick your ass all fucking day long."

Lily shivered, goosebumps pebbling her arms.

Grey's pale eyes blazed with heat, and I nodded toward our bedroom door. He smirked, adjusted the tent of his shorts, and led the way.

I lusted over every flex of his backside while rubbing Lily's.

"We're going to have you at the same time," I told her.

She made a throaty hum that caused my dick pressed tight against her core to jerk. "Yes, please."

"Think you can take us both in that tight pussy of yours?"

"Oh God," she whimpered.

"Because I want to feel Grey's cock sliding alongside mine, coated in your cream. I want to feel you come around us before we fuck you full of our cum." Fuck, did I lust for that, making her ours once and for all.

"Holyshitandallthingsholy," she breathed the words all in one big slur, and I grinned. "You've been spending too much time with Grey—filthy mouth."

"You love it." I nipped her earlobe.

"Damn right I do."

I set her on her feet at the edge of the bed.

Grey sprawled naked in the center beneath the lights he'd dimmed. His dick leaked in his hand, already glistening with precum. "Strip her down, B."

I nosed over her delicious-smelling neck while gathering up her dress, easily slipping it off overhead. It was like she came prepared for a quick strip down. She'd even worn flip-flops which she never did. They got kicked to the side without effort.

Arms wrapped around her middle, I rested my chin on her shoulder, my focus on Grey while he slowly stroked himself.

"He's so fucking hot," I muttered, my hard-on digging into her lower back.

"Mmm *hmm*."

I inhaled until it hurt, so overrun by *positive* thoughts and emotions for the first time in over a week that I felt like I'd entered our heaven's gates again. The garden of life blooming in my heart from Lily's presence lay beneath bright, twinkling starlight from the man waiting for us. I decided in that moment that I would start seeing a therapist, because I wanted complete healing...

Grey fully inside my head—and body.

But that could wait for another night. We had our girl to love on.

"Go sit on his dick, Lily," I whispered against her ear, ready for the next step in our relationship. Dual claiming, a raw marking, a physical acknowledgement of where all three of us belonged.

Together.

43

———

GREYSON

Lily had moved into my heart as easily as she sank onto my aching length. One smooth glide that rolled my eyes back into my head with exquisite pleasure. Without effort, she'd solidified her place in my life, and I refused to exist another day without her beside us.

I pulled her down, taking her mouth in a slow, languid kiss when I would have rather devoured her until she lay spent atop my body.

We would get there...but we had a ways to go.

Blaine and I had spoken in the shower while jerking each other off about double penetration in the way she'd fantasized over.

And fuck, did we both want it.

We'd unloaded our balls in record time thinking about fucking up into her pussy, skin on skin.

Fuck.

My dick jerked inside her, and I motioned Blaine closer without tearing my mouth from Lily's. I might have found release in Blaine's hand a half hour or so earlier, but my need approached detonation within seconds of her hot clasp around my cock.

Blaine pressed a thigh between mine, and I opened, giving him room to rest his knee on the bed.

"Mmm." Lily moaned into my mouth, gyrating her hips, her slick pussy walls dragging along my cock.

"Gorgeous ass," Blaine said. His hands slid down over my balls and away again, caressing us both. "Is she wet?" he asked, his fingers gliding around where I stretched her, the sloppy noises of my slow thrusts answer enough.

"Fuck yeah," he groaned. "Perfect. So damn needy."

She abandoned my mouth, rising up onto her hands. Panting. Eyes hazed with lust.

I buried deep and held her gaze. "Be a good little girl and let him in too." I pinched one of her nipples, and she whimpered, her head tipping back.

"Please, baby. Please..." she begged.

The sound of the lube cap snapped.

Blaine pressed a slicked-up finger into her tight sheath along my length, and we both groaned.

"So fucking tight," I said through clenched teeth, unable to help from fucking up into her along Blaine's calloused finger as he stretched her out. "Need your dick in here so bad, B. Give our girl what she's been dreaming about."

Blaine lifted Lily onto her haunches, his arms wrapping around her body, his mouth on her ear. "You want both of our dicks inside you, pumping you full of cum?"

"Yeah...oh yeah." She panted, her luscious lips parted, eyelids fluttered shut. "So bad. You have no idea."

"Think you can take us both?"

Red flushed her check, neck, and face. So fucking beautiful my heart ached. "Fuck yes. Do it."

He pressed her forward down onto my chest, and I held

her close, fighting to keep my hips still so Blaine could work his way inside her. The head of him smeared pre-cum and lube over my firmed balls to where I penetrated Lily.

Our gazes caught over her shoulder, his eyes dark with hunger I experienced deep in my core.

Make her ours.

He pushed—notched.

"Oh fuck...fuck. God!" Lily whined and stiffened, her head tipping back again.

"Shh." I rubbed my hands down her spine. She shivered beneath my light touch as I held Blaine's hazed eyes with my own, just the feel of his thick head pressing against my dick inside her tight sheath making my balls tingle. "I have you, sweet girl. Relax and let him in."

Easy. Gentle.

Blaine released a slow exhale before trying for more.

Lily gasped and trembled, nonstop curses spilling from her lips as his length pushed in another inch.

"Baby..." Blaine bent over her back, sinking in a little further. "You feel so good wrapped around us like this."

"Oh *God*." She bit the word out then hissed between clenched teeth. "Too much...fucking hell, it's like you're ripping me apart."

"Need us to stop?" I asked, cradling her face in my hands so I could see her expression.

Eyes wild, she stared down at me, shaking her head. "No. I want this. I-I'll stretch. Just go slow."

Blaine pushed forward, and I eased back, allowing him to slide in deep along my throbbing head still buried in her tight sheath.

"Ohholyshitandfuckinghallelujah," Lily spewed words in a mumbled mess that twitched my lips upward.

"Okay?" I asked, and she moaned.

"Yes. Oh yeah. Do that again."

I pushed back in, slick, hot skin gliding against each other as Blaine retreated.

Her pussy cradled us better than any hand job, mouth, or ass. Lily's body had been shaped for us, the final piece I hadn't realized we'd been missing until she blew in like an ocean-swept breeze.

One body, I realized we'd become in that moment of coming together. One being.

"I fucking love you both so damn much," I choked out, grabbing hold of Blaine to sandwich Lily between us.

They both panted and whimpered something along the same lines, but the words got lost in the lust-driven sensual dance of three bodies offering the physical expression of their love to each other.

No selfishness sent us racing toward the finish line, no need to empty balls in a spine-tingling sensation.

I wanted Lily to come apart between us, fully sated, her fantasy fulfilled. Nothing mattered in that moment but giving her what she'd dreamed about.

"Come all over our cocks. Need your cream dripping down my balls, baby." Sliding a hand between our sweat-slickened skin, I found her swollen clit.

"Oh God." Lily turned her head, her cheek on my shoulder. "So good...so full." A puffed exhale ghosted hot breath over my pec. She licked her lips as though desperate for moisture.

"You like being stuffed, don't you?" Blaine kissed her shoulder, every ripple of his abs while fucking in over my dick making my mouth water.

"Yes. So much."

I groaned, ready to blow my fucking load. A few flicks of my fingertips over her slippery clit, and Lily clenched.

"Fuck." I ground my teeth together, fucking needing her to come. "Lily. Please"

"Kiss—"

The word didn't even finish passing her lips, and Blaine smashed his mouth onto mine.

Lily whined a loud cry and erupted, her pussy like a pulsing vise squeezing us together. Hot wetness slickened our thrusts, dripped from my tight balls, and Blaine let go, his groan leaking into my mouth.

His dick pulsing against mine.

I grabbed hold of his ass and thrust hard, all trace of nicety gone from my mind. My lovers had found their release, and I pushed forward with mine, snapping my hips, moving Lily atop me.

"Love...fuck!" Cum erupted from my dick, shooting deep inside Lily to mingle with Blaine's. Even while spurting, ears ringing, I imagined both of our scents, our mark, coating her insides.

She'd branded herself onto our hearts, and we'd done the same to her.

———

We lay spent, sticky and sweaty in a tangle of limbs. Cum coated my dick, smeared between Lily's thighs, but none of us made a move to get up.

Euphoric waves of delicious rest kept me still while facing her. Eyes closed. Smiling like an idiot.

"I want you to move in with us," I said what I'd been thinking about for days on end.

"What?" Lily roused from the verge of passing out like she usually did after we fucked her senseless. "No command?"

"You're moving in with us," I amended as she opened her eyes. "Tomorrow."

She shifted her head back on the pillow, closer to where Blaine had his face buried in her hair as usual so she could meet my gaze. "You don't think it's too soon?"

"If I did, I wouldn't have asked."

"*Demanded.*"

I chuckled, sliding my leg between her thighs to rub my foot over Blaine's calf muscle. "Our bed is empty when you aren't here."

"Hardly," she snorted, her brown eyes waking with laughter and the kind of joy that made my heart ache.

My grin faded. "I'm serious, Lily. We're head over heels and want you with us. Always."

Blaine snaked a hand between us, his caress over her belly rubbing his knuckles along my abs. I flexed beneath his touch. "Please," he whispered against her neck

One word from him, and I saw the decision in her sleepy eyes.

Anything to please him.

She smiled, her gaze soft as she tucked my hair behind my ear. "Anything for him," she all but repeated my thought. Perhaps that silent communication thing had sprung to life between us as well.

"Are you reading my mind now?" I asked, running my hand down over her hip. So satiny smooth...

"Yep." She popped the P and pressed her lips against mine.

"Is that a yes?"

"That would be a yes."

A few kisses lazed among the three of us until the stickiness became too much. I carried Lily to the shower, and we washed her from head to precious little toes, paying homage to our girl.

Blaine's time for attention came next, and while I'd have loved to lather his backside with sensual glides of my palms and fingertips, I avoided that area of his body.

I owned a part of his heart, but even if I never got a piece of his ass, I would be content with what he allowed. Lily's lathered hands took over cleaning his front while I held him against me.

Blaine rested his head back on my shoulder. "I'm going to see a therapist."

Inner relief swept through me over his openness, and my throat tightened.

"I—I want to be free with you, Grey. Be able to give myself to you fully some day without the darkness rising to steal it away."

I swallowed hard. He'd told me Lily knew vaguely about what all had happened to him, which solidified in my mind how much she meant to him. Talking about it in front of her would be okay. "I don't need that to be happy, B. I'm perfectly content to bottom for you the rest of our lives."

"*I* need it."

"Then I'll support you and do everything I can to help you overcome whatever hurdles lay in our path."

Lily peered up at us from where she knelt to wash his legs. Full-on lust simmered in her big brown eyes.

I snickered. "Someone's buttons just got pushed."

Blaine lifted his head to peer down at her. "You want to watch Grey own my ass and heal me from the inside out?"

"Boundaries and all that," she breathed, "but oh my God, yes. A thousand times yes, when you're ready."

"Shit." Blaine's dick stirred to life, and Lily glided her hands up the insides of his thighs to cradle his balls. "Can we..." He swallowed audibly. "Grey...would you touch me. There? I-I want to try that. Now." His words stuttered out, stirring my groin to life again.

"Anything for you," I said against his ear, then turned my focus on Lily. "Suck him."

She obeyed like a good little girl, and I smoothed my hands over Blaine's backside again, keeping my chest against his back, my mouth on his ear. I told him how strong he was, murmured words of edification and encouragement that would usually turn his face a sexy shade of pink.

And when I finally moved a fingertip over his hole, I slid my tongue into his mouth. He shivered, one of his hands coming behind my neck to hold me tight.

"Grey," he moaned against my lips, and I rimmed my finger around his hole, tapping, and pressing without breaching.

"I have you, baby. You're so fucking perfect, B. Love you so damn much."

Lily whimpered around her mouthful of cock.

"Can you come again?" I asked, pulling away enough I could see Blaine's pupils blown, the gold-green of his eyes eaten up with darkness—but not from the turmoil he buried inside. Those pupils had blown out from lust, pure and simple.

"Yeah. Fuck yeah."

I pressed again, the wet tip of my finger breaching enough that he trembled. "B?"

"Yes. Fuck!" He jolted back toward me, sinking my finger in to the first knuckle. His ass spasmed around me, sounds of Lily choking on his cum jacking lust through my balls. "Grey...fucking hell."

My heart soared with him, and I knew one day I would

be able to sink myself fully into his body while losing myself in his gaze.

Blaine went lax, and Lily kissed her way up his shivering belly and over his pecs. "You're so yummy." She sighed and stood on her tiptoes to kiss his slack mouth. "And you." She lifted an eyebrow my way, her lips curled in a smirk. "Naughty, filthy man."

I narrowed my gaze at her but couldn't help my grin. "You love it."

"I love *you*," she corrected, draping her small frame over Blaine's front, her soft hands reaching around to cradle my ass.

A spent Blaine in my arms, a gorgeous girl all up in our space...

Life didn't get much better than that.

44

LILY

EIGHT MONTHS LATER

I clasped Blaine's hand and stepped outside the courthouse into the biting March wind. Fucking New England and its cold as *fuck* spring.

But I didn't scowl at the weather I couldn't wait to escape for the California sunshine.

A grin stretched over my face—same as Blaine's, same as Grey who stood on his other side with his hand on our boy's lower back.

Abraham Quell had been found guilty on all the charges brought against him without Blaine even needing to testify. Sarah had sat tall and proud on the witness stand as had others who'd been emerged from beneath the cult leader's teachings.

Theft.

Rape.

Murder—of his first wife and Blaine and Sarah's parents as expected.

The fucker had gotten the maximum sentence and would rot behind bars until he breathed his last.

While the three of us would have preferred he be skinned alive, his genitals cut off, and his tongue ripped from his mouth, we took solace in the fact he would never hurt another innocent ever again.

Sarah exited the building behind us, tucked tightly against her fiancé's side.

A sea of press stood in wait at the bottom of the steps, already hollering out their questions, but Higgins and a couple of his friends from a protection agency saw us safely to Grey's Dad's SUV and Franklin and Sarah to his grandparent's.

Mr. Scott drove, and Grey and I sandwiched Blaine between us in the back seat. Two sets of hands clasped tight atop his thighs.

Silence settled as we pulled away from the fiasco, and a collective release seemed to fill the car's interior.

"It's over," Blaine whispered. "Truly over." He tipped his head back, a smile on his lips.

He'd been seeing a therapist for seven-plus months, and the results amazed us all.

Nightmares no longer visited him when he lay sleeping in our bed.

Rarely did darkness haunt his eyes.

Talk and news about cults and child sexual abuse didn't cause his stomach contents to erupt over the kitchen floor.

He worked hard for the progress he'd managed down the path toward healing, and Grey and I had held his hand every step of the way.

We would continue to do so until our hearts stopped beating.

I rested my cheek against his arm and closed my eyes. Contentment like I'd never expected flooded me with happiness. The trial was over. We were finally free from the shroud of bullshit to continue on with our lives.

Fear of losing Grey or Blaine had long since diminished, even when they loved on each other while I watched, and I rested in the knowledge they wanted me there.

Always.

Forever.

Enough time passed quietly in the SUV that I wondered why we hadn't gotten to the Scotts' home where we'd been staying.

I opened my eyes and watched the trees along the highway speed by. Shifting, I peered out the windshield. A sign let me know we headed toward Boston.

"Where are we going?" I asked, but Mr. Scott merely glanced at me in the rearview mirror.

"Grey?" I turned to find both my lovers looking at one another. Sharing their secrets. "What are you two up to?" I asked, sitting forward as far as my seatbelt would allow to better see their faces.

Grey caught my eye first. He grinned. "Do you trust me?"

One of my eyebrows raised as I truly considered his question. With my heart, yes. My emotions, absolutely. To not pull some sly plan to get what he wanted… "Sometimes?"

Blaine barked out a laugh and tugged me into his side. He kissed the top of my head. "We have a dinner date."

"With?"

"An old friend of yours," Grey said. "I made a few phone calls—"

"You and your taking charge," I muttered, baffled as to what he'd set into motion.

"We've been invited to dine with Mr. and Mr. Sipe this evening."

Levi.

My breath left in a rush. "What!" I squeaked, my eyes popping open, adrenaline rushing to my stuttering heart. He wouldn't...

Fuck, he definitely would with how I'd explained the relationship Levi and I had and the extent we'd gone to sow some supposed wild oats. My boys knew I held no bitterness toward my ex and that we'd remained friends and spoke at least once a month.

Grey had also overheard me tell Boo that I missed him a few weeks earlier the last time he'd called.

Grey angled around Blaine and grinned at me. "We wanted to meet these old lovers of yours since you go on and on and on about them—"

I leaned forward to back hand him across Blaine's chest. "I do not!" I choked on a laugh and glanced up at Blaine. "I don't!"

He tipped his head back and forth as though weighing my adamant statement. "You kind of do."

"You will not be all possessive and act like assholes!" I stated sternly—or tried to, rather, with how my insides shivered and shook. God knew my boys never behaved that way.

They laughed, and pure happiness swept through me.

"I can't believe you did this." My voice went all wobbly, and Grey reached around Blaine to cradle my cheek in his free hand.

"You really think we would bring you back east and leave without you seeing him?"

I knew he spoke of Levi. Zeke and I hadn't ever been friends per se, but we'd become closer since they'd married, and Levi and I stayed in touch.

"We figured your finally being able to see the two of

them together as happy as you are would bring one extra added layer of contentment in what the three of us share."

As if I needed something more.

My eyes welled, and I let out another laugh while shaking my head at their thoughtfulness. "What sort of man insists on his woman spending time with an ex?"

"Your God of Fucking and Blaine of the Thick and Juicy Cocks," he whispered, heating my face at the nicknames spoken out loud in front of his father.

I tore my attention of Grey's pale, twinkling eyes for the rearview. The same smiling orbs, the same color blue. It didn't seem he'd heard, thank God.

"I think I love your son too much for my own good," I told him.

"There's no such thing, young lady."

My cell rang, and I ignored it to eyeball my grinning lovers until it stopped. "Seriously. You two..."

The phone started back up, and I groaned, digging it from my purse.

Haley.

"Shit. I forgot to call her!" I swiped to answer. "Hey. So, you probably already heard?"

"Yeah. It's all over the news. So glad that fuck face got at least a tiny bit of what he deserved."

It had been my cousin's suggestion that Quell had ought to have his tongue forcibly removed from his body without a numbing agent.

"What?" she hollered but muffled as though she'd put her hand over the speaker. "Go suck a dick!"

I snorted a laugh, settling back into my seat. "What's all that about?"

"Garrett."

Another laugh escaped me. The roommate she'd found after I moved into Grey and Blaine's house drove her insane—but she refused to kick him out. The cute guy, while a gay cuddle bug who'd weaseled his way behind her walls, didn't know when to stop pushing her buttons. He teased her relentlessly, and she pretended to hate it.

But he was a good fill-in for me, Haley had claimed after telling me she secretly had a massive crush on him. A good listener, gorgeously built, smelled absolutely divine—but only liked dick.

At least they had that in common.

"When are you coming home?" she asked. "I need a girls' night out with *all* the wine."

"Soon." I shot a glance over at Grey who still watched me. "Then again, knowing these two, who the hell can say. I just got the surprise of the century dropped into my lap."

"Do tell," Haley murmured as though settling into the couch with a glass of chardonnay.

"Someone called an old friend of mine and made dinner plans."

"Get. The. Fuck. Out. He didn't!"

"He did."

"Oh my God." Haley snorted with laughter. "Awkward much?"

I could imagine...

But it wasn't.

Levi opened their home's front door before I even started up their front walkway. His face lit up the second our gazes landed on each other, and it was like no time had passed since I'd hugged him goodbye at the airport when he sent me off to seek out my two lovers.

"Boo!" I squealed and sprinted forward.

Grinning and gorgeous green eyes glistening, he swept me up into his arms just over the threshold of his and Zeke's house. "Lil." He choked on my nickname, squeezing me tight.

Although I recognized the feel of him holding me, his toned body no longer felt like home, nor was he my best friend who used to know me inside and out. At one time, I'd thought I would spend the rest of my life with him, but our terrible choices and the resulting heartache had been worth the pain.

We laughed, tears wetting both our cheeks when he finally set me onto my feet. I grabbed hold of his face, peering into his beautiful eyes. Any hint of haunted sadness had diminished due to the man I saw in my periphery, and what had once been a childhood crush had become pure, platonic emotions.

"I can't tell you how happy I am, how perfectly things have turned out for both of us," I told him, smiling brightly, my insides still jittery with excitement.

Levi pulled me in close again, and I rested my cheek on his chest, his heart thrumming beneath my ear.

Once upon a time, I'd believed it beat for me, but I knew better. Zeke stood off to my left in the foyer, grinning at both of us.

"Thank you for loving him," I stated quietly, still hugging Levi's trim waist.

"Thanks for making him give me another chance," Zeke said, stepping forward to clasp the back of Levi's neck. "Come on in," he called, and I realized I'd left my boys outside in the cold when I'd gone scampering toward the house without them.

"Shit." I laughed and pulled away from Levi but

threaded my fingers through his, familiarity in the feel of his palm pressed against mine. "Boo," I said, turning to face the men who filled my heart to overflowing, "there are two men I'd like for you to meet."

THE END

———

ABOUT THE AUTHOR

USA Today bestselling author Lynn Burke is a CrossFit and coffee addict. Her three spawn dictate how often she can be found hunched over her Mac, typing as fast as her fickle muse cooks up hot stories.

You can find more about Lynn at her website: www.authorlynnburke.com

ALSO BY LYNN BURKE

Abel's Obsession

Divulging Secrets

Healing Storms

In Between

Reluctant Lumberjack

Resisting his Mate

Billion Dollar Love Anthology

Blood Born Series

Bonds of Worship Series

Dark Leopards MC

Darkest Desires Series

Devil's Outlaws MC

Elite Escort Series

Elite Escorts MM Series

Fallen Gliders MC

Forbidden Obsession Duet

Found by Fate Series

Midnight Sun Series

Missing Link Series

Pippen Creek Series

Risso Family Series

Sandy Ridge Series

Sinful Nature Series

Vicious Vipers MC